STEVEN SCHWARTZ, the author of two highly
praised story collections, has received numerous
honors for his writing, including an NEA Fellowship,
a Nelson Algren Award, and two O. Henry Awards.
He teaches writing at Colorado State University and
lives in Fort Collins, Colorado, with his wife and two
children.

ID668526

Therapy

a novel

Steven Schwartz

A PLUME BOOK

PLUME
Published by the Penguin Group
Penguin Books USA Inc., 375 Hudson Street, New York, New York 10014, U.S.A.
Penguin Books Ltd, 27 Wrights Lane, London W8 5TZ, England
Penguin Books Australia Ltd, Ringwood, Victoria, Australia
Penguin Books Canada Ltd, 10 Alcorn Avenue, Toronto, Ontario, Canada M4V 3B2
Penguin Books (N.Z.) Ltd, 182–190 Wairau Road, Auckland 10, New Zealand

Penguin Books Ltd, Registered Offices: Harmondsworth, Middlesex, England

Published by Plume, an imprint of Dutton Signet,
a division of Penguin Books USA Inc.
This is an authorized reprint of a hardcover edition published
by Harcourt Brace & Company. For information address
Permissions Department, Harcourt Brace & Company,
6277 Sea Harbor Drive, Orlando, Florida 32887-6777.

First Plume Printing, July, 1995
10 9 8 7 6 5 4 3 2 1

LIBRARY OF CONGRESS CATALOGING-IN-PUBLICATION DATA
Schwartz, Steven.
Therapy : a novel / Steven Schwartz.
p.   cm.
ISBN 0-452-27431-1
I. Title.
PS3569.C5676T48   1995
813'.54—dc20
95–734
CIP

Printed in the United States of America
Original hardcover design by Lori J. McThomas

PUBLISHER'S NOTE
This is a work of fiction. Names, characters, places, and incidents either are the
product of the author's imagination or are used fictitiously, and any resemblance
to actual persons, living or dead, events, or locales is entirely coincidental.

For Benjamin and Jeannette Schwartz,
in memory

Acknowledgments

I wish to thank the National Endowment for the Arts for its support; my editor, Claire Wachtel, for her valuable suggestions; and the following people for their encouragement and insight: Robert Boswell, John Calderazzo, David Cantrell, Wayne Carpenter, Ann Cummins, Mary Golden, Elise Goodman, Deanna Ludwin, Liza Nelligan, Toni Nelson, and Terrie Sandelin. I am especially grateful to Emily Hammond, my wife, who guided this book home.

Part One

into the world

Chapter One

THEY WERE BOTH IN THEIR FORTIES AND HAD COME TO BEING PARENTS with a determination to succeed where their parents had failed, a wish to fail where their parents had succeeded, and a hope that the baby would love them regardless.

Perhaps because they were older, they noticed that people took a particular delight in telling them *it will change your life*. Until they couldn't stand to hear it from another person. Sixteen years of marriage had given them a certain confidence in their limitations as sufficient strengths. Before, when asked (by everyone) when they might have a family, their standard reply had been pleasant yet firm: "We are a family." Queries stopped. So did invitations to the parties of friends' children. It puzzled Wallis. How was she as a childless woman of forty perceived? Pity? Fear? Envy?

"Oh, why not," she'd told Cap, and on her forty-first birthday had pushed her hand through an angel food cake with lemon frosting. She examined the arm, the icing like streaks of candle wax down her wrist.

"I should tell you something," she announced to Cap, who wore a party hat with the number 1 circled in gold leaf. "I haven't had my period in a while. It's either one or the other."

It wasn't menopause. They were alternately shocked and elated. They'd done nothing different. "It happens," said their doctor at the fertility clinic, a place Wallis and Cap had raced to on occasion, getting there within thirty minutes so their commingled fluids could be processed and tested to see whether her mucus was rejecting his sperm, twelve-inch stainless-steel needles inserted into her womb on "probing missions" like some uterine Star Trek: the whole humiliating analysis of inexplicable barrenness that had lasted ten years.

And then she conceived. They didn't tell anyone the first months, then told everyone. "Do you feel sick?" people asked. "Absolutely," said Wallis. "I'm radiantly nauseous." But in private she fretted. "I'm too old, I'm too old, I'm too old," she said to Cap. Their obstetrician didn't seem to think so. "Good femur," he said, when Wallis was five months along. "Nice and long. Oh, and there's the cardiac activity. Swell, very strong." Cap and Wallis stared at the white dot winking at them amidst tiny ribs that surrounded it like a miniature birdcage. "That's the heart?" asked Wallis. "The very one," said their doctor, a man close to seventy, who looked as if he'd gladly take a bushel of apples for payment: patient, gentle, if a little folksy and old-fashioned. "Can you tell the sex?" asked Wallis. "I'll see," he said, and he doused her belly with more jelly. "Boy," he said, "boy to the world!" "Really?" said Cap. He'd been hoping, but not too hard, of course.

They went out to breakfast afterward, sat together in a booth and held hands. Wallis ordered scrambled eggs and couldn't eat them. "I guess we need to pick out a name," she said.

"Sam," suggested Cap.

"No."

"Samuel."

"No."

"Samson."

"*No.*"

He'd once hated the name, but over the years had become stuck on it. They'd named their two dogs Sam, or variations of it. "We're not naming our child Sam."

"Bob."

"No one is named Bob anymore."

"You can spell it backward the same as forward. He'll read and write early, foolproof."

She saw it was a joke, about himself—his reading disability. Maybe, too, a fear the baby could inherit it. "Okay, come on, what else?"

"What do *you* want to name him?" asked Cap.

"Do you like Claude?" The name had just popped into her head. Such a nice old-fashioned name, respectable yet warm. "Please say you like it."

"It's not bad," said Cap, taking the eggs off her plate. It wasn't eating that bothered her, but mastication; if she could just bypass chewing, straight to digestion. "Claude. Little Claude."

"Claude it is," said Wallis. They toasted water glasses. She pulled the lemon out and sucked on it. Delicious.

One week past his wife's due date, Cap woke up at six-thirty in the morning and couldn't find her. She wasn't in the bathroom. She wasn't in the baby's room, where she liked to read when she couldn't sleep. The room was ready: coverlet on the crib, diapers and wipes stacked on the changing table, a lullaby light on the new dresser—even the "stim" cards set up. Some friends at the baby shower had given them these rubber cards (for chewing too) with their geometric designs and silhouette shapes in black and white. Cap picked one up: a hairless, polished head with large, alien eye sockets. Infants were supposed to like this?

They'd also been given books, puzzles, a beginning block set, rattles, a Snugli, a bouncing baby seat, six months of diaper service. Cap had noticed that the two childless couples who had come (two others had not shown up) hung in the background. They clearly felt uncomfortable as the conversation went easily from pregnancy to breast-feeding to sleepless nights to pediatricians to teething to day-care schedules to children's clothes catalogs to inherited allergies to whether a cure would exist for AIDS when their children would be having sex to all the things the parents had sworn they'd never do. "It's shocking," said Phyllis, who taught eighth grade with Wallis. "I used to live on a macrobiotic commune in Chama, New Mexico, and sell rice tamales to the tourists. Do you know what I served my kids for lunch yesterday? Jimmy Dean miniburgers. And do you know where we're planning to go on vacation next Christmas? Baby Med in Mexico. And do you know what's sitting in plain view in my living room right now? A La-Z-Boy rocker. I used to think those things were the equivalent of corrective shoes in furniture. Now I ask you: Who in the world is this person called a parent?" She let out a booming laugh and gave Wallis a hug. "You're going to be a great mother. I wish you were *my* mother." All of which had made Wallis blush. Cap had slid over toward the childless couples and asked them if they wanted anything more to drink, more of the strawberry bread he had made. No, they really had to go. They left. One of the couples had given Legos as a gift and been told by another guest that it was a little advanced—by about four years. Cap felt sorry for them. The world of parents, even prospective ones, was so utterly self-absorbed, and he remembered why he and Wallis had conveniently arranged to be out of town for baby showers. It wasn't anybody's fault. The parents couldn't help themselves. And he did feel the tug toward them now, away from the old order, curiosity about how exactly you *did* change a diaper, or take a one-year-old's temperature ("Under the arm—put a video on," Phyllis had said), or know if they were too cold or too hot and when to put them on solid foods; and what happens if they roll over on their faces and can't breathe; and what did Wallis mean when she said don't worry if at first the baby's hands and feet turn blue and he secretes milk from his nipples or has jaundice—how could you *not* worry about such things? Wasn't jaundice right up there with tuberculosis and hepatitis?

Blue feet? Milk from his nipples? What was that—some kind of dairy stigmata?

The baby shower had made it all real somehow. All the gifts. The tours of the baby's room. The jokes about no sleep; about intriguing tributaries of spit-up on Wallis's black blouses; about Cap conducting sessions with little Claude on his lap; about the reactions clients would have to his abandoning them for his own child ("You can't overestimate their resentment," warned Dick, his associate and a father himself of three nearly grown boys, having started twenty years before Cap).

He went downstairs now and looked out in the backyard. Sometimes Wallis liked to get up early on summer mornings and work in the garden. But there was no sign of her. Last night he'd come home from work and found her sitting out back on the white bench. He'd joined her, and they'd sat waiting until well after dark, Wallis with her hands on her belly, her head leaned back in discouragement. She wasn't tall, and her belly had had nowhere to go these last months except straight out. It seemed ages ago that she'd declared herself radiantly nauseous.

She'd gotten up from the bench and plopped down in the high grass that Cap needed to cut. "When I sit down, my bottom hurts," she'd told him. "When I stand up, my legs ache. The only position that offers me any relief at all is on my side, and I'm sick of lying on my side like a plattered fish."

They'd called Dr. Lutchman again.

"Well, this happens, of course. Especially with first births." He had paused for a moment. "Let's wait another day or two and see where we are. We can induce over the weekend if necessary."

"Is there anything more we can do?" asked Cap. He had turned on the speakerphone so Wallis could hear too, but she was glaring straight ahead at the TV, mad at him, at Lutchman, at everyone, the whole world. The day before, when they'd checked in with Lutchman (who was receiving full blame for this delay), she had said, "This is silly, this is completely silly—having a child at forty-one. I just can't believe how silly this all is." When she got nervous, she became mad. When

Cap worried, he became more persistent. "Anything you can think of at all, Dr. Lutchman?"

"Exercise sometimes helps."

They'd walked miles last weekend.

Wallis tapped her foot impatiently, still glaring at the TV. A show about the rain forests of South America. A thirty-foot anaconda had swallowed a pudu deer. The snake, its jaw unhinged (Wallis had said "You fat lug" under her breath), would spend the next month beside a tree, digesting the deer.

"Well, I guess we could try walking some more," said Cap.

"*You* walk," she muttered.

He was sure there was something else short of inducing labor chemically. Something they were all overlooking—some trick position, a breathing technique, a simple natural remedy, something. "Is there anything we could take, an herb, perhaps, that might help?"

"An herb?" said Dr. Lutchman.

"Something internal but natural."

"Well, that's not my department."

The enormous, bulging anaconda had slithered from the screen, replaced by a ludicrous five-foot-tall rhea, a fat ostrichlike creature that could run up to thirty miles an hour but was incapable of flying an inch off the ground. Wallis looked ready to shoot it. Cap had the thought that they would never get up from the couch again.

"I'll tell you a little story," said Dr. Lutchman.

"Oh, wonderful."

Cap covered the speakerphone with his hand. "Please, Wallis. He's just trying to help."

"I don't want his help. I want a baby!" she said, as if the two were mutually exclusive.

"Have you ever been to the University of Chicago Medical Center?" asked Dr. Lutchman.

"No," said Cap dully. He felt himself wearing down.

"Well, if you ever go there, look at the pillars in front. Six of them display the busts of famous medical discoverers. There is a seventh pillar—without a bust. Do you know for whom that pillar is reserved?"

Wallis said, "You?"

Dr. Lutchman's laughter echoed through the speaker. "No, my dear, no. It is reserved for the individual who discovers what precisely starts labor. I'll leave you with that little story and wish you a good night. I'm on call this evening, so allow me to be optimistic and say I hope our meeting is imminent."

The phone rang now, and Cap hoped it was Wallis. Where could she have gone at this hour of the morning, nine months pregnant?

"Any news?" His parents. The first of ten calls they would make today.

"Not yet," he told them. "I'll let you know as soon as anything happens." He hung up before they could get a word in.

His parents had been out to see them only a few times in Colorado. They didn't like to travel and expected Wallis and Cap to come to Philadelphia. "I thought you lived on the Rocky Mountain," his father had said the first time they visited, it having taken them almost eight years to come out here. Cap explained that they lived on the Front Range, where the Great Plains met the foothills of the Rockies. The actual Rockies—it was more than one, by the way—were an hour's drive west. It was as flat here as in Philadelphia, flatter, unless you went up in the foothills. "So dry," his mother said. "You have a lot of snakes here?"

Cap gave them a tour of Pierre: the bike paths and walking trails that ran along the river; the new indoor ice-skating and swimming center; the two-hundred-acre nature preserve; the redeveloped down-town with its outdoor mall and street performers; the flower gardens of the university. He brought them to the town museum in Skookum Park, right across the street from his office. Out back of the museum was the original log cabin of the French fur trappers, the brothers Pierre, who had founded the town. "Where can we eat?" his parents had said, unimpressed.

He took them to a delicatessen, or Pierre's version of it.

"Is it lean?" his mother asked the clerk about the corned beef.

His father, looking at the glass case, made a face. "You have any fresher potato salad?"

"We just made it today, sir."

"But you got more in the back, right? That's the real fresh."

"We don't have any other, sir," said the clerk.

Cap's father winked and spoke hoarsely. "*I'll bet my shorts they got some in the back*"—an attempt at whispering that drew the same attention as if he were talking through a PA system.

Cap sat down with them. His mother removed the bread and sniffed her egg salad sandwich. She wrinkled her nose. "Feh, who can eat such chozerai?" She looked around the restaurant for sympathetic supporters, and finding none, only a normal lunch-hour crowd engaged without crisis in their meals, she turned to Cap. "Did you see that corned beef? Like *wax*." She picked at a seed on her rye bread, then scanned the restaurant again. "Is that good?" she said to a young woman sitting at the next table.

"Pardon?" asked the woman, who was trying to read the *Denver Post* and enjoy her lunch.

"Your sandwich, it's what you want?"

"What I want?"

Cap's mother turned back to him. "What? Nobody understands English here?" She opened her arms toward the heavens. "They all repeat what you say in this place!" From the restaurant bathroom, down a long, resonant corridor, Cap could hear his father groan and curse. "Listen to that. See what I mean?" his mother said. "All the time he's like that." His father spent ten minutes urinating. An enlarged prostate. When he came out, he said, "The place was filthy. I tell you

I wouldn't have been surprised to see a snake pishin' in there next to me. I had to open the door with my elbow."

Cap drove them back to their hotel for a nap. Then he went home and collapsed—at one o'clock in the afternoon. He canceled his afternoon appointments, something he hated to do, but otherwise he would have had to sit in front of his clients a deflated thing, a dented, airless kickball, offering insights such as: "So your parents ignored you. Lucky you!"

When they'd learned about the pregnancy, Cap's mother had said, "A miracle! It's a miracle! What I've been waiting for all my life. I'm going to call Ellen Levitz at the temple and get it in the next newsletter!"

His mother wanted to come out for the birth and to help with the baby. "I'll have an abortion first," Wallis had threatened. "Really, Cap, this is a stressful time. Do you want to be taking care of your mother too?"

"I thought she could help." He honestly had envisioned his mother spelling them, doing some cooking and laundry, assisting them—but that was someone else's mother, he had to agree.

"She'll criticize everything I do—*we* do."

"All right," he said, and called them to explain that he and Wallis needed time alone with the baby to bond.

"You want bonds, go to a bank," his father said, dismissing the entire core of Cap's profession in a single platitude. "You think the little fella is going to care how many people are standing around watching his diaper be changed? How long are you talking about? A week?"

"A month," said Cap.

"A month!" His mother broke in on the extension. He couldn't remember ever having a conversation with just one of them. "He'll be in college by the time we see him!"

"When's the bris going to be if you wait a month?" asked his father.

"Well, Dad"—he'd been preparing for this moment—"we've decided not to circumcise."

There was an unsettling silence on their end. He thought perhaps they'd both fainted.

"All right," his father said—a low, dying voice. "If that's what you want. God knows you're two grownups. We knew there would be problems, of course."

Against his better judgment, Cap asked, "Problems?"

"When you married her."

They always called Wallis "her" when they were mad at him. "Fine," said Cap. "Let's not discuss it further."

His mother spoke up. "You'd think, even being from goyim, she'd want the poor child not to be teased."

"We need to drop the subject right now," said Cap. "If you can't drop it, I'll have to hang up."

"He's giving us the two-minute warning again," said his father.

His mother, meanwhile, had started to cry. Through her tears, she managed to say, "You can't answer me one question? I don't deserve one answer from you?"

"All right." Nausea was rolling up from his stomach to his throat, but he was reluctant to hang up on them and have to deal later with their hurt feelings. "Ask your one question."

"What happens when he goes to the Jewish Y and all the kids make fun of him in the locker room?"

"There aren't enough Jews in Pierre for a minyan, let alone a Jewish Y! And regardless, no one is going to make fun of him here or anywhere else."

"What if God forbid he gets a serious infection and winds up sterile like your uncle Eddie?"

"Look, Cappie, forget what your mother says. I know better. Half the boys today don't have it done anymore. I read the papers. It's not like in your generation. I'm sure Wallis has got good reasons. But the bottom line is *he won't be a Jew!*"

He hung up. Surprisingly, they didn't call right back. In fact, they didn't call for three weeks (he'd never gone more than a week without

hearing from them). Finally, he called—haunted by headlines: PSY-
CHOLOGIST'S PARENTS FOUND DEAD THREE WEEKS. There would be a
picture of them lying at the foot of the refrigerator, dead of dual heart
attacks, a pound of not-so-lean corned beef near their heads.

They acted as if nothing had happened.

"You're all right, then?" he asked.

"Fine. What should be wrong? We're fine here. A little hot, maybe.
Your mother's legs are bothering her. I can't get the cable fella to come
out and fix the set so I can see the game, but life goes on."

"How's Strawberry doing?"

"He went three for three last night." It was the one subject he could
talk about with his father (one more than his brother, Allan)—sports.
Born in New York before the Dodgers moved, his father had remained
a loyal fan all his life.

"All right," said Cap, satisfied to know they were still alive. "I just
wanted to check on you. Everything's fine here," he said, speaking in
generalities because it was safer that way. "Wallis stops teaching for
the summer next week, and we'll probably go up to the mountains for
a long weekend. We're getting ready here. I'm cutting down on my
hours, letting slots go unfilled if clients terminate. Claude is doing
great, kicking up a storm—"

"Claude? Who's Claude?" asked his mother, on the extension.

"Claude's the baby."

"You're naming him Claude?"

"That's his name, Mom. That's the name we've decided on."

"Who names a baby Claude?"

Cap blew up. "Who names somebody Casper! You think that's a
better name?"

"It's a very distinguished name. A million times I've told you. Casper
Kaplan. Everybody says so. Like a governor's name it sounds."

"It's the name of a ghost, for Christ's sake!"

"You came first. The ghost we didn't know about. Claude. I don't
know any Claudes. You know any Claudes, Murray?"

13

"I'm looking through the synagogue directory," his father said.

"Claude Rains. There's a Claude. An alter kocker."

His father broke in. "An uncircumcised French alter kocker—that's what you want for a son? What's going on here, Cappie? You want to make a freak out of this child before he's even born?"

Wallis had walked into the room at that moment. She recognized the distress on his face and took the phone from him. He gladly gave it over, his only other choice being to hang up again. Wallis began telling them in detail, with no more transition than a trebled hello, about the baby's room: the sheets and matching coverlet, the clown night-light, the bright-yellow striped wallpaper, the mobile that played "It's a Small World," the curtains she'd sewn, the white crib they'd bought, and in no time she had them distracted and calmed down and off the phone, happy, in a way that Cap could never accomplish. "You've got to talk at their level," she had told him again, and when he asked what level was that exactly, she said, "About here," and put her hands an inch away from her face, as if nearly blind. "They just want to hear a story," she'd said, "like my kids after lunch. They defy psychology. Or they're immune to it. In any case, it does no good to argue with them."

And what of Wallis's parents?

Her mother enjoyed the distinction of being the foremost designer of feminine-hygiene boxes in the world. "What are feminine-hygiene boxes?" Cap had asked Wallis on their first date at the university in Boulder. "Tampons," said Wallis. She also informed him that *tampon* in French was a masculine noun. He'd burst out laughing. "I like your laugh," she'd said, and she did. He laughed with his whole face, with his long body and dark eyes. People in her family didn't laugh like that or do anything with their whole bodies. Her father, an architect in Berkeley, specialized in designing rental-car lots at airports. Like her mother, he traveled often. Her mother used to bring Wallis sample tubes of toothpaste and soaps from the hotels she stayed in. Wallis never used any of them, instead storing them in her closet. When her parents got divorced—Wallis was nine—the sample toothpaste boxes and soaps and little shower caps and shampoos filled a laundry basket to the brim. She'd lugged the basket downstairs to the living room, where her mother was packing up the silver. They were moving to a smaller house. The housekeeper, who had raised Wallis, would be going with them. "Here," said Wallis, pushing the basket toward her mother. "This is all of it."

"I had no idea you were collecting all those," her mother said. "Whatever for?"

"My hope chest," said Wallis. "I just wanted you to see before I threw it out."

Then she dragged the basket back up the steps, opened her parents' window, and dumped the contents on the well-fertilized front lawn. Her mother never said a word about it. Instead, she picked up the items and put them in a trash bag, which she hauled to the alley. "It was the way we dealt with anger in our house, with any emotion," she told Cap the night he proposed to her, so he'd know what he was getting himself into. "We stored it up for years, in neat little sample boxes, then dumped it all in the trash, worthless."

He had met Wallis when she signed up for a perception study that he was supervising in graduate school at Boulder. He'd walked her home, over the stone bridge with its duck pond, through the university's tree-lined quad, the cherry blossoms in bloom, past the outdoor theater, staging *Othello* that summer, where he was already imagining bringing her, sitting close to her in the dark.

A graduate student in education, she still lived in a dorm, but she liked it. She was a resident adviser there. It gave her a little extra money; she'd taken pride in paying for college, her parents both willing to give her money but always complaining in the same breath about their debts. He kissed her. She kept her eyes open. "Do you like Moroccan food?" she asked, as if he hadn't kissed her at all. She seemed to have absolutely no response. "I like you," he said. "There's a great Moroccan restaurant on Pearl Street," she told him, "where they give you a five-course meal. You don't use silverware. You sit on pillows. I've always wanted to go. Okay?" She disappeared inside.

Afterward, unable to sleep in his apartment, the tenant downstairs trying to play Jimi Hendrix on an acoustic guitar, he lay awake thinking about her dry humor in that exacting voice. She left no room for uncertainty, and her sureness intimidated him. He thought about her small hips, her round bottom hardly moving in her long muslin skirt as he watched her run straight up the dorm stairs.

His last relationship had been with a girl from Philadelphia, like himself, someone he'd met his junior year in Boulder on a rafting trip. By his senior year they were engaged. As he got closer to graduating, she had urged him to apply to medical schools. "Why go to all that bother of graduate school and an internship when you could do almost the same amount of work and become a doctor?"

But he didn't want to be a psychiatrist. He didn't like the reliance on drugs, the orientation toward traditional medicine, the posturing of psychiatrists as supreme judges of mental disorders, the last word on sanity. It was 1970, and he'd read too much Fritz Perls (Lose your mind and come to your senses), R. D. Laing, Carl Rogers, Alan Watts, Rollo May. He wanted to find a profession that combined the spiritual with the psychological. "Well," Susan had said, with only a little irony, "you can always work in a Jewish hospital."

It had occurred to him then that Susan was the woman his parents wanted him to marry. She was studying to be a recreational counselor, and with her he'd learned to ski and camp and kayak. A Jewish blonde, tall and athletic like himself, she had a husky voice, that familiar Cheltenham accent, heavy on the *r*'s, which barked instructions easily. One day he'd gone to watch her intern at a youth activities center. She wore denim shorts that showed off her long, tan legs, and a sleeveless white T-shirt that slid up to her ribs as she unselfconsciously did back flips and one-handed cartwheels for the kids. She appealed to the jock in him, and he had imagined settling down out here with her, starting up his practice while maybe doing a little intramural coaching for kids, driving with her in his Volkswagen van up Boulder Canyon to remote hiking trails or music festivals or arts-and-crafts fairs tucked away in little mountain towns.

What had finally broken them apart was planning the wedding. She had wanted to get married in Philadelphia. He wanted to have the wedding out here. Their friends were here, and more important, the place meant something special to them both: represented their love affair with the West, an awareness of nature they'd never had in Philadelphia. Cap felt he'd made major decisions about the direction of his life here, a place that felt like a spiritual home.

"Why do you always say that?" Susan had asked.

"Say what?"

"Spiritual this, spiritual that."

"I don't say it that much."

"Well, it stands out. You sound like you want to go join boy wonder up the street." The thirteen-year-old maharishi, the boy guru, lived with some of his followers a block from them in a large white house, the Divine Light ashram. "Sometimes I worry you're too affected by this place. To be honest, I'm glad we're getting out of here."

"Since when are we leaving?" Cap asked.

"You said you wanted to leave after you finished school."

"Yes, but I didn't mean leave the West."

She had looked at him for a long time and then gone into her room and quietly shut the door. Two months later, she was engaged to someone else, a law student. Cap's mother became ill after the wedding was called off. Her joints swelled. Her blood pressure shot up. His parents had gotten to be friends with his prospective in-laws and played bridge with them regularly at the Jewish Community Center in Philadelphia. It was all Cap's fault, according to everybody. He was afraid to grow up and settle down. What was so terrible about coming back to Philadelphia? Susan had told her parents (who told his parents) that he wanted to keep his hair long and run around barefoot in mountain meadows of wildflowers.

"That's ridiculous," Cap told them, his mother cutting in to say what a lovely girl Susan was, the beautiful healthy children they would have had together.

"How are you going to support a family with that kind of attitude?" his father added.

He ran into Susan one day while he was crossing campus on his way to the library. Her fiancé was with her. Susan wore his fraternity pin. He was a sammy named Sam, and he had a faint, contemptuous smile, as if to say, So this is the loser you wasted four years of your life on. His hair was sleek black curls, parted slightly in the middle and dipping into a sheen of wings. He wore new flared jeans, still creased, shined cordovan loafers with a matching maroon V-neck fraternity sweater. Cap, meanwhile, was at his worst, his hair in clumps from the warm Pepsi that had exploded minutes earlier in his face, his eyes red and lidless from the amphetamines his new room-mate, Perry, had given him to help him study for finals, his zipper (he discovered at the library urinal soon afterward) halfway down.

Susan was repelled. She kept her distance and wouldn't look directly at him. She told him that she still had his Traffic album. (Keep it, he mumbled, his mouth foully dry from not eating or drinking anything that morning except the warm Pepsi.) He really would have to come to the wedding, she said, if he ever got back to Philly—a last dig. Then she fled with her future husband, who pointed his thumb and forefinger like a gun and said, "Take 'er easy, Casper, my man," and he could picture the two of them rolling around on Susan's bed (she had been athletic in sex too), having a good hoot over his name, Susan's titan legs over the sammy's shoulders, their mutual cries of Casper the ghost!—fucking each other into eternity.

He decided that if he ever had a dog, he'd name it Sam; it was a good name for a dog—a dog could give it a little dignity.

It had been the low point in his life so far. But it got worse. To save money, he had moved in with Perry, a junior from Georgia, who had advertised for a roommate. On Perry's twenty-first birthday, the two of them went downtown, played pinball, had a few mixed drinks at a bar to celebrate, then brought home the remainder of a pizza. The light was off in the stairway. They would later learn that the bulb had been unscrewed. Cap thought nothing of it at the time. It was only his second week in the duplex. But suddenly Perry, who was in front of him, going up the stairs, began to whimper. And then Cap was grabbed and thrown into his room, shoved facedown on the bed. Guns were pointed at him, silver-plated twenty-two pistols. Two guns. One was in his kidney and one at his left temple. Three kids—they couldn't have been more than seventeen—in jackets with the collars pulled up demanded that he give them all his money. They rifled through his pockets, found two dollars, and threw the empty wallet at his head. He didn't have any more. "Where is it?" He turned around, and they slapped him in the head. "Where's the shit?" Perry was crying in a heap next to him. "Where's the shit?" they kept asking, and he realized they were talking about drugs and that perhaps Perry was a dealer— where else had the amphetamines come from?—or they were mixing him up with somebody else who had lived here.

He turned around again; it was a natural reflex he would later explain as a need to see what's jabbing you: he couldn't keep himself from looking. The gun in his back—the one pointed at his kidney—popped, and he felt a sensation at once searing and dull: as if a thumb were poking hot bread. The phrase "lodged foreign object" occurred to him—and then he blacked out. Years later, when he would have women clients who had been raped as children during incest or attacked as adults, he would go back to this place to understand their despair, their thorough psychic destruction. Back to the instant when the bullet ripped through his jacket and sweater and skin with ease, when his robust body, which he'd trusted as immutable, the one solid and reliable constant his parents had propagated—when this finest self would become a powerless blank of absolute pain.

He was told after the bullet was removed that a hair closer and it would have shattered his kidney. His parents flew out. They came into the room and patted his shoulder tentatively. He had expected them to be angry, somehow to blame him for what had happened, but instead they were timid in the face of such violence. They treated him as a totem object, some ceremonial deity who had survived death, their greatest fear, the one that ran their lives. In their deference, he felt a power over them, an understanding that their love, pocked as it might be with anxiety, was a constant plea that he survive. Every generational cell leaned toward this moment of a bullet in his back, had expected and dreaded and waited for it, and now that it was here, in the face of it they were just small children, his mother crying in her hands, his father patting her arm, their heads bowed as if they were all in judgment before God.

He had felt a tremendous sorrow for them, for all their weaknesses now made flesh, for how it tormented the soul like nothing else to know that you had brought children into the world to die. He was aware, too, in that moment, with a fat wadded bandage on his back, plugging a hole where his life had nearly seeped out, that he had taken a step beyond them and that in their frailty they were on their way back to childhood, as he was jumping ahead into manhood. It was a moment of passing, and they would never know each other quite this way again.

Susan came to visit him. She had left her fiancé home. She brought Cap a gift, an updated edition of *Hiking Trails in Colorado*. "To encourage you to get well quick," she told him. It was a peace offering. As with his parents, toward her, too, he felt generous now, and when she lingered, her eyes teary, he patted her hand gently, without desire or regret, and she looked at him curiously and said, "You don't love me, do you?" not with rebuke but with surprise, as though she had been tricked. She left when the nurse came in to check his blood pressure and give him his antibiotics. He never saw her again.

He and Perry (who had been spared any physical violence) looked at hundreds of pictures of juveniles at the police station. They couldn't recognize anyone. The robbers were never found, and Cap soon moved into an apartment of his own.

It was almost two years later that he met Wallis. He took her to dinner at the Moroccan restaurant, where they sat on the floor and ate with their hands. She sucked the apricot sauce off his fingers. "You shouldn't waste any," she said, without any suggestion of lewdness. It was strictly a frugal gesture. When they got back to the dorm, they sat downstairs in the lobby and talked about his program and her teaching. She wanted to find a job out here in Colorado, never return to the Midwest.

She stood up and walked to the water fountain. She was only a few inches over five feet tall. He supposed they made an odd couple walking together. He was over six feet tall, with broad shoulders. His curly dark hair met his beard somewhere indefinite on his neck. He had been more a match for Susan, with her strapping athletic body, than for this compact if spunky girl, whom he was afraid he'd crush.

On her way back, she did a little jig, mouthing some words of a song, though it didn't seem so much for his benefit as her own—as if she'd do this anyway, alone in her room. She did seem like an only child, used to an audience of one. Her hair, braided in a long, coppery rope, bounced on her back between her shoulders. She tossed her head, and the braid swiveled like a weight to the side.

She sat down cross-legged on the couch and faced him. He had the uncomfortable thought that she'd had many lovers, was very "loose," and liked to smoke grass before going to bed with guys.

"What are you thinking about?" she asked.

"I'm wondering . . ."

"What?"

"Are you interested in me?" asked Cap.

"What a question!"

He was surprised he'd asked it himself. "I mean, we're very different, aren't we? I must seem ponderous to you, phlegmatic."

"Phlegmatic! Oh, not that bad, I hope."

"Bad, though?" He never remembered being this unsure of himself in his life. Why couldn't he stop asking all these direct questions!

Wallis turned away and burped politely in her hand. "I love that food, but it's a nightmare to live with afterward. Listen, Cap the Phlegmatic . . ." She reached over and took his hand. It was such a natural gesture.

He was trying now not to lose his head about Wallis's whereabouts. He called their neighbor next door, a woman who had retired this year from teaching at the same school as Wallis. No, she hadn't seen Wallis this morning at all. Were the dogs around?

The dogs! He hadn't thought about the dogs! Thanks, Jo, he said, and quickly went into the backyard to check. But the dogs, the two Sams, were under the deck, out of the sun. In desperation, Cap asked, "Where's Wallis, for God's sake?" and they thumped their tails against the wooden posts at the sound of her name, anticipating a walk.

He called the hospital. No, nobody under the name Wallis Kaplan had checked in. "We have her preregistered for the delivery, but that was arranged a month ago."

And then he saw her—swaying down the sidewalk. He ran out to meet her. "Where have you been?" but she looked up at him, surprised by the question, as if he should know. She'd been up since four A.M.—that's when her contractions had started. She hadn't wanted to wake him. "What I'm trying to say," she said, smiling, patting her stomach, "is that we're ready."

By Cap's estimate, they'd walked around the hospital's fifth floor a hundred times already. Five hours had passed since they'd checked in and been assigned to a room that except for the fetal monitor and the portable delivery station hidden behind closet doors could have been a motel room. Cap had massaged Wallis's shoulders, back, and feet; they'd done exercises; Wallis had squatted and stretched and taken a shower; she'd sat in the whirlpool, before her water had broken. Her contractions had stopped the minute she entered the hospital.

They switched on the TV—*Mister Ed* on cable. "Wilbur, my life has no meaning," the horse complained. "I want to be remembered for something." Cap watched Wilbur and Mister Ed work it out. Wallis had gone into the bathroom. Mister Ed was depressed, a midlife crisis, no goals that excited him anymore, stuck on a gentleman's ranch, unable to connect with other horses, and Wilbur listened like a good therapist, validating the animal's feelings.

Cap hit the mute button and watched Mister Ed's muzzle contort to the side; without sound, the poor creature looked as if he had polio of the mouth: those rubbery dark lips, viscous gums, and large, blinding picket teeth. Was this a portrait of therapy with the sound off, without language? Without interpretation? The tormented mimicry of an intellectualizing horse brooding over an accident of evolution? It was horrifying, monstrous, and he jumped up to shut off the set just as Wallis came out.

They resumed their walk around the hospital, stopping to look out the window at the mountains in the west. Then down to the opposite end: the eastern plains, the expanse of grazing land, horses, normal animals—not the mutant Mister Ed—bowing their heads toward the gathering rain clouds, rolling over the mountains for an afternoon shower.

Wallis leaned against Cap. "I'm scared," she said.

"It often takes a long time with the first child."

"Not always. I was born in an hour. My mother barely had time to get her makeup on."

When they got back to the room, the nurse took Wallis's blood pressure, then measured her.

"Is he crowning yet?" asked Wallis.

"Sometimes it just takes longer," the nurse said. She was kind, patient with Wallis's frustration. In another twenty minutes, her twelve-hour shift would end; then they'd get somebody new.

Dr. Lutchman came in, full of good cheer and hearty hellos for the hospital personnel who had converged on Wallis's room—an orderly to restock the bathroom, a candy striper who delivered a bouquet of cut flowers from the teachers at Wallis's school, and the new nurse. For a few minutes both nurses buzzed around, elevating Wallis's bed and taking her vital signs, adjusting the fetal belt around her abdomen, while Cap stood in the background, downing a cup of bouillon that Wallis had rejected.

"Well," said Dr. Lutchman. "So the little fellow won't play ball?"

Cap closed his eyes. He feared Wallis would lunge. She hated sports metaphors and was certainly in no mood to hear her baby compared to an intractable child in gym class. "It's been six hours," Wallis said. "Six hours and forty-five minutes and too many seconds."

Dr. Lutchman put on a rubber glove. Cap looked away. Did any husband ever get used to seeing another man's hand, even a doctor's, up his wife's vagina? "Well, let's see what we have. We're about one and a half."

"Too bad I'm not bearing an ant."

Dr. Lutchman exploded in laughter. The nurse who had taken over the shift smiled politely and helped Wallis to sit back up. Dr. Lutchman said, "Let's talk." He sat down in the chair next to the TV, and maybe because the image still lingered in the air, or maybe because Cap had not eaten anything since six this morning besides the bouillon, he saw Mister Ed's face, that long, twisted snout, torturously trying to make words. "Pitocin," he heard the doctor say.

Then they were suddenly alone, the doctor gone, the nurse busy with another maternity case, who was making good progress—already eight centimeters dilated after just three hours; Cap and Wallis could hear her grunts and screams across the hall. Wallis looked dejectedly at her enormous belly, no longer even having a sense of humor, as when she had whistled and coaxed, "Come on, baby Claude, time's a-wastin'."

"Well?" said Cap now. "What do you think? Should we do it?"

"We already did it," said Wallis.

He sat down on the very edge of the bed. Wallis was making no effort to allow room for him.

"This was supposed to be different, Cap. I did everything right. I went to all the classes and practiced, I walked five miles a day, I'm in terrific shape for being a forty-one-year-old woman having her first child. I completely made sure I was prepared. I did my part."

She put a sucker in her mouth, her fifth one, all she would eat. Her lips had turned bright red. "And what if the Pitocin doesn't work? You know what that means, right?"

"If it happens, it happens. You have to remember what we get out of this."

"We?"

"Wallis, you've got to let go of how you expected it to be. So it's not going to be completely natural. Big deal. Is it any more natural to endanger yourself and the baby?"

"I don't want a C-section."

"We're a long way from that."

"No, we're not. My water already broke."

"We still have plenty of time."

"Oh, God, I hate this. I'm ready to push. All I want to do is push this baby out and hold him, and nobody will let me *do* that."

Cap could hear Dr. Lutchman making his way back down the hall, his commanding voice coming toward them. When he walked into the room, he wore a scrub suit. He was about to do a cesarean—a woman having twins.

"All right," said Wallis, taking one look at him. "Shoot me up."

They were able to walk around the halls, just as before, the only difference being that they had to bring the Pitocin with them. The IV hung from a pole on wheels. Their "tall friend," Cap called it. The sheriff who was going to get this labor moving. But nothing had happened for an hour, even with Pitocin, and Wallis became discouraged again. She was too nervous, too old, too small, too unlucky to have a baby, and Cap listened, and made jokes about a tall fella that kept following them, and told her to try the visual imagery they'd learned. Imagine herself blooming, a rose opening, or try to picture airy, expansive vistas. They'd gone to the window again and looked out at the foothills, the mountains in the distance. Wallis had said that when she closed her eyes she didn't see blooming roses or open meadows, just a movie she'd shown to her class last year of a newborn calf with chains around its legs, being dragged out of its mother.

Thirty minutes later, the Pitocin kicked in. Wallis said, "Uh-oh." In two hours the contractions were too strong for her to leave the bed or even want to squat. The fetal monitor beeped, and their nurse, who had been steadfastly reassuring, looked at it for a moment, then went over to Wallis and took her pressure. The baby's heart rate had dropped to 50 during her last contraction. It had been hovering around 120, sometimes going as low as 90, but Cap hadn't seen it make this kind of dive before.

"Here," the nurse said, and shifted Wallis in bed. "His cord may be bent because of your position."

But the heart rate increased only a little, up to 65.

"What's wrong?" asked Wallis, breathless after yet another strenuous contraction.

"I'm sure it's fine," the nurse said. They all watched the monitor, which flickered up to 100 eventually but then started coming back down. The nurse picked up the phone to page Dr. Lutchman.

He showed up in less than a minute. "Let's take a look," he said, and reached inside Wallis.

"Why's his pulse so low?" A sucker bulged in her cheek now, the stem writing in the air as she talked.

"Oh, he's ready to come out, all right."

"Do you mean a C-section?"

"No, no. We're ready to push," said Lutchman. As if on cue, the nurse opened the closet doors and wheeled out the examination table.

Hot towels, blankets, syringes, sterile instruments, a scale, all appeared from their hidden places. Tall floor lights were placed on either side of the bed. Lutchman instructed Wallis how to bear down (no need to turn purple) and when to breathe. Despite their course, Cap felt woefully underprepared. He glanced at the monitor. "What about the pulse?" he asked. It had risen to 90, but was still below normal.

"Well, he's been in there a while. He's having some stress about it. But let's see if we can get him out fairly quick."

Wallis took the sucker out of her mouth. She put her hands back down on the bed and started pushing when Lutchman told her to. The nurse stood alongside her and said, "*Go go go,*" her voice surprising in its force and sudden authority.

Cap joined in, all of them telling her to push, while Wallis made a high-pitched grunt, a kind of screeching yodel. "Was that me? I sound like a poltergeist," she said, and then another contraction started. She bore down, then alternately pushed and rested for twenty minutes more, and suddenly Lutchman told her, "Reach down and touch your baby's head," and Wallis put her fingers there and felt the skull and said, "Oh my God, let me see, let me see," while the nurse held a mirror for her. And Cap could see too, the very top of the head, a furrowed surface, waxy and milky blue, and then it disappeared, retracted into its familiar home. "Push," Lutchman said again before Cap had a chance to think about it, and Wallis, ready, inspired by the touch, strained harder than ever, her face contorted with the will to push forth an arkful of creatures if necessary, and the nurse said, "Great great great *amazing!*" upping the praise, and Cap kept telling her how terrific she was, and Wallis responded, then rested a moment.

"*Big-time* push now," the nurse told her, and suddenly Lutchman was using the syringe, and Cap could see the face: the eyes, veiled with their thin soft lids; the matted dark hair, the delicate mouth, as if placed on at the last minute like a cake flower. Wallis shouted, "Take a picture!" Cap tried to remember where he'd put the camera, Wallis always thinking of these things, even now. Out came the shoulders—

they looked like latex, so unreal!—and then the whole body, all of Claude, and Lutchman brought him up to Wallis's chest. Wallis exclaimed, "Hi Claude! Hi baby!" while Cap took pictures without even looking through the lens.

Except Claude wasn't moving.

And suddenly there were two other nurses and another doctor—the pediatrician on call—in the room, and the baby was taken from Wallis's arms to the examining table, six feet away. "What's wrong?" Wallis asked, and Cap heard the pediatrician say, "Do you have a pulse?" to the nurse who was standing over Claude with a stethoscope.

"Tell me what's happening," said Wallis, but Cap didn't know himself. "What's wrong?" she said to Dr. Lutchman, who was attending to her but was distracted by the activity, glancing over at the table. "There's some distress," he said. "They're taking care of it," but he didn't sound confident.

Cap stood rooted between the baby and Wallis, not knowing what to do. Where should he be? He went over to the table and saw Claude lying there, ash-colored, his extremities blue-gray, not crying as he should, his chest concave. Cap shuddered, and whether from fatigue or fear, his whole body began to shake. He grabbed onto a metal cart to steady himself.

"Do we still have a pulse?" asked the doctor again. He had put an air bag over Claude's face, a mask with a black sack like a bellows attached to it. He kept squeezing it with his hand, making the baby's chest move up and down. "Do you still have a pulse?" The nurse with the stethoscope nodded, while the other two worked on the baby's arms and legs, vigorously rubbing them, flicking their fingernails at the soles of his still feet.

It had become deeply quiet in the room, a cavernous chamber filled with hushed probings and manipulations, as silent and impenetrable as if all this were a secret initiation rather than a medical emergency. "They're giving him air," said Cap, going over to Wallis's bed. "You did a great job!" he added, as if this could soothe her, but he'd started to cry himself now, and Wallis asked if she could get up and see. Lutchman said no, stay down. She had to birth the placenta yet; it would be all right; they were doing everything possible.

Then Wallis spoke in some helpless voice Cap had never heard from her before. "Please let me hold my baby before he dies." A dark liquid rose up in his throat, acrid and thick, sucked through a long tube from a deep brine pit of terror, and he found himself praying—not in years—never that he could remember, not even in college when the muggers had pushed the gun in his back. He had promised himself never to pray out of desperation. He'd cultivated the faith of one who understands God more than he believes in Him, who considers himself more a consultant than a supplicant. But what was belief if not desperate? And his own chest ached with the hunger of breath for a son. How little he'd let himself want that until this moment. He heard himself forming long-forgotten words. A little boy again, playing with his father's tallis strings. His father rocked back and forth, chanting Kaddish for lost souls—his breath sour, his lips dried with thirst, the steady drone of exhortations for God's mercy.

The pediatrician kept pumping oxygen into Claude's little body— his chest inflating, the bag breathing for him. Cap moved his lips, his own breath rising, words bursting from him. *"Shema Yisroel Adonai Eloheynu Adonai ehad,"* pleading and hypocritical, but he couldn't stop. Let him live, let him live, let him live, please, and the skin on Claude's chest changed color from gray to mottled patches of red and white. Claude let out a cry. Then a long squall. He was breathing on his own.

"Okay," the doctor said, and stepped back to take a breath himself.

They let Wallis hold Claude for a minute, then took him to the special care nursery. Cap followed behind. They took X rays. There had been a rupture of the lung. Air had seeped into the chest cavity, a weak spot evidently on the alveoli—the little air sacs on the inside of the lung. One of these tiny sacs had burst, probably with Claude's first intake of air. Maybe the stress of the long labor had caused it, but they didn't really know. The pediatrician showed Cap on the X rays the leaked air, the hole in the lung. If all went well, the oxygen they'd pumped into Claude would keep his injured lung full of air, allowing it time to heal the tiny rupture. Claude would be just dandy.

"Just dandy!" He ran to tell Wallis. He held her, kissed her, told her everything he knew, and then, fleet-footed as a Roman courier, he rushed back to the special care nursery to watch over Claude. By the time he got there, the nurses had hooked Claude up. Cap counted ten wires in all. To keep up his blood pressure, an IV had been stuck in his scalp. Another IV had been inserted into the top of his tiny fist. A blood pressure meter was wrapped around his arm. A heat sensor was attached to his thigh. EKG electrodes like fat silver parade buttons lay on his chest. A metal clip pinched his big toe; it would measure the oxygen level of his blood by directing a beam of light to peer at and compare the layers of skin color. Worst of all, a tube ran under his rib and into his lung.

A nurse was probing Claude's belly below the severed umbilical cord, trying to get yet another needle in, but it wouldn't take. "Is all this necessary?" Cap said, his voice pitched near hysteria.

"Yes, I'm sorry, it is," said the nurse. "Be patient. We're only trying to help," and her calmness disarmed him just enough so he could control his rage while he touched the incision under Claude's rib with the tip of his finger, wiping his own eyes with the back of his other hand.

Then Cap was told he'd have to take his finger away. A Plexiglass hood that looked like a cake box lid, with holes for arms and legs, was fitted over Claude.

He understood now that he'd made a bargain, if not with the devil, then with God. Back-room bribes went on at the top as well as the bottom. He'd given up a claim that he'd always reserved—that everybody reserved, even those who, like him, didn't need or want or even think about exercising it until it was forbidden. He had to live for someone else now. He'd relinquished all rights to self-extinction, to the only choice we ever have. He'd promised in the simplest of prayers to give himself to this boy if he survived, to never desert him of his own free will. You couldn't witness a struggle like this to live and not be moved to surrender a fine, dark piece of oblivion, kept like a ticket in the heart's pocket.

He ran down the hall to Wallis's room, his footsteps resounding at one A.M. in the empty hospital corridor.

"I want to see him!" Wallis said, and they got her into a wheelchair and Cap took her down to the special care nursery. She put her hands to her face and burst into tears when she saw Claude attached to so many wires, even though Cap had tried to prepare her. "He's healthy," said Cap. "His lungs are fine," and as if to prove this himself, Claude at that moment had begun flailing his arms and legs, pulling at the wires. He was mad. Good, Cap thought. A healthy burst of neonate anger. Keep it up.

And then Claude knocked his cake box lid completely off. The nurse headed over to replace it.

But Cap had already begun embellishing the incident, making it the first story of his new family. He pictured telling Claude the tale of his birth—the way he fought back from a hole in his lung to karate-kick his oxygen hood out the fifth-floor nursery window.

My God, he had a son!

And Wallis said, "I want to hold my baby!" She leaned into Claude's bassinet and fitted herself to him, his wires vibrating with excitement.

Part Two

therapy

Chapter Two

CLAUDE KEPT FALLING ASLEEP AT WALLIS'S BREAST. CAP WOULD HAVE to rub his head (which barely made Claude stir). Claude's nose was stuffed up too, the dry Colorado air, so Cap squirted some saline up his little nostrils to loosen the mucus. Claude wailed, really wailed— they'd never heard such a sound from any being before, not at least from one they had to console at two A.M. Cap felt as if he were abusing the poor child. "Sorry, Claude, we have to do this, it's for your own good," he said, amazed that only one month after his son's birth, he'd broken his vow never to use the platitudes of his own parents.

Finally, at three A.M., they'd gotten Claude's nose cleared enough for him to nurse, but by then Wallis had developed a plugged duct and they had to wake up their pediatrician, who groggily told them to use hot compresses on the "down breast," as if it were a computer malfunction. Cap heated water on the stove to make the compresses. Waiting for the water, listening to Claude cry upstairs from hunger and lack of sleep and frustration at wanting a breast that eluded him, Cap heard the newspaper thud on the porch. It was morning already! He was sure he'd remember the sound of that newspaper all the rest of his life. He'd remember, too, standing at the stove, splotches of spit-up on his sweatshirt; feeling overwhelmed by what should be the simple business of trying to get an infant to nurse and breathe at the same time; seeing old tea bags, which Wallis used on her sore nipples for the tannic acid, stuck to the breakfast table. And he'd remember the useless baby swing with which they'd tried to soothe Claude, only to have him tip out the side like a melon; and the big electric breast pump that they'd rented from the hospital so Wallis could build up her milk supply and that, with its tubes and suction cups and powerful vacuum motor—a "double collection system," which serviced both breasts at one time—made Wallis appear as if she were locked into some technological upgrade of Puritan stocks.

All that kept Claude happy, after he'd finally been able to nurse, was Cap's pinkie. He spit out the pacifier they offered; only Cap's little finger soothed him. "*He wants flesh*," Cap whispered to Wallis as they both lay in the dark with Claude between them on the bed, their eyes wide open. *Doctor Mom*—a book they'd consulted frequently over the last four weeks—claimed that babies woke so often at night because they needed frequent human contact. "As a therapist, I should appreciate that more," said Cap, his finger bobbing in Claude's mouth like a float, "but to be honest, I'd give our life savings right now if I could fool him with a pinkie prosthesis," and Wallis grunted, unable to laugh she was so tired.

They'd all fallen asleep. But every time Cap tried to remove his finger, gently, stealthily, millimeter by millimeter nudging the tip out, Claude would wake and bleat out his anguish, and Cap would quickly plug the pinkie back in again, sending Claude instantly back to sleep, while Cap lay there and watched and waited and drifted off for a few minutes at a time, his finger making the link to this new life very real, a dependency far more intense than he could imagine with even his most needy client. (He thought of his father saying, "You want bonds, go to a bank," and imagined biting down on the old man's own pinkie.)

Somehow, he made it to the office. His first day back. He sipped tea at his desk and looked over the appointment log.

Julian. The boy was twenty, a student who had moved out West from Baltimore. An epileptic, he'd been free of seizures for two years. His last major seizure had occurred his freshman year of college, at Ohio State University. It had been the worst one of his life. At the end of his freshman year, he'd returned home to stay with his parents. He believed he could never live by himself, but after being back in Baltimore for a year and working for his father, he decided he wanted to try college again. Having always imagined he might like the West, he'd gotten up the courage to enroll at the state university in Pierre. He'd been seeing Cap for a few months, since first coming out to the university for the summer session. He had told Cap that he thought his seizure at Ohio State had been related to being separated from his parents and was intensified by his fear of meeting someone of the opposite sex. He'd been afraid the same situation would happen out here. Cap had been impressed by the boy, his dark good looks, his articulateness, his quiet determination to figure out his problems. A month after they had been working together, Cap found out that the boy's mother was a survivor of a concentration camp.

Julian had forgotten to tell him this.

Surely not, Cap had said.

The boy insisted he'd just forgotten. They'd talked about Julian's father mostly. He didn't like to talk about his mother.

"Let's talk a little about her," Cap had said gently.

It turned out the mother suffered numerous phobias, including a fear of driving and of using the phone. She had no friends in the community and had depended on Julian, an only child, to make calls for her, whether to the doctor or the plumber or the maid. By seven years old he'd become practiced at calling the pediatrician and making his own appointments—adept at deflecting surprise or bewilderment by stating that his mother had asked him to help her out and could he please have the possible times? He'd pick one himself and promise to call back if this wasn't suitable, which it always was, because his mother was waiting next to him by the phone and would nod at what he had written down. Even Julian's father at work she wouldn't call. Julian had to get him on the line before she'd talk, because the cashier might answer. His father, a pharmacist, had his own drugstore and spent long hours there, eight in the morning until seven at night on weekdays. An American soldier, he'd met Julian's mother after the war near a displaced persons camp, married her in England, and brought her back to Baltimore. They'd been childless for twenty-four years, and then, when Julian's mother was forty-three (close to the same age as Wallis, Cap couldn't help noting when taking down the history), Julian had been born. In third grade, Julian had his first seizure, though he recalled having absence seizures before this, which had been mistaken by the teachers as poor concentration or "nodding off" in class.

His mother blamed herself for the seizures. Not her age, but her experience during the war. She'd been operated on by Nazi doctors and, she believed, sterilized. Pregnant with Julian, she'd waited nearly five months before seeing a doctor. She'd avoided looking down in the shower. She'd worn loose shirts. She claimed to be ill (which she was). Her belly itched and stretched with the life, but such an occurrence was impossible. The Nazis had seen to this. She'd been told she would never have children. A doctor at the camp informed her of this when she woke up with burning pain in her womb after an operation in Auschwitz. The doctors had implanted viruses that attacked the reproductive organs, and her ovaries had been permanently damaged. She was fifteen years old.

Cap had stopped Julian at this point and asked if he believed, as did his mother, that her operation was the cause of his epilepsy.

Julian shrugged. "Somehow she had a child and it wasn't normal."

He couldn't let the slip go by. "You said, 'Somehow she had a child and it wasn't normal.'"

"I meant it wasn't normal for her to have a child."

"But you said the child, meaning you, wasn't normal."

"Well, I don't know." Julian reached for his cup of tea. "Anyway.

It wasn't normal for her to have a child. Look, I'm just telling you what I grew up believing."

"Do you ever blame yourself for your mother's unhappiness?"

"She was unhappy long before I was born."

"I agree. I'm just wondering if you really believe it."

"I'm not following."

"If your mother was supposedly unable to have children, the one she did have would carry a tremendous responsibility."

Julian took a sip of tea. He'd insisted that Cap show him the box from which the tea bag came, to make absolutely certain it didn't have caffeine. Caffeine was on his list of items that he believed could trigger a seizure. "I'm not following you."

"If you were really born out of sterility, out of barrenness—a miraculous birth—that would make you very special, wouldn't it?"

"I suppose."

"And you'd have a special obligation too, knowing how much your mother suffered as a survivor. You'd owe her something, some compensation, for all that suffering."

"They take care of me. They pay for my school. They've provided for me all these years. What compensation have I ever given them?"

"You've been your mother's sole emotional support, her single contact to the outside world. She was depending on you as a seven-year-old child to make phone calls. According to you, she had no friends, no life outside yours. I'd say that's quite a lot of compensation you've given her."

"I don't want to talk about my mother anymore."

"It must be very painful to remember all this."

"It's not painful. I just want to figure out how to keep the seizures under control. That's why I came."

"It's all connected, Julian."

"I just wish you'd try hypnotizing me."

Cap shook his head. "You know that won't solve anything."

"If it prevented the seizures it would."

"Well, I think we both know that hypnosis wouldn't do that."

"How do you know? Have you ever tried it?"

"Julian, there are deeper issues here. You're wanting hypnosis to be the magic cure. It isn't. Even if your epilepsy were suddenly cured, what about your other fears? Where do you think they're coming from?"

"The epilepsy. I'd be able to look a girl straight in the eye without worrying that she saw what was wrong—or would find out soon."

"There are many people with epilepsy who have comfortable, close relationships with the opposite sex. It doesn't stop them from getting on with their lives. It's not what's stopping you."

"So you're blaming all this on my mother, then?"

"I'm not blaming anybody. I'm trying to help you find the right box to open. Until you do, it's going to weigh you down, keep you depressed and anxious and looking for magic cures." Cap paused. He made a note to himself to find out if Julian's parents were going to be in town at any time. If he could interview the parents, have a session or two with the whole family together, they could break through these impasses much quicker. "I don't know why your mother had been unable to conceive for years and then could. I know it wasn't a miracle, though." He thought carefully about whether to say something, then decided it could help in making a bond with Julian. "My wife and I tried for many years before we were able." Cap paused, wanting this next fact not to be missed. "Wallis is almost the same age as your mother was when she had you."

"Are you saying she's lying about what happened?"

"Of course not. All I know is that they didn't successfully sterilize her, otherwise you wouldn't be here. Unless you think you're adopted."

"You never know."

Cap couldn't read the tone here. It seemed almost spiteful, but not spiteful about being adopted. About something else. "If you're adopted, why wouldn't they tell you?"

"Are you kidding? They would never talk about something like that. They never talk about anything to do with the war. I had to find out everything from my aunt Tula. Even my father wouldn't say a word to me. Only that he would never buy a Volkswagen as long as he lived. That was our revenge. A boycott."

"Do you have a picture of your mother?"

He did. He showed Cap a photograph taken after the war, when his mother arrived in Baltimore. She was striking, with dark hair, glistening black eyebrows, a wide, unsmiling mouth. "You look just like her," said Cap. "It's indisputable."

"Well, I just know what I was told."

"Look, Julian, you're not adopted, and you're not an immaculate conception. You're her flesh and blood, and I imagine that has been enough of a burden without believing you owe your life to the angels."

Cap walked out to the waiting room now to get Julian. The boy stood up and followed him back.

"Congratulations."

"Thanks," said Cap. He'd sent a letter to his regular clients, telling them when he would be back in the office. At the bottom he'd put a P.S. announcing that they'd had a seven-pound boy, Claude. The birth still made him shudder—a lingering afterimage of Claude's limp body on the table, gloved hands swarming all over him, trying to give him life. Seeing Julian now, after six weeks, he realized how much he'd missed the boy. Despite all of Julian's problems, Cap would be pleased if his own son turned out to be as sensitive as Julian. All those years of tending to his mother had developed at least a strong dose of devotion. Cap was touched by that and wanted Julian to know it was something to value and hold on to.

But Julian looked particularly anxious today—the fall semester had just started for him, so he'd be feeling the stress of that—and Cap felt protective. He wondered if it was already the effects of having a son. "We're not sleeping a lot, but we're getting by."

Julian nodded. "I haven't been sleeping much either."

"Why's that?"

"I've been bowling."

"Oh?" said Cap.

Julian looked away. "I haven't told anyone about this. I'm really embarrassed."

"Tell me about it."

"I haven't bowled in years, but I always liked it when I was younger, one of the few sports I did enjoy. I'd go by myself on Saturday, when everybody else was playing football or basketball. Anyway, one night a couple weeks ago I couldn't study, and I went over to the student center. I got a lane to myself and I stayed until morning. I've gone back every night since."

"What's wrong with that? Sounds as if you found something you enjoy and you want to do it a lot. Happens to us all. You get a new car, you want to drive it all the time."

"It's more complicated. I have to take the exact same amount of steps every time up to the line." Julian stopped. He was wearing a tan sweater—the weather had cooled off these last days of August—and he'd pushed the sleeves up his arms. Julian's right forearm, the one he bowled with, did look as if it had been exercised regularly. Cap thought he was exceptionally handsome. His hair was dark brown with a gold tinge to it, thick and wavy in back. His olive skin set off his brown eyes, a deeper shade than his hair. He had full red lips that pronounced each word carefully. "It feels better to talk about it. I couldn't wait until you got back."

"You could have called me, Julian. I've told you that." He guessed the bowling had started because he'd been away, Julian feeling deserted, needing some way to deal with his anxiety. "Why didn't you call?"

He shrugged. Pulled his sweater sleeves back down. "You just had a baby. I didn't want to bother you."

"You know, I didn't forget about you, Julian."

He looked away. "Anyway, it's pretty complicated. You sure you want to hear all this?"

"Of course."

"I have to bowl alone. I have to take the right amount of steps. I can never go over the line. I have to score at least two spares or one strike in the first four frames, and my total score has to be divisible by four."

"What happens if it isn't?"

He smiled—almost proudly, it seemed. "It always has been. I make sure it is. I know how many pins to miss if it's looking bad."

"Bad meaning not the magic score divisible by four."

"Exactly."

"Okay," said Cap. "So you do all this, and then what?"

"I've made it harder each time I've gone back. Last night I had to have a spare by the ninth frame, but a spare made on a seven–ten split, which is almost impossible."

"Did you do it?"

Julian nodded. "Yes. I did. I had to. I'd already done the four–six, seven–ten combo the night before, so I had to make it harder for myself."

"Sounds punishing, Julian. I'm wondering why you have to be so severe with yourself." He got up and sat next to Julian on the couch. He could see the boy shrink away. Julian had told him, after Cap tried to hug him goodbye once, that he didn't like to be touched. He didn't mind touching people, but he tensed up when anyone touched him. It's why he couldn't imagine being with a girl now. How could you be with a girl and tell her you didn't want her to touch you? But recently, before they'd been interrupted by Claude's birth, Julian had started letting Cap put his arm around him. It had been real progress. When Cap reached to do it now, though, Julian sank into the corner of the couch.

"Are you mad at me for going away?" asked Cap.

"Why should I be? You have a baby. What are you supposed to do, not take time off?"

Cap laughed. "I'm not asking you whether it's legal. Just whether you're angry with me."

Julian looked down. "I don't know. I don't think so. If something's necessary, it's pretty hard to get upset about it."

"Sleep is necessary, but that doesn't stop Claude—to take one recent example—from waking us up five times a night, unreasonable as it may be."

"He's an infant."

"You were too, at one time. Or were you allowed to be?"

Julian pinched flat the empty paper cup from his tea. "I think we're getting back to my mother, and I really don't want to talk about her."

Cap shrugged. It was quarter to eleven, and he was feeling the strain from last night. "Would you do something for me?"

"Depends."

"Call me instead of bowling tonight."

Julian shook his head. "I can't."

"Why not?"

"I just can't. I can't take a chance."

"Can't take a chance on calling me?"

"No. On not bowling."

"Why not, Julian?"

"Because I'll have a seizure if I don't."

So that was it. He should have known.

"I've got it in my head that bowling can control my seizures."

"Better than medication?"

"Medication has failed before."

"And bowling hasn't?"

"It's just extra insurance."

"But it's only been two weeks, Julian. You've been taking medication for how long now?"

He was silent.

"What's wrong, Julian?" Tears had come into his eyes. "Tell me what I said that made you sad."

"Twelve years I've taken pills. I was eight when I had to start."

"Yes," said Cap. "That's a long time for a little boy."

Julian wiped his eyes with his sleeve. Cap handed him the tissue box. "Tell me what you remember about that time when you were eight." He'd been trying to get Julian to talk about his seizures in detail, but the subject was as off-limits as discussion of his mother. Except for being at a special camp when he was sixteen, Julian had been secretive about the disorder all his life. It had been a big step just to tell Cap, let alone go into specifics. But Julian looked more ready today, not as closed as when Cap had brought it up before. Maybe the separation had actually helped—made Julian feel the absence acutely enough to realize he trusted him.

"I didn't know what was happening. The first time."

"I'm sure you didn't. Where were you?"

"On the playground. Then I was in the nurse's office. That part wasn't so bad. I had to go to the doctor; there were tests over the next four days. My father took me. My mother stayed home. The doctor said I had something called idiopathic epilepsy, which meant my epilepsy didn't have a cause—but what I heard was "idiot," and I thought: *retarded*. And I shouldn't think of it as a disease but a symptom of disturbed electrical activity in my brain. He tried to make all this sound like okay news, before he told me the bad news: I'd have to make some changes in how I played. I'd have to stop swimming for a while. He didn't think football was a good idea either, or any contact sport. I shouldn't stand on tall places or ride my bike alone. I would have to take medicine three times a day. I might have some side effects—problems with my gums, dizziness, maybe an upset stomach or jitters. If I had any of these, he'd adjust the dosage, though my father, being a pharmacist, could do that too. I'd have to expect some discomfort getting used to the medicine. It would be hard, but this was my only choice.

"It was true what he was saying, and I knew he meant it. I was different, really different now, from all the other kids. I'd been different anyway because of my mother, but now what had been on the inside, hidden at home, showed on the outside. They all could see."

"What do you mean, 'They all could see'?"

"The next day, when I came back to school, the other kids looked at me and were whispering. That was okay. I just sat on the steps and played with a gyroscope I'd brought in my lunch box. It was funny, now when I think of it, that I'd insisted my father stop for a gyroscope on the way home from the doctor. I'd seen one in the window of the toy store a few weeks before. Anyway, I insisted he stop. He didn't want to. It was late. I started screaming that he'd better do it. I never did that. I was always well-behaved, especially around him, because he was always so tired from work and sad around the house. He kept saying, We have to get home. Your mother is waiting to hear from us. He couldn't call her, of course, from the doctor's office, because my mother wouldn't or couldn't answer the phone. But maybe that's partly why I insisted. I didn't care if she was waiting. She should wait. Anyway, he gave in and we stopped for the gyroscope and I played with it all night, pulled the string until I could get it to spin on every surface in the house—wood, Formica, steel, up walls and down the banister. I was fascinated by it. Its *balance*. Not surprising, I guess, considering what the doctor had just told me—something I didn't understand about my body shaking and stiffening. And that I would sort of fall asleep and there would be this electrical storm in my brain and then when I came out of it I'd feel very tired, very, very tired, and maybe relieved or peaceful, and I should stay in one place for a while. I might tip over too, lose my balance and fall down, and I should make sure if I started to feel funny—he said my arms and feet might feel tingly or I might see spots in front of my eyes—I should get to a safe place, away from sharp objects or open flames. I was listening to him and thinking he can't be talking about me, he must be talking about somebody else, a pretend friend I had or a puppet. But maybe, too, I heard only the word 'balance,' and that's when everything all started—I mean, these kinds of compulsions. Maybe the gyroscope was the first one. I've had others I haven't told you about, and when they wear out I find new ones.

"I brought the gyroscope with me to school, and I was sitting there playing with it on the concrete steps, making it bounce all the way down from the top to the bottom one. Nobody was coming over to me like they usually might, especially considering I had a new toy. But I heard giggling, and then I looked up at the jungle gym and there was Tommy Eberhart at the top, leaning backward against the bars, and he was—it was this unbelievable ugly sight—he was jerking his hands and arms and making his whole face twitch as if he had some awful tic, and drool was coming out of the side of his mouth and the kids were laughing and glancing at me, and I knew then that was me. That was what I'd looked like yesterday. That was the missing piece. That piece of time that had disappeared. That animal, that ugly sub-human thing Tommy was imitating, was me."

"Can I hold you?" said Cap quietly, and Julian let him put his arms around him, while the boy cried. He drew away after a few minutes.

"It's not good for me to get upset like this. It could start something."

"I disagree," Cap said, stroking his arm, talking gently to him. He'd been moved by the story and found himself choking up, a lump in his throat. It had made him think about his brother, Allan, the teasing and humiliation he'd endured. "I think, Julian, that it can only help. Getting all this out finally will only take off the pressure."

"It won't. I take the pressure off by *never* thinking about it. When I start thinking about it, that's when it happens. I panic."

"Yes, but not in here. In here, we take care of your panic together. You bring your panic to me. I'll handle the bomb. We'll defuse what's been ticking for so many years now. You're panicking because you've been trying to handle this by yourself, ever since you were eight.

That's an awfully hard experience for an eight-year-old to undergo alone, to hold everything in by himself."

Cap looked at his watch. They'd already gone over their time. "You did good work today, Julian. I'm honored you're telling me this. I know how hard it is for you."

Julian kept his head down.

"Will you do something for me, Julian? If you want to go bowling tonight, call me."

"Why?"

"I'll go with you." He couldn't believe he had made this offer. Wallis would kill him. "I'll go with you, and we can just bowl. We won't count. We'll step over the line together. I'll be with you the whole time. Here . . ." Cap got up to get his notepad. "I'm going to write something down for you. I want you to put this in your wallet and read it later." He wrote at the bottom of his pad and tore off the slip of paper, handing it to Julian.

Bill Sable came in. A first visit. He was forty-four and separated from his wife. He'd been going through a custody battle with her, and Cap had been asked by the courts to file a recommendation about which parent was suitable to have full custody of their two children (neither was willing to go along with joint custody). Sable's wife, Millicent, claimed her husband verbally abused them all and had on occasion hit her. He countered that she frequently left the kids while seeing a series of other men.

When Cap had spoken to Millicent, he'd found out the series of men included her brother, who had been dying of lung cancer. She'd gone down to visit him for a week in Colorado Springs. "As for leaving the kids, yes, I did that, so as not to interrupt their schooling, but I left them with my mother."

He'd asked her about the "other men."

"Once, just once," she'd told Cap, "I went out on a date, folk dancing at the university. And yes, I spent the night with him, a stupid mistake.

After years of being under Bill's heel, I just wanted to know what it felt like to be free for a night. Meanwhile," she asked Cap, "how do you think my husband found out about it? Because he followed me. He follows me all the time, then denies it. That's the kind of man he is."

So he talked to Sable now. Next week he would interview the kids, and then Millicent and Sable again, if necessary, before writing up his report.

Sable gave polite answers to Cap's questions. He worked five days a week, ten to six, as an appliance manager at Sears. On weekends he squeezed in coaching Little League, Scouts, church, and chores. "I know I work a lot, but I'm on call for my kids twenty-four hours a day. I understand how to love them and set limits at the same time. That's the kind of father I am," he answered, eerily echoing and rebutting his wife's accusation.

This would be harder than Cap had thought. He wanted to be fair; he didn't automatically assume mothers should have custody of their children. In some cases, especially with boys—and Sable had three boys, ranging in age from two to eight—fathers sometimes made the better choice. He decided just to let Bill Sable talk about his feelings in the remaining minutes, rather than ask any more background questions; the man was almost too good at answering questions about himself, as if on the floor at Sears, with quick responses about the merits of a refrigerator.

"So how are you feeling about all this personally?"

"What do you mean, Cap?"

"How has the breakup of the marriage affected you?"

"Well, Cap, I'm a soldier. I'll come through this just fine. It's the kids I'm worried about."

"Any feelings about your role in the separation?"

"You know, Cap, I tried my best. I'd love to give it another chance, if only Millie would."

"You've been in counseling?"

"Oh, sure, we went that route, yes; geez, yes."

Sable was so affable, Cap didn't know what to do with him.

"Would you be willing to take some tests?" asked Cap.

"I'm not the best student in the world, Cap. I only made it through one year of college."

"These wouldn't be those kinds of tests, Bill. They're personality assessments. Sometimes they can help us make a better recommendation."

"Would Millicent have to take them too?"

"I would ask her also, yes."

"Whatever you say then, Cap." Sable stood up after Cap did. "You know, I had a roommate my first and only year in college named Kaplan. You're no relationship to him, are you?"

"There are a lot of Kaplans out there, Bill."

"Just thought I'd ask," he said, shaking hands warmly. Cap would have bought a refrigerator from him in a minute. It was going to be a difficult decision. He hated custody cases that demanded one parent be declared less competent than the other.

Maureen Kels sat in his office, in black stockings and black knit skirt, her feet pulled under her on the couch. She lit a cigarette.

"Maureen—"

"Sorry. I keep forgetting where I am. Seventy-five dollars an hour, and it doesn't even entitle me to enjoy a cigarette." She stood up and dropped the cigarette in the coffee mug on his desk. It sizzled in the dregs. The mug was his favorite; she somehow knew this, he guessed.

She was his most difficult client; he'd braced himself for the visit. He'd intended to relax first by taking his lunch hour, but his sessions with Julian and Sable had gone over and set him behind.

"What's been going on?" asked Cap. He noted that Maureen hadn't said a word about his new son. Cap knew by now, after working with her for two years, that the lapse was no oversight but a conscious omission. The baby would mean more if she could make a silent issue

THERAPY

out of it. They'd eventually get around to both her jealousy and her resentment of him for having his own child now. It was going to be the theme of the month, he could see, with all his clients.

She'd turned thirty-six just recently, had never been married, and had no promising prospects (though many affairs). She insisted she wasn't interested in having children, but nevertheless she had found a reason to walk out on the session when he first told her that Wallis was pregnant.

"I'm not really here today."

"Oh?" said Cap. "Who am I talking to?"

"My answering service." A dig at his refusal to give out his home number. He made clients use the answering service, though he encouraged them to call if necessary. It was the only way he and Wallis could get any peace. If clients needed him quickly, they could place an emergency call. Maureen had told him it was humiliating to make an emergency call, to tell some flunky answering-service operator "This is an emergency," just so he'd call her back right away. "What about all your 'unconditional positive regard'?" she'd asked. Unconditional positive regard doesn't mean being invincible, he'd explained. Even therapists have limits, especially therapists, and his acceptance of her was unconditional within those limits. "Oh, Casper," she'd said, the only one who called him Casper, having seen his full name (everyone thought Cap was short for Kaplan) on his doctoral degree, which hung on the back of his closet door—he'd found her in there "looking around" one day after he'd gone down the hall to get some tea. "Unconditional within limits. Sounds like 'minor emergency.' A nice oxymoron if I've ever heard one." Maureen was a professor in the environmental economics department at the university. She'd grown up on a farm near Port Arthur, Texas, where her parents had been pecan growers. They'd been poor, preoccupied with the farm, which was always losing money. On more than one occasion she'd told him she'd gone into economics as a means of understanding their poverty and had never figured it out. "Maybe we can think of some more," Maureen had said.

"Unconditional prevaricator. Wait! That's not an oxymoron—that's hyperbole. I mean, there's nothing unconditional about the lines you hand me, is there? They're all based on my good, solid payment for such insults. If I'm fool enough to hand over seventy-five bucks a week for horse poop like 'unconditional within limits,' then I can't really blame anyone but myself."

He stuck with her. Rode her anger, a bull out of the chute. Her pattern was to sabotage relationships with men when she became frightened of being too emotionally involved. After a grace period, when she could be charming (Cap had seen this side, and he never knew what he would get in the therapy), she'd find her lover's weakness and step on it, on her way out the door. He'd confronted her about her pattern of dropping men before they had the chance to drop her.

"Has it occurred to you," she fired back, "that the behavior you claim is my defense against being rejected is simply my waking up to what losers most men are? Hmm?"

By the time she came to Cap, she had already been through four therapists, two in Pierre, two in other places where she'd lived. It was hard, almost impossible at times, to sidestep her attacks and not take them personally. It helped to know that she would have found something wrong—anything—about his character in order to undermine their work. He knew the two other therapists in town, both male, whom she'd seen for a short period. One had flat-out told her, after two sessions, that he couldn't work with her. ("You're just figuring that out, Sherlock?" she'd said as her exit line, leaving him with a fine-tipped, personalized dart.) And the other, whose intelligence and critical acumen were irreproachable—he was a recognized scholar in his field—she had informed, "Physically—well, this shouldn't matter, but it does to me: I mean, I have some issues around sexuality—physically, I just can't take you seriously. You're like talking to a pudgy little brother." She'd left. A Denver therapist, prior to these two, had been "overtly simple-natured" and lacked "the requisite darkness." Only her first therapist, from Minneapolis, was truly a gem, a man who had "tuned me up and turned me on—healed my body-body split the minute he opened his gorgeous mouth," but he'd died.

She'd done the same with Cap, compared him to the idealized, if conveniently dead, therapist, while checking him off the list like others she'd found wanting. But it had not been his appearance that she'd maligned. Indeed, as she reported frequently, she often masturbated fantasizing about him. He was keeping the flames going down below. That was worth the price of admission alone, since nothing else he did earned it . . . by the way, did he ever masturbate over her? ("No," he told her honestly, knowing that if he avoided the question she'd think otherwise.)

She'd tried insulting him in small ways at first: his bad taste in office furniture ("Neat—my grandmother has a lamp like that with a cute doily underneath it"); his choice of teas ("Umm, Lipton, how original"); his clothes ("That shirt would go well with elephant bells"); his voice ("You stutter sometimes, did you know that?"); his sex life ("Can't have kids or can't manage it?"); even his choice of magazines and of soap in the bathroom ("Irish Spring, how . . . pungent").

Through with the petty insults, she went for the bigger stuff. Once when he'd asked her why she found it difficult to sustain a healthy reciprocity with a man, she'd said, "Wow. 'Sustain a healthy reciprocity.' I wish I could talk like that. Will you teach me to speak like a social scientist, Casper?" He'd meant simply to ask her what happened inside when someone paid her a compliment, told her he liked or loved her. He admitted the stuffy jargon, but she wouldn't let him forget it. "Why can't that man sustain a paradigmatic, intergalactic, oceanic copulation?" she'd said, complaining about one of her lovers, who suffered from premature ejaculation and on whom she wasted no sympathy, as she did on no man. "I bet you wouldn't have all that wordiness of yours in bed, Cap dear, would you?"

It took her a year to get him. Her sensor had worked overtime. Finally, she found it. It was a spring day. He'd just come back from enjoying a walk across the street at Skookum Park, stopping there to eat his lunch. He'd been glad when they'd changed her appointment slot to two P.M., so he could take a lunch break first. A full stomach, some exercise—a quick game of racquetball with Dick—it helped him to face the afternoon, especially on Wednesdays, with Maureen. He'd been feeling pretty good, satisfied with the progress he'd been making with clients (Maureen excepted), happy about where they lived, guiltless about being so far from his parents, resigned to having no children, and resigned about his brother, Allan, who was thirty-seven, schizophrenic, and still lived with Cap's parents in Philadelphia. Cap was explaining something to her, a little awkwardly—distracted by the nice day, the budding lilacs, the apple tree in crisp white blossom outside his window, the sudden sharpness of a Western spring born from a winter with windchill temperatures of twenty-five below— explaining a concept of parental introjects, when she interrupted him: "You're a plodder, aren't you?" He'd frozen, stunned. He could see in her eyes, the soft, almost tender and solicitous way that she'd said it, that she knew she'd found the key, turned gold back to lead, the prince back to the frog, peeked at the warty, ugly bottom of her man. Bingo.

It was what his father had once told him: "You're a plodder." One step above being a schlump—a schlump's slightly better off cousin. But no natural smarts. You'll work harder than five men and still be selling shoes to old ladies when you're forty.

It wasn't enough; no matter how much he did, it wasn't enough. And Maureen had seized upon this fact, having been searching from the first session for his prized vulnerability. He believed that anyone else who worked as much or as hard as he (Oh, he should be doing so much more for not having children! was how the loop went) would be famous, a zillionaire, and loved the world over.

Every bit of personal volition, every ounce of professional commitment . . . it had taken these and more not to leap down her throat—he wanted to kill her; he'd never felt such murderous rage for a client—and then afterward not to boot her out.

She stopped coming. No explanation. No phone call. Nothing. It wasn't a surprise, when he thought about it. Now that she'd made the hit—and he could only think of it in terms of mafiosi, a vendetta, her ego just a hit woman for her unconscious—she had no reason to return to the scene. Her assumption was that he was dead. Dead to her, at least. (How did she know, he wondered, how did she know the *exact* word? She'd even said it with his father's inflection; he had to admire her inductive skills, though they were in the service of such foul ends.)

He'd thought about calling her. He'd consulted with Dick about the case and received rare direct advice. "Don't, Cap. A client like her will claim harassment and malpractice. And it's doing exactly what she expects. You're fulfilling the pattern of the scorned suitor, the father over whom she has power only by rejecting." He'd been convinced and let go of it. It was sheer ego to think he'd do better than any of the other casualties. For Maureen, the only good therapist was a dead one.

Eight months later, in a wet January, during the Iraq war, he ran into her at the supermarket one evening. Their eyes met, and she dashed off to another aisle, but he saw her at the checkout stand and went up to her. Small talk. He asked about her teaching (she was on leave). They discussed the war for a few minutes. She'd broken away from the TV, had to get out of the house and do something else, a little shopping. Cap picked up his groceries. "You're welcome to return anytime," he told her. Her face reddened. She turned and fled.

The next week, after calling for an appointment, she came in to see him. For the first part of the session she raged at him: why didn't he leave her alone, why couldn't he get off her back, who did he think he was, approaching her like that in the market—some old boyfriend? "Why the hell did you say that to me?"

"Say what?" he asked.

" 'You're welcome to return anytime.' "

"I meant it."

"How could you say it, after—" She stopped.

"After what happened?" he said, completing the thought.

"*No*, after what I *looked* like."

"What?" said Cap, not remembering.

"I'd run to the store for some exercise. I had to get away from all those 'smart bombs that performed sensationally' and that could 'impressively' find their way down the air shaft of the military bunker, aka family bomb shelter, killing only a few thousand children. If I had to see Wolf Blitzer's face one more time—I just wanted to grab a razor and start shaving him—or Fred Francis in his little Pentagon picture booth, if I had to hear one more paean of praise for our new generation of weapons, saving millions of lives with their surgical strikes, *I* was going to start shooting. So I went for this long run to the store. I smelled terrible, once I got there. I had on my ugliest green sweatpants because the spandex ones—the ones I'd lost ten pounds for, to be MTV slim—were dirty, and my hands and face were muddy because some goddamn jerk *guy* had driven by on the way and splashed me. I looked like shit."

"I didn't notice," said Cap.

"Of course you didn't notice." She wiped back her tears. "It doesn't matter to you, it really fucking doesn't matter to you, does it"—and he couldn't tell whether she was more disappointed than relieved about this. She was casually dressed, jeans and a white blouse, a single gold strand around her neck, no heavy eyeliner, no wild perm (she'd had three different styles since he'd known her), nor the usual black molded skirt, tight leotard top, and dark stockings—her dragon costume, which she admitted she wore only to therapy. She would change from the more tasteful outfits in which she taught to the dragon costume before coming to see him. Behind the getup, Cap thought, she was attractive, stylish and slender, with fine, sharp features. She had light-green eyes, blonde hair, a gentle sloping neck that formed delicate, soft hollows into her shoulders. Occasionally, she'd show strong white teeth in a smile. So much was attractive, in fact, that he'd often have to remember that his first impression of her had been one of beauty, not made-over vulgarity.

She pleaded, "What more do I have to do?" A question she had asked him frequently, trying to get him to take her up on her standing sexual offer.

"Nothing, Maureen. That's the whole point. You don't have to do anything. You don't have to sleep with me. You don't have to impress me with your sexual charms. You don't have to dress up or down— or lewdly. And you don't have to worry about destroying me with some terrible insult. I still want to work with you."

"I *know* I hurt you."

"Yes," he said, confirming even what he hated to admit, though it crossed his mind to lie. "But you didn't destroy me. I'm still here. Healthy. Alive."

She just watched him, surprisingly wordless for once, as if she was actually taking his words at face value. He decided to make use of her interest (her trust, finally?) before the window closed. "Don't you think, this little hiatus aside, it's time we get to the truth about your rage?"

It had been the turning point. It was then that she told him something that moved them ahead dramatically, an incident from her childhood that had influenced her life more than any other but that she'd never spoken about to anyone, not even her sister.

When she'd been four years old, she'd almost drowned at the pond on her parents' farm. Something else had happened that day, which she couldn't remember. She only knew it had made her afraid of her father for the rest of her life. "He'd do other things too," Maureen said.

"Sexual abuse?"

"No," said Maureen. "Surprisingly enough. Implied maybe, but not any acts I can remember. He'd do things to scare me, intimidate me. Once, when I was fifteen, he got me in a headlock on the living room floor and told me he could break my neck if he wanted, snap it in two. My mother walked in at that moment, and he let me go. Sometimes I think he would have gone through with it if she hadn't come in."

"What else?"

"One night I woke up and he was sitting on the edge of my bed with a butcher knife. I was too frightened to scream. The next day he walked around the farm with it, tapping it against his leg before he slit a pig's throat."

Maureen looked down. She wiped her eyes and blew her nose. All the air seemed to have gone out of her, the fury. "Maureen," Cap said, "we have to stop. I'm sorry we do, because obviously this is extremely important."

He thought they'd turned a corner, which they had for a while, but then he started preparing her for his paternity leave, a term that she spit back at him with derision—since when do men do enough to warrant a paternity leave?—and he knew they were back to fighting her resistance again, himself the hostile, uncaring father.

Now, sitting in his office, she wore a short knit skirt, a black sweater with scoop neck, stockings with silhouette designs—the familiar vamp outfit. He knew they'd have to work through this latest setback, his absence.

"Tell me what you've been doing," said Cap.

"Not fucking anyone. Unfortunately."

"Umm," said Cap.

Maureen was silent. She would stare at him until she saw it didn't make him uncomfortable.

"Maureen, why don't you tell me directly how you feel about the baby."

"Baby?"

"You got the letter I sent."

"I love form letters. They're so . . . touching."

"I wanted to let you know what happened. It was the best I could do under the circumstances."

"Right. Unconditional with limitations again. Personal and caring but qualified by your very busy life. Kind of like being proposed to by voice mail."

Cap smiled. "All right, Maureen. I take your point. You might remember, though, I wrote you a note at the bottom." He thought he saw a faint hint of appreciation cross her face, a crack in the retributive facade. "What about your mother's visit? You mentioned that she was planning to visit with your stepfather." Maureen's father had died ten years ago. "You were going to talk to her about the incident from your childhood."

"They never came out."

"Why not?"

She shrugged. Her sweater hung provocatively over her right shoulder, which she kept turned toward Cap. "They couldn't leave their dog."

"You're kidding."

"No; they couldn't leave their dog with somebody else for a while. That's what's become of them. They don't like to travel unless my aunt who lives nearby can house-sit for the mutt. And she wasn't available."

"So they canceled their trip. Chose the dog over you. Along with my being unavailable, that must have made you pretty furious."

"Don't flatter yourself," said Maureen. She tossed back her hair, not curled anymore. She was wearing hoop earrings nearly the size of Claude's head. Cap had a thought of him asleep on his shoulder. He missed him.

"Thinking about the little spud?"

"Pardon?" said Cap.

"You were thinking about Claude, weren't you?"

He hesitated a moment. "Yes," he admitted, impressed by how tuned in she was to him.

"That's all right. What the hell. I'll just leave now and save you the boredom. Get some young stud to fuck my brains out."

"Maureen," said Cap, "I think we should try talking to your mother."

"Are you crazy? She wouldn't get within ten feet of a therapist's couch."

"I don't mean talk to her in person, although that would be useful if you can ever get her in here. I mean talk to her inside you."

"Yeah, right, inside this whore is just an uptight Farmer Jane, dying to get out. What if I just came over there and unzipped you? What would you do?"

"That's not going to happen."

"Just put my hand lightly on your fly. Maybe nuzzled you through your jeans a little bit. Not take it out yet, just play with it from the outside. My warm breath heating up your crotch. What if we start there?"

"Does it make you nervous when I want to speak with your mother?"

"Does it make you nervous when I want to suck your cock?"

"She doesn't like to be talked to directly, does she? She's trying to hide behind the prostitute."

"I bet your cock would like you just to shut up for a while and let me talk to it directly too. You could come right in my mouth. In a minute. Real fast. I'd swallow it, and nobody would ever know. I'd walk out of here, my mouth shut tight, all your hot come in my throat. I bet Wallis never swallowed your come."

He took a breath, tried to control himself. "Maureen, we're crossing a line here."

"I already crossed it, Casper. I'm waiting for you."

"I want you to listen to me," he said shrilly, his muscles too tense. "It's important that you let me speak to your introjected mother."

Maureen burst out laughing. "Introjected is right! Gee, social scientists have the sexiest jargon." Cap flushed. She had him again.

He reminded himself that he was therapist number five and she would be saying this, or something similar, to anyone. He'd stuck with her for two years, which she couldn't discount. "Maureen, we've been meeting a long time now. Aren't you ready to stop attacking, testing, and demeaning me and get to it?"

"Get to it? Does that mean s-e-x? Have I finally triumphed?"

"It means your rage. What are you so afraid I'll find out if you stop trying to seduce me?"

She hesitated and reached reflexively for a cigarette. He'd stopped her finally, and righted himself in the process. "Shit, I want to smoke. Why the hell can't you let me smoke in here?"

"We need to work with the split-off parts of you that are keeping you in costume here. I want to talk with your mother about that day at the pond."

"And if I don't let you? What are you going to do? Get me in a headlock and make me scream 'Mother'? Please do. It runs in the family anyway."

"Maybe we should reevaluate the therapy if you don't want to work with me."

She stiffened at his words, then yanked off the hoop earrings. "Nice threat, Casper. Unconditional acceptance. Uh-huh. Right, sure. As long as we play by your rules. You're just another asshole, authoritarian, patriarchal, gender jerk, with a whip in your mouth instead of your hand." She stood up abruptly. "I have to change for class," she said. "I'm going to use your bathroom. I want to wash out my mouth too. The very thought of your come in my mouth is enough to make me vomit."

"I want you to return next week, Maureen."

"Fuck you," she said, and walked out.

Maureen's alter ego came in. Wilmella Hoder. If Maureen was a taloned temptress, Wilmella was a declawed kitten—never having let herself enjoy a single good swipe at anyone, her paws bloodless, cushioned artifacts. She was sweet, polite, attentive, deeply grateful, and complimentary—filled with a frustrating willingness to please. Admiring, forgiving, modest. And hopeless in her goodness. He'd been trying for months now to get her to say a bad word about anybody. "Oh, no, he was just tired," she'd decided about her son, a bum who had gotten her to loan him money so he could buy a pickup (which he managed to drive into a Wyoming lake) but who had overslept when she'd needed a ride to the airport, making her miss her flight to see her daughter and only grandchild in Seattle.

Cap expected she would be just as understanding with him now. And indeed, after forty minutes, they'd exchanged the usual pleasantries, with ten minutes, ten *long* minutes, left to go in the session. She was by far his most tedious, if agreeable, client, steeping him in small talk; he had begun to suspect she was a master of passive aggression, keeping him away from any dangerous areas even better than the more virulent Maureen, with her claw-hammer seduction lines.

At the moment, she was still cooing over Claude's baby picture, newly installed on Cap's desk. She had thanked him excessively, gushingly, for the same form letter that Maureen had loathed, and had waved away his question about whether she was still having heart palpitations and dizzy spells, hearing loud, booming noises at night while she slept, and seeing shadows move behind her. She was seventy-two years old and in good health, according to her doctors. They had referred her to Mental Health, which gave her the names of three psychologists in the area. She'd picked Cap because of his first name ("Is that short for Captain?"). Her husband, before he died, twenty years ago, had been a captain in the merchant marine. He was rarely home. There weren't many ships in Lander, Wyoming, where she'd grown up. She'd pretty much raised her family herself, but that was just fine, because she was used to hard work from growing up on a ranch near Lander. She now drove 140 miles round trip every Wednesday from Laramie, where she'd retired to. She never missed an appointment. She was always on time. She paid promptly. And she still had all her symptoms: headaches, dizziness, loud noises, and fears of going into basements. He'd made little progress with her in examining them, because she always deflected the conversation to how "basically good" things were in her life.

"Wilmella," said Cap, "maybe we should consider stopping therapy." He was getting rid of clients left and right today. Whew. Cleaning house. "I don't think you're getting what you need from me, and to be honest, I'm frustrated at not being able to help you more."

"Oh, but you are helping me, Mr. Cap." She insisted on calling him this, even though he'd told her that Cap was, in fact, not short for Captain. "I so look forward to these sessions. They've helped me so much."

"How have they helped you, Wilmella?"

"Well, it gets me out of the apartment and down here to do my shopping. We don't have all the malls in Laramie that you do in Pierre. And I see my daughter more who lives out in Wellington—I hardly used to see her before. And I get to exercise the Plymouth on a long stretch of road. It's not good to let all that sludge buildup in the oil pan, you know."

"Wilmella, these aren't good enough reasons to pay me seventy-five dollars a week."

"But I don't mind. You're a nice man, always so kind to me, and it's not as if I don't have the money from the ranch."

"I really think you can do all those things you mentioned without my services."

"Mr. Cap, are you firing me?"

"Wilmella, people—clients—aren't fired in therapy."

"But that's what you're doing, isn't it?" She actually had a tear in her eye. Her small, powdered face, her thin neck, a freshly pressed blue dress, her hands neatly manicured, her white hair thinning at the sides, so that he could see the pale pink flesh, her glasses magnifying her light-blue eyes . . . She was a child! Her hands folded patiently in her lap, she sat on the edge of the couch as if being interviewed, her false teeth polished to a glistening teacup white, bravely trying to smile this out. God, he was heartless. And yes, he was firing her!

"I just feel that we're wasting each other's time and your money, Wilmella."

"I just don't see it that way, Mr. Cap. You've given me so much *motivation*."

"Motivation for what? To drive your Plymouth down here?" He felt himself getting testy. He needed to control himself. It had been a long day. He would be old himself sooner than later. "And you have serious symptoms, Wilmella, that continue to intrude upon your life."

"But I've learned to live with most of those. I just won't go in basements or close my eyes for more than five minutes at a time. If I wake myself up frequently at night, I don't see those things anymore. You taught me that."

"Wilmella, I taught you no such thing."

"You told me to watch my thoughts and pay attention to when I became upset. So that's what I've been doing."

"But it was so we could try to discover what's setting off your anxiety."

"Yes, that's right. Sleeping, going into basements, looking over my shoulder too quickly, knives on the counter, elevators—"

"Those are all symptoms, Wilmella. What's causing them—"

"That's right. That's what I'm trying to avoid. I put away a knife now soon as I use it, because my heart starts beating so fast to see it up on the counter. And it really isn't hard as you think to wake myself up every five minutes. I just keep a clock beside my bed and push the button on top. I do that all night. Keeps the trouble away."

Cap shook his head. "We're going in circles."

Wilmella looked at him blankly. "I really thought you'd be proud of me for how well I'm" —she hesitated, groping for the word, then smiled at him—"cognitating myself."

"Okay, Wilmella. It's time for us to stop now."

"Oh, well, it's all just mud pies and beaver tails to me. I'm just trying to do what everybody tells me. If it weren't for my uncle, none of this would be a problem anyway," she said out of the blue.

"What?"

"Please?"

"Your uncle? What about your uncle? Which uncle?"

Wilmella glanced at her watch. "Oh, look what we've done—we've gone over our time by a minute."

"Hold it, Wilmella. What's this about your uncle?"

"Oh, nothing. He just used to make some trouble on the farm. You know, give a girl a hard time once in a while."

"What kind of hard time?" asked Cap.

Wilmella stood up, smoothed down her skirt as if it were a gingham apron. "Nothing worth talking about. I guess you're right about me not coming down. I'm just wasting everybody's time. I always am. That's what my daughter keeps telling me when I talk like this. I won't bother you anymore."

"Next week, Wilmella, we're going to start by talking about your uncle. All right? Are you prepared to do that?"

"Mr. Cap, I just can't, in good conscience, impose on you another minute."

"Therapy is the only business where the client is always wrong," Armond had once told him. Armond had been his therapist when Cap was doing his internship at a psychiatric hospital in Denver. "Use the intuition like a witching stick," Armond had said. "It will start to quiver when you're in a bad spot—but the right place." And Cap hadn't fully understood the statement until he'd begun practicing himself and spent months—years—breaking down resistances, often losing clients before he ever did.

Armond, who talked in riddles that would take Cap years to figure out, had told him, "A dunce hears the same lesson and can never learn it. He gets two plus two drilled into him every day and comes up with five. If you keep hearing five and you're afraid to hear four, you should check what's hiding inside your own pointy dunce cap."

He meant the therapist had to ask what countertransference was happening. What about the client's situation and conflicts made the therapist uncomfortable or caused him to react negatively? What in the therapist's own life distanced him from the client and kept the client stuck? Armond, who was Indian, a Brahman who had rejected the caste system and been educated in England and then lived in the States for twenty years, and whose father had been a medical doctor, had told Cap in their first session that Western psychology had one main advantage over Eastern asceticism, an advantage that should not be underestimated: it believed in grudges. Grudges against God. Grudges against man. Grudges against history. Grudges against one's birth. Grudges against parents. Grudges against nature. Grudges against the post office, the phone company, and the airlines. Eastern philosophy, meanwhile, believed in amends. Wars and genocide and passionate love slaps in the cinema had come from grudges. No-fault insurance from amends. "So you see the advantage?" Armond had asked Cap. It was the week before he and Wallis were to be married. Cap would be moving up to Pierre to open his own office and terminating his therapy with Armond. He'd resolved, or thought he had, his major issues with his parents and his brother Allan. Armond was trying to explain this grudge thing, and Cap was wondering why they were wasting their last moments together with such a cryptic and obscure exchange. He wanted Armond to tell him that he'd miss him, or to invite Cap to come back down to Denver occasionally to see him, or to pronounce Cap the best client/trainee/friend/student/man Armond had ever treated. Instead, Armond simply said, "If you remember you are both a therapist and a person with a grudge, you'll make a good living."

Make a good living? That was it. Nothing else. How did he mean that, exactly? Make a good living as in money—or as in peace and contentment?

He'd seen Armond only once since, two years ago at a professional convention, an abysmally disappointing encounter. Armond had been standing in a corner of a meeting room, listening to a panel on the terminally ill in therapy, and Cap had walked up to him, Cap without a beard now, in a suit instead of bell-bottoms, his hair much thinner and receding, so that if he'd been wearing a headband, as he had in the early seventies, when he'd been seeing Armond, his head would have looked as if a quoit had landed on it. Armond, meanwhile, wore no suit or even appropriate casual attire—say, slacks and sweater; instead, he'd dressed in plaid shorts over his fat brown legs, and a windbreaker, "Valtano's Electric" on the front. Could he still be practicing? But why else would he be here? Cap, in fact, had been amazed at how much Armond had changed, and in some way, some significant way, Cap had certainly expected Armond to notice and recognize the years that had passed—and Cap's progress, if not his own. But Armond had only said, "You left your umbrella in my office."

Sixteen years of not seeing one another, and all he could say was that Cap had left his umbrella! What was he, a crackpot now? "Do you remember me?" asked Cap, sure he'd misheard. "Yes. I told you, I still have your umbrella." "Well, fine," said Cap, feeling irked. "You might as well keep it," and because he couldn't resist, he added, "I'm moderating a panel here on negative countertransference," a subject that had come up in their discussions many times. It was perhaps his way not only of recalling their past work but of letting Armond know the professional progress he'd since made, grudges or not. And also, perhaps, yes, to show him up. He'd felt his competitive hackles rise at the snub. "I guess you're not doing any panels yourself," said Cap. Armond scratched his hair, gray as when Cap had first started therapy with him; he'd been Cap's present age then. His flat black eyes registered no response. Cap fired ahead, giving him the big one: "I've been running a group for child oncology patients and their families." Surely this would get some response! It was the reason, in fact, Cap stood in this very room, listening (or trying to, in the face of Armond's unnerving indifference to him) to the panel on the terminally ill in therapy.

Indeed, he'd been written up in both Denver newspapers for his work with child cancer patients and their families; one of the group sessions had been taped for the local PBS station and broadcast twice now. He could not believe Armond had missed seeing the publicity, especially since Cap had sent a videotape of the PBS show to his office, though it had never been acknowledged and Cap had too much pride to call and ask if it had arrived and what Armond thought of it. He was convinced Armond was now withholding approval out of professional and personal spite. (Did he fear Cap's accomplishments—the son exceeding the father, the very focus of his and Armond's work together, Cap's father always feeling competitive with his sons, fearing his sons would grow up and shame him with their achievements, their father a vending machine king who had never gone beyond the eighth grade, Allan shrinking from the battle, no match with his paranoia and instability for the father, while Cap jumped in the ring, the first-born, his loyalties great enough that he wanted his father to share in his accomplishments and be proud of him, though his father never asked a single question about what Cap did as a psychologist, because it all seemed like mumbo-jumbo to him—God! His sessions with Armond were rushing back to him; how could the man *not* remember. . . .) Cap said, "I guess you never got that tape I sent."

"Your umbrella is missing two of its spokes. I let another client use it, and that's when the damage occurred." Then Armond excused himself to visit the bathroom, and Cap never saw him again at the conference.

What did it mean that he let another client (more loved than Cap?) use the umbrella? Take Cap's place? Was it some kind of put-down? Some message about Cap's neediness? That goddamn idiotic umbrella!

Cap went home and fumed for an hour in front of Wallis, who tried unsuccessfully to calm him down. "I wasted three years in therapy with that nut!"

It meant nothing. Some banal remark purporting to be useful information, manipulative in its stupidity. Maybe in his twenties—during the sixties—he might have fallen for such riddles and Zen chestnuts, but not now. India or not, Armond was no guru imparting special divinations. He was a dazed old man, perhaps destitute (should Cap have treated him to lunch?) or suffering from Alzheimer's (why did he think only Americans developed that?) or a tumor, or maybe just rude. A joke. Disappointing, but still a joke. Write it off.

The next day, up at six as usual and working on his presentation to a church group about his oncology project, he remembered all the old anger—directed at Armond back then. In therapy, Cap had accused him of not listening, of falling asleep (Armond's eyes would close briefly on more than one occasion), of being patronizing, of thinking that Cap was stupid and inept, a big, dumb jock who couldn't even get himself married (Susan) or mugged right (whoever heard of getting shot in the kidney?), who would never amount to anything.

He'd projected it all onto Armond, a successful transference if there ever was one. Armond did act bored. Was he? He did seem to frown when Cap admitted that he had "sort of" cheated on his statistics final as a senior and bought a copy of the previous year's exam from a fraternity file. But Cap had done it because of his disability; he couldn't read the questions fast enough. Or was the frown really concentration, not judgment but pained empathy, as Armond claimed.

Was this the process of transference?

This was the *problem* with transference. It worked on trust alone. You put your life in someone's hands and then had to believe him when he said he was taking care of it better than the first people, who had done such a bad job. The whole messy nexus of psychotherapy was right there.

What choice did he have? He had to believe Armond when the man said, "I would consider myself rich if I had a son like you."

Rich. Yes, he'd said this! Said it when Cap had voiced his fears that Armond secretly despised him, found him inept, and actually shared the same low opinion as Cap's father, who had proclaimed after Cap failed ninth-grade algebra, as he would struggle with statistics years later, that Cap could look forward to a nice career as a caddy.

He'd done so poorly because the unfamiliar combination of numbers and letters in word problems intensified his usual difficulties with reading; the contrasting elements seemed to be at war on the page, annihilating one another. That was before Cap had known about his disability, of course, diagnosed about the time he'd started seeing Armond, a diagnosis that Armond sympathetically assured him (one more reason to trust him) would have made a vast difference had his teachers and family been aware of it while he was growing up.

For two weeks after running into Armond at the conference, Cap couldn't concentrate. Could it be? His whole therapy amounted to a broken umbrella? A man in a Valtano's Electric windbreaker? Were the results of therapy so ephemeral that they equaled a conversation he could have had with the office janitor? He started getting chest pains. He was forty; his last physical had been five years ago. He went to see his doctor, who gave him tests, took blood, examined his prostate, listened to his heart and lungs, collected specimens. Were they still trying to have children? Yes, Cap said. "You're fine," he told Cap. "Just suffering stress, something in your department." He needed to slow down. He'd been too busy. All the conferences. The therapy group for families of child oncology patients. The speaking engagements. He had even thought about writing a book lately—an onerous, nearly impossible chore, given his impairment. But he could do it if he drove himself. A well-known self-help book (he couldn't but notice) had been on the *New York Times* best-seller list for 472 weeks. Nine years!

A therapist and a man with a grudge. Resentment. Jealousy. Was that what fueled his ambition? Proving himself still to his father, who was intellectually, socially, academically, professionally, emotionally inferior but could ask Cap, "So how much did you pull down last year?" and in a single sentence obliterate all Cap's advantages. "Sub-

stitute the word 'love' every time you hear 'money' and you'll understand the family sickness," Armond had once told him.

Cap stopped running the oncology group. One of the other therapists took it over. If he was going to start purifying himself of his
reckless ambition, his workaholism (he reflected that indeed his own
father had married his vending machine business), this seemed the best
place to start. Oh, he'd done good, no question about it. He'd helped
many of those children and certainly their parents. But he'd exploited
the situation too, caught up in when the next offer would come in to
appear on a radio talk show or present his findings at a conference;
when the phone didn't ring, when he didn't get a letter in the mail
thanking him for his selfless, dedicated work, he'd be perturbed and
wonder if the phone was out of order, his mail stolen.

Okay. His work. One broken spoke.

And the other? Well, he and Wallis had been "drifting apart." How
many times he'd heard those words from the couples he counseled,
while he sagely instructed them in the ways of intimacy, avoiding it
himself.

Their sex life had dropped off to nil. The surest test. How were
they supposed to have a child like that? Or maybe that was why they'd
been avoiding it, embarrassed and turned off by their failure. His mind
was always somewhere else when he was with her—planning his next
project, impatient around her until he could get back to his office or
on the phone to promote his career.

The following summer they went away together. They took their
first real vacation in two years, somewhere other than to the mountains.
They went east to Nantucket and chartered a private boat one day for
a tour of the sound. The captain, a black man with a full white beard,
who looked like an African Santa Claus—they would later joke about
his being a visiting angel—had told them, "You all gonna remember
this day," and Cap thought he just wanted a bigger tip, the usual
tourist stroking.

They couldn't find his flat-bottom trawler the next day. Wallis had left her favorite scarf on it. Nobody at the harbor or at the dock's tourist information booth had even heard of this man or his boat. It was impossible, they had said, because the harbor wasn't that big and somebody was bound to know him. But nobody did, and finally they had to go back to Colorado.

A month later, Wallis was in the supermarket and dropped a jar of artichokes. Cap hadn't been there. She told him later that that was when she knew. There was no reason why she should drop a jar—a typical certainty of hers, but it had validity, because, he had to admit, he had never seen her drop anything. She was so careful, or exact, or lucky. She rarely made mistakes, at least not ones of carelessness or neglect. Her mistakes were those of excess, an insistence on perfection: piling too much work on her students until parents complained, or speaking out in faculty meetings about other teachers being remiss in their grading, or following a recipe exactly and having the lamb curry taste flat and dull and making the recipe three more times before she wrote to the newspaper where the recipe had appeared and chastised the writer for leaving out the two tablespoons of parsley—Wallis had discovered this in her own experiments—that lifted the flavor. Or her frequent headaches, sometimes migraine, from the unending pressure she put on herself to do things right and perfect—which, she had once explained to Cap, were not the same thing: right was for others, perfect for herself.

But when she'd dropped the artichokes, the glass shattering, the small green hearts scuttling across the floor, she'd felt neither perfect nor right, just confused, and had stood over the smashed jar. The shards had spread everywhere. The supermarket clerk cleaned up with his mop, patting her arm once. "It's okay, ma'am," he assured her. "Things break all the time in here. We lost three bottles of seltzer today alone. Kids especially are careless," and whether it was the word "careless" or "kids," she didn't know, but it prompted heaving sobs. The manager walked up and asked if there was anything he could do. He called Cap for her, and he came right over and took her home.

They found out the next day that she was six weeks pregnant. They traced it back to that day they'd gone on the tour boat with the African Santa. That afternoon, right after the boat ride around the island, when they'd both felt so (there was no other word for it) horny, they'd rushed back to their room to make love—pulled their clothes off and grabbed for each other with a hunger they hadn't felt in a long while, Wallis's scarf gone in exchange for this new seed, this tiny life they'd been trying to make for ten years.

On the birth announcement he'd sent Armond, Cap scratched at the bottom, "Thanks for telling me about the 'umbrella'!" Giving him the benefit of the doubt. Amazingly, Armond wrote back. A chatty letter, but with no mention of having seen Cap at the conference. All about going back to visit his family in India, the hero's welcome he'd received, about the two Arabian horses he'd just bought and was boarding on some land up north around Cap's way ("I got two for the price of one"), about the new car he had ("it has dual airbags—does yours?"), about how many clients he had to turn away these days. It was filthy with self-promotion, every line full of unabashed self-aggrandizement, the paper virtually burping with materialistic gluttony. There was barely a line devoted to the baby ("Good job on little Kaplan"). At the bottom, Armond had written, "Umbrella? What do you mean?"

He'd been tricked! He'd changed his life because of some stupid remark that the man didn't even remember. Nothing! It meant nothing!

In the end, he decided it didn't matter. Therapy was therapy. There were no rules. That was the problem. You came out the way you went in, only more so, but with your spurs turned out instead of in to strafe yourself. Was that better or worse? Could you count on any one insight lasting into eternity or even until the next Wednesday? Was it a faith? It spoke like one, it felt inside like one, it had the urgent calling of one, it had adherents and converts and naysayers and heretics and denouncers and high priests (472 weeks on the best-seller list!), but it insisted it was simply an aid for living—like a juicer or a microwave, not the vegetable or meat itself. It was only a protective container: Tupperware for the psyche. Or a soft glove for the embattled human spirit—a system for coping with living, but not the living thing. No, indeed, it was not a faith, but finally, he believed, it was.

He had five minutes before his next client. He called Wallis in a near panic. "I think I'm having a reaction to being back," he said.

"Your parents are here," said Wallis. "They came in early."

"Wallis, I'm not prepared to see them—"

"And pick up some nursing pads on your way home. And a fluorescent. The light is out in the basement, and there's a ton of laundry waiting down there." She lowered her voice. "Claude shrieked when he saw them."

"Wallis—" he said, but she'd already gotten off, and Cap, with no time to indulge his own childlike fears, stood up to let in his next client.

Part Three

breath and spirit

Chapter Three

ON JULIAN'S FIRST DAY AT OHIO STATE, HE'D HAD A SEIZURE AND AN ambulance had been summoned. The next morning his picture was on the front page of the student newspaper with the caption: "Frosh collapses during orientation." His rescuer had been a blonde sophomore with an irrepressible smile, an agronomy major (there was a sidebar about her). She was used to taking care of sick livestock—she'd grown up on a farm outside Columbus, Ohio—and what she'd done, getting the victim's tongue out of the way so he wouldn't bite it off, wasn't that much different from reaching in and tossing a pill down a sow's throat. She liked helping "all kinds of people," especially when a life was at stake.

For weeks afterward he avoided the biology building, dropping his class so he wouldn't have to go by the spot. He saw himself lying there, an outline of his body like a chalk drawing, a crowd watching his grunting, stiffened form, his twisted mouth expelling foam and vomit, his eyes rolled back, while the heroic agronomy major reached bravely in his mouth for his tongue—a completely unnecessary gesture, matched only by the embarrassment of the ambulance's arrival to cart him away.

He'd woken up in the student clinic. They'd already figured out that he was epileptic, but they insisted on keeping him overnight for observation. It was university policy that anyone ill enough to be picked up by ambulance needed at least one night of supervision.

He'd lain in his hospital bed, listening to the mixer parties going on outside in the quad. Music of a volume so high it sounded like a hot roaring wind blasted from speakers set in the dorm windows. There were shouts and howling laughter, all the primitive calls of initiation, and as the night went on, the noise became more savage and unrestrained.

At three A.M., tired of staring up at the ceiling, he had left his bed and walked to the end of the hospital corridor. Only one night nurse remained on duty. Otherwise he was alone in the ward. He watched a couple standing at a tree in the quad, the boy's back against the trunk, his hands lifting the girl under her buttocks, while she straddled him.

He'd looked down at himself in the hospital gown open at the back and thought he'd never survive this, that the humiliation had been too devastating this time, had shoved him back beyond a point he'd passed years ago. Since grade school he'd been spared seizures of this wallop. There was no explaining it other than stress: going away to college, his courses . . . the dorm food? The explanation could be anything or nothing, a thousand contributing factors or just one, something obvious or rare: too much caffeine or too little sleep, frayed nerves or an allergy to some new Ohio plant—or just a coincidence, a synaptic time bomb set years ago for his first day of college. He could (and would, if he didn't make a powerful effort to stop) drive himself crazy trying to figure it out so he could make sure it didn't happen again, though he knew there was no certainty, this being the worst consequence of what had happened: not even his medicine, strictly taken, could guarantee that he wouldn't wind up with June McCormick's fingers (his agronomy savior) in his mouth, like some pathetic 4-H project gone bad, on the front page of the school newspaper again.

The incident had blackened anything good that might have happened thereafter, the proverbial drop of ink in the water, inextricable. All he could see were the "negatives," as his father told him in a letter, encouraging him to try harder, to persevere. Most kids have problems adjusting to college, his father wrote from Baltimore.

But "negatives" were all that he'd known here: The bone-chilling cold while trying to make his way across the sprawling Ohio State campus on a winter day, a cold he'd never felt in Baltimore, a wet, penetrating Midwest cold that he would walk into with his head down like an ox, tears streaming from his eyes. The kids in the dorm who knew each other from high schools in Ohio and sat in tight, exclusive knots with their girlfriends, also from high school, at the student center. The Saturday football madness, while he stayed in his room and cranked up the volume on Ten Thousand Maniacs, pitying himself. The fraternity rush parties, a few of which he attended, standing along a wall or with his back to everyone, nervously picking up cheese cubes and potato chips, trying to look natural drinking a beer, when he knew alcohol was among the things that set him off. One of the brothers at Delta Tau had come up to him and tried to be friendly and finally asked, "Where have I seen you before?"

Julian shrugged; he knew where—the front page of the newspaper. The brother looked at him curiously. "Well, I guess it must be someone else I'm thinking of." And Julian, sounding curt when he meant only to be evasive, said, "Probably is," and excused himself to get away and out the door.

He was never invited back, of course, not asked to pledge anywhere. An abyss had opened up, one he'd been relatively protected from by his parents. Despite their own anxieties, he'd known the way through them, known where to stand, how to act, what he should do on weekends, who would protect him. If the worst happened, they'd take the brunt of it, bear the costs of his humiliation, make the explanations. But out here there was no one, nothing to cover himself with, nowhere to avoid the picture of himself pinned to the ground. He had failed here, and he had failed so badly that he couldn't even feel ashamed about it; his fear of having to return to that moment—that instant of dropping, helpless and splayed like some foaming animal—was great enough to make him sure he'd never leave home again.

But he did leave—breaking a pledge to himself in favor of some overriding want of experience, some hunger for travel that stood up and refused to be bullied by one of his strongest convictions: change is bad. A long-cultivated crop in his garden of fears. Change will destroy you. It will humiliate you first, as it had done at Ohio, and then it will atomize you into vapor.

He went even farther away. After a year back in Baltimore, he transferred to the state university in Pierre, Colorado. A sophomore, he was able to find an apartment within walking distance of the university.

He'd always wanted to go out West. Something about the mountains laughed at his predicament. Their absolute immobility, their disregard for time and space. They held their ground, moved aside by no force. Indeed, they seemed to be the planet's rulers of time and space— dimensions he exited from and returned to without the slightest control during his seizures. But mountains . . . well, he felt he could learn something from them.

He gave up plans to follow in his father's footsteps as a pharmacist; or rather he decided to combine business, science, and a growing interest in the environment— now that he was out West—by majoring in environmental economics. The professor of his Affording the Global Atmosphere course had told them that research showed the present ozone depletion was caused by CFCs released twenty years ago. It took at least that long for degrading chemicals to reach the upper atmosphere. "It's like a star—twenty light-years away. Even if all CFC production were cut immediately," she'd told the class the first day, "we'd still have to contend with the damage already done over the last twenty years from aerosols, insulation, air-conditioning, heat ex- changes, and many other sources just now exerting their effects. How are we going to keep them from destroying what's left of the ozone layer?"

This had been the class's initial assignment: to come up with a cost-effective solution. Julian wrote his paper in a long feverish trance (he did, in fact, have the flu and a temperature of 103), claiming there was little that could be done about the existing CFCs, but as for adding more ozone to replace that which had been depleted, smokestacks could be built. Ozone was a by-product of common industrial waste, a component of smog from cars. Funnel up the ozone trapped below. The very problem that had caused the mess would solve it. Twenty-mile-high smokestacks that would reach the upper atmosphere.

They had to read their papers to the class. No one, to his surprise, laughed at his. Rather, they asked him questions afterward, and he found himself answering them, one by one. As to the height . . . well, yes, that was a problem; it would be almost a hundred Empire State Buildings, or seven Longs Peaks, the fourteen-thousand-foot mountain that could be seen from the campus in Pierre, but it could be done with a kind of space-station factory.

No one else in the class had come even close to anything so preposterous. His teacher called him up afterward and asked him to see her in her office. He thought she would reprimand him for taking a frivolous approach, wasting the class's time. "Well," she said, laughing, sitting on the edge of the desk while he stood in front of her, a pen in his hand, "somebody's got to be willing to think loony. Absurdity is the back door to genius. So you have my admiration."

Two days later, following class, she asked him back to her office again. Would he like to work with her on a summer research project? He'd be paid well and he'd be doing important work, a study of environmental impact costs from waste-water runoff. Nitrates and bacteria from animal wastes were remaining in the water table and causing an increasing degree of toxicity. Her findings would eventually wind up in a book she was writing, *The Last Family Farm*.

She put her hand on his shoulder, lightly, then just as softly removed it, as though a leaf had come to rest there and fallen off on some indoor thermal current. A shiver went through him, an electrical gas, mildly pungent, stinging the nostrils—that smell in the air, in fact, of ozone after lightning has struck. She touched him again, this time between the shoulder blades, just held her hand there and let it drift to the middle of his back, while he remained absolutely still, a sheet of pins crossing his skin, ever so gently marking him and leaving fine lines of blood. He wasn't sure for a moment if the sensations meant a seizure was starting, but he decided it was different, not the usual tingling and lightness in his extremities, but something outside his knowledge, some aura confined only to his flesh—his brain locked out. "Anyway," she said, moving to the other side of the office and leaning against the window, "we need to talk about this further." She had closed the door. "If you're interested, that is."

That same day he ran into her at his therapist's office. He had just told Cap in detail about his first seizure. The session had drained him. So he'd walked around the corner to have lunch and try to . . . well, he didn't know exactly. Forget about it? Understand what had happened? He'd been crying in the office and had felt good right afterward, but now he wasn't so sure. He'd eaten, then discovered he'd left his jacket in the waiting room, and when he'd gone back, she'd been sitting there, about to go in. Awkwardly, he excused himself, picked up his jacket (which to his even greater embarrassment was on the back of her chair), and fled. She'd seemed amused by the whole encounter.

A week later, she invited him over for dinner, noting that since they had the same therapist, why not share some food? He brought a bottle of wine, which he didn't drink. He kept pouring for her. Tell me more about yourself, she asked. She wanted to know about his life before the university. Had he lived in Baltimore until college? What did his parents do?

His father owned a pharmacy in Baltimore. His mother he quickly skipped over. She was a housewife.

Did he have lots of friends out here? Any special friend?

Special? he asked. What did she mean?

They became lovers.

He spent the night at her house, but unable to sleep lying next to her, he had slipped out quietly in the early morning. He went straight for the bowling alley at the student center. Even one frame would take off the pressure, just so he could smash the pins and—like firing a gun to set off a controlled avalanche—preempt the explosion that was building inside him.

But the center, always open all night, was closed. He banged on the door. A janitor came. No bowling this morning. A gas leak had been discovered. The fire department had closed the center until they could check it out.

Please, Julian said. Just for a while.

It's all closed now, son, said the janitor. Come back tomorrow.

He felt himself panicking. To be closed now, of all times! But he saw it was futile to plead.

He wandered near the campus, passed restaurants that were just opening at six A.M., stopped for a freight train that ran through town. Pierre had grown to over ninety thousand people, but long freights still went straight through town ten times a day, backing up traffic on either side of Central Avenue for miles. There had been talk of moving the tracks, but nobody could agree on where to relocate them.

He watched the long freight train go by now, standing so close that the cars blurred and the draft whipped his hair against his cheek and the wheels sparking the rails filled his ears and he could barely hear the shout of the brakeman, waving him back. He'd always loved and feared trains, their power and noise and great forward motion through time and space—mountains that moved—and he'd been thrilled to find a town with trains through its heart. He had come down here often just to watch them, though never this early, the sun rising behind him and starting its journey over the mountains. He could throw himself under the train like Anna Karenina; he'd read the book nonstop one weekend, fascinated by Anna's bad luck (how fitting that his own mother was named Anna). He would not let himself fall in love, not get torn up inside—not be part of the world, because he had never really belonged here anyway. As long as people could stick their hands in your mouth and compare you to a sow or stand on a jungle gym and let spit dribble down their chins, he couldn't be with anyone.

He watched the train, this train that wouldn't end. He saw the cattle cars from Wyoming, and he thought about his mother. She'd been in a car like one of these, on a long train like this, adults and children dropping all around her, dying of thirst, hunger, and exposure—suffocating and going mad. And he was here today. By all rights, he shouldn't be. He shouldn't exist after what had happened to her. This whole long orderly procession of cars, all linked together, the rattling steel scream of the wheels in his ears, the rush of blood, the panting and grappling and sweating and terrible wet stickiness and flesh hugging her bones, none of it should be, and oh he was in love, oh God he was in love. He wanted it to go on and on and on. He would never take her for granted, never make her regret having chosen him. He would suffer for it, but he couldn't stop it now; he couldn't stop it from beginning.

He walked across the tracks and bought a muffin at Hannah's Bakery. A rack of fresh-glazed cinnamon rolls had just come out of the oven, and he devoured one of those too, swallowing a pint of milk quickly. He'd been too nervous to eat last night, the homemade pasta she'd cooked for him with shrimp and red peppers (and couldn't spicy food set him off?). She'd gone all out and he'd felt bad about not being able to swallow more than a few bites, but he'd been afraid that if he ate too eagerly he'd have to explain why he wasn't drinking the wine—he'd taken one sip—so it was better to pretend that he was just generally sick, without an appetite. It was so complicated being him! All the little diversions, deceptions, and excuses. Why couldn't he just tell her he didn't drink? But then she would say either Fine or Why not? He drank another milk now and ordered a poppy-seed muffin, finally starting to fill up, the smells of the bakery washing over him, the cinnamon roll's stickiness on his fingers—she'd sucked each of his fingers last night, then unzipped his pants and sucked his penis too. Nobody had ever done that. Even Luchesca, the only other person he'd slept with—unstable, wayward, orphaned Luchesca—had never done that.

He'd made sounds, something else he never did with Luchesca, low at first, then louder as he exerted himself, his breathing quickening, his heart bucking against his chest, and he had to tell himself this wasn't a convulsion coming on, this was *another* it, a wondrous it, this was absolute pleasure, and then her hands dug into his back, her mouth twisted to one side, and she thrust up against him, pulling him deeper into her, so he felt her squeezing him below, her breath catching— her body jerking and going limp with exhaustion.

A bit of foam had settled in the crease of her mouth. He stared at it in awe of her satisfied release, knowing what this wetness had always meant on his own chin.

He lay beside her, not moving. She reached down and felt him. He was still hard. "You didn't come."

He shook his head. "I didn't want to," he said, trying to make it sound as if it were some manly show of self-control.

"That was good," she said, "just as good as gold," and she pressed against his hard penis. "You want to try something different?"

He'd pleased her and satisfied her, he'd actually made her come, once, twice, an amazing eruption in any case, and he was completely mixed up as to whether there was anything more he should expect or want. He was afraid that if he got too tired, something would happen; it would all be taken away from him, in payment for his lapsed vigilance. "Maybe we should rest awhile," he said.

She stared at him.

He felt his erection sinking. "I just mean you must be tired."

She threw her head back against the pillow and laughed. Her right arm was draped across her chest. She looked sated and bemused. He wondered how many men after sleeping with her had said, "I just mean you must be tired." He knew the answer.

She got out of bed and went into the bathroom, shutting the door. When she came out she wore a bathrobe. There were pictures in her room of herself and of someone who looked like her—her sister? There were books on the floor and a stack of reports, which he realized contained his latest paper. He resisted the urge to see if she'd graded it yet and instead put his head back to see above the headboard. A wall-size poster of a black jazz musician loomed there, sweat flying off his face, his eyes squeezed shut as he played his sax. Above the poster hung a long computer banner: ECSTASY: BLOW.

She sat on the edge of the bed and crossed one of her legs over her knee, inspecting a toenail. Her robe opened, and he could see her breasts, their long nipples, the pimpled brown circles, her shoulders rounder and her breasts fuller than Luchesca's skinny, pale body. He wondered how old she was. He reached out and pressed her belly, fitting the swell to his hand. She looked up, startled. "Why'd you touch me there?"

"I don't know," he said, and withdrew his hand.

"So," she said, "what's wrong?"

"Nothing's wrong."

"Don't you like me?"

"You must be kidding," he said.

"Then why didn't you come? Why don't you want to fuck me again?" She started to play with him now. "You know, Julian," she said, "I like you. I think about you a lot," and the words went straight to his groin—delighting in the praise!—and his erection shot back up. She reached for a pillow (while he watched and pretended to know what she would do with it) and then put it at the opposite end of the bed and wrapped her arms around it, hugging it to her chest, murmuring her approval when he entered her from behind. She turned her face to the side; he could see the down on her cheek tipped with blue light from outside, a breeze coming through the open curtains.

It had started turning cold, though it was only early September. He thought about Luchesca and his parents and bowling pins smashed out of formation and all the things Cap had tried to tell him about letting go into his fears, and about Tommy Eberhart drooling high atop the jungle gym and the agronomy major grabbing his tongue and how he needed to hold it all back, and then he didn't think anymore.

When he returned to her apartment, she was still asleep. He took off his clothes and got into bed beside her, under the quilt, the room freezing from the open window. Her back and buttocks were warm. Shivering, he curled up behind her. "You poor baby," she said, waking and reaching behind her. He'd come so many times already he didn't think he could do it again, but he was instantly hard at her touch and wanting her. She turned around and kissed him and he tasted the sleep in her mouth, remembering that he hadn't taken his medication this morning, that in fact he'd brought only one dose of Dilantin with him, not expecting to sleep over, and that with all the sugar from the cinnamon roll and no medicine, he could be in trouble.

He pushed into her and she told him yes, yes, there, keep going, and soon her head was off the bed, her hair hanging down. Her chest, he saw in the morning light, was freckled, her long white throat swallowing dryly. Only her legs were on the bed, her skull touching the floor—wasn't she getting dizzy?—the blood rushing to her head, but no, she said keep going, don't stop, and he held on to her hips to keep her from disappearing below completely, and then, at her command, he thrust into her ("Hard! Hard as you can!"), and she moved herself back up to the bed.

He looked down at her. "Hi," he said. He hadn't come. Maybe it had been seeing her in the daylight and realizing she was his teacher. Or maybe, too, how hungry she was, her desire so available, and how much he could have of her, how he'd passed through some barrier once so impermeable, how possessively she reached for his cock. But he knew that what he'd really been distracted by was watching her—

her body's contortions and tension, its release and explosions, its disquieting similarity to seizures. Sex was epilepsy's cousin, its joyous, wicked, insatiable cousin, amused in its reckless abandon by its embarrassed, secretive relative.

"I have to hurry," she said, looking at the clock, and he was disappointed that she wasn't going to help him come like last night, but he didn't say anything, just watched her go into the bathroom and heard her turn on the shower.

He lay on the bed. He had to get up too—for her class. An eight o'clock. Would they go together? He hadn't thought about the logistics of any of this. Whether they should appear in public. His books were back at his apartment, and he hadn't slept since seven o'clock the previous morning. He could take a very brief nap now while she used the shower. Maybe she could drop him off at his apartment so he could rush up and get his books. . . .

When he woke up, the clock said three P.M. and he was completely disoriented, unsure of where he was, whose house it was or why he didn't have any clothes on (he slept in pajamas, a habit from adolescence, when he'd started to have seizures in his sleep and didn't want anyone to find him naked).

The blinds were still drawn, unopened from the morning. A note lay on the middle of the kitchen table, with two Hershey Kisses as paperweights at the top.

Julian—

Here are two sweet kisses to tide you over until we get
back together. Make yourself at home. But don't leave!
Not all day. I'll call you soon for a mystery date.

Maureen

A P.S. at the bottom said, I'll excuse you just this once from class. But don't let it happen again. Or there will be "consequences."

He'd gotten hard reading the note. It was horrible! A simple note. Some provocative hint of "consequences" (he could see her tongue slipping out when she wrote the word), and already he was aching for her. And now an image from last night: her legs up over his shoulders while she reached underneath him and gently squeezed his balls, coaxing the come out of him until he exploded into her, his body collapsing over hers, drained and relaxed, his very bones crying with relief.

He thought about masturbating now. This was excruciating, sitting stupidly on her leather couch, his legs parted to give his swollen balls a rest, his penis sticking straight up and listing toward the door, as if it were a dog eagerly awaiting its master.

Hadn't he had enough? He'd come four times last night! So what if he hadn't this morning. So what?

But it wanted more. There was no stopping it now. It was greedy, all right. Find her. Bring her back here. Get her legs open. Do it!

He took a shower. When he stepped out, the phone was ringing. He picked it up, thinking too late that no one knew he was here.

But it was her. Did you sleep well?

Yes, he said. Where are you?

The Holiday Inn, she said. Room 516. She wanted him to pull on his jeans and join her.

How did you know I wasn't wearing any?

Oh, I have my ways. And leave your underwear off when you come.

Come? he said, thinking two could play this game—how easy it was to talk dirty when all your thoughts were dirty.

What do you look like? she asked.

Big, he said.

Oh? Could you describe yourself in more detail?

Well, he said, *very* big. You sure you want to hear about it?

Are you, by any chance, touching yourself at this moment?

In fact, he said, looking down at his penis, which was up around his navel and listening with great anticipation to the conversation, I'm afraid to do that. We're on the verge of a meltdown here, very, very hot, and could use some cooling off.

Is that something I could help you with, perhaps?

I really hope so, said Julian.

Sounds like you need me, she said.

Yes, he admitted. I do.

Desperately?

All over.

Can't wait, can you?

No, I have to see you now.

I better make you wait.

No! he said. You can't.

So impudent. I don't know. I might have to punish you.

Please, he said.

She laughed, and he felt as though he'd just received an A on a quiz.

Why don't I prepare myself, Mr. . . . ?

Tower.

And she laughed again, and he realized there was nothing better than making a lover laugh, and how free and womanly and teasing and knowing was her laugh.

Of course, Mr. Tower. How do you think I should do that? I'll follow your orders. Would you like me to wear something special— or nothing special?

Take off all your clothes and turn over on your stomach, he told her, amazed he could talk to anyone, let alone his teacher, like this.

He opened the door. Recklessly, enticingly, she'd left it slightly ajar. She was under the quilt on the king-size bed. He could see only her dark-blonde hair spread out on the pillow. She was on her stomach, as he'd instructed. Her arms were at her sides. They were acting out some game that he'd learned only today but was already compelled to play. He'd had no thoughts on the way over. Nothing. His brain a windy tunnel dropping straight to his groin. He wasn't afraid of having a seizure anymore. That was somebody else. He wanted only to touch her and then to be inside her. He wanted to feel his fingers clench her shoulders and the hard rise of her back curled under his chest. He wanted the pressure of her hips against his, the palms of her hands flat and stiff against his, her mouth loose and slick and pushing against his, making sounds, not words, just noise vibrating against his lips— her whispers answering his while he moved in her and found a rhythm and his mind tucked itself up inside her.

He'd never had a rhythm before, never been in a groove, as a dormmate at Ohio State had said happens when sex is really hot, never thought his body could be cranked up to full power without it short-circuiting and turning against him, never had his bones jumped or his lights fucked out, never understood the infinite clichés people used when trying to describe the ecstasy of sex.

He went over to her and sat on the bed. He pulled back the sheet and looked at her. She didn't speak. He put his hand on the small of her back and left it there. He couldn't move it. He could feel her becoming restless, not wanting to spoil something but wondering what was going on. It was too strange for him, though, too unsettling to see her lying here like this, so still, stripped, ready to be taken, and he caressed her buttocks, moving his hand down between her thighs, but his heart was beating too hard now, working against him, and he saw someplace far away, some dismal barracks office with smoke and a small daybed and high black boots off to the side of a desk and a door being opened and a woman being pushed inside and her feet with wooden shoes stuffed with newsprint, and he could see her lying facedown on a couch and her arms stiff like this at her sides while a hand with stubby fingers, one of them missing, grabbed her legs and tore them open.

He screamed.

Maureen bolted up. "What's wrong? Julian, what happened?"

He was covering his face, embarrassed to look at her, not knowing what to say. What could he say? "I got scared for a moment."

"Of what? Was somebody at the door?"

He looked at the door. "Yes," he said. "That must have been it."

She stared at him. He felt as though he'd disappointed her. He'd ruined something. But she merely pulled him down onto the bed with her and put her arms around his neck. "I missed you," she said. "I could hardly stand not seeing you in class." She reached for his penis, but he felt little except worry, a coldness inside, and though he tried for a while, kissing and rubbing against her, nothing happened. Finally she said, "I guess I'm tired too," and she rolled over and was asleep instantly—resentfully, he felt—while he lay there and thought about what he'd done wrong.

Chapter Four

Cap lay trapped in the bedroom, listening to his mother cleaning, rummaging through cabinets, and talking to herself. "Oh, *there's* my little friend."

Her "little friend" was a green porcelain pig (maybe a warthog, if one dared examine it closely enough), its back and sides perforated with so many holes it looked as if it had been machine-gunned in some gangland massacre. The toothpick holder had been an anniversary gift from his parents. Unbelievable! Impaled with tasseled toothpicks, it appeared to be less a pig than a dying bull riddled with a picador's lances. His mother had tried to "show it off" last night, use it for appetizers, when Dick and Sarah had come over for dinner. Wallis had spared them all. "It's special," she said, sweeping it away by its fat neck. "We want to save it for a more important occasion."

And now, at five-thirty A.M., while the rest of the world rose gently toward consciousness, Claude and Wallis both sound asleep next to him, his father downstairs snoring, here was his mother already cleaning and babbling to herself.

Was she delusional? Some organic malady, perhaps? A tumor or a blood clot? Her own singular disorder? Page 578 of the DSM-III:

"Cap's mother: An acute character disorder. Symptoms: bad taste (e.g., a fondness for toothpick-holding porcelain pigs); uncontrolled dusting; paranoia about fatty foods, esp. corned beef; compulsive use of the word 'feh'; rampant pessimism. Recommended response: hide."

Which was exactly what he was doing. He could be taking care of correspondence or exercising on his stair climber or just enjoying the morning alone.

But what disturbed him most was that the two of them *were the only ones awake.* Equally driven to be busy, in their respective compulsions. So what if she dusted while he wrote a high-sounding letter to the president of some foundation? Was it any different? Why was her puttering any less meaningful than his? Oh, but he had people depending on him! Didn't that make his work significant, his job essential, his life *purposeful?* Or did it just make him more busy, yes, more apprehensive of stopping, because at any moment that notepad in his hand might turn into a dust wand. "Excuse me, is that a duster in your hand?" one of his clients would say. And he'd be caught—having to face his worst moment, the transformation complete. All these years he'd been on guard against becoming his father, and now, lo and behold, standing there with her fuzzy blue slippers around his big hairy ankles, he'd become her.

He turned over and looked at Wallis. They'd given up trying to make Claude sleep in his crib. "Don't get them used to sleeping in bed with you," their pediatrician had warned. "You'll never get them to leave." But the man's own kids were grown, and he didn't have to lie awake listening to a screaming infant. "Just put your hand on his back." As if this did anything besides make Claude arch his spine and cry harder. That was the problem with developmental theory. The individual always defied it. So then you tried a new theory, from pediatrician B, who claimed that the child now *needed* to sleep in the same bed but would outgrow his need (say, by college?) and would have—according to the best minds in attachment theory—a secure basis for later forming healthy relationships.

In the end, it didn't matter. "Of course he's going to sleep with us," Wallis had said, and that was the end of the subject.

Now she had her arm slung over Claude's little back, rising and falling with each sleepy breath, the two of them cozy as kittens, oblivious to his arguably crazy mother yammering downstairs: "Where *are* those salt and pepper shakers we gave them?" Yet another heart-stopping oddity: two humpbacked creatures, one "Saltie" and the other "Peppie," lugging sacks of their respective goods out of some black, bottomless, spirit-breaking mine shaft. He'd thrown those away long ago.

Ah, but they were supposed to leave today.

One more meal with them, and then they'd be gone. Would they come more often now that Claude was here? "If that happens," said Wallis, "we'll change our names and go into the witness protection program."

He took the remark seriously. Yes, surely there was a special category for protecting grown children—thousands of them with new names and identities, hiding out in obscure Arizona desert towns, waiting until their parents died.

A horrible thought! But he couldn't help it. Why did Freud think such hostilities were buried? His own were right on the surface, as unrepressed as a whole SWAT team. And why did the great man think it applied oedipally to the father only? Cap wanted them both dead!

Claude's birth had done this to him—stirred up his own childhood conflicts. And then, too, Wallis was a wonderful mother, underscoring his own mother's failings. "We talk, we rub noses, I blow on the top of his head and tell him, 'That's the wind on the ocean,' " said Wallis when Cap had asked how she and Claude spent their time all day. "We sing, we tickle. Sometimes I take his diaper off and we lie in the sun on the window seat. We smile at each other. When he sneezes, I sneeze. When he sticks out his tongue, I stick out mine. We're falling in love. I feel as if we're lost on an island together."

And Cap had wanted to weep, for pleasure—and envy. It was perfect mirroring. All these things Wallis did naturally without studying a bit of object relations theory. Attunement. Joined Claude's world. Became his twin. Gazed at him with admiration. Claude's baby self a joyous fact he could take for granted because "when he sneezes, I sneeze."

It was that simple, and that impossible.

Who has time for such things? His mother's voice. She'd taken up residence in his head since getting here. You change them and feed them and bathe them and get them to bed, and with what's left you fall dead asleep on your feet. Who has time to sit around and be a mirror? What is that, some kind of peek-a-boo game you wanted me to play with you? Joining? Join what? I got no time even to go to Hadassah meetings. Attunement? Boy, were we ever tuned in to you. A wild Indian if I ever saw one. God help me, I should have been able to tune you out once in a while. Twinship! What are you, nuts? Can you imagine what poor Sophie Levin went through, raising those two identical hellions? We stayed up with you when you were sick and we wiped the vomit off your face, and you tell us now that's not enough? From all this what you got was something called a "narcissistic wound"? What is that—some kind of kinky sex crime? When you got shot in Boulder, *that* was a wound. This other stuff, vulnerable this and toxic that and shame this and inner that—should I have shopped, cleaned, and cooked, and had all this figured out by Saturday night too? Didn't you turn out well enough? A nice family of your own finally, thank the dear Lord, and a good job, even if you listen to meshuggenehs all day, not that I wouldn't have a few things to say myself about my own parents, but that was life back then, with nine people in a family. You didn't have time to sit around wondering if somebody wasn't getting cuddled enough and would grow up depressed. . . . What you should know is this: I lost three sisters before I was ten years old! An unhappy childhood? Half of us didn't even *make* it out of childhood!

And he thought, Yes, that's the crux of it, no time for admiration and mutual gazing and cooing and sneezing together and being the wind on the ocean and discovering an infant's special language when you have to worry about surviving, when your own grandparents had died of starvation in Hungary, when your mother and father had seven children to feed and no bathroom in their seventh-floor cold-water walk-up, and when you moved six times as a child because the store went bankrupt again and again and your parents couldn't pay the rent. . . .

It didn't matter that he was a psychologist and could explain this all to them. (Had this been the whole motivation for his profession?) His would always be a pretend world to them. Much as they'd killed themselves to get it for him, schlepped and sacrificed to make it possible, they still looked at such a vision, and him with it—their grand creation—from a distant shore and said, in the words of his aunt Milva with her bad feet, "Very nice. Now take me home."

He could hear his mother talking on the phone now. Who could she be calling at this hour? It was too much for his curiosity. He put his robe on and went downstairs.

When she saw him, her hair up in a net, the fuzzy blue slippers on, her pleated housecoat buttoned to her throat, she said, "Oh!" and then, into the phone, "Just a minute." She put her hand over the receiver. "I'll be off soon." She waved him away.

He wandered into the living room, looking back toward the kitchen. He couldn't hear. When she wanted to talk softly, she could. Was she having an affair? Calling her lover at six A.M., eight o'clock back East?

The thought thrilled him. How wonderful. How out of character. His mother . . . his mother having sex? Impossible. He couldn't imagine it. He'd walked in on his parents one night when he was four. Both their shapes had been rustling under the covers, and he'd been delighted. Great! Mommy and Daddy were roughhousing! True, it was late, but maybe this was the only time they could find to wrestle. He'd jumped right on. His mother screamed. No—howled! A piercing female alarm sure to confuse and stunt any male sexual development. His father took him out of the room and explained something about how he'd been "helping Mommy find her cold cream."

It was as if he'd been a snake—or Oedipus himself disguised as a snake. Her awful noise—that gelded cry, as if his surprise visit had castrated *her*. God, was he ever confused! His first introduction to sex. Couldn't they have just taken him aside and been a little more honest than cold cream? Armond had said about the memory, "That's when your brother was conceived."

How would he know?

His mother came out of the kitchen now.

"Who were you talking to?" Cap asked.

"Oh, nobody." She started straightening the magazines on the credenza.

"Leave those, Mom. Who was it?"

"If you must know"—she looked over her glasses at him—"it was your brother. He's home by himself. Well, Mrs. Adams is checking in on him."

"Allan? What's Allan doing alone at home?" The last time they'd left Allan home alone, he'd set fire to the couch because it had spoken to him. He'd been diagnosed with schizophrenia in adolescence, though he'd shown signs much earlier. As an adult he filed all day at his father's business. Sometimes he would answer the phone too, but that was more iffy, because he might hear voices telling him to hang up before the telephone caught on fire, in which case he'd want to use one of the fire extinguishers (under lock and key at the company). And on very bad days, he couldn't even file without having symptoms. The pink sheet of the invoice would glow radioactively, smearing and leaking onto his fingers and burning his hand. Or he'd suddenly see his name at the bottom of a letter: somebody was impersonating him, writing to his father, accusing him of arson again. Or he'd have to cover the stamp with a paperweight because he'd seen a tiny alien peeking out at him.

When Allan was fourteen he'd set fire to the couch. Cap was supposed to stay home with him, but he'd been lured away by a basketball game. When he came back from playing, fire trucks lined the street. The family room had burned to the ground. Fortunately, a neighbor had seen the fire start and called the fire department. Allan, who had stood frozen, watching the flames, had been dragged out. His parents never let Cap forget it—how he'd deserted Allan, let them all down.

Now they had left Allan alone themselves. Without the housekeeper, Mrs. Adams, staying there. It was unbelievable.

"He's on a new drug," said his mother. "Cap, you wouldn't believe how well he's been doing this time."

Cap frowned. He'd heard it before. Allan had tried a whole series of antipsychotic medications, none of which stopped his symptoms; in most cases, they only caused unwanted side effects: the restless pacing and agitation of akathisia; the tics, spasms, and tremors of tardive dyskinesia. His parents, meanwhile, vacillated between acute anxiety and outright denial of the seriousness of his brother's condition. "I'm just amazed you'd leave him alone," Cap said.

"You wouldn't believe the change. He's going to write you soon."

"About what?"

His mother drew a zipper across her mouth. "He made me promise not to tell. He wants to tell you himself."

They went out to breakfast before driving to the airport. When Wallis lifted her shirt to nurse Claude, Cap's mother cleared her throat. "You're not worried?"

"Why?" Wallis asked without looking up. She'd discreetly covered herself and Claude with a cloth napkin. She had made it through his parents' stay here by excusing herself at six P.M. to go upstairs and by sending them on frequent errands. "Oops, we need orange juice. I think you'd both better go," and she'd gently push them out the door. She treated them exactly like her eighth graders, a firm and unflappable hand on their shoulders, and they seemed to appreciate the direction.

"You're not worried about the board of health?" his mother said.

Even Wallis had to look up. "What?"

Cap's mother, her eyes squinted so she wouldn't have to fully see, nodded at Claude, enjoying his meal. "They could make trouble for you, doing that in here."

His father was in the bathroom again. His oatmeal was getting cold.

"Is breast-feeding *still* a felony in Colorado, Cap?" asked Wallis.

His mother saw no humor in this. While her schizophrenic son stayed home alone, she was terrified of the board of health running them out of town for a natural act. "Really, this is a nice place. Don't you want to come back?" she asked.

"We'll be fine, Bernice," said Wallis, flashing a tense smile. "Your own food needs some attention."

Cap's mother gave a big, heaving sigh and put her fork down. Two nights before, Cap had taken them to Pierre's best Mexican restaurant; they'd talked about nothing else since—what a terrible experience it had been. They'd ordered fajitas, thinking it was the falafel they'd once eaten on International Foods Day at the temple, but after tasting some jalapeño, both of them fanned their mouths for the rest of the meal, saying Never again! Never again! as if they were talking about the Holocaust.

Cap turned toward the wall. Photographs showed the restaurant's site years ago. A horse pulled a plow through a sugar-beet field. Mountains, open prairie, and endless sky filled the background. The caption said: "Pierre County, 1946." Less than fifty years ago. He loved this area of the West for that reason. It was still relatively new and undeveloped and, compared to Denver, unpolluted, if people wouldn't destroy it as they did everywhere else. Even his parents had been more impressed this visit, and alarmingly had inquired about retiring here. Still, they'd been afraid to venture outside the city limits, collecting their souvenirs at the Holiday Inn gift shop.

"Are we ready?" Cap said as soon as he saw his father emerge from the bathroom. He'd already paid the check. Their luggage was in the car. All he had to do was take his parents to the Denver airport, where they'd board a flight to Philadelphia and then be gone. Gone! He pulled his mother up by the arm. "What's the rush?" she said, deciding now to have a bite of her omelet.

They dropped Wallis and Claude off at the house, where there was a tearful goodbye—on his mother's part. She refused to let go of Claude, bathing the child in wet kisses. To Cap's surprise, his own eyes became moist as he watched. His parents were old enough now, both of them in their seventies, that this could be the first and only time they saw Claude. His father seemed reluctant to leave too, standing near Wallis and thanking her for putting up with them. Their candor was remarkable and even touching.

"Come on, Mom," said Cap gently. He helped her into the car and gave her a tissue. Wallis waved Claude's little arm at them, and Cap drove away.

He felt a heaviness in his chest. And a crazy urge to take them condo shopping. They could stay here forever! Make up for the lack of family. Wallis had none. No siblings. Her mother stalling them about when she would come out. Her father somewhere in India on some endless bike trek. She wasn't even able to get in touch with him to tell him about the birth. His brother Allan was lost. Claude didn't have a single aunt or uncle who would pinch his cheek. But he had grandparents! They were right here, in the car. It would take nothing to find them a place to live close by. Housing was cheaper here than in Philadelphia. The weather was milder than people thought. They'd at least liked the Denny's he'd taken them to! He could see it. Himself swelling with generational pride while he introduced them around town as Claude's grandparents. His oldest fantasy: he was actually from a very, very happy family—Mom, Dad, Allan, all of them at the dinner table (where else)—Norman Rockwell's major Jewish work.

It was silent in the car. They weren't talking. Were they upset about leaving?

"Sorry you're going?" he asked. They both sat in the backseat. It felt to him as though they were in mourning back there. "You'll be here again soon," he said, trying to comfort them. "Or we'll visit you in the East. I promise."

They didn't answer. He turned his head to look at them. They were huddled together in the corner, like refugees. "Are you okay?"

"Where are we?" his father said. "This isn't the way to the airport."

Instead of the interstate, he'd taken County Road 5, which wound through Timnath and Windsor. He wanted to show them some more of the countryside, give them a final look at the mountains and the empty prairie right outside Pierre, the red buttes in the distance and the streams and cottonwood groves—maybe they'd even catch sight of some golden eagles and red-tailed hawks. When did they get a chance to see anything like this in Philadelphia?

"It's a back way—more scenic."

"There's nothing out here," his mother said. "There's not even a tree."

"Plenty of trees—cottonwoods, junipers, Russian olive. You have to look."

"Not even a gas station."

"We'll be fine," said Cap.

"You sure you know where you are, Cappie? It's already eleven-thirty," his father announced.

It was nine-thirty. Although he'd been here over two weeks, his father insisted on not turning his watch back.

The paved road became a dirt one. He must have taken a wrong turn. But he could find his way south to the airport easily enough. He'd been out here many times. He reached to open the glove compartment. "I'm just going to look at a map here a minute." Cap's shoulder was grabbed so hard that his head jerked back.

"What do you mean, map? We have to make a plane! Where are you taking us!"

"We have plenty of time—"

"God help us," said his mother, "we're lost! We're in the middle of nowhere!"

"Please calm down. Both of you. I've driven here so many—"

"A house! Over there! Stop and ask!" demanded his father. The farmhouse was nestled beneath a bluff at least two miles back from the road.

"I'm not stopping to ask directions," said Cap. "I know where I'm going."

"He'd rather die than ask directions! He's always been like this!" his mother said. She rolled down the window. "Help!" she shouted from the backseat.

"What's wrong?" said Cap, thinking she must be having a heart attack.

"There! Up ahead!" His father pointed to a milk truck coming from the opposite direction. "Honk your horn! Honk at him!"

"Will you please sit back and be *quiet!*"

His father unstrapped himself and lunged forward; he pounded the horn as the truck rolled past them.

"Stop that!" said Cap, trying to peel off his father's hand and drive at the same time. But his father wouldn't let go. *HONK! HONK! HONK! HONK!*

Now his mother stuck her head out the back window and began shouting. "We're lost! Somebody help us!" *HONK! HONK!* "Help us! Please somebody stop!"

"Red alert!" his father screamed at the cows. "*Red alert!*"

"It's the wilderness! For God's sake help us! We're lost!"

By the time he got home, it was one o'clock. Wallis and Claude were napping. His parents' plane had been late departing. They'd made it with time to spare. Cap stiffly kissed them goodbye and sent them on their way. They were all smiles once they entered the jetway, waving gratefully to him before they disappeared down the long tube.

Home. They were on their way. There was no mention of the car ride down; he'd found the right road shortly after they'd had their panic attack. Such hysteria, he remembered, had always been the way they avoided their sadness at anyone's leaving. He guessed they felt abandoned, even though they were the ones leaving him. Perhaps that's why they rarely complained about Allan, a permanently dependent child—or had been until now. The plane ride would put their defenses all back in place, and soon, at home, they'd be complaining at a comfortable distance that Cap never visited them. Their instant crisis shouldn't have surprised him, but it did. Shaken up, he lay down next to Claude and Wallis.

He woke up ten minutes later, realizing he had an appointment with Julian at two.

The boy was waiting for him on the steps outside. He was smoking.

"I didn't know you smoked," said Cap once they were indoors.

Julian shrugged. "I just started."

Cap nodded. What to do? Should he pursue it? Julian wore an embroidered white blousy shirt, exotic for him, opened three buttons to his sternum. His hair was different too. It no longer sloped in dark, easy waves over his ears but flew straight back in oiled quills. Cap hadn't seen him for two weeks, since they'd talked about Julian's first seizure. Julian had missed a session, inexplicably. "Any reason why you're smoking?"

"I decided I like it."

"All right," said Cap. He could accept that. Or not. "So what's going on that you need to smoke?"

Julian took a breath. "My . . . this new person in my life smokes."

"This new person you met is a girl, I presume?"

"Yes."

Cap waited, then said, "Are you still bowling?"

Julian shook his head. "I was able to stop that. I'm over that now. Everything's fine."

"And you're still taking your medicine?"

"No," said Julian. "I'm not going back on it. I don't need to."

"Your doctor told you this?"

"Nobody told me. I just know it. I can control it."

"Smoking."

"It helps." Julian looked down at the cigarettes in his shirt pocket, as if they had been placed there by a waiter. "The medication can have side effects, you know. Sexual problems."

"Oh," said Cap. "So you're afraid it will make you impotent. Julian, anticonvulsants, unlike some blood pressure medications, do not—I repeat, do not—cause impotency. Can we make an agreement for you to go back on your medication?"

"I have to tell you something," said Julian, switching the subject. Cap would let it go, for now. He was getting too parental anyway, and Julian would just resist, until they could work this out together. "Two things. One is that you know this person, and two is that I don't think I'll be coming to therapy anymore."

Cap rubbed his cheeks. He hadn't had time to shave today. He wished he looked more presentable, more dependable for Julian. What could he say to get them back on the right footing? "Julian, if you could let yourself imagine anything, what would you most want from me right now?"

"A smoke," said Julian.

A deadpan. But the boy was serious. It didn't even sound like Julian. He seemed completely transformed.

"Besides a cigarette."

"I don't want anything. I've got everything I need. I just want you to let me go."

"Let you go?"

"Tell me I can leave."

"You're the one who decides that."

"No, I don't. Not really. I guess I don't want you to resent me for leaving. I've appreciated what you've done for me. It's meant a lot. I'm just ready to go."

"You know I'm not going to resent you, regardless. I'm very fond of you. I've told you I'm honored that you're working with me." He waited to see if the boy could take this in, but it seemed to have little effect. "Why now? Why do you suddenly have to leave therapy now? Is it because we're starting to get to some tender parts of you? You'll remember that we talked last time about your first seizure. That must have been painful for you. What was your reaction?"

"Maureen Kels."

Cap blinked. "What about her?" he snapped, caught off guard.

"That's who I'm seeing."

He thought for a moment, some crazy interpretation of the comment, that Julian meant he was in *therapy* with Maureen. It was easier to accept.

"We're lovers," said Julian, his face flushing.

"I'm not sure what to say. I'm not at liberty to talk about another client."

"I know that," said Julian. "That's why I think it's better if I stop."

"Can I ask how the two of you got together?"

Julian rubbed his eyes. Along with the breezy white shirt, he wore jeans with holes in the knees. He'd been a spotless and conservative dresser, expensive cardigan sweaters and laundered shirts with button-down collars. He'd once told Cap he still laid out his clothes the night before classes. It was important to have control over his appearance, he'd insisted. It made up, just a little, for how disheveled he felt inside. "Maureen is my teacher. I didn't know she was in therapy with you until two weeks ago. I forgot my jacket, and when I came back for it, I ran into her. Anyway, we've talked about it, and we both think it's better if we drop out."

Is that so? he heard himself about to say, but rejected it as too biting. He felt furious at Maureen; it was good she probably wasn't going to show up this afternoon. "You and I have a relationship too, Julian. It's independent of the one you have with Maureen. I feel it's an important one for you, since it concentrates exclusively on your needs."

"I wish you wouldn't do this," said Julian.

"Do what?"

"Make me feel guilty."

"That's not my intention. It won't work if you're coming here from guilt. But I wouldn't be doing my job unless I challenged you about your reason for leaving."

"I'm so *busy* lately. I hardly have time to study." Julian looked down. "And I'm spending a lot of time with Maureen. She's gotten me involved with so much."

Sounds as if Maureen is running your life, Julian, my friend—but he rejected that one too. Any similarity here to your mother? Reject. He needed not to get locked into a triangle with the two of them. "Julian, why don't we make a contract for three more sessions. After that time, we can evaluate where we are and you can make a decision."

"I just don't think it's necessary."

It was unnerving: he could almost hear Maureen's voice in him; how much she'd influenced him in so short a time. It was no surprise. Julian adapted so well to another's identity. He'd had so much practice from childhood; and it was no surprise, too, that he'd wound up with an older woman, repeating the past on all counts.

Julian leaned forward. He rested his hands over the holes in the knees of his jeans. "I feel as if I'm finally getting out of this box I've lived in for so long. Maureen's helping me. Do you understand?"

"I understand it feels that way to you, Julian."

"School, my classes, the environmental work . . . other things: it's all finally coming together."

Cap couldn't help but notice the play on words. Come together. The original mother-child union, the mutual adoring gaze, the bliss of oneness, that mirroring Wallis did for Claude so well, the return to Eden and all the archaic childhood urges recaptured—attached, bonded, healed. Sex. It would make Julian think he *could* go home again. He'd possess what he'd lost a long time ago; his mother would finally look up from her terrible past, pleased and cured, and know him. Come together. It wasn't a fantasy, after all.

"I'm afraid you're setting yourself up here for trouble," said Cap.

"Don't you understand? I'm finally living—not sitting around all the time thinking about how screwed up I am."

You've replaced one compulsion with another. Reject. "Julian, we talked about some pretty important stuff last session. How did that make you feel?"

"I don't remember."

"We talked about your seizures. Your shame about them. About how it felt to be alone as a little boy with the problem."

"It's fine. I told you, I'm off my medicine now, and I don't worry about it anymore."

"Why didn't you call me, as I invited you to do?"

Julian looked away. "I did. You never returned my call."

"When?"

"The week after our session. I was going over to Maureen's for dinner, and I was panicked about it. I wanted to talk to you."

"I never got your message."

He suddenly had a picture of his mother frantically cleaning, and he wondered why *that* had popped up—his mother's compulsion being like Julian's? his own compulsion to overwork? Oh, Christ. It wasn't that at all. It was literal. She'd been up early, cleaning the house. She'd thrown away the messages Wallis took while he'd been at a baseball game in Denver with two of his old oncology group clients, who were in remission. The next morning his mother had told him blithely, "I finally threw away all those scraps on your desk!" She'd laughed, her high nervous laugh, and he should have known something was up. "Just the same as when you were a boy—never able to throw anything out, have to save every snip of paper," and Cap had dismissed it, only half listening, because he was trying to change Claude, who was screaming. "Julian, I know what happened. It may not help to say this, but it was a mistake that I couldn't prevent. I didn't know about your message until right now. I'm sorry."

"It's too late," said Julian.

"Why is it too late?"

"I can't do what you want. I can't be with Maureen and see you too."

"But why not? I'm not asking you to make a choice between us. Is Maureen?"

"No. That's not it. It's me. I have to make the choice. I have to choose. It's my duty."

Duty. Afterward he understood. Make the wrong choice and you get killed. Trust the wrong people and you'll never live to tell about it. A single phone call could be critical. His mother's legacy. Cap had lost his chance. The boy was gone.

He sat in his office without eating. His lunch lay open on the desk. The food didn't interest him. He was taking this too hard. He'd rarely had a case get to him so, one that he blamed himself for as much. Maybe it was the strain of his parents having been here. (Had he let his mother throw away those messages? Conspired with her in some way to get rid of them for him?) Or being a father. It was as if he'd herded his clients in closer, surrounding his own son: take no hostage to fortune or take us all. Or maybe he was just doubting the whole profession again, a periodic flare-up.

He went down the hall and saw Maureen waiting there.

"You look like you've seen a ghost, Casper," she said. It was her, all right.

Settled in his office, she said, "I want to do what we talked about last session."

He remembered they'd talked about sex. Today, however, she

didn't have her dragon costume on. She wore a hip-length white ribbed sweater over a yellow dress. And glasses, for once. She looked as if she'd come straight from teaching. "What do you mean?"

"You should review your notes better," she said. "You're slipping."

"To be honest, I wasn't expecting you."

"Oh? Why not?"

Was Julian fabricating this affair? He didn't seem to have those tendencies. "I don't know how to say this without violating confidentiality. . . ." He was hoping she'd say it for him.

But she wasn't going to make it easy. He'd push it. "Are you involved with a client of mine?"

"Oh, that." Maureen put a finger to her lips. "We're having a fling."

He wondered if the whole relationship had been engineered by her to get his attention. With Julian, she'd certainly raised the ante.

"Oh, I bet you think that I'm doing all this for your benefit, don't you?" she said.

He remained impassive, though it was difficult. She was baiting him. Could he really go on being her therapist? She'd finally made it impossible.

"But to be honest—and you know how easy that is for me—I had no hidden motive. I can see you don't believe me."

He didn't.

"How many therapists do you think there are in Pierre anyway, Casper? Have you looked at the skinny column in the phone book? I've already gone through three of them, counting you."

He said nothing.

"Do you think I'd be here if I had another choice?"

"I was under the impression that you and Julian 'agreed' to leave therapy."

"I've been leaving therapy for the last two years. But be that as it may, don't you think we should at least say goodbye?"

"Maureen, don't you think you're being irresponsible and unethical?"

"Aren't we judgmental today."

"He's your student, Maureen."

"Well, it's not as if he's my *client*." She smiled and took out a hairbrush from her bag and began stroking sharply, agitated. "And really it's none of your business. He's cute, smart, and legal. So butt out."

"Why are you with him?" Cap persisted.

"I told you—he's sweet and safe. Know many men around like that? Young men?"

"I don't think so, Maureen. He's easy. Vulnerable. And you've got too much power over him. Couldn't you find someone your own size?"

"Size. Now you're talking. Listen, Casper, you can make up all the quickie analysis you want for why we're together, but it doesn't mean a thing. We like each other; it's as straight and twisted as that. And I daresay you seem jealous. Of something."

His only hope was that she'd lose interest fast and spare Julian too much hurt. Cap would hang on with her, though, because he could do more good involved than not. Or maybe he just was being stubborn himself, not letting her go because he refused to concede the defeat that had happened to every one of her other therapists. "All right, Maureen, what did you want to talk about today?"

"I've gotten you mad, haven't I?"

"Yes. I don't like what's happening. And I'm not sure yet how I'm going to deal with it. And before you say anything else"—she'd started to speak—"you should understand that whatever goes on between you and me is fair play. But I'm not going to knowingly stand by and let a client be damaged."

"You're threatening me. My shrink is threatening me. How traumatic."

"What can I help you with, Maureen?"

"I told you. I want to do what you suggested last time. Turn into my mother."

———

111

"Mrs. Kels, how are you today?"

"I'm fine. I don't know why I'm here."

Cap shrugged. "You tell me. What's on your mind?"

"Really, Doctor—are you a *real* doctor?"

"You can call me Cap."

"Then go ahead and call me Adele. Cap. What's that short for?"

"I think you know, Adele. I think, too, you're a little uncomfortable here, aren't you?"

"It's not the kind of place I go to, if that's what you mean. Crazy people come here, don't they?"

"All right. But since you're already here, why don't you tell me a little about yourself. Tell me about your marriage."

"Oh, that."

"Did you have a close relationship with your husband?"

"Oh, no. Not at all."

"Why not?"

"He was hard to get close to, always blowing up a storm about one thing or another."

"Why did you marry him?"

"I wanted to get out of my house."

"And why was that?"

"Well, we never had much money, and my father was always unhappy. It felt like I was just another mouth to feed."

"Just like with your husband."

"Out of the frying pan and into the fire."

"What was your relationship like with your daughters?"

"With Josie . . . well, Josie did everything she was told."

"And Maureen?"

"Maureen was a rebel from day one."

"And how did that go over with your husband?"

"Well, to tell the truth, he didn't want another girl. He wanted a son, to help him out on the farm. He never seemed to take to her because of that."

"Was that the reason?"

"What other reason could it be?"

"You tell me."

"Well, she did give him a hard time about everything. She wouldn't knuckle under."

"No, she wouldn't. Did you knuckle under?"

"I knew how to handle him."

"How was that?"

"I knew how."

"Tell me."

"I could be pretty tough about things in my own way."

"How's that?"

"You sure ask a lot of questions."

"Just the same question," said Cap. He couldn't help but be impressed, in spite of his feelings about her, at how well Maureen had picked up the role. He had guessed she had this ability; she took too much in, he knew, not to be able to spread out these family selves before her like cards—though cagily.

"A woman has her ways."

"I'm sort of thick about all this. Why don't you be more specific."

"She can withhold certain favors. Or threaten to give them out to someone better."

"So you made him jealous."

"I didn't have to make him. He just was."

"Adele, can I ask you about something that happened one day when Maureen was four?"

"Seek and ye shall find. That's what I always told my girls."

"Exactly. Now, why don't you tell me about the time Maureen almost drowned. Where were you that day?"

"Up by the house, washing clothes."

"You were outside?"

"Had one of those old wringers right by the side of the house, a tub next to it full with Azal's coveralls."

"So you could see the pond?"

"Lord no; that was off by the east fence."

"A mile, say?"

"Oh, not that far."

"In hearing distance?"

"I could hear pretty good."

"What did you hear?"

"I heard her screaming."

"How long did she scream?"

"Quite a while before I got down there."

"A minute? More?"

"A couple minutes."

"Were you concerned?"

"No."

"Why not?"

"Because Azal was down there with her."

"Your husband?"

"Yes."

"And what did you do after you kept hearing her scream?"

"I went on down to see what all the fuss was about."

"What did you see, Adele? Adele?"

Maureen stood up abruptly. "This is silly. This is absolutely the stupidest thing you've ever put me through!"

"Why'd you stop, Maureen?"

"It's ridiculous! That's not my mother! I made it all up!"

"Of course you did. How else would you tell me so much?"

She paced around the room, took out a cigarette, then threw it back into her handbag. "This is like a jail. Worse! At least in jail you can smoke!"

"Whatever happened to you back then, it must still be very frightening."

"Oh, Casper," she said, standing at the window and pulling back her hair, which she never stopped fixing in his office. She'd regained her composure. "You believe the wildest stories. Next time I'll be Cleopatra. I'll bring my asp, and we can play with it on your couch. Wouldn't you like that better?" and she turned around and lifted her chin toward him for a phantom kiss.

"Maureen," he said, and thought to make one last plea for her to stay away from Julian, but, knowing it wouldn't help, just said, "We have a lot more to talk about."

He got back to the house late that evening. Wallis had just finished putting Claude to bed. A couple he'd been treating, the Johnsons, had come in for an emergency visit. They'd just found out that their first child was going to be born with neural-cord damage and might die shortly after birth. On the other hand, the doctors couldn't tell them exactly how serious the disorder was until the delivery. The wife wanted to keep the baby; the husband wanted to abort.

Cap had found it wrenching to listen, not to take sides (even though he did side with the husband) to help them decide if they would go full term. Bereft afterward, he'd had to sit through a session with Wilmella, who told him her Plymouth had just had an eighty-thousand-mile checkup and was as good as new. Once more he suggested terminating therapy, and once again she declined, in the politest but stubbornest terms. He didn't remember until afterward that there had been something about an uncle the previous session, which he'd wanted to follow up on. Again, he hadn't had time to review his case notes.

Now Wallis met him at the door and told him Shh. She led him into Claude's room. He was asleep in his crib. The first time. "What prompted this?" asked Cap.

"He fell asleep there. I think he wants his own bed. I put him in there, and he looked at his mobile for an hour." They stood above Claude and watched him awhile in silence, Claude in his pajamas with trains and trucks on them, his breathing so quiet they both leaned forward at the same time to make sure his back was moving. Cap kissed him, and Wallis put the blanket up around his shoulders. They went upstairs and turned on the baby monitor.

They still spoke in whispers. "You can talk louder," Wallis said. "So can you," said Cap, but neither did. They continued to speak in hushed voices.

"What a day," said Cap. He told Wallis about driving his father and mother to the airport, his father honking at the milk truck, his mother leaning out the window, shouting, "It's the wilderness! For God's sake help us!"

"After seventeen years it's still hard to believe that they're really my in-laws."

"My mother said Allan was going to write me."

"About what?"

"She wouldn't say."

Wallis shrugged. "What a peculiar family. But however peculiar they are, at least they're in your life."

Cap nodded. "I'm sorry about your mother."

"My father upsets me even more. He hasn't even called. He knew the baby was due around this time."

"They're hopeless," said Cap. "We'll just have to lean on friends around here to take their place."

"I have a confession," said Wallis.

Cap took off his shoes. He fell back on the bed, his feet hanging off the end. "I'm ready. Lay it on me."

"I called Bombay tonight. Not just once, but three times, trying to track him down. I don't want you to tell me how much the bill is when we get it."

"How long did you talk?"

"Let's put it this way. I learned how to speak beginning Hindi."

"Come here," said Cap, and pulled her down on top of him. They hadn't made love since Claude had been born. They'd been tired, and shy. "Is this all right?" said Cap.

"I think so," said Wallis; her voice sounded soft as a child's. "I'm going to cry, though. Don't stop just because I do. You promise?"

"Yes," said Cap, kissing her hair, smelling her skin, seeing, too, when she took off her blouse that her milk was leaking.

"Great," she said. "This makes me feel sexy as a cow."

"Come here," said Cap, and felt the milk trickle against his own chest.

He woke up shouting. He'd been dreaming about people being brutalized, drownings and gassings, Nazis and screaming mothers, babies dying after their first breath. Wallis patted his shoulder and he fell back asleep. Later—he didn't know how long it was—he woke up again, with a start. He jumped up and got down on his hands and knees, looking under the bed. "Where'd you put him?!" he said. Wallis sat up. "What are you doing down there?" He was looking for Claude. "He's downstairs," said Wallis. "In his crib. Remember?" "Oh," said Cap, awake now. "That's right. I forgot. I'm so used to him sleeping with us."

He got off the floor and lay awake, remembering—of all things— taking bar mitzvah lessons with Cantor Zommick. It was seventh grade, and although Cap weighed almost one hundred fifty pounds and could have started as fullback for the junior high team, he had to drop out of the squad because he couldn't learn his haftarah. A short section it would have taken a more fortunate student one week to learn, but the cantor needed to meet with Cap four times a week for remedial lessons. "No!" shouted the cantor, a childless man, whose nostrils were as hairy as Cap's underarms and whose musty office smelled of wet wool. "Again," he'd say, opening his dark mouth with its rows of silver fillings. A tallowy finger would point to the word on the page, which would disappear for Cap into a nest of snaky squiggles. "*Up!*" The cantor jabbed the air, as if trying to poke angels awake to help this poor case. "Ahhh*hhhhheeeeee!* Like that!" instructed the cantor, reaching the high, tremulous note that Cap immediately flattened—

not sure whether to read what he saw or just follow after the cantor. The cantor dropped his head in the despair that comes of hearing so many mistakes, a rash of guesses at inflections and vowels and indecipherable sounds. On more than one occasion, the cantor had informed Cap that he was the worst student in the history of the temple. Finally, the cantor made a tape of the entire service, including the *maftir*, his Torah portion, and Cap had listened to it for hours until he knew it by heart. At his bar mitzvah, he only pretended to read, hoping his memory wouldn't jump ahead of the *yad*, the silver pointer that he moved uncertainly through the scroll.

He had felt nothing less than retarded. He'd refused to leave his room for days afterward. Only Allan, who was four years younger and worshiped him no matter what, would Cap allow in. He swore never to enter the synagogue again. Never utter a word of Hebrew. And suddenly now he was dreaming in Hebrew, speaking it almost as if in tongues, making an invocation over his clients' dead child, and then he was performing a ceremony, a rabbi marrying two people who he realized were Julian and Maureen, and it was too late to stop; he was asking them if they understood the Jewish word *nefesh* in all its meanings—had they studied it?—and they said yes, they knew it meant both breath and spirit, and Cap said, Oh, but there are more meanings! He would tell them if they came closer, and he knew that at the moment he brought them up to touch their bowed heads, they would be married. He could see Cantor Zommick pointing up up up! Hit the high note! he was saying, and he smiled at Cap, something he'd never done, the bridge of his nose clean of fingernail marks from where he'd pressed his fingers in pain at Cap's practicing. But all these people are dead, Cap thought, watching himself in his dream: the cantor is dead, the baby is dead, Julian and Maureen are dead, and he heard himself say quietly, Come closer, come closer, I will tell you all that the word means, and at the moment he touched their heads, he blew a cold breath onto them.

Chapter Five

JULIAN SPENT ALL HIS FREE TIME AT MAUREEN'S—HE'D MOVED HALF HIS clothes over there, his books and music. She had a piano but couldn't play; he had lots of music but no piano. "What a convenient arrangement," Maureen said, and they sat together playing "Fire and Ice" at three in the morning, Julian teaching her how to do the melody while he improvised low chords for a bass. He played Mendelssohn's "Consolation" for her, a wandering, romantic piece that his mother had performed at her middle school recital in Budapest, a pleasant memory that she told him about over and over and that he always listened to as if it were the first time. Maureen watched from the couch behind him. Afterward she draped her arms over his bare shoulders. "I love watching your back while you play, all the way down to here," she said, and traced his spine to his tailbone. It gave him goose bumps, and he felt himself flush. An only child, he wasn't used to people seeing him naked, let alone commenting on it. Privacy had been abundant in his house. And encouraged. Bodily functions were secrets; nakedness was a rumor. His father seemed always to be dressed for work. Julian wouldn't have been surprised to see him showering in his pharmacist's blue tunic. His mother took two hours every day to dress; she'd emerge from the bedroom—the door wasn't locked, but he wouldn't have dreamed of entering—fully attired, a different dress or skirt and blouse each morning. Unfortunately, she never went anywhere.

Maureen, meanwhile, had mapped every mole and hair on his body. Charted it with her tongue and hands. Once, she'd touched the gully of his upper lip and said that in Texas, where she was from, there was a term for this, a "ditch." And once, she'd tapped the scar on his chin, a tiny white raised thread only a lover would care about enough to lazily run her finger back and forth over: "How did you get this?"

He'd told her it was from a bicycle accident when he was seven. What he stopped short of saying was that he'd fallen off his bike during an absence, seizures that had been called petit mal when he'd been growing up. He'd had as many as ten a day, without anyone figuring out the problem, until he'd had a grand mal seizure in third grade. His second-grade teacher had thought he lacked concentration. She'd sent a letter home with him: *Julian drifts off in class. He frequently loses his place in the reader and stares into space. Is he getting enough sleep and having a proper breakfast? Perhaps, too, you should have his eyes checked.* . . . He had no idea himself what was causing him suddenly to go blank or to hear the beginning and the end of a sentence but miss the middle.

Once, as he was coming, Maureen put her finger up his ass. He didn't like it. "Don't do that again," he told her—the first time he'd been upset with her for anything. She'd tried to make a joke about it: "A little uptight back there?" and she'd reached behind him teasingly. "Don't," he said, grabbing her wrist so hard that she cried out, "You're hurting me!" What he didn't tell her was that it brought two things too close together, two things that had to stay apart: sex and seizures. As a child, he'd imagined that was where the button was, the on-off switch that started these things up, in his rectum, and if anybody touched him there, this most shameful place, this place where shit came out, the gross material equivalent of his seizures, he would be set off. Feces and convulsions went together. When he looked at one, he saw the other. They were equally mortifying to do in public and, much to his shame, had happened together on three occasions.

He thought it was remarkable how much time he now spent with his clothes off; he felt as if he lived in the tropics, rather than Colorado, and was descended from a sensual people uncomfortable in clothes. He was enjoying the feel of his skin for the first time, its taut smoothness, its seamless muscle; he'd often sit in front of the mirror, fondling himself, remembering Maureen's mouth or fingers on some part of his body he hadn't known existed until it jumped under her caress: all these lost parts she'd stitched back together, with lips for a needle and saliva for thread. He'd even considered, at Maureen's prompting, that he might pose for an art class, his leanness being desirable for life studies. He'd never looked at his body this way, and certainly had never loved it before.

He stopped by his apartment on the way to class to check his mailbox—overflowing from days of neglect. It was already the end of October. A thick letter from his mother. She would comment on all the classes that he'd told her about. She'd describe in detail the begonias, dahlias, and gladiolas she'd taken inside for the winter and bedded down in straw, the bulbs she was planting this fall, a bird feeder that was giving her trouble with squirrels, or she'd enclose a particularly difficult anagram she wanted his help with. She would warn him to take his medication, to do his laundry with nonallergenic soap (he was prone to rashes), to remember they loved him and thought of him always. She would pour her life out to him, a life squeezed into her room-to-room existence, her ventures into the garden and, very occasionally, the world. How far he'd come from her! Or maybe because of her. And he could tell her nothing, just jot down a few lines and feel guilty—she had put her heart and soul into her letter.

He remembered her coming once to his elementary school. The class had been doing exercises in their arithmetic workbooks, and he was trying to figure out how 9 times 10 plus 10 could equal a hundred just as 10 times 10 did. It seemed wrong, or misleading. He knew this because when he got 100 on his papers it didn't mean the same as it did for Ellen Hasp, the only other person in the class who regularly got A's. He could take no pleasure in it; felt no joy; had no thought of waving his paper proudly in the air as Ellen did on occasion, running to tell her mother after school. When he looked at his 100, he saw it as if in a mirror, 001, himself the last digit, preceded by zeros. He also saw the green number on his mother's arm, which during the hours he'd sat in silence with her (she would stare off into space for long periods of the day and just as abruptly come out of it, though her absences weren't due to seizures) he had configured to be 100, as well as zero, through complicated permutations that bore no resemblance to the laws of mathematics he learned in grade school.

When his mother came into his third-grade classroom that day and stuck her head in the door, he didn't see her at first. He looked up only when he heard his teacher asking, "May I help you?" His teacher wouldn't know his mother, of course. They'd never met. His mother had never been here. She couldn't drive and rarely left the house by herself; it was his father who picked Julian up when he was sick. It had been his father who had come to get him just two weeks before, when, on the playground, he'd had his first grand mal seizure. And it was his father who took him to school when he missed the bus, as he did frequently, because he hated and dreaded school.

"I am here to see my son, Julie," said his mother in her crisp English, squeezed by her heavier Hungarian. *Julie.* It rang through the classroom. A girl's name. At home it didn't matter. But here, not here! He heard giggling. His teacher said, "Julian, can you come up?" But he couldn't move. He didn't want that to be his mother. He wanted her to go away, get back in the house, she wasn't supposed to be here, no one came into the classroom like this, she should go to the office first. Didn't she know the *rules?*

And then she was stepping toward him, in her black rubber boots that she stuffed with a little wadded newspaper. Newspapers had been all she had during the war to keep her feet warm. She did it out of habit and memory, a ritual he could only partially understand. Her mother had put them in her shoes when she was a child. And Julian could hear the newspaper rustle as her boots squeaked toward him, and then she reached out her hand with a brown paper bag, and he thought, Why are you doing this, I have my lunch, and he realized it wasn't his lunch at all but his medication. He'd forgotten to bring the medicine he'd just started taking twice a day at home and once at school, in the privacy of the nurse's office, and would be taking—the doctor couldn't promise it wasn't true—for the rest of his life.

And then she'd left. But before she had, he'd seen her eyes, how terrified they were, how confused, how worried about him, how hard it had been for her to come up here—the gauntlet of terrors she'd run to bring him his pills. His father had been out of the store. She couldn't reach him with her coded telephone ring. She'd waited and anguished and finally walked the mile in the rain to his school, her toes gripping the wadded newspaper, all for him, and all he could think was Go away, hide yourself, go back, *run!*

Now he put his mother's letter back in its envelope but then found inside a postcard she had forwarded. It was from Luchesca, informing him that she'd finally made it back home to Italy, was "happy, some-what," and would love to hear from him. She gave her address and phone number in Rome. He zipped the postcard and his mother's letter inside his pack and hurried off to class. He didn't even have time now to go upstairs and check his apartment, much less write to anyone—his mother included.

His class was in the engineering building; the halls were jammed with students. Originally an agricultural school, the university was nicknamed Moo U. He had applied to both the university at Boulder and the one here and been accepted at each. But when he visited Boulder, the trendiness bothered him; it was as if he were back in Baltimore, with the competition to look good, something he wanted to get as far away from as possible. And though Boulder was beautiful—he'd never seen a prettier campus—it felt crowded to him, the town's back right up against the mountains. Pierre, on the other hand, was open, farther east on the plains, its residential streets as wide as a four-lane highway back in Baltimore. They'd been planned that way, Maureen had told him, so that horses and their carriages could make turns in the middle of the street.

He could finally breathe here; it had been his original reason for going to Ohio—to spread out, move his limbs, and contact nothing. Somehow (his reasoning had gone), if he could escape into such vast open space, he'd eliminate the pressures that squeezed and built up inside and inevitably exploded. Except he hadn't gone far enough (or wide enough) by going to Ohio. But Pierre, with its oversize streets, long views to the mountains, room for rodeo parades and slow freight trains, could contain even his uncertain fusions.

But still he became uncomfortable here occasionally, the students often from small farming and ranching communities (Boulder attracted the more worldly and the out-of-state students)—all the people in his classes who had never been outside Colorado and were surprised to learn that Baltimore was near water. Most had never met a Jew before college. When his sociology teacher asked if anyone would be absent for the Jewish holidays Rosh Hashanah and Yom Kippur, everyone had looked around the room as if searching for the lone Jew. Julian had kept silent. He wouldn't take off for the holidays. He never had. His mother and father had never set foot in a synagogue, not with him at least, and yet he knew because of his mother that he was more a Jew than anyone here could imagine.

He sat down in the back row. Maureen hadn't arrived yet. He had a moment of wondering what had happened, where she was, trying to picture her every action in the fifty minutes since he'd last seen her. It distressed him to find he couldn't account for all her time. She was friends with her apartment manager, who had come by several times to fix things—a garbage disposal, a faulty doorbell—while Julian had been there. Maureen had introduced Julian as her student. It bothered him. Why didn't she say he was a friend? Because you're my student, she said, and it's safer to be honest. My student over at my apartment plays better than my friend (who happens to be my student). Get the difference? He didn't. It was their second disagreement, not long after the incident of her finger up his anus. Was this what couples fought about—how lovers introduced you and fingers in the wrong places? He'd never been in a relationship. He apologized to her, but he wasn't sure why or for what. Maureen said (a sort of apology that sounded more like additional evidence for her side), I'm sorry too, but I'm up for tenure this year and have to be careful.

Now she came into the classroom, and for a moment, a split instant, because it had turned so cold and was supposed to snow and Maureen was wearing high-laced boots, he saw his mother in the doorway and suffered the same tearing forces, recoiling at the sight of her but wanting to run to her, too, and weep, and he felt himself being pulled asunder for Maureen, for sex and love and for sickness over what he was doing.

She took the roll, talked for a while about when their papers were due, and then she lectured about carbon dioxide released into the atmosphere from the burning of Amazon forests. Julian took notes. He had moved his seat to the back row after they'd become lovers. He always tried to screen himself behind a girl whose hair blossomed out like Dolly Parton's, catching sight of Maureen occasionally through the O of a blonde ringlet.

"Listen," said Maureen, sitting on the desk and crossing her legs. She had the full attention of the class. "Do you know what one of the most damaging greenhouse gases is? Methane gas. And do you know where much of that methane comes from?" She slid off the desk and stood right in front of the first row of chairs. She had just taken off her coat, and Julian wanted to help hang it up for her. She was his teacher. She was his lover. He suddenly noticed the buttons peeking out of the flap of her jeans and had the startling thought that he'd buttoned them for her today, one by one.

But she was absolutely untouchable when she lectured. He couldn't stand being behind the barrier.

"From factories?" said one student, Gaylon, a tall and talkative boy with long, prematurely gray hair in a ponytail. He always stayed after class, as did many of the students, to speak with her. Julian, meanwhile, would wait in the hall until the second before she came out, then quickly disappear so she wouldn't see him. He felt awkward standing among the others, but he worried if he didn't. She was a popular teacher because of her subject, her activism, her sharpness of tongue, her looks; he'd have to get used to it.

"No, not from factories," and Julian thought of his twenty-mile-high smokestacks for producing ozone, an idea that had started the whole relationship. How could it be traced back to that? How did that come out of the formula? Ten times 9 plus 10—why this arrangement; how did it add up to him? "It's from cows."

"Cows?" someone said, and laughed.

"Exactly," said Maureen. "Cows produce methane gas during digestion. Sixty million tons of it a year. They burp, and up it goes."

The class laughed. She boosted herself back on the desk, looking down at the floor. Everyone waited expectantly. He felt annoyed with her for making a show, for performing like this—performing for others. He put his pencil down in protest. "That's twelve percent of all methane gas from all sources. Cows. Plain old cows."

"How can that be changed?" asked Gaylon. He'd earned some prerogative whereby he didn't need to raise his hand like the others. Sometimes he seemed to carry on a private dialogue with her. Julian had once mentioned that he found Gaylon a little overbearing, and Maureen had said, "Oh, Gaylon, he's just a hippie who should have been in my generation," and Julian thought, So now we're going to play the age game.

"I'll tell you in a moment. But first you should know some other facts: To produce one-half pound of steak requires hundreds of gallons of water. Half the water consumed in the United States is used to grow feed for cattle. You should all appreciate that, living in an area where water is so scarce anyway. Cattle also consume nearly seventy percent of all grain produced in the United States and almost one-third of the entire *planet's* grain harvest. Meanwhile, one billion people in the world have chronic malnutrition. How many of these people could be fed, how many starving children, if we just cut back our cattle production by a third, let alone half?"

"What are you saying, then?" asked Gaylon.

"What I'm saying is this: The costs of being a primarily meat-eating culture are financially and environmentally staggering in a way they weren't even twenty years ago. It will get worse, too, as land becomes overgrazed and feed crop is depleted. You have to change people's ways of thinking about what they eat. And there's no better place to start than right here at Moo U. In Colorado alone, over three million cattle a year are slaughtered—that's three billion pounds of beef."

Julian sat and listened. Maureen went on, writing the name "Olton" on the blackboard: "Pregnant women and infants can't drink the water anymore in this little eastern Colorado town. That's because fecal coliform bacteria has entrenched itself in the water table and can't be eliminated by the usual leaching of the municipal water system. The bacteria comes from manure, from livestock operations dumping waste, from hog and cattle farms, mostly, that allow it to sink into the ground-water. These large cattle operations claim they'll just dig a big pit and slowly let the wastewater seep in, controlling and confining it until the nitrates and bacteria dissolve."

She paused and walked right up to Gaylon's desk, in the front row, grazing it with her thighs. "Well, folks, it just isn't working that way. We're not going to have any water to drink soon, and we're losing our breathing air because we eat too much meat. Anyone interested in helping out should see me after class."

He resented that she hadn't told him anything about this before-hand. Why hadn't she mentioned the project? That had been the original motivation for his getting to know her better. They'd work together on writing her book about the death of the family farm. But now she tickled his balls or bit his shoulder whenever he tried to talk about the work she was doing. "All work and no play makes Julian a dull lay," she'd told him. "Let's," she warned, teacherly, "not become dull."

After class he stood with the rest of the students, listening while she outlined an on-campus "meat-out" they could organize. She didn't look at him once. She walked down the hall with the group, their numbers dwindling as they went outside and came closer to her office, until it was just Gaylon and Julian. Finally, Gaylon left, after a discussion about desertification through farming practices in third world countries, a discussion Julian just watched.

"Well," said Maureen, "top of the morning to you."

"You want to go out for coffee?" He didn't even drink coffee, but he felt desperate to be alone with her, to have her full attention for a little while.

"Sure," she said, and smiled at him knowingly, and he forgot everything—how remote and unreachable she'd been in class, all the things he'd planned to tell her in a spate of anger and confession. She had a faculty meeting in a half hour and a lecture to prepare after that and a doctor's appointment this afternoon, but she could certainly have coffee now.

A man called her from across the plaza. Julian recognized him as one of Maureen's colleagues. He came toward them. "We have to go over these recommendations before the meeting," he said, and then they talked awhile about the new graduate curriculum, a Ph.D. in environmental ethics, about the endorsements they'd received from national programs in California and Oregon, and about how many students they could realistically expect to recruit.

Julian listened with interest, then grew bored and then irritated. She'd forgotten he was here. And she hadn't introduced him to her colleague. He was invisible. Suddenly she turned to him. "I'm sorry," she said, without so much as calling him by name. "We'll need to have our conference later," and he had the crazy urge to grab her, to pull her toward him by her just-washed blonde hair, to yank her briefcase out of her hand and toss it into the fountain behind them. But he just nodded and watched her go off with her colleague. He could not stop watching her back; he kept hoping she'd turn around and give him some signal. And then she disappeared around the corner of Atmospheric Sciences.

He went inside the student center but couldn't face the crowds there. Students bumped into him while he stood in the middle of the cafeteria, trying to locate a free table. He decided he'd skip lunch and go bowling, but all the alleys were full. He went back upstairs. His heart was starting to pound, his breathing to shorten. Someone called his name, and he turned, expecting to see Maureen, but it was Gaylon. He was coming at Julian with his notebook open, saying something about signing up for table duty—Gaylon's tall head weaving back and forth as though it were on a stick at a carnival. Julian turned and ran, bumped into a student coming out of the copy center. "Watch it! I just had all these collated!" she said, and got down on her hands and knees to pick up the scattered papers. Julian backed away from her, not helping. People were staring at him. The atrium had tables with class rings for sale and season tickets to the basketball games and blankets from Peru and subscriptions to the Denver newspapers and tie-dyed T-shirts and handmade jewelry and crystals; and someone tried to hand him a pamphlet about God; and military recruiters stood with their hands locked behind their backs, watching him sternly; and a Native American Studies video of dancing and drumming flashed and pounded. . . . He couldn't find the exit. He saw two campus policemen coming along the corridor, and he backed into the popcorn wagon and heard laughter. He started running and could hear handcuffs rattling and nightsticks and guns. If he stopped he was dead, they'd shoot him—who could imagine that? He could. They'd shoot him, and he mustn't stop. He ran to the edge of the campus and dashed in front of cars that honked at him, and he made it to the other side of the street, into an alley behind a fraternity building, and crouched down beside a dumpster, shaking.

He stayed there for an hour, shivering uncontrollably. Snow fell on his head and melted in his hair. When finally he stood up, his legs felt weak, but the panic had gone. He could breathe. His heart had slowed down enough so that he could think about what to do.

He walked to the end of the alley and saw a gas station. A canopy of snow, like a white pagoda, covered the pay phone. He opened his wallet, found Cap's number and the message he'd never read:

I'm here for you. I care about you and won't desert you.

"It's an emergency," Julian heard himself explaining to the answering service. He gave the number of the pay phone and waited, sat on the curb with his head lowered. Snow floated down, heavy wet flakes that stuck to him like notes pinned to his clothes. In five minutes the phone rang. It was Cap. "Come right over," he told Julian. "Can you make it here all right?" "Yes," said Julian, and slid along the street to Cap's office.

When he got back to his apartment, Maureen was waiting for him. She sat shivering on the stone steps, huddled in her coat, her knees locked together. The snow had piled up around her legs, and seeing her in her hat, her cheeks red, her nose running in the cold, he knew he could never leave her.

He'd told Cap everything about the last six weeks. And then Cap had talked. The panic attack, he had said, was probably set off by Julian's having no way to deal with feeling rejected by Maureen—the same overwhelming anxiety he'd had as a child when he felt alone and his mother had been lost to him, withdrawn into her own excluding thoughts. He'd coped with it then by turning inward or to compulsive rituals, but now the fear of being abandoned threatened him all over again, and much more strongly because of the sexual involvement. His defenses just weren't up to it.

Nor could he really protect himself from the hurtful imbalances in the relationship: Maureen was older, already established in her career, a member of many organizations and committees. Literally every step she'd taken on the way to her office had made him feel left behind and inconsequential. It wasn't a fair situation, nor would it ever be. "There's too much catching up to do, and frankly, by the time you get even with her, she'll be gone," Cap had said. "And, too," he added, never mentioning Maureen's name but talking about her as a hypothetical case, "let's say this individual had been mistreated in her life. She'd be likely to find someone she could use in the same way, make an object of that person in turn, especially if that person were unusually vulnerable, as she had once been. It wouldn't be intentional, maybe, but it would be irresistible in order to regain power in the original situation of her own past. Those circumstances would attract you because of your experience taking care of your mother, a role that required you to be a little adult. When a child fills this role he becomes mechanically reliable—that is, he doesn't have needs, impulses, bad behaviors, inconsistencies, temper tantrums, unreasonable demands. He's dependable, like a butler or a machine. He acts to please others over himself. He can't ejaculate for his own pleasure"—and Julian had winced hearing this, because it was true—"or even know when he is feeling pleasure. He gives up his self to gain any kind of attention or love he can, on terms he must take. It's all bound up with what the other person wants and is pleased by. I suspect, too, that your seizures made you feel even more objectified. In your situation now, it sounds as if you have a sexual role, one that requires that you be unconditionally available for pleasure. And one that engages you unquestioningly, until a rupture like today's occurs."

What had affected him, though, more than anything else Cap had said was his parting remark. "You'll know you're in love when you feel more of your self rather than less, Julian." It was true; he'd been feeling less around Maureen, especially whenever they were in public, anywhere with other people. He couldn't feel then the lovely, dizzying grandness that her touch ignited in private.

He'd had it all straight, and then he saw her on the steps and forgot everything. Completely. Always. Snow had settled on her eyebrows; he kissed her lashes, tasted the wetness, licked her lips until they were warm. He moved his rough cheek against her face: she'd lately wanted him to grow a beard, and the follicles had sprouted dark and tight overnight, as if each pore couldn't resist trying to please her. She put her hands around his neck, curled a finger through his hair, and said, "Take me inside, Julian. I have something to tell you."

Maureen got under the covers and shivered. She told him to lie down beside her. He had the feeling he was going to hear something that would matter for the rest of his life. She was too quiet, silent as his mother could be when she slipped into a dead space in her memory.

"I'm pregnant, Julian. I found out this afternoon. It's your baby, and I'm going to keep it." She'd answered all his questions. He had nothing to say. He lay there looking straight up at the ceiling, thinking its color matched the snow outside; inside and outside, he was being swallowed up.

He fixed her dinner, spaghetti and meatballs. She was ravenous for meat. She agreed it contradicted her lectures and values. "But I enjoy certain irrational prerogatives now," she said, and put her plate out for more. Julian heaped spaghetti on and the one meatball that was left. She gulped down a large glass of milk so fast that it left a white mustache on her lips. She didn't even wipe it off before digging into her spaghetti again. He'd never seen anybody eat like this, not even in the school lunchroom. Some hungry force inside her was rushing toward existence, devouring his spaghetti, and maybe he'd less than secretly (never once offering to use or asking about birth control) wanted to create it as much as she did. He couldn't blame her.

Gaylon called during dinner. The protest? Oh, yes, the protest, Julian said. He'd like to participate somehow, he said vaguely, feeling Gaylon's insistence. When Julian got off, he told Maureen that Gaylon wanted to have the meat boycott soon, before Thanksgiving. "Sorry," she said. She couldn't help out herself. If how she felt now was any indication, she'd be too tired to do anything but the absolute minimum—show up for class, talk, and then come home and conk out.

She fell asleep shortly after dinner. She'd asked if she could spend the night at his place, too tired to go home. She'd driven here straight from the doctor's. He watched while her blonde hair spread out on both pillows, the covers up to her shoulders, her thumbs folded in front of her lips, as if she were about to whistle into them.

They had talked over dinner about the baby: when the due date would be (over summer break—she could complete the school year), what she might tell people ("Nothing—artificial insemination makes the scarlet letter obsolete"), even how close in age the baby would be to her new niece, her sister's baby, just two months old now. But they'd avoided any mention of what this meant for them as a couple until Julian said, "I'm not sure I want to be anonymous. I don't mean that we have to tell everyone right away, but afterward, when the baby comes . . ." He stopped. He'd just comprehended what she'd meant by artificial insemination. *He* was obsolete. She'd gotten what she needed from him, and he had no part in the process anymore. Was this her way of telling him to go away?

"Come here, silly," she'd said, just before she'd fallen asleep. Cap would want Julian to break off the relationship (even as a father now); he'd want Julian to resume his medication; he'd want Julian to talk about his mother and feel things that happened years ago and that were of no consequence compared to the amazing events overwhelming him now.

Chapter Six

CAP CAME HOME THROUGH THE SNOW, STOMPING HIS BOOTS ON THE porch. Wallis was cooking dinner already. He picked up Claude to play Runaway Elevator, lifting him in the air and letting him drop like a stone—catching him just before he hit the couch.

"Don't get any ideas about taking him outside," Wallis warned, training her eye on Cap from the kitchen.

Last week he'd brought Claude outside in the middle of a windstorm. Balancing him on the pedestal of his palm, Cap had turned him around like a little ice folly. Claude had been utterly still and transfixed, watching the tree branches whip from side to side, undulate, and discharge their remaining leaves, which swirled up in the currents of air. Wallis had called for them from the porch, concerned Claude would become chilled or get dirt in his eye. But Claude had loved it, as he loved being flown through the room when Cap played Superbaby. Superbaby, aka Claude Kaplan, protected babies everywhere: he snatched electrical cords out of their hands; he ripped plastic dry cleaners' bags off their heads; he halted baby carriages just as they were about to tumble off the rim of the Grand Canyon.

"How do you think of these things?" Wallis had asked him.

He didn't know. He supposed it did mean something significant that all the games he played with Claude were disaster scenarios: Earthquake Escape, Space Station Alert, Mud Tidal Wave. Partly it was a way of replaying his own childhood, but the other part, he had to admit, came from work, he supposed, some fantasy translation and purging for him of the disorder, chaos, and hardship that always threatened to wipe away his clients.

But he'd toned it down lately. Instead of Superbaby, snatching babies from the paths of speeding cars, Cap had Claude spend some quiet time as *Supper*baby, a very lazy baby who liked to just loll around with a good rattle. "He's kind of a blob," said Cap, who had explained the new arrival to Wallis after she requested gentler and less inclement activity than playing with Claude in a cyclone.

So now he let Claude lie on his back, kicking his legs and flapping his arms like an overturned bug. "See," said Cap, calling to Wallis in the kitchen. She was making stir-fry for dinner. "He just wants to fly."

"Don't you dare take him outside in this snow!" said Wallis.

"He'd love it. What a great primal memory it would be."

"Cap—"

"How about if we go into the garage to look around for the snow shovel?"

"Five minutes, Cap. And bundle him up. It's freezing out there." He got Claude all ready, putting him in his baby bunting, blue with red piping, his arms sticking straight out like a scarecrow in the stiff sleeves—but a handsome outfit compared to the snowsuits of Cap's childhood, which looked as if air had been pumped inside for eight hours. Cap folded Claude over his shoulder, like riding backward on a train, and they went outside and rummaged around for the snow shovel he'd buried deep in the garage last spring. The storm had already dumped fourteen inches. Only November 5, and it had snowed twice in the last week.

When he came back in, Wallis handed him the phone. "It's Allan," she said. "He has something he wants to tell you." She shrugged, not knowing what it was.

Cap took the phone. His brother had been calling him more often in the last couple of months, without any reason other than to say hello. His symptoms had been in remission for over half a year now, longer than ever before.

"Wallis says it's snowing hard out there," said Allan.

"It is," answered Cap. He tried to be friendly and encouraging, but he still found himself listening for a delusion: an operator was monitoring their call, or the phone cord had tiny electrical charges that were going to shock him. "How's Mom and Dad?" asked Cap.

"They're fine. But there's someone else here with me now."

"Oh?" said Cap, bracing himself.

"Joan."

"Joan?" said Cap. "Do I know her, Allan?" He felt himself slipping into his office voice, guarded. Joan of Arc?

"Not yet. But you're going to meet her soon enough. Our wedding is June third."

"Pardon?"

"I wanted to wait until we'd picked the date before I let you know for sure."

It didn't sound as if Allan were joking or imagining this. "Where'd you meet her, Allan?" His voice felt thick with disbelief, but Allan scarcely noticed.

"She's from my therapy group. We're both druggies."

"What?"

"Clozapine. We've been on it together. Do you want to speak to her, Cap?"

"I . . . well, yes, sure." He was dumbfounded.

In a few seconds he heard a soft voice, "Hi, Cap. I'm Joan."

"Yes," he said, lost for words, then recovering himself. "It's good to talk with you."

"Allan's told me a lot about you. And Claude and Wallis too."

"I'm afraid he hasn't told me much about you yet."

She laughed, for which he was grateful, because he was afraid there was some irritation or condescension in his voice. She seemed very comfortable, however, quietly generous in putting people at ease. "Allan wants to speak to you again. It was good talking to you, Cap. I'm looking forward to meeting everyone."

His brother got back on the phone. "So anyway," Allan said, sounding like their father, "we'll see you in June, if not before?"

"Of course," said Cap. "Absolutely." He slid off his down jacket, shifting the phone to his other hand. "Allan, is Mom there?"

"Yes."

"Can I speak with her, please?"

"Sure. I just wanted to let you know, Cap."

He'd almost forgotten! He could see Allan was waiting. "Congratulations! It's great news!" he said, hoping it sounded sincere.

"Thanks, Cap. Thanks a lot. You can't imagine how excited we are. Joan is a lot calmer than me, but we're both thrilled about it."

The first thing his mother said was, "Isn't it wonderful!" Now Cap knew it was really true. He spoke with his mother for a few minutes, before his father got on the extension to ask about the weather—he'd been following the storm on the weather channel—and then Cap got off.

Wallis stood waiting expectantly. "Well? What was *that* about?"

"Allan's getting married."

Wallis stopped slicing a carrot. "You must be joking."

"I'm not. He's marrying someone named Joan from his therapy group."

"Was he . . . lucid?"

"Yes, he was perfectly clear and logical. And then I spoke to Joan herself, who sounded very pleasant. The wedding is in June. Can you believe this?" He himself couldn't. He couldn't even imagine his brother holding a girl's hand without thinking it would turn into a spider, let alone Allan accepting all that marriage meant.

"Is this all because of that miracle drug your mother mentioned?" asked Wallis.

"Clozapine. I suppose. I guess," said Cap, clearly baffled by the normalcy of all this. "It's so sudden, or feels that way out here, not having seen him since all this started changing."

"Do you remember it took me two hours to get Allan back from the park in Philadelphia because he was afraid of the cracks? I had to draw a hopscotch grid every few feet with imaginary sidewalk chalk, a net to protect him from them, just to coax him home."

"I remember," said Cap.

"Things change fast when they do." Wallis turned back to the stove. "So how do you feel about it?"

"I'm not sure," said Cap.

"I'm not sure either. My first thought is where will I get a dress and what size will I be then. And it's seven months away. That tells you what state of mind I'm in."

Cap laughed. He took Claude into the living room while Wallis finished cooking dinner. Cap lay on the floor, Claude crawling over his chest. The snow had already blotted out the skylight at the top of the stairs. His brother's news should have delighted him, but all it did was fill him with apprehension. He could see himself rising to object at the wedding ceremony, the only one who had any problem with the unexpectedness of all this.

The phone rang again. "I'll get it," said Cap, and stood up, carrying Claude over his shoulder.

"If it's Phyllis," said Wallis, "tell her I'll call her back." Phyllis and Ed were coming for dinner on Saturday—only the second time they'd entertained since Claude was born. They'd talked about going out, too, alone, getting a baby-sitter for Claude, who was almost four months old now, but Wallis wasn't ready for that step yet. Nor, frankly, was he.

Cap picked up the phone. The answering service. "I have an emergency call from Bill Sable," the woman said. "Do you want his number, or should I patch him through?"

"Put him through."

"How you doing, Cap? Bill Sable."

It took him a moment to absorb the name. He was still thinking about his conversation with Allan. "What's up, Bill?"

Sable cleared his throat. "I was wondering how you've been doing with my case."

He couldn't believe Sable had called him at home about this. It didn't seem exactly urgent.

"I was just sitting here getting curious," said Sable; it was the same smooth voice he'd used in the office, the salesman's pitch that reminded Cap of a Popsicle after it had melted awhile.

"I can give you more information tomorrow, if you'll call me during office hours."

"I thought you might have something for me tonight."

"I'm sorry, but I don't."

"That's too bad," said Sable.

Something shifted in the easy chumminess; a piece of grit had come into Sable's voice. "I think you should call me tomorrow, Bill. We're getting ready to eat dinner here."

"How's your little boy, by the way?" Sable laughed. "Keeping him warm enough? Claude, right?"

A shiver went through Cap. How did Sable know Claude's name? "Is there something you need to talk to me about in a session, Bill? Would you like to see me tomorrow?"

"Not really, Cap," said Sable. "Just thought I'd give you a buzz to see what progress you've made, how my tests came out."

"Even when I get them I won't be able to share them with you directly." In fact, they were on his desk. He'd received them late today. But he didn't want Sable to know that; he didn't want Sable to know a thing more than he already did.

"Apologies to you, Cap, if I disturbed your evening."

"You can call me tomorrow if you want to talk further."

"Maybe I'll do that, Cap. Maybe I will." He hung up.

Cap held the phone in his hand. A draft blew through the house, the storm windows not yet up. The cold and his own reaction to the call made him tremble.

He went in to see Wallis. Claude pulled at the back of his hair.

"Who was that?" Wallis asked.

"A client," said Cap, not sure what else to tell her. "It was a strange call."

She stopped, holding sliced ginger in midair above the wok, its oil sizzling and waiting for more ingredients. "What kind of strange call?"

"He just wanted to know if I'd gotten his evaluation results yet. It's a custody case."

"And he called you at home?"

Cap nodded. "No big deal. I'll set the table." He took the plates from the cabinet.

Wallis turned off the stove. "What else did he say?" She must have heard something in his tone.

"Nothing important. It just felt a little as if he were pressuring me."

"Pressuring how?"

"Maybe I mean something else. He brought up Claude's name."

"Why?"

As soon as he'd said it, he knew it was a mistake to tell her, but it had been the part that bothered him the most—the inappropriateness of it, the unctuous, facile interest: *How's your little boy . . . Claude, right?* "Just to ask about him, I guess."

"You don't sound sure yourself."

"He's a salesman. Suppose we give him the benefit of the doubt. Maybe he always remembers kids' names, like salesmen do—to flatter the parents."

"Had you told him Claude's name?"

"No."

Wallis stared at him. "This is weird, Cap. You're sure you never mentioned his name."

"I only saw him once." They were silent a moment, then Wallis said, "I feel like calling the police or something, Cap. I know that's overreacting, but this is our son you're talking about, a baby."

"Think about it from his perspective. It's a tense situation. Maybe he's just bumbling around, trying to get on my good side." Still, Cap wasn't sure. It wasn't the first time a client had tried to manipulate him, but it was the first time that Claude's name had been brought up. "Anyway, I'll check into it further tomorrow."

"How?"

"I'll look over the tests. I still have to talk to his kids' teachers and his neighbors and some other names I have for the custody references. By the end of the day I'll have a very accurate profile of him. Don't worry."

"I don't like this, Cap. Something feels wrong."

"I'll check into it," he repeated, remembering the piece of grit, the scratch of malice, he'd heard in Sable's voice.

He took Claude and headed into the living room, making sure the doors and windows were locked. The snow muffled all sound outside and amplified the noises in the house—the furnace going on, the creak of the floorboards, the hum from the fluorescent light in his office. He stood at the window. It snowed so fast out here in the West, so deliberately, without taking a breath, the streets already deserted and left to the plows with their yellow beacons and their loud shovels pawing the ground until the house shook.

When he went back into the kitchen, Wallis had put the salad and the stir-fry on the plates. "I've lost my appetite," she said. "Between Allan's news and this guy's call, it's been quite a night."

"Nothing's going to happen," said Cap, but he stood beside the cutlery block, one hand resting casually below the black-handled knives, realizing that he hadn't stopped looking at them since he'd come into the kitchen.

In the morning, Wallis watched the sun come out strong. By noon water dripped from the remaining leaves on the trees and from icicles that hung from the rain gutters. Strong as scabbards earlier, the icicles by midday had melted into tiny tubes, fragile as the legs of glass horse figurines. The snow on the front lawn shrank into a small continent, darkened by the blue shadows of the afternoon. It was sixty degrees by two P.M. Up fifty from last night. Extremes like this had taken Wallis years to get used to. Snow came this early in Chicago, where she'd grown up, but it stayed, rudely, along with the cold. Now she just accepted the rapid shifts in climate and dressed Claude in a yellow-and-white-striped cotton jumpsuit and took him to the doctor with her.

Her period had just begun again. It would be odd, after so many years of not using anything, to have to worry about birth control, something they hadn't done since the early years of their marriage, when they thought children would happen according to plan.

A young nurse called her name, and Wallis followed her back to the scale, then into the examining room.

Dr. Lutchman soon came in, jolly as ever. The nurse held Claude while Lutchman measured Wallis for a diaphragm, then helped her sit up. She took Claude, who had started to cry, back in her arms and went over to the chair to nurse him.

Lutchman quickly recited a list of irregularities, including headaches and swelling and uterine pain, and Wallis said no to them all. Everything was going fine, Claude very healthy coming up on four months. For a moment she wanted to tell Lutchman about the phone call from Cap's client last night—it had been on her mind all day—but she restrained herself.

Cap never talked to her about his clients. He had in the beginning of their marriage. Anonymously. But even that became too much, too contentious, because Wallis always had suggestions, simple, impatient ones (that he wouldn't take) for what was wrong with them and how they could be fixed (get a new job, stop drinking, lose weight, move out). His cases populated the house after a while in ways that made them both uncomfortable—his clients' needs and problems hanging from the ceiling like strung meats. Navigating their own marriage was difficult enough without bumping their heads on all these other obstacles. So they'd made an agreement not to discuss his clients, unless it was unavoidable. Occasionally, Wallis would be in a supermarket line and wonder if the person standing in front of her was a client of his; it was likely in a small city like Pierre. Did her husband know this woman's most intimate secrets? Did she regularly discuss her orgasms with him? Tell him things she would never have dreamed of confessing to her own husband? But mostly she didn't want to know. And Cap, too, after a while, after he no longer worried that her silence on this matter meant she was uninterested in his work, didn't want her to know either; it only doubled the burden.

Claude nursed hungrily, particularly noisy in the quiet room. Wallis was grateful, though, for the distraction, something filling the silence while Lutchman made notes in her chart and the nurse prepared the room for the next woman. Phyllis had claimed nursing released some kind of mothering hormone. "How else would nature get someone like you to sit still for so long?" she'd told Wallis. She was right. It was the most patient she'd felt in her life. What a relief (and how unexpected) not to care about *everything*, to believe things could get done without her. Yesterday afternoon she'd stood at the window and watched Claude's stroller collect snow. An unthinkable event before Claude, the front porch always spotless, the yard clear of the tiniest leaf. We'll get it in the morning, she'd thought about the stroller. Maybe we'll just let it sit there until the snow melts.

In an odd way, having Claude gave her the confidence *not* to do things. She even wondered if her difficulty in becoming pregnant had resulted from her own mixed feelings about being a mother. Maybe she'd wanted to put it off until the last possible moment—for fear of not being able to do it right. What models did she have, after all? Her own mother couldn't even bear to visit them and meet Claude. Maybe it reminded her too much of being a mother herself, the disappointment it must have been, along with the whole marriage. Wallis had spoken with her three times since Claude's birth. Each time, her mother promised to give her a definite date when she could visit, but then "couldn't commit." An industrial designers' convention. A flood in her basement. An operation on her knee. Wallis's silence made no impact. Her mother took it as acquiescence.

She sighed. She'd have to let go of it. If she could watch the stroller vanish under the snow, she could do the same thing with her parents. A short mental leap. Granted, she argued with them all day in her head, couldn't stop thinking about how heartless they were. It was one thing to ignore her, but to ignore her child . . . Still, she could do it. She could make them disappear under a smooth, shapeless white mass.

She thought about Cap playing his disaster games with Claude last night—Submarine Attack ("Dive! Dive! Dive!" she'd heard him saying, changing Claude into his pajamas for bed) and right after dinner, Earthquake Escape, maybe to distract himself from his clients, particularly the phone call that had bothered her. He'd rumbled and tripped around the living room with Claude, who remained motionless and serious and appeared to be holding his breath with the excitement of an amusement ride, while Cap saved them from the earthquake by sliding down the long face of a mountain and leaping across molten lava to a French farmer's field, where they landed safely in a haystack.

Perhaps she was jealous—jealous of Claude. In a different way, Cap had flown her around at one time, concentrated his gaze on her, listened so well, out of his training and love, that she had taken off, blossomed as she never had with a man, believing she could go about her life and not have to keep her distance. His kindness and humor and patience with her impatience all helped, but mostly she just didn't feel alone with him, as she did with others, who always wondered why she was so "busy." Admittedly she'd kept herself that way. Unapproachable: another favorite description when she'd been growing up. While other girls had been described as having great smiles and sweet dispositions, the caption under her yearbook picture had read: "Hard, hard worker," the repetition of "hard" speaking volumes about her perceived personality.

It wasn't jealousy, exactly. Just confusion. Some part of her stood outside and felt left out of all this. A spectator at what she'd always wanted, a reluctant winner of family love.

"Everything looks swell," said Lutchman, who wrote out a prescription for a diaphragm and cheerfully gave the slip to Wallis.

She drove to school with Claude. She'd been here only once since he'd been born, to show him off to the teachers. It had been lunchtime, and business as usual: monitors looking for kids in the halls; Teresa Harkins, with an upset stomach, waiting in the office for her mother to pick her up; a budding eighth-grade gang, who'd spray-painted the bathroom with graffiti, being escorted en masse to the principal's office; and of course the weak and garbled PA system—still not fixed after a year—which made everything sound foreign and monotone, as if the office secretary were dully reciting a recipe for German potatoes rather than announcing this year's newspaper staff.

Wallis walked down the A wing to her office in Language Arts and found it empty. It was four-thirty, and she was supposed to meet Phyllis here. A new teacher had taken over Wallis's cubicle and put up pictures of her own young family; Wallis experienced a twinge of laziness, feeling uncooperative, insufficiently dedicated. After all, this young teacher didn't let her children—not one but two—stop her from being here every day.

She knew why she avoided the place. Coming here only made her more unsettled about her decision to stay home. It had worked out well that this was her sabbatical year, but now she wondered if she'd want to return at all, and the thought filled her with trepidation about money and loneliness and everything she'd invested in this job for the last sixteen years. She'd started here right after they'd moved up from Denver, following Cap's internship. How easy it seemed now to take the few remaining books from her shelves, the photo collage of her last class of eighth graders, the plaque that had honored her two years before as the school's teacher of the year, and the decade-old pack of cigarettes she still left for security in the back of the bottom drawer (she wondered if the new teacher had discovered it).

Claude had pulled her away from this place, as she had never anticipated. If anything, she'd expected to feel the opposite—that she'd want to return here early, reduce her sabbatical. But she'd become used to the slow pace of her insular life with Claude, and he still seemed so young to her, too young to entrust to anyone else, though she knew many people who did it all the time, out of necessity or choice. But every time she pictured being here and sitting in on a curriculum meeting, she thought of Claude after a bath, his sweet smell and his pinkish, warm skin. When he watched her, his brown eyes dug so deep that she felt as if rich, dark earth would pour forth from her heart and grow enough fruits and vegetables to feed every starving child. It was such a surprise, such an uncontrollable love, so lush, so different than with Cap, with anybody, refusing to be quelled or exhausted, even as she herself became exhausted, bored, frustrated, hungry for adult company.

"Hi, sweetheart," Phyllis said to Claude as she bent over to peek under his hat. He'd fallen asleep on Wallis's shoulder. "And what's wrong with *you?*"

"Nothing," said Wallis. "Why? Does something seem wrong?"

"A little like you got caught in somebody's headlights. This is your old home, remember?"

Wallis shifted her weight. Claude was getting to be a heavy baby, already fifteen pounds; he was taking after Cap, in the ninetieth percentile for both height and weight. For starting off so precariously, he was roaring ahead through infancy. It gave her immense pleasure to see him thriving after such a fragile start. She thought again of Cap's client last night, asking about Claude. She'd gotten up three times when she heard noises. Standing at the window, she'd watched the snow come down in the orange haze of the streetlights, the slow passage of cars. "Would you think I was a terrible person if I told you I wanted to leave school?"

"Leave?"

"Quit."

Phyllis looked amused, but that was the way Phyllis acted when she was annoyed: the slight smile of detachment, the arms firmly crossed. Her brown curls quivered a bit, like a jester's jeering bells. "So you're deserting us?"

"I'm just thinking about it," said Wallis.

"No, you're not," said Phyllis. "You've already made your decision. Now come on and let's get out of here, before I decide to use my teenagers as an excuse for quitting too."

"I'm *not* using Claude as an excuse—"

"Oh, stop it, Wallis. I'm on your side. But once you know what you want to do, that's it. I'm going to try like hell to talk you out of leaving. Not to mention you're only four years away from a retirement pension. So what if it's the mistake of your life and once Claude starts running amok, dropping the cordless phone in the toilet, you'll chain yourself to the trophy case here, begging us to take you back. You're *still* going to do it, and frankly I've never seen you so . . . well, the word isn't 'happy'; it's more like 'beguiled.' Maybe lack of sleep, or too much drool to wipe, but I think it's a spell you're under, and far be it from me to interrupt your enchantment."

"You stayed home with Jamie and Carolyn when they were younger."

"You're absolutely right. And look what happened to me. I used to lie on the carpet and let them throw Nerf balls at my head. Sports for exhausted parents."

Wallis smiled. "I know you didn't regret it." Claude woke up with a cry. He'd want to nurse again. "Anyway, I've got some months to decide." Phyllis just rolled her eyes and pulled her out the door, down the corridor that already looked less familiar.

Cap spent his lunch hour looking over Bill Sable's tests. Sable, according to his MMPI, had quite a revealing profile. His L scale, the one that measured lies, was elevated. It reflected a defensive responding, an effort to cast himself as more reasonable than expected or even possible. The questions were ones that a confident and self-assured person would be willing to answer truthfully: Do you ever yawn in public? Have you ever wanted to cut another driver out of a parking space? But Sable's scores, when the K scale was included, demonstrated a goodness that was unlikely, a halo effect. Cap remembered that in the interview Sable had made himself out to be faultless too—his church and Scout work, his tireless devotion to his boys. More disconcerting, though, was his Pd scale, the paranoia measurement, up around 65. Sable was someone not comfortable in social situations, ironic for a salesman. The overall assessment was that of an individual with traits of marked repression, evasiveness, rigidity, intolerance, and a general lack of psychological comprehension of self and others.

Cap looked through the folder. The kids' teachers were listed, as were two neighbors and Sable's boss at Sears. They would all need to be interviewed. He shut the folder. It was twelve-thirty. Julian had canceled his appointment for today. Last week Julian had come to him shaken up, having made an emergency call, saying he'd been sitting in the snow for an hour. He'd had a panic attack, triggered by Maureen's going off with a colleague. They'd hashed it all out, and Cap had truly felt they'd made progress, but then Julian had sent him a note—significantly not even a phone call—explaining that he wouldn't be in for his session today. It was clear he didn't want Cap to call him back, otherwise why a note slipped under his door? And of course he didn't expect Maureen today either, but that was mostly a relief.

He paced around the office, then walked across the hall and looked in on Dick, who wasn't there, gone for lunch. He went back and did some billing work, returned a call from the Johnsons, only to receive the sad news that they'd lost their baby, shortly after its premature birth, to anencephaly, a neural-tube defect. They wanted to see Cap soon. They'd been warned that this would probably happen, but it was devastating anyway. After Cap hung up, he sat motionless, depressed himself by the news—they had lost a previous baby in a miscarriage two years ago. He wondered what he could say to them that would sound empathetic, in light of his own lucky fortune with Claude.

For a half hour, he worked on two insurance forms. When he finished he was restless, more than restless. He realized it was Sable. The tests. The phone call last night. Thinking about the Johnsons, and even Julian missing his appointment, somehow only made it more obvious that he couldn't just sit here and wait an hour and a half till his next appointment. He would force this out into the open.

It took him ten minutes to reach the mall, the parking lot empty for a Wednesday afternoon. A couple of mothers sat by the fountain with their children in strollers. Several car dealerships had the new models on display. Three times this month alone, Cap and Wallis had been here, because the place seemed to relax Claude when he became fussy at night. Before Claude, they might have come three times in a year.

Cap went into the appliance department at Sears and opened a few dishwasher doors, pulled out the racks, checking occasionally to see if anyone was around. He'd picked a bad time. One-thirty. Sable could very easily still be at lunch.

"Hello!"

It was Sable, in a white shirt and blue tie, his sleeves rolled up.

Sable stuck out his hand. Cap shook it, then leaned back against the dishwasher. He wished he'd thought this out more. "I wanted to speak with you about last night."

"I've been meaning to call you about that," Sable said. "I'm working things out with Millicent."

"You're what?" said Cap, unable to control himself at the surprise of this news.

"We're working things out. Oh, not about us! But about the kids. We've agreed to go through mediation and find an arrangement we're both comfortable with."

"Is that right," said Cap.

"So I'm sorry about all that work you did. How did your report come out anyway?"

Cap could hear the edge in Sable's voice. He could either confront the man or dispose of the issue. "I haven't made my decision yet," said Cap.

"Well, I'm sure that won't be necessary. Now that we're handling it ourselves."

"I suppose not," said Cap, feeling cowardly and enraged all at once, wanting to jump down the man's throat, wipe the salesman's grin off his mouth and stick Sable's shiny face in the dish rack. But he couldn't make a case of it. What could he prove: that Sable had asked how Claude was, that his MMPI and TAT showed he wasn't to be trusted? Nothing more would even come out in the custody hearing now. Cessation was the best he could hope for.

"I guess this means you won't be calling me at home anymore," said Cap, prepared to be more specific if Sable missed the warning to stay away. Sable put his hands out expansively. "No need," he said. "No need now."

Cap turned to go.

"Just a second," said Sable, calling him back. Cap stood a few feet apart from him in the narrow aisle between a wall of refrigerators and an embankment of stoves. "You know that college roommate of mine

I told you about?" said Sable, smiling under his mustache. "The one named Kaplan like yourself?"

"What about him?" said Cap, hearing the funny scratch back in Sable's voice.

"Well, he was a Jewish fella too. Just like yourself, Cap."

"What's that supposed to mean?"

"Nothing," said Sable. "Nothing at all." Sable turned his back to Cap and cheerily greeted a customer who had just come up. Cap stood a few seconds. He felt himself turn inside out with a willingness to commit some foolish act he'd long regret and still had no basis for; then he thought of Wallis and Claude and left.

Chapter Seven

"MEAT SUCKS!" GAYLON SHOUTED IN FRONT OF THE STUDENT CENTER. "Want to see what beef does to your arteries?" He waved a section of a mud-clogged garden hose. The crowd leaped back. Julian and Celia, another of Maureen's students, sat at a table bearing leaflets, bumper stickers, and buttons that displayed hamburgers slashed with red diagonal lines. Gaylon picked up a second prop: a five-foot spatula made from poster board. "Hamburger Helper, anyone?" he called out. On the front, a caricatured man was stuffing a triple burger into a gaping mouth full of piano-key teeth; on the back (Gaylon turned it so the small crowd that had gathered could see) was a blown-up photo of a starving African child, her belly grotesquely distended, flies swarming around her mouth.

"What are you waiting for!" he yelled at the crowd. "Come and get it! Fill your stomach with the truth about meat!"

He shouted at two women who had just left the student center and were carrying Hardee's lunch bags. "How many trees got chopped down so some fat cow could become your lunch?" The girls giggled and walked on. "Isn't that sweet, Kelly and Kitty Carnivore off to lunch." Some low laughter came from the crowd, which had grown

152

as Gaylon became more reckless. He rushed back to the table and dug into a box for yet another prop, a cookie sheet (he'd rehearsed his performance to the last detail) filled with "snake" fireworks bought in Wyoming. He lit them until they sizzled and curled into black crisps, then tossed them wriggling into the crowd, which screamed in enjoyment but retreated to a safe distance. "Meat!" Gaylon bellowed. "Live meat! Hot off the grill!"

A tall boy wearing a black felt cowboy hat with a falcon feather yelled back, "Hey, why don't you light yourself on fire, Bacon Lips!" and this drew a bigger laugh than anything Gaylon had said. Julian shrank down in his chair. Gaylon reminded him of an embittered comedian facing a hostile audience, or a drunk magician out of control at a kids' birthday party. Certainly he'd defeated their cause by now.

Gaylon considered himself an environmental militant, like the members of Earth First!—a monkey-wrencher, a guerrilla ecofighter. He'd once stayed at Edward Abbey's house and learned all the tricks of the trade from Ed, as Gaylon familiarly called him, though all Julian could tell from the lack of details was that Abbey, before he died, had let him sleep overnight in a backyard filled with cactus, somewhere out in Arizona.

"You got to shock people into recognition of their *ignorance!*" Gaylon had pounded his fist in his hand, the tendons in his neck popping out like links of sausage. "Blow up their comfortable little worlds right in front of their noses! Shove their faces in their selfish habits!"

This had been at three A.M., at their organizational meeting. Gaylon had argued everyone else down. The five other students present had walked out. Julian stayed because it was his apartment. He didn't know why Celia stayed. She'd sat quietly in the corner and waited until after Gaylon left and then asked Julian if he could take her home. She didn't have her car.

"You're mysterious," she told him. "You never say much in class, but you always seem to be thinking hard about things."

"I don't drive. I'm sorry. I'll call a cab for you," was all he could respond, and he'd waited outside with her for the taxi, silent so as not to dispel her impression of him as mysterious.

A week after they'd all met at his apartment, Julian had helped Gaylon distribute leaflets and put up "Meat-Out" posters around town. Gaylon had wanted to keep going—knock on doors, talk to radio stations—but Julian had headed home, tired and missing Maureen. It was cold in his apartment; the heat had been off all day. Frost had formed like turreted castles inside the single-pane windows, and all Julian could do was sit and watch the ice soften and melt as he waited for Maureen to come over after her class.

Now, in the midst of all that had happened, he wondered why he'd agreed to be part of the protest, sitting dumbly at the table while the crowd grew more hostile, Gaylon verbally sparring with the small mob. Meanwhile, Julian sank deeper into silence with Celia, whose interest in him he could no longer ignore. After asking him in class (she sat next to him in the back) what his plans were for Thanksgiving ("Nothing," he had said, wanting to be vague because he was unsure what Maureen wanted to do), she phoned last week to invite him to her family farm in Alamosa for the holiday. Maureen, during the conversation, had awakened and called out to him. She spent more time at his place now. It was out of the way, less conspicuous than hers, and she slept better without her books and computer around to remind her of work. He quickly clapped his hand over the receiver; Maureen had become sloppy about being careful. Sometimes she took his arm on their way to class, and lately she didn't think it mattered if they separated before going into the building.

The young cowboy who had called Gaylon Bacon Lips was engaged suddenly in a shouting match with him. Julian saw some friends of the cowboy under the student center's long portico. They were lighting something. He stretched up in his seat but couldn't see any better. The argument became more vocal, and the cowboy's friends came over from the portico, surrounding Gaylon and shouting at him, while

Gaylon returned the insults. Should he join Gaylon? He stayed in his chair.

Gaylon rushed back to the table and grabbed a transparent plastic globe. It was a beach ball that Julian and Celia had shopped for at Woolworth's (Gaylon had given them the list) and that Gaylon had then cut open and resealed like a bottle with a ship—except that it contained not a vessel but a bloody, defrosted T-bone steak, dripping its juices all over the planet's insides. "Here, scum!" called Gaylon, and threw it in the cowboy's face.

What happened next, Julian would tell the police, made no sense to him at all—but of course it did. It made sense in some way that only he would know. His mother would know, of course, because it had happened to her. She would warn him afterward in a long letter not to get involved in any more trouble, and his father said how disgraceful, how terrifying that such a thing could occur on a college campus in a civilized country: "Like the Nazis all over again"—a phrase that had echoed throughout his childhood, not from her, who never spoke of them, but from him, who spoke for her. Julian's phone at his apartment would ring off the hook until he disconnected it. Ironically, the protest would be an enormous success. Even *Time* would report it: "Anti-Barbecue Protest Sizzles on Campus." From all over the country, people would write to Gaylon in an outpouring of sympathy and outrage. There would also be morbid requests for pictures, as well as several marriage proposals and lots of money sent. Many people wanted to join his group. What could they do to help, to continue his fight, to contribute to a cause that had become successful beyond their wildest dreams—or Julian's nightmares.

But the main incident Julian would remember would not be what everyone else talked about. It wouldn't be the young cowboy who, after getting hit with the plastic globe, grabbed Gaylon and threw him on the ground. The two of them grappled for a few moments, while Gaylon's ageless gray hair flew loose from its ponytail. The cowboy's hat fell off, to reveal his own hair problem, premature balding. This young rancher, it turned out, was not even a student at the university but a kid from out of town, whose father had died years ago and left the ranch to his mother and him. He had heard about the protest and brought some buddies with him from eastern Colorado. In a statement to the police, they would admit that yes, they'd planned to do this; it was premeditated. But they'd only meant to *scare* the guy, not really knock him down and hog-tie him with a rope—well, maybe they'd planned that part. They wanted to make him *think* about what he was doing, taking away people's jobs, but no, not the other part: it just happened when he provoked them and called them scum and threw that beach thing at them. They were only going to show him the branding iron, get it red hot in the bag of coals, hold it over him and spook him until he cried for mercy. They didn't actually intend to rip off his shirt like that, turn him over on his belly, and brand his back so the flesh seared and the smoke rose into Julian's nostrils. He knew that smell of human skin, knew it from inside his bones. The smell from ovens working overtime. The smell he'd inherited and that left its trace in the air when he woke from the electrical burn of his seizures. He heard Celia's long scream: *Noooo* . . . and saw her pick up the large hamburger poster and wildly slap the ranchers. They had squatted over Gaylon and pinned him down with their knees so nobody could see what was happening. Two students threw up once they saw. The ranchers ran away then and left only Celia kneeling over Gaylon.

Gaylon babbled in shock. "Save my world! Save my world!" Over and over he said it. Not until afterward, not until the police had come and caught the ranchers, not until the ambulance had rushed Gaylon to the hospital, and not until Julian fled to Maureen's apartment because reporters were camped outside his own, did he understand that Gaylon didn't mean the world but meant only his plastic globe with its encased steak: he wanted it back. He wanted to hold it like some blanket or favorite bear, because when real terror came, the response was always the same frightened cry. When your legs were roped together and somebody was branding you, you didn't think about causes or honor or loyalty or nations, such as heroes died for in books. You thought only of being rescued. And when no one came, you clutched objects that were right in front of you—a spoon, a piece of bread, a scrap of cloth—as if you were holding your mind together.

Compared to his own Thanksgivings, Celia's family's celebration was an extravaganza—a Mexican-American epic with extras coming out of the walls (Julian had yet to meet all the family, more arriving every minute) and people eating in shifts, the older family members lapsing into rapid Spanish. *"Hija, ven acá! Hijo, trae otra silla!"* called Celia's mother, directing traffic. The tables stretched from the front door through the living room and the dining room, all the way to the kitchen. One group of relatives stood behind the first ones seated, talking, laughing, waiting their turn to eat. Celia's oldest brother (he was forty) said a prayer. Julian bowed his head respectfully. "Thank you, Lord, for bringing those far away home to us. And for bringing newcomers into our home to share this happy occasion." He stopped and looked at Julian. So did everyone else. *"Siéntate! Siéntate!"* said the mother, getting more people into their seats. The kids fought in the living room around a TV that collected cans of beer on top and showed nonstop football. Metallica blasted from the youngest brother's room upstairs in the rambling farmhouse that had seen four additions. A moving knot of women brought not just turkey and stuffing and fresh cranberries to the table but green chili and chicken molé and full plates of tamales, all of which vanished as quickly as it arrived. There was more activity than he'd seen in a lifetime at his home in Baltimore.

They asked him one question after another, and Julian, not used to being the center of attention anywhere, having always made sure that he avoided such predicaments, found he couldn't escape these people's interest. Celia had talked about her family the whole way down. Close to fifty relatives were here, all asking questions of him. Where was he from? How many children in his family? (One? That started a long discussion in Spanish he didn't understand.) What was he taking at school? What did his father do? What did he think of Celia, and this had set off a yowl of laughter from everybody, while Julian sat with his napkin in his lap, the relatives surrounding the table and looking over his shoulder, patting him on the back, chattering in Spanish.

After dinner Celia's six-year-old nephew, Teddy, took out his trumpet and played "The Swallows"—"Las Golondrinas." The elderly relatives wept, called out, *"Qué lindo! Qué angélico!"* Applause thundered from everyone, including Julian, who for all his practice at the piano had never played anything with such fluidity and passion. Six years old! Each note soared and arced. Teddy, his eyes squeezed shut, blew a sharp blast. He'd hit a high C. Six years old! Marlon Zalk, who had played first trumpet back in Julian's high school orchestra, couldn't even manage a high C—let alone thread one through like this with such sharp purity. Teddy, with his black hair falling in his eyes, stood on the chair where he had climbed so all could see him play. "He's deaf," whispered Celia, and Julian reeled back, disbelieving. Impossible! "He's inherited the same condition as my father. We call him Gabriel's wonder." Teddy blinked his eyes while the applause grew louder. Julian could see he'd heard not a single handclap.

Julian suddenly remembered he'd promised to call Maureen. She'd gone to visit her sister in California for the holiday. He hadn't wanted to go with her. He needed to be apart from her for a while—to think by himself, as he never seemed to have a chance to do. And then, also, earthquakes, always a possibility where she'd be, had too close a personal meaning. He'd told her he was going to spend the holiday with his parents in Baltimore. Meanwhile, he'd promised Celia he'd join her for Thanksgiving at her family farm. He'd felt guilty about what happened to Gaylon and responsible for how shaken up Celia had been, so he reasoned, in his circuitous, tormented way, that he owed her the visit. By a series of lies, omissions, and good intentions, he'd been trying to please everybody—including his parents, whom he'd informed that he couldn't come back to Baltimore because he had volunteered to serve Thanksgiving dinner to the homeless. Even to Gaylon, who was recuperating at his parents' house in Indiana, Julian had lied: he would be sharing a vegetarian meal with a group of Greens visiting from Germany, whereby Julian could learn more about starting up the environmental party on campus.

It came so easy to him to lie, not from malice but from a desire to make them all happy and to escape their watchful eyes. He couldn't live with anyone's bad opinion of him. Even someone like Gaylon (he would certainly be contemptuous of their eating turkey), who wasn't around. It was maddening to care so much about what people thought. Half the time he had no idea what his opinion was exactly. Hell is other people, Sartre had written. Nothing made more sense. Celia, at least, only seemed to care about what *he* thought, not people she didn't respect or know. That cut down on ninety-nine percent of the world. How much easier his path would be if he just admitted he despised Gaylon, self-made martyr or not, and that the man annoyed him to tears.

He thought now about Celia's brothers butchering the turkey earlier. Two nails on a tree stump held the bird's neck in place while one brother lifted a hatchet and chopped the turkey's head off. It convulsed for five minutes, blood spurting in rivulets from its severed neck. The brothers put the bird in a tub of boiling water for a minute, then pulled it out and dropped it in a tub of cold water to stop the cooking. All the feathers were pulled off. A knife was stuck in its neck, then its anus, and the bird was eviscerated. Its claws were severed. The brothers hung it from the back porch to cool down for an hour before Celia's mother would cook it. Julian couldn't escape the image of the headless turkey jerking. Those awful death convulsions. It was what he imagined himself to look like on the inside from all the lies he had to tell to satisfy everybody. That bird: it was the real source of his anxiety. Himself headless on the ground, desperately thrashing and spilling his blood.

———

After the tables had been cleared and the dishes washed, Celia took him outside to show him around the farm, the barn, the cottonseed pile for feed, the fields and pastures that stretched into the basin of the San Luis Valley. The family had been in this valley for over a hundred years. The wind blew against their faces as Celia pulled him along by the hand. She wanted to show him something else.

They went over a rise and looked down on what appeared to be swampland, a marshy area with birds swooping nearby and long, shallow tubs built of lumber. "There's my father," said Celia. He'd come right out here after dinner.

Julian saw him walking among the rows of tubs, throwing pellets into the water from a burlap sack. Hundreds of fish leaped up. They broke the surface and flung themselves in the air, then disappeared back into the water. "He's made a wetlands back here," said Celia. "He recycles all the waste, all the manure, all the runoff water from the farm back into the pond, and then processes it through scrubbers before it floods the marsh. Then he grows fish for food and to put back in the stream."

Celia had changed into her jeans and a high school T-shirt that said "Alamosa Rams"; she'd tied her hair up with a black velvet bow. Her brown arms, with their delicate veil of dark hair, were folded across her chest while she looked at her father. She had a gentle, broad face, like her mother's, and strong legs that seemed to stride in leagues across the property. How relaxed and content she seemed here! Not so much quiet and shy, which was how he thought of her at school, but appreciative and watchful, as if she were memorizing everything —every motion of her father's, the direction of the wind, the pattern of the hay bales in the fields—remembering it all to take back to school as love and comfort. "Why does your family call you Weda?" he asked. They'd greeted her with this, smiling slyly at her and glancing at him.

Celia laughed. "It's slang for white. It's because I brought you home."

"Oh," he said, not knowing if this was good or bad.

"Come on," she said. "Let's go see my father."

They went down the hill. Celia's father, feeding the fish, looked more like a grandfather (which he was too), his face a nest of wrinkles, the bristles of his beard white as the tips of pine needles in the bright sun.

He gave Julian some fish pellets, and Julian threw them in, the fish making their crazy leap. The power to make fish rise from the waters! Celia's father motioned for him to do it again, and Julian threw more in, laughing. God, he hadn't laughed in a long while! He loved seeing these crazy fish leap for their supper, and this time when he tossed them food he jumped with them and shouted "Yeah!"

He could have done this all day, but Celia pulled him along. They had gone a ways before he realized they were still holding hands. She let go to open a gate that led into a pasture with several horses. Julian stayed back. He'd never ridden a horse, not a full-grown one at least, only some ponies at kids' birthday parties in Baltimore.

"Come on over," Celia told him, and introduced him to Sadie, her mare. The mare nudged Julian's hand, looking for carrots, which Celia gave him from her pocket to feed the animal. "We can ride tomorrow," Celia said.

"I don't know how to," said Julian, backing away from the overly friendly horse.

"I'll teach you."

"But I don't even drive."

She laughed, stroking the mare's nose. "Well, you don't need a license, silly."

But he'd meant something else: Was it okay to take a chance if it involved only his own life?

They went back to the house. When it got dark, they played Pictionary. He had to draw England. All he knew was that it was an island. "Is that an amoeba?" asked Luis, Celia's oldest brother. "Maybe a giant fungus," offered Katharine, a cousin. "I draw better than him," said Dorie, Celia's four-year-old niece (Celia was an aunt eight times over). More laughter. They patted Julian on the back. "What's the easiest place to draw?" asked Victor, a nephew. "Florida," someone said, and they told Julian to try drawing Florida, forget England. But Florida came out looking like a skinny loaf of French bread, a baguette. He couldn't draw to save his life. It was true.

Afterward Celia took him upstairs to where he would be sleeping. Five men from her family would be up there with him. It was a long room with dormers on either side and violet curtains. Sleeping bags were stacked on their ends like fat corks. Celia unrolled one for him and placed it next to the heater. "You should be warm enough right here," she said, and unzipped the bag, smoothing out the soft flannel with her hand and putting two towels at the foot. She sat down at the end of the bag. "Are you having a good time?" she asked him.

"Great," he said, and he was; it felt so easy to be here, to spend time with her. She made him less a liar just by her presence.

"I hope you didn't mind them teasing you."

Julian shook his head. "I *am* terrible. In elementary school my trees always looked like porcupines and my animals like very low sports cars. After a while my art teacher wouldn't even stop at my desk. She got tired of telling me to use more of my space. I'd draw everything in one small corner of the picture."

"That's sad," said Celia.

"Is it?" Julian asked. He had meant it to be funny.

"It doesn't sound like you felt very free as a child," said Celia. "I used to make big loopy faces festooned with giant pineapple earrings."

He laughed. "Anyway, I'm not very good." And he knew she was right. Of course he hadn't felt free, and naturally it would show up. But he hadn't cared here. He'd enjoyed being teased about it, in fact. For once, he'd had fun being inept.

"They all like you," said Celia. "It's just their way of accepting you."

"Yes," said Julian, and he yawned, then excused himself.

"You're tired. I could talk to you forever, but I'd better let you go to bed." She looked at the door a moment, then back at Julian, as though waiting for him to say something personal.

Suddenly he remembered Maureen. "Is there a phone up here?"

Celia shook her head. "Just the one downstairs." It was in the kitchen, where everyone was still talking. He'd promised Maureen he'd call by six. It was already nine o'clock in California. "Do you have to call someone?" she asked.

He waved the question away. "It's not important," but he realized he'd have to get up after everybody went to sleep.

"I guess you are tired," said Celia.

"I'm getting there," said Julian, wanting to be friendly but feeling the strain of the day, this big family.

"Let's not talk anymore, then." She kissed him quickly on the lips and left, waving to him at the door.

It felt like only minutes later when he woke with a start, but it must have been hours, because it was dark in the room and he could hear snoring to either side of him. The curtains had been closed, but he could see a scrubbed and yellow moon, three-quarters full, floating outside the window.

He got up and stepped over a sleeping body and went down to the end of the hall. The stairs were steep and creaked with each of his steps. From the bedrooms he could hear snoring or coughing or springs squeaking as people turned over—or did other things. He didn't know all the connections of this huge family, could only feel their sleeping, weighty presence holding the house together.

The phone was on the kitchen wall, and he guided himself to it by the glow of a clock. He took out Maureen's number from his wallet and held it up to the face of the clock, memorized the number, then dialed the digits, including his credit-card number. When a female voice answered, he said, "Is Maureen there?" and the person, after a pause, said, "Just a minute."

Maureen got right on, sounding groggy.

"Hi," he said.

"Julian? Where are you? It's three in the morning."

"Here," he said.

"At your parents'?"

He nodded, as if this would be an easier lie, more gentle if she didn't have to hear the words, if he didn't have to speak them. "Did you have a good Thanksgiving?"

"It was grand," Maureen said. "Wish you could have been here. My niece is adorable and has turned me into a blithering maternal mess. I couldn't let go of her. In fact, I burst into tears when I saw her." Maureen paused, and he knew what was coming. "Did you tell your parents yet?"

"I haven't found the right time."

"How about now? You could wake them up."

He tried to laugh but felt it catch in his throat. "I'd better get off."

"Give me your number before you do."

"Why?"

"So I can call you tomorrow. Why do you think?"

"But I might not be here."

"So? Can't your parents take a message?"

"My mother doesn't use the phone."

"Huh?"

Why had he disclosed this? True and private, admitted now, it was a panicky piece of information, a decoy for a lie. "She doesn't like to use the phone."

"Well, we don't have to have a phone-a-thon. Can't she just tell you I called?"

"No, I mean she can't talk at all on the phone." He felt that if they went on much longer, he would start babbling everything. "And my father works."

"Julian."

"What?"

"You're not at your parents' house." He held his breath. "Are you?"

"No," he said. "I'm not."

There was a long silence, during which he could hear all the noises in the house closing in on him—the refrigerator humming, the radiators clanking, the clock ticking, the floor settling—and all the farm sounds outside: whinnying and barking and lowing, a cowbell ringing close under the kitchen window, a rooster crowing, all the twittering morning calls of birds, the murmur of the dirt itself, the quiet shriek of a farm waking.

Liar liar liar. Your mother's skin is on fire, they screamed. *We got her now.*

"Do you want to tell me where you are, then?" Her tone had turned professorial. A late paper: Can you give me a good reason why I should accept this?

"I'm at Celia's house in Alamosa."

"Celia?"

"Celia Trujillo. From your class."

A loud expulsion of breath. "Why?"

"She asked me to come here."

"She *asked* you?" Another long pause. "I asked you too, Julian. And you know what else? I can't believe this. I just can't believe you'd do this to me!"

"I'm sorry," he said. "It's just a friendship. With Celia, I mean."

"That's sweet," said Maureen, and for a moment he thought she was going to accept it, and then she added, "Fuck you and your little friend!" And she hung up on him.

When he turned around, he saw Celia's father standing in the doorway. "I was just making a call," said Julian, and then he remembered that her father couldn't hear, as Teddy couldn't hear. But Teddy could hear music or the vibrations of notes or the sounds of imagined tones—so why couldn't Celia's father hear deceit in his own house? Julian looked at Mr. Trujillo's rough hands and his white beard, his full head of gray hair, uncombed from sleep. He was ready to go to work. He would not want Julian near his daughter. The deaf must know all about lies and would not bear them so easily—could not take their sound for granted.

He touched Julian gently on the arm, then picked up his work gloves from the counter and took his thermos from the refrigerator. In a second, Celia's father was gone, leaving the doorway open and hazy with the dawn.

"I'm really sorry," said Celia. She was driving Julian to the bus. "Are you sure you can't stay until Sunday?"

"I think I'd better go back."

They reached the bus station, a small shelter built on the backside of a grocery store in Alamosa. Hardly anyone was there. A man, smelling of too many nights in the cold, slumped against a wall, his eyelids red-veined and swollen shut. A sign above him said SLEEPING PROHIBITED. VIOLATORS WILL BE REMOVED. How could you prohibit sleep? That's all he wanted to do himself. Get home and sleep. Wait for Maureen. Beg her to forgive him. Make it up to her somehow. Sleep with her. Be inside her again and touch her, touch her, touch her—touch her until he didn't have to think anymore and he could stop feeling such loathing for himself. Sex was the only thing that could stop it.

"You seemed to be having such a good time until this morning," said Celia, clearly baffled by his sudden announcement that he needed to return to Pierre. He wished he could explain. He liked her enough not to want to lie to her.

"I was—I did," said Julian.

He saw his bus outside the station. He wanted to get on it and sink into a stupor, his mind in tune with the drone of the engine. It would take nine hours to get back, almost twice as long as to get here, because the bus had to stop in every local town along the Front Range, but that would give him plenty of time to plan a suitable apology.

He kissed Celia on the cheek. Her arms went around his back, holding on tight. She smelled of the farm, of all the smells of the kitchen, of the barn and the hay bale they'd sat on, talking about her growing up in Colorado. He'd sounded like a normal person when he spoke with her. He should stay and let her hold him, but then he saw Maureen, with her pale breasts, waiting for him on the bed where they'd made a child, and he hurried up the steps of the bus.

Chapter Eight

SPORTS. IT WAS THE SUBJECT OF THE DAY. FUNNY HOW A DAY'S WORK fell out that way. Sometimes it was sex, sometimes divorce, sometimes children, sometimes careers, sometimes adultery, sometimes drinking, sometimes stepfamilies, sometimes absent fathers, sometimes domineering bosses, sometimes rape, sometimes beatings, sometimes suicide, and sometimes love.

And sometimes it was just sports.

Only it wasn't just sports. Cap hadn't had a single man in therapy who said to him, "It was just sports. Just fun. Good old fun and sportsmanship. Cooperation. Built character. Loved my coach. Best years of my life. Wish I could've married the team."

Irv Cafferty, pushing forty-three himself, like Cap, had come in today, sat down on the couch, looked at Cap, and said, "Do you know what I've been thinking about? This is really crazy, but I was thinking about the time I had to lace up Coach Perry's sneakers. He got a new pair of Converses, and he said, 'Irv, come over here a minute.' And so I went over and he handed me the sneakers and he said, 'Lace these up, will you. Be a good fella.' And you know what? I did it. Laced his sneakers up. Off his feet, of course. But still I laced them up. And

I never forgot it. I never forgot it because I wanted to tell the bastard, 'Go fuck yourself,' but I didn't. Another time, he made me go out and scrape gum off the court during halftime, in front of everybody. That was twenty-eight years ago, Cap, and I can still feel myself squatting down and poking those plastic tips through the eyelets while my team-mates shot layups in practice."

So they had spent the session talking about how it made Irv feel to be a whipping boy for the team. Every game they lost, somehow Irv wound up paying for it (though he rarely played). And why had he let himself be put through this? Because his father had forced him to play; not asked, not demanded, not insisted—forced. "Like by the ears," Irv told Cap. "He lifted me up by them one day when I said I wouldn't go to any more practices."

"So your father is like Coach Perry," Cap pointed out, but Irv rejected this. His father was nothing like Coach Perry. The connection, though plain as Irv's own bald spot, would not be acknowledged today, or perhaps for quite some time. So Cap would use Coach Perry next session to get some of the feelings out of the mute whipping boy, humiliated at having to scrape gum off the court in full view of his father and his friends. Eventually, if they were lucky, they might get to the anger he felt toward his father, if Irv didn't terminate therapy first.

And then another client, right after Irv. Peter Bridleman, who was in his late thirties, divorced twice, and working as a printer's assistant, and who was seeing Cap because of "commitment problems." Cap had asked him to lie on the couch and imagine himself going down floors in an elevator, starting with his present "floor" of thirty-nine years. He could get off at any floor that caught his attention. And the one that finally caught it was the sixteenth—eleventh grade. He was a great football player, a fullback. He could always find the hole, run right through the other team. It was a wonderful time. And Cap had waited. Yes? Was there anything more? Any further reason why he had stopped here? Yes; he broke his collarbone that year and was out for the rest of the season. When he'd come back, in his senior year, he wasn't outstanding anymore; something had changed. He'd been a hero briefly before the broken collarbone; girls had called him for dates; even his teachers had treated him differently. He'd never been that good again at anything.

Cap looked out his window. It was December 9, sunny, one of Pierre's mild winter days. The Christmas lights were all up; the city had installed a ring of three tall electric candles around every street-light. Earlier, before Peter had come in, Cap sat watching the workers navigate the metal hoop onto the pole of the streetlight, repairing this one. He had the urge to be closer—out of his office and in the street, staring up at the men like a small boy. Free of all troubles for the day. Maybe even get a ride up in the cherry picker.

"We have to stop here for today," he'd told Peter. And Peter had gotten up heavily—heavier than when he'd come in—and walked out of the office. Meanwhile, Cap had understood that the last thing he needed to do was work regressively with Peter; no more elevator rides for this client. That was Peter's problem: he slipped from the future to the past and up to the future again, somehow missing the pres-ent—his third wife and his four children from previous marriages, his cocaine usage, his dreams that went back and forth and never stayed put and always faded into some excuse like a broken collarbone, never his fault, something "out there" that had taken his jobs and children and happiness from him. And Cap wasn't going to join him back there anymore (a misdirection apparent on their fifth session), because the past for the Peters of the world was too mined with excuses, not reasons. That slight but significant difference—which a client like Peter resisted accepting. No, it wasn't every client you wanted to jump with into the teeming past. Some just needed to be grabbed by the ankles and moved forward an inch at a time so they could see where they were stepping and own up to their feet.

But there was no getting away from sports today. His next client, Frieda Larson, told him, "You know, I really was that person who

was always the last picked." She'd gone on to describe the embarrassment of batting, her terror of the ball, the pop fly that would hit
her in the nose, her throw that dropped like a shot put before it got
anywhere near second base. "Everybody thinks it's only boys who
suffer about athletics," she'd told Cap, "but it's girls too. We just give
up earlier and pick a male to champion our losses. I hate sports. I woke
up thinking about it today. Maybe because I'm dating this guy who's
a real jock. I mean, he has no idea yet the klutz I am. And I don't
think he's the kind I can make a joke about it with. I'm going to wind
up on *teams* with this guy. He'll expect me to be good. Do I really
have to go back and live this stuff all over again?"

And Cap had wondered, after Frieda left, what there was about
him today. Was he looking particularly physical? Like a coach himself?
Why the sports stories? Maybe they were the antithesis of therapy on
a long, if mild, winter day, this sedentary season made even more
thick and bottom-heavy in his office. Action. Dreams of forgotten glory
and tales of disgrace on the playing field. And what of himself? He
was better than good. He'd played all three sports in high school, the
big three. There weren't any others back then. Soccer was something
that happened in other countries, in stadiums with crazed fans. La-
crosse was for girls. Cross-country for human slide rules, studious
types with willowy bodies, polite kids whose hands and feet were
outsize and who would crack like a stick if he, Cap, all six feet two of
him, had run into them. He'd let it all out on the field; it had been all
right there to be dumb and fierce, to feel anger but not know it, to
make up for the humiliation of being a slow reader and by implication
a slow thinker, to have his hand up in class always a second behind
everyone else's (or more likely not at all), and not only to *not* get the
answer but to be still reading the question when everyone else had
already finished.

All along it had been a reading disability that made him lose track
of the words. He didn't transpose letters, a *B* for a *P*, or a *D* for an
O. His trouble was more with misplaced pieces, gaps in a chain of

worded logic. He'd forget what he'd read a few seconds before and have to reread a sentence over and over—five, six, seven times, until his neck burned and his thick shoulders hunched toward his dry throat and the teacher said, "Time." He'd have to hand over his paper: blank, blank, an answer, blank, blank, an answer, the rest blanks.

It had not really been diagnosed until after college. His teachers back in public school, during the fifties and sixties, weren't alert to the problem. His homework would be frequently returned to him to do over. He attended summer school regularly to make up failed subjects. In college, accepted on probation, he knew he would have to expend an extraordinary effort to stay in. He took in every word spoken in class. He went to extra study sessions. He came in during office hours and chatted with professors after class. He tied his knowledge together from different sources: films and tapes from the library, lectures from related courses that he audited. He spent twenty-five hours a week in classes, almost twice as much as the average student. He'd lay down one clue after another just to comprehend a simple chapter that was never a mystery to most people. He missed no opportunity to overhear some remark, even a stray one, from a student who might have a handle on what Cap himself couldn't plainly read. When the professor announced at the beginning of the semester how much each of the elements of the course would count—tests, papers, oral reports, class participation, additional reading, attendance—Cap crossed off reading and tests and went right up that first day and asked if he could do an extra project or help his grade in any other way. He usually was granted the request. And through all this he himself didn't know anything was wrong, only that he was slower and had to work harder. *Grind* was the word. These maddening little steps, the extra work, the hustle to get information off the page, the organizing of his whole day so he didn't lose a spare minute—it all had to be done if he was going to survive college.

When he did read anything, it was always at the same pace, whether it was the Sunday comics or his Social Learning Theory text. It wasn't just that he underlined passages; it was that he underlined, then made columns of key terms, then added more facts under these columns. Seeing the term "Bipolar disorder," for instance, on a test, might produce a whole flood of associations that he'd cross-check against the time, place, course, professor, subject, past material covered, current and anticipated use of the term. Eventually he'd make a guess as to what the hell the test question was asking.

But in the end it was always guesswork; it had to be. He'd read a sentence that would begin: "Parental care . . . ," and then there would be a phrase between commas, in apposition to the main clause, "withheld in early infancy," and he would lose it, as if it had passed through a butterfly net with a hole. Gone. He couldn't make the parts of the sentence stick together. He could see them. He could count them. He could even diagram the sentence if someone would take its components apart for him and lay them out like ingredients on a cutting board or like matching clothes on a bed. But he couldn't make it have meaning.

When the problem had finally been diagnosed, he'd been given intelligence tests administered orally. His I.Q. was actually very high. The difference between his listening and his reading comprehension measured just how smart he was, and how disabled. He then had the additional problem of accepting that his intelligence could be so bi-furcated. What happened in between? Where did his mind go? The jump from hearing/thinking to reading/absorbing remained a myste-rious descent into a ballroom of cloaked symbols, which unmasked themselves at midnight, only to reveal more disguises underneath. True identity teased and eluded him, like a kiss through the mouth hole of a mask, lips protruding ever so slightly before they disappeared back inside.

He had finally overcome it, or at least learned to decode the word clusters faster and not overload his memory so much. But he'd never been truly free of the difficulty. He knew he'd picked a profession where talking and listening were more crucial than reading and writing. He'd been determined to become a therapist (he could have opted out altogether and worked with his hands—the field still required plenty of reading). After a year of graduate school in Boulder, he'd switched to a program at the University of Denver. He'd chosen to get a Psy.D., a doctoral degree that emphasized practical clinical experience more than the extensive research and writing required for a Ph.D. All those years of asking good questions of professors (he *must* find out the answer; he had only this one chance to hear, nothing in a book to back him up), all those years of watching for how pieces of language went together and formed an elusive whole, had made him a superior clinician, able to translate gesture, nuance, and tone. In private practice he wouldn't have to read out loud in a group (a nightmare, from elementary school on up to seders, where he'd be asked at the table to read a portion of the Haggadah and he'd feign a sore throat, no glasses, etc.), or do loads of paperwork as an administrator, or do anything except work on his correspondence in private and sweat over it. But he would still have to grind. It was the dirty secret behind the plodder Maureen had caught.

Ironically, Allan had been a gifted reader; at six years old he could read eighth-grade books. And Cap had thought more than once that the same gene that screwed up Allan resided in him too—only it had entered the back door instead of the front, some cruel experiment by the gods to see what would happen to brothers with opposite gifts and afflictions. Cap could read people; Allan, books. Cap struggled to find meaning everywhere to make up for what he couldn't get off the page; Allan was assaulted by too much meaning. And Allan feared sports as deeply as Cap sweated opening a book.

Sports. He'd known there was something in it for him today too.

He had a memory of Allan at home plate, ready to bat, in seventh-grade gym class. Cap was already a sophomore and driving with his learner's permit. School had been dismissed early, and he'd driven over to the junior high to pick up Allan. Cap had stood on the track, watching. Allan let the first pitch go by, as though the ball were a mere curiosity. A sphere with stitching, not a ball to be hit. The outfielders were talking to each other. The first baseman was tying his shoe. The second baseman was throwing a stick of gum to the third baseman. Only the pitcher paid any attention, and even he just seemed to be doing his job—five pitches, unswung at, until Allan could sit down by default.

Then Allan hit the ball, smashed it, a wallop, over the center fielder's head. Complete disbelief. Suddenly everyone moved at once, the opposing team and Allan's team, who had leaped up and were cheering him on. And Allan began to run, wobbly, awkwardly, with the bat in his hand, but nevertheless he did run, while the center fielder retrieved the ball, and Cap stood on the track shouting *Run*, desperately wanting his brother to make it around the bases.

But he got caught in a rundown between third base and home and was tagged out. That was it. The next year, fourteen years old, Allan set fire to the couch at home and was diagnosed as schizophrenic, and he didn't participate in gym anymore. He went to a special school. He was still a fine reader, but there was another dimension now: voices were attached to everything, and they wanted to eat him alive or warn him of plots against his life.

Meanwhile, Cap knocked them dead on the playing field.

He closed up his office and stopped on the way home to pick up some wine and flowers. In the checkout line he saw someone who reminded him of his fifth-grade teacher, Mrs. Howton, with her weak chin and her small eyes. She would give them monthly reading comprehension tests, which Cap would invariably fail. He'd spent much of his life, it seemed, trying to escape Mrs. Howton's shouting "Time!" and his being caught short. Julian had once told him about a teacher reprimanding him for staring blankly in class, the teacher not knowing that Julian was having a seizure. No wonder Cap had gotten a lump in his throat, fiercely identifying with the boy, though Julian, thoughtful, slender Julian, with his silky eyebrows and dark curled lashes and fine-boned fingers, was clearly not a plodder. It bothered him more than he cared to admit that Julian had dropped therapy, over a month now since their last session, when Cap had tried to steer him away from Maureen. Julian had been mentioned in the local paper among those participating in a meat protest, a classmate of the boy who had been branded. Cap had sent Julian a short note asking if he was all right but got no response.

After leaving the florist, he put the flowers—a dozen yellow roses —in the back seat, next to the bottle of wine, and headed for home. Tomorrow he would talk with Dick, always a calming influence. Maybe, too, he'd cancel his appointments and take the day off. He could drive up to the mountain with Wallis for some cross-country skiing, put Claude on his back and get out in the woods before the holidays hit—regroup, as the term went. His first special-reading teacher, when Cap was already well into graduate school, had said to him: "We are going to teach you how to regroup the language. You need to do mechanically what other readers do automatically. Grab the words from space and anchor them." As he would later do with clients.

Wallis could hear Cap singing to Claude in the bath. She resisted going in there to supervise. Cap's idea of giving Claude a bath amounted to making shoulder pads from the bath bubbles. Claude howled when anyone tried to wash his hair, and Cap dealt with it by never trying. "Once a week," he'd told her. "Once a week is enough." "It isn't," said Wallis. "Not when he has applesauce in his hair." It would never occur to Cap that Claude's nails needed cutting occasionally. He was, however, very concerned about Claude's penis. Any small rash, any stippled pattern, any change in color or shape, would give him pause. "Does it look a little red to you?" he'd say. Or, "Look at that vein up the middle. Isn't it awfully blue?" "Veins *are* blue," Wallis reminded him. "Maybe," she had said, "you're still having trouble with Claude being uncircumcised." "Not at all!" he'd protested. "I would never

want to put him through that trauma. Since when have I had trouble?"
But she wondered.

She'd made the mistake of once saying, "Well, you would know
more about having a penis than I do," and watched Cap jump for the
phone. In the study, she'd heard him talking to Arthur, their pediatrician: "Well, it looks a little odd to me. Should it be *so* blue, Arthur?"

When he acted like this, it was the same as being around his parents,
with their enormous anxiety level. The first time she'd met them was
at the Philadelphia airport. As she got off the plane, they'd come at
her with spread wings and devouring grins, shouting untoward fa-
miliarities: "There's our darling!" and "Can you believe how tiny she
is!" They'd scared her half to death. They were as gushing as her own
family was stiff, and though she should have been pleased by the
difference, it made her want to run back inside the plane. At the house,
his parents leaped up every five minutes from the dinner table, finding
something else to bring her—little tins of pickled foods to try. She'd
never experienced so much hovering in her entire life. She should have
loved it after all the years of her own indifferent family, but she was
mostly repelled and wondered how much of them was in Cap.

Her second night there, she'd cooked dinner, a plain one, baked
chicken and salad, because Cap had prepared her about their bland
appetites. They'd fawned over the meal—and her—the whole evening.
"What a salad!" Cap's father had said. All she'd done was add some
romaine lettuce. Cap had warned her that they ate only iceberg, but
she'd been daring. His father had gone on to talk about the baked
chicken (breaded from a mix) and the green beans: "This is a professional platter!" His mother had gushed over Wallis's clothes, calling
her cutoffs and tank top a "cute little ensemble." She could do no
wrong. It made her think of various possibilities: (1) they were crazy;
(2) she was terrific; (3) they had something to hide, perhaps about Cap;
(4) they were actually very sweet, if smothering; (5) people like them
didn't exist, and Cap had hired actors to entertain her.

In the end, she'd gotten used to them, but with less appreciation for their attention than yearning for her own parents, who seemed sane if frigid by comparison.

Now she went into Claude's room for his pajamas, and then upstairs to the bathroom. Cap had brought home flowers and wine and had touched her secretly throughout the evening. She was surprised at how far her thoughts still were from sex, despite the diaphragm, whose egg-blue case she tapped with her nail, as if trying to hatch awake her interest from inside it. She'd always liked sex with Cap; he was a good lover, and whatever quiver of family worries he'd slung over his shoulder and taken out West, he at least didn't bring them to bed with him. He was relaxed and patient, eager to please without being overbearing—like a good dancer who knows how to lead and can follow a little too.

She'd had a few other, brief relationships, one with a boy who had planted flowers with her when she'd worked her freshman summer on a grounds crew at Grinnell College, where she'd gone as an undergraduate. He wore coveralls with no shirt. His hair, long and lightened by the sun, hung down to his shoulders. He invited her over to his apartment once after they finished work and they smoked grass, which disoriented her enough to make her want to leave, but he'd encouraged her to stay, and they'd spent the night together. His name was Jeremiah (he'd changed it from Kevin—it was 1969), and in the morning he'd made her runny scrambled eggs with tofu. The dish was waiting on the table. She was wearing a green-plaid flannel shirt she'd found in his closet. Her hair was pushed to one side like a dented helmet, and she felt sticky between her legs, desperately wanting a shower. He'd put the food on a telephone spool table that was already crowded with organic gardening books and beer-making equipment. She'd looked at the yellow eggs with their denuded lumps of tofu and felt sick. She hadn't had a great track record with boys in high school, so she'd made up her mind that in college she would be pleasing or concerned or sincere or agreeable or lighthearted or whatever it was boys liked. And she'd eaten the eggs. Which wasn't the worst of it. They'd gone down relatively easy. But as she was leaving, Jeremiah told her he needed to see lots of "different people," meaning girls, she supposed, to keep his music alive (he played guitar). She'd gone home and promptly thrown up the eggs, feeling like a fool.

It was a year before she ventured out from her privacy again, this time with a more serious student, a history major who seemed to have missed the sixties and who wore corduroy sport coats with turtlenecks instead of denim work shirts and overalls. Like her, he wanted to be a teacher—in his case, a professor. They talked about working in the same VISTA program to help pay off their student loans. Before they knew it, they'd made plans to spend the rest of their lives together, without discussing marriage somehow. Two years went by. She was a senior. Corman always called before coming over, planned her birthday well in advance, and offered her a selection of travel brochures for their vacations from school. A better cook than she was, he made well-thought-out dinners with spices he grew in a little window box in his apartment (they joked about the tofu and runny eggs—the masses, especially the hippie masses, were so amusing). They listened only to jazz: Sonny Rollins, John Coltrane, Zoot Sims, Art Blakey, Horace Silver, Miles Davis—shunning and frowning on any interest in the Beatles, Led Zeppelin, and Steppenwolf. He was, she realized, just before they broke up to go to separate graduate schools—she in the West and he in the East—a little too much like her father: attentive, precise, even cheerful at times, but always from a distance that would never be bridged.

She heard Claude crying. Bedtime.

Downstairs, she turned off the music. Cap was on the couch. Claude, who'd settled down, sat on his lap and pulled himself up by Cap's two extended fingers, then plopped back down. Up, down. Up. Nobody could try harder. She couldn't imagine Corman being this energetic or affectionate. It was unsettling to think that she'd almost married him. How cold he'd been. How easily their two years had blown away, like salt tossed in the wind. And, most troubling to her, how familiar and at home she'd been with his sparing intimacy.

"I'll put him to bed," Wallis said. She took Claude into his room and lay down with him on the daybed and nursed him until he was asleep. His rippled breathing culminated in a single deep sigh. Then he was out, a stillness that continued to startle her in its abrupt taking over. She carefully detached him from her nipple—if he was going to wake, it would be at this moment—and went upstairs to their bedroom.

She took her clothes off and stepped into the shower. She needed some time to herself, wasn't ready to just hop into bed. Maybe she should go back to teaching, after all. She'd talked to Cap about it and they'd decided to just wait and see. They could manage financially; she'd get a lump sum of money from retirement that they could put into savings. But that meant she'd be home all the time with Claude, and how would she feel about that a year from now, as Phyllis had pointed out. Would she be climbing the walls? On the other hand, she couldn't imagine going back into a classroom; her mind was so singularly focused and she couldn't divide it, even between a husband and a child these days, let alone among twenty-four hormonal eighth graders.

Opening the shower curtain, she stretched her shoulders and then stepped dripping wet onto the bath mat, wanting to feel her flesh grow goose bumps, glisten with drops of water that would run down the curves of her legs, find little channels of excitement.

She was trying. Trying to will herself into the mood—to no avail. A book was all she wanted, and her own pillow, with just her head on it. Was it terrible to feel this way? Didn't all the women's magazines talk about it? Then why did it seem as if it were only her problem, some unnatural failing? Desire fossilized or, worse, run off into a thousand little tasks, unsexy as cleaning Claude's ears. What if her libido had just gone, no room for it in the new mothering machine?

She wrapped herself in an oversize marigold towel, which Cap had bought her for a present—she loved plush towels—and went over to the sink. A glass of white wine was there. Cap must have snuck in while she was showering and left it for her. Seeing this, she felt her shoulders loosen and smiled. She hadn't lost the weight from her pregnancy instantly, as some women seemed to—baby one day, old firm tennis-net stomach the next. But the more she sipped the wine, the more she liked the way she looked. Her face was less thin but more relaxed. Her curves weren't as exact, but they filled her clothes better. She smoothed lotion on her arms and chest, her legs and shoulders, observing herself in the mirror, pleased by the feel of her own hands, wishing she had time to let them drift. But even masturbation seemed some remote activity you went away on a retreat to learn.

She finished off the wine, inserted her diaphragm, and went out to the bedroom.

The lights were off. Cap wasn't here. Was he downstairs? Had she misinterpreted his interest? Imagined it? She had a moment of feeling utterly foolish, all this getting ready and in the mood, for nothing. Then she saw him—once her eyes got used to the dark. He was lying on the bed, naked, with one of the yellow roses he'd brought her on his chest, nestled among the dark hair. He looked so funny that she burst out laughing, and he did too. What a relief to see he wasn't taking this as seriously as she was. She walked over and plucked the rose off his chest.

In the morning, the phone rang. For once they'd all slept late— seven A.M.! Wallis got up to answer it. Cap was still sleeping soundly. After they'd made love last night, she'd curled up against him and told him that it had been too long.

"This is the answering service. We have a call from a Detective Atkinson. Should I put him through or take a number?"

"A detective?" Wallis said, unable to imagine what this could concern. "Put him through, I guess."

"This is Detective Atkinson at the police department. Is Dr. Kaplan home?"

"What is this about?" asked Wallis. "He's still sleeping." She hated to wake him. He needed the rest; he seemed especially tired lately.

"There's been an accident," the detective said. "We found Dr. Kaplan's business card in the victim's wallet. We need him to come down and identify the body."

Wallis shook Cap awake. "Cap, a detective is on the phone. There's been an accident."

"What?" He leaned over for the phone and said hello and then nothing else for a minute, just "All right" softly before he hung up.

"What happened?" asked Wallis.

He didn't answer; he stared at his hands. Wallis sat down next to him on the bed. "Cap?"

"A client of mine is dead."

"Oh, Cap, I'm sorry. Who?"

"Julian Katz."

Wallis followed him into the bathroom, but he waved her away; he wanted to be alone. He turned on the water and splashed his face. She closed the door behind her, just standing idly on the other side. Then she heard him crying, the same soft way he had the night Claude was born and almost died.

Chapter Nine

MAUREEN HAD BEEN LEAVING HIM NOTES ABOUT HIS SURPRISE. "WHAT'S white and blue and goes right through you?" Julian confessed to having no idea. She left him another clue on her bathroom mirror, in lipstick: "It's plain to see you're way out in left field." Tickets to a ball game? A fielder's mitt? No, no. What then? Another clue: "Stop using your head; your feet are way ahead of you."

"Hiking boots!"

"What?"

"Your birthday present to me—it's hiking boots!"

She splashed water on him. He could see the growing curve of her belly through the glass door of the shower, the water dripping off the ends of her hair, the arch of her spine and sudden slope of her buttocks as she leaned her head back to wash off the shampoo, then brought her arms up behind her and squeezed out the excess water until her hair was a tight blonde cord, her breasts rounder than even two weeks ago.

Now he walked out to her bedroom and saw the six-foot giraffe he'd given her. He'd shown up at her door with the animal after Thanksgiving. "For the baby," he'd said.

"Lucky for you," she'd told him, "that my hormones have rendered me hopelessly sentimental."

She'd taken the animal, let him inside, and then extracted confessions and promises from him: No, he'd never touched Celia; yes, he would stop seeing her even as a friend, if Maureen wanted him to; no, he had no idea why he had gone to her farm and not to California, unless it was because he couldn't face up to the responsibility of being a father. Maureen seemed satisfied with this last answer, and they made love for only the third time since she'd been pregnant, Maureen not feeling as sick now. He promised he'd spend all of Christmas vacation with her.

She stopped the car now and reached over to remove the blindfold. "We're here," she said.

It was the county airport outside Pierre. "Are we going on a trip?" Final exams started tomorrow, December 10. He couldn't imagine why they'd come here.

"*You're* going somewhere," Maureen said. She had put the blindfold on him as soon as he woke, brushing his teeth for him, dressing him: "I'll make you completely dependent on me today," she'd told him.

They went inside a hangar and were greeted by a man in a flight suit. "Happy birthday," he said to Julian, shaking his hand and introducing himself: Al, a large man with a full black beard and soft red skin around his eye sockets. "Ready, skipper?"

"For what?" asked Julian, alarmed by Al's eagerness.

"I haven't told him yet," said Maureen, who squeezed Julian's hand. "You're going to jump."

"Jump?"

"Skydive. Remember you told me you'd love to try it."

"I did?"

"You said you couldn't imagine ever doing it."

"I can't!"

"But you wanted to—you thought it would be a wonderful test of courage. Well, what better occasion than on your twenty-first birth-day?"

"Come on up," said Al, who would soon be strapped to Julian's back for something called a tandem jump. "You won't even feel my two hundred fifty pounds!" Al's voice thundered through the hangar as Julian followed him.

They watched a fifteen-minute training video. He would be sitting in front of his instructor on the floor of the plane; they would use the same parachute, with a reserve chute as a backup; they would push themselves out of the plane when the time came by shimmying forward (he would not be forced to jump); they would free-fall for about a minute from twelve thousand feet. Julian would have an altimeter with an alarm set to go off when he needed to pull the rip cord; he should not drop the pin, however, as they reused these; he should know that there had never been any casualties at this location (at others!), but nevertheless he would be asked to sign a release form.

The screen went black.

"Feel more confident now?" asked Al.

"No," said Julian. Maureen had her hands on his back; she was being so affectionate to him. She wouldn't, he realized, though, let him back out of this. Why was it so important that he jump out of a plane?

Julian got up to walk downstairs.

"Whoa," said Al. "Got to get your John Hancock on this, Slim, before we go." And he gave Julian the release form. The third item on it was: "Do you have any medical history of convulsions or seizures?"

Julian stared at the question. He could answer yes and get out of this, or he could lie and go up twelve thousand feet and jump out of a plane, strapped to a two-hundred-fifty-pound weight. What better conditions for a seizure.

"Good-o," said Al, giving the sheet a quick glance and seeing all the "no" boxes checked. Maureen squeezed his hand. How could he do otherwise? He'd have to explain to Maureen: *By the way, I forgot to tell you something about me.* . . . He thought of his father and mother knowing about this, after all the years of warning him not to go swimming or ride his bike too fast or climb to the top of the ropes in gym. (Only halfway, his father had told his gym teacher, and sure enough, the gym teacher would blow his whistle when Julian went up half the distance, the other kids saying, Hey, let him go all the way, he was about to make it, and Julian sliding down and explaining he felt tired anyway, to cover himself. God, what would they think—they would never even imagine such a thing, skydiving . . .)

"Let's go," said Julian. It was nice weather for December, and he'd worn only his light jacket. He put his hand on Maureen's neck. He was twenty-one and about to be a father, the lover of a grown woman—what more did he have to do to prove he could run his own life now? He'd quit taking his medication, and no dire predictions from anyone had come true. He could do anything, including fly. Icarus had the right idea but not the right equipment—which Al was now checking thoroughly. "You can't believe how hard it is to pack a parachute to fail," he told them, winking and snapping the chute closed.

Fifteen minutes later, Julian was "put together;" as Al called it, and ready to go. Maureen took their picture. He and Al were strapped front to back like two loaves of fresh-baked bread. They both wore helmets and had to walk together, a large, four-legged insect, to the plane. Maureen kissed Julian full on the lips, as if he were going off to war.

It took them twenty minutes to get up to the altitude they needed. The pilot circled over a large open field west of the county airport. Al shouted over the noise of the engine for Julian to look down and see the target. That's where they'd be headed. Most important was to arch his back. Just pretend he was doing a swan dive. And relax, have fun. Enjoy the free fall. Pull the pin out when he heard the alarm. Al pushed Julian's goggles down. Anytime now, said Al.

Julian looked down. They had edged along the floor so that now

Julian was actually more out of the plane than in. He put his hands on either side of the hatch. He couldn't find the airport below. "ANY-TIME YOU'RE READY!" Al yelled in his ear. There was something familiar about this, Julian thought. The only difference was that he would stay conscious (he hoped) and have to let go voluntarily. After years of doing everything in his power to avoid losing control, he'd now undergo what he no longer could think of as skydiving but regarded only as a massive, inside-out seizure. "ANYTIME!" Al said, and then shouted, "I SEE YOUR HONEY DOWN THERE!" And Julian leaned out, just enough to start falling, and had the distinct impression that Al had used this little trick frequently.

They did a somersault out of the plane, then righted themselves, the noise of falling so much louder than he had expected, swelling and filling his ears as if they were inside a tornado and Dorothy's farmhouse would soon fly by them. He'd been able to see the plane pass above his head, so he knew they were going down, but otherwise he wouldn't have had a clue: the noise entered and surrounded and so completely infused their falling that it took the place of all sense of sight. He had no idea that sixty seconds had passed or how far or fast they'd fallen until the alarm went off on his altimeter. He reached for the pin and found it immediately, pulling it out, and the chute opened with a *whomp* that snapped them up.

And then it was hushed and still, a silence so at odds with the rushing air seconds earlier that he began giggling and trying out one trick after another, pulling himself to the left, to the right, turning spirals by holding one side, then stopping in midair by pulling both straps at once. In the distance, a faint buzz: the plane flew in circles above them. With so much air rushing in, all moisture had evaporated from his mouth, and it felt dryer than at the dentist's when cotton logs were stuffed in his cheeks. He could see the target now and made his way left. Driving this amazing contraption when he couldn't even drive a car! He'd done it, he'd really done it! They glided faster toward the target, and Al said, Pull down! All the way! Lift your knees! And Julian made a perfect landing on his feet, right in the circle.

Maureen came running over from the fence. She threw her arms around Julian's neck, kissed him and jumped all over him like a teenage girl, much to his delight. Al slapped him on the back. "Outstanding jump! Hell's bells, Julian, you're a natural at this!" And Julian thought, yes, so true; he'd been practicing for years and he hadn't known it.

He shook hands with Al, who congratulated him again, encouraged him to come out for more lessons to get certified as a jumpmaster, and then Maureen whispered, "Let's go. I can't wait any longer." She wouldn't let go of him all the way to the car, her arms locked around his waist. "You were incredible," she said, and then, "I love you, Julian."

He proposed. He'd been feeling so confident after his jump, so exhilarated and pleased with himself, that he asked her to marry him as they were about to exit for Pierre. He said it quickly: "Let's keep driving up to Wyoming and get married."

Maureen got off at the exit.

She had no plans to get married, not even to the father of her child.

"Is it because of our ages?" asked Julian.

"It's because of mine, at least."

"What's that mean?"

"It means I've lived too long this way and can't imagine it being different. I always pictured a child, but not a family. One is company, the other a sentence."

"But we already spend all our time together."

She put on her blinker to turn down her street. "Not all. Married is all."

"What are we going to do, then? Have two apartments? What about the baby?"

The gates went down at the railroad tracks. "Shit," said Maureen. "I wish they'd move these tracks already."

"How can we have two apartments with the baby?" Julian repeated, hoping it made the question clearer.

Maureen turned off the engine while the freight train rolled slowly past. She straightened her seat belt. Her belly had grown larger, and she was unmistakably pregnant, though she could still disguise the fact with the right baggy sweater for class. They had only one more week of the semester left, and then they could figure out what to do about next year. At least he wouldn't be in her class then.

She reached over and put her hand on his leg. "I know exactly what I'm going to think about as soon as this train gets out of the way and we can get to bed. Your dropping out of the sky. It's the way I used to feel about horses as a little girl, all that power and style in one animal. I think I could get hooked on your doing this."

"Why won't you answer my question?"

"We're having such a nice birthday," she said, and he heard the professor's tone creep into her voice. "Why do you want to spoil it? All this nonsense about marriage and living arrangements. What's the point?"

"Do you intend to let me see the baby?" The train passed. The gates went up.

"I need to tell you something," she said. "When I was in California, I had lunch with an old friend from graduate school." Julian knew without asking that the friend was a man. Maureen seemed to have no women friends besides her sister. "He told me about a two-year position opening at the University of California in San Diego, where he teaches. It would be half time, for as much money as I make here. I could take care of the baby and—this is the real draw—I'd be near my sister and my niece."

"And what about me?"

"You could transfer."

"But I like it here," said Julian.

Maureen smiled, unmoved. "Sometimes we have to make tough choices."

He could see her marrying the old friend and the two of them raising his child together. "I'll have to think about it," said Julian, just to be difficult, and because he knew that people—people unlike him—always said such things in these situations to throw their weight around. He knew, too, that he'd follow her anywhere she went.

"Wait here," she said, as they pulled into the garage under her building. "More surprises."

In a few minutes she came back down for him. "Ready?"

He walked into her apartment, to find a cake with twenty-one lit candles. "Make a wish," she said. He blew out the candles, wishing for once for something other than an end to his disorder: he wanted them to be a family together. "Now find your wish in the bedroom," and she pushed him gently from behind when he seemed reluctant.

"What is it this time? An octopus to wrestle?" She gave him a slap on the butt when he wouldn't move. "Go ahead, silly. It won't bite, though I might."

On the bed was a large gift-wrapped box. He sat down next to it, tried to shake it (no sound, very heavy), and then tore off the paper. He couldn't believe it. She'd bought him an Apple computer. "Maureen—"

"Just be quiet. I'll spend my money any way I want. Look behind you."

"Where?"

"On the desk."

It was a photograph, enlarged and in a silver frame, of the two of them on top of Tanner's Rock. They'd climbed the mountain back in October. At the summit, Maureen had set her camera on remote and they'd thrown their arms around one another and kissed. "It goes with the computer," she said. "To inspire you. So what do you think?"

"I'm overwhelmed," he said.

"No; what do you think it all means? That I don't care about you?"

He looked at the computer. "Can I set this up?"

"Just like a man," she said, and pushed him down on the bed. "You're not finished being the birthday boy yet."

She cut two pieces of chocolate cake (he had only a moment of worry about the caffeine) and brought them over to the bed. Maureen licked the chocolate off his lips. "I bet you never imagined you'd be in bed with your pregnant professor on your twenty-first birthday." She fed him a bite of her cake. His last birthday he'd spent with his father and mother. They'd bought him two wool sweaters to wear for working at his father's store. Already the customers had started calling him Mr. Katz, assuming he would soon take over the store and give them the same discounts as his father. His parents were probably trying to reach him right now at his apartment to wish him a happy birthday. This would be beyond their comprehension. It was beyond his.

"I have one more surprise," Maureen said, beckoning him to follow her.

They went into the room that Maureen used as her office. It was tiny, the size of a large walk-in closet. Here she kept her computer, a filing cabinet, and a shelf of reference books. She had told Julian it was off limits—she was still his teacher, and she didn't want him or anyone else messing around with her papers.

On the floor, she unfolded an Indian batik bedspread. She put a brown paper bag in the middle, its top rolled down like a closed lunch sack. "Promise?" she asked.

"Promise what?" he said, and for a moment he thought, I should be studying for finals. He had two tomorrow, Maureen's at eight o'clock in the morning and his sociology exam in the afternoon. But he felt what had become a strangely comfortable fluttering of fear and desire, and he understood that he wanted to make her happy at any cost, that all his pleasure now came from never disappointing her, even on his birthday, especially on his birthday, that pure joy was giving himself over to her wants, surrendering, and that he hadn't surrendered enough yet, not enough. "Yes," he said.

"Open it," she said, and he unrolled the brown paper bag. "Look inside."

She slipped out of her clothes, out of her jeans and black union shirt with its long row of buttons, then curled in a ball, hugging her knees. She almost looked shy, as if she were reluctant to be here. He started to take off his clothes, but she told him no, just her.

"Take out the candle," she said, "and light it with the matches in the bag. Don't touch anything else in the bag. Sit next to me," she told him. She stood up and turned off the overhead light, then sat back down on the bedspread, with its purple veins jutting out from an orange center. The candle flickered and cast shadows on the ceiling. "Tell me something that isn't a lie."

"What?" The question jolted him.

"Tell me something you've never told anybody. Something that frightens you."

Julian's chest tightened. "You tell me first," he said.

"My parents never celebrated my birthday," she said without hesitating.

"Why not?"

"They didn't want me, so they ignored the day completely. Or pretended to forget, then promised they'd make it up to me, a cake, gifts, a party. It never happened. They didn't want to spend the extra money either. Maybe now you understand why I made such a fuss over yours. . . ." Facing him, she walked her fingers like spiders across his shoulders, until her hands locked behind his neck, tangled in his hair. Then she unlatched her hands and ran her fingers lightly under his chin. He leaned toward the caress, toward her proffered kiss, the taste of chocolate on her upper lip. Her mouth moved against his: "Your turn," she whispered.

He pulled back, wanting to avoid his turn completely, prolong hers. "That doesn't sound like much of a secret."

"No; you're right. You catch on fast." She was right next to him, holding him around the neck, but it felt as if they were talking across a large dinner table. "My father punched me in the stomach on my birthday once."

"What? Jesus."

"You heard me."

"Why?"

"Because I was fifteen years old and pregnant by my boyfriend. I was hoping, foolishly, that the baby would get me out of the house."

"But why did he punch you?"

"Because he didn't want me to have a baby. That was his abortion technique. It worked. Nobody ever knew that, not even my mother. She thought it was a miscarriage—nature correcting its own mistakes."

He remembered the first time they'd slept together—how she'd jerked back when he'd touched her stomach.

"Your turn," she said.

"It's hot in here," said Julian. The walls of the room pressed against him. It was too small and overheated, warm air pouring out of the register at his back. He felt his lungs shrinking into small, seedless hulls. He wanted to roll on the floor and cover himself with the cool parachute that he'd opened earlier. "I'm having trouble breathing. Maybe we should talk about this later."

Maureen laughed ruefully. "It's perfect in here, hot and sealed. You promised, sweetheart."

"I don't have any secrets."

"You're a liar."

Liar liar. Your mother's skin's on fire.

The candle's flame weakened. Not enough oxygen. "All right," he said. "I'm not what I appear."

She laughed. "Are you gay? Could have fooled me."

"I'm epileptic." He couldn't believe he'd told her. He'd had only one secret, and lies born of it like children. They kept the secret alive; they were its survivors.

"I didn't expect that," she said.

"No, I imagine not. Who would?"

"What's it mean?"

"It means I have seizures. Sometimes."

"I know that. What's it mean now, though? Do you take medication?"

"Not anymore. I need to get out of here," he said.

"Are you going to have a seizure?"

"No, no, I just need some air."

She put her hand out. "Soon. First you have to do something for me, now that we're accomplices to each other's dark parts. You wanted to marry me, right? Well, we'll marry in the name of shame."

"Maureen, let's stop. It's not fun anymore."

"It never was just fun," she said, and told him to open the bag and reach inside.

He did so and took out a small mirror.

"Break it," she said.

"What?"

"Break the mirror."

"How, exactly?"

"I don't know. You're the man."

He banged it on the carpet, but it stayed in one piece.

"Use your shoe," she said.

He stood up and stomped the mirror with his heel. Nothing. He smashed it again. It broke into odd-size shards.

"Ah," she said, "now we're married. You smashed the glass. Let's drink the wine."

She spoke so bitterly it made him shiver.

"Pick up a piece of the mirror," she said, and he followed her instructions robotically, taking the shard with its needle point between his thumb and forefinger, his hand unsteady. She stretched one leg out on the batik sheet.

"Cut me," she said, and pointed to a place high on her leg, just below her crotch. "Come on. You wanted to marry, didn't you?" she said. "We can do anything."

She moved the candle alongside her leg so he could see, as though it were a surgical procedure. He heard her breathing quicken, a shallow panting, the long, taut muscle in her thigh laid out, the shard slipping between his sweaty fingers, his head ringing. He saw, too, the swell of her belly, the movement of life inside her. "I can't," he said. "I can't."

"Give it to me, then," she said, in a voice filled with impatience and reproach. She drew the point swiftly across the skin, as if opening a tiny zipper on a doll purse. Blood seeped from the line on the inside of her thigh. She sagged back against the wall. Released. "The fine pleasures of wakening pain," she said, almost as if reciting. "The dull comforts of edging self-annihilation. Unknowable unless you've been there." He knew all about it. "Put your mouth over it," she said. "Stop the bleeding."

He did as she told him, and tasted her blood.

"If you do it right," she said sweetly, stroking his hair, "it never leaves a scar. It's the only thing that stops me from hating myself." She bent down and whispered in his ear: "I can't marry you, Julian. I can't love anyone."

Julian sat up. He felt chills now, feverish hot chills. His head was spinning, and he heard himself asking a question, as if in a dream. "What about the baby? You'll be able to love the baby, won't you?"

"Ah, the baby," she said, and put her head back against the wall, a drug stupor of sorts. "Do you still have seizures?" she asked, unwilling, he could see, to answer his worry.

"Not recently, but yes."

"You've been afraid to tell me, right?"

"Yes."

"Afraid I'd leave you."

He looked down at her skin; the blood had stopped. "It doesn't mean the baby will be epileptic. Only five percent of children inherit the disorder," he said, mechanically reciting a statistic he wanted with all his heart to believe. "What are you going to do now that you know?" he asked.

"Now that we know about each other," she said. "Don't give up your trump card so easily. I never handed one out before. I'd hate to see it go to waste."

He was starting to breathe again, but now he had a headache, trying to keep track of everything: what he said, what she said. What could they have left to say to each other after such confessions? "It's been quite a birthday."

"People should get whatever they want on their birthdays. Even pain, if that's what you want—pain that they own. You wouldn't hurt me, would you, Julian?"

"No," said Julian, not wanting to be asked to mutilate anybody ever again.

"Unless I asked you to."

"Maybe not even then."

"You wouldn't punch me in the stomach, would you?"

He shook his head wildly.

"You don't understand any of this, do you?"

"Yes, I do," he said.

"I don't know about us, Julian. You play both badly and too well for our own good. I'm not sure we have a future."

"Neither am I," he said, and marveled at his own honesty.

He couldn't sleep. He should be studying for his final exam to-morrow in Maureen's class. They should be making plans for the baby. He should go see Cap again. He should take his medication, get some sleep, not drink wine as he'd done tonight when they'd gone back into the bedroom and made love, Maureen pushing against him so hard he feared for the baby. "Obviously the events of the day—and I mean all of them—have excited me," she said afterward, spent and lying alongside him. She'd moved on top of him, pushing him back and biting the fleshiest part of his shoulder. She slumped over him, her hair falling in his face. He'd failed to come again, but it didn't bother her anymore. She'd gotten used to being the one who was fully satisfied all the time, and she was too tired to help him along. His penis—he understood finally what Cap meant about it being a form of impotency—was scared stiff of failing to please her, unable to relinquish its vigilant attention to her long enough to satisfy himself.

And because of the pregnancy, the extra weight, the changes in her body, her lack of sleep, whatever, she had started snoring—like a man in this too.

He got out of bed. The kitchen clock said three-thirty, too early to get up for breakfast but too late to have much hope for sleep. He looked around at their clothes on the carpet. Maureen had been all over him, pushing her tongue into his mouth, taking his hands and putting them on her breasts, telling him she'd been thinking all day about him skydiving, how he looked in his blue flight suit with its brass zipper from crotch to neck, his perfect landing, and how when he took off his goggles and helmet, his hair, which she wouldn't let him cut, fell out in waves onto his collar. How she wanted to fuck him right there on the ground. That's why she'd taken him into her office.

It was a kind of apology for what happened. She knew he had hated it. He didn't tell her, but she knew, as she knew he didn't like her finger up his rectum, as she knew she'd gone too far, even with him, and that he was drifting, standing outside himself watching, waking up from the beguilement of endless fucking and wondering how to escape from some monstrous fusion of sex and space.

He blinked at the clock. A minute had gone by. He realized he'd just had an absence. His first seizure in two years. More would follow. They always did.

He didn't want her to see him like this or risk having a massive seizure in front of her. He'd go back to his apartment. Sleep. In the morning, first thing, he'd call Cap. Then he'd have his father express-mail some Tegretol. Tegretol sometimes gave him a neck rash, but at least it wouldn't keep him awake like Dilantin. And anyway, he wouldn't have to lie about the rash; he wouldn't have to lie anymore at all. He'd told Maureen; he'd done the hard part. From here on he'd do everything right.

A fine glaze of ice covered the sidewalk. He moved slowly, sliding along, taking baby steps down Wilcox until he turned the corner, out of sight of Maureen's apartment, and onto West Martin. A police car went by him, slowed down, then pulled away. He was cold, and his teeth chattered. He concentrated on the sound, the light tapping of his back molars, a little tinny, it seemed, his hands and feet numb and tingling from the cold—or an aura; he couldn't tell which. . . .

He heard a train whistle. Student apartments lined either side of Central, where the tracks ran down the center. How could anybody live so close? The train rattled windows and shook walls. The horn had to be blown every few seconds because there were so many intersections through town. It was so loud it could blast through brick.

He was half a block from Central, and he could see it coming: two engines, one facing forward, one rear, a long, long train; he'd have to wait twenty minutes until it all passed, freezing, standing out here alone. He could make it across the intersection if he ran fast enough. He had flown today! Opened his arms and fallen through the sky. "Use your fear," Al had told him on the way up. Use your fear to concentrate. Do you realize you just flew a hundred and eighty miles an hour with nothing above or beneath you? Pretty good for a boy who's been so scared of dropping all his life.

Arms out, head up . . .

Arch.

Pelvis out. Your crotch, your balls, your cock. Stay with it and use your fear. You can't escape it. Not up here. You won't disappear through the trapdoor up here. You can't *not* exist in the sky. Fold your arms across your chest, rock back, fall forward. Arch arch arch arch! *Fly*, my love. . . .

———

Her name was Luchesca, and she'd been born in Italy. When she was seven years old, she'd been in a car accident and thrown through the windshield. Her epilepsy had started a year later. She wore her hair, neither red nor brown but some oxidized mixture of the two, cut sharply off at the neck and shaved over one ear. An onyx bracelet circled her wrist. She'd read somewhere that onyx was good for the nervous system; she thought it might keep her from having so many fits, though she didn't really believe in any of that New Age junk. A recent brain operation had worked for a while, but then she'd had two bad convulsions. She liked sex because it made her forget about being so different. She thought the only good thing about this camp for teenage epileptics was that it got her away from her foster parents. When she told Julian all this, she stroked his penis, as if it were the most normal thing in the world, chatting while she held him swollen and throbbing.

Julian lasted only a minute once he was inside her. Luchesca had lain completely still. Afterward she told him she could hear his blood move into hers, all their fluids intermingling, their bones rubbing. It was one of the powers she had, to go so deep inside herself that she could feel their souls touch. She believed it was because she visited death when she had a seizure. Sex was like that too, but it didn't go quite as far—it was only the first circle. Yet if she lay perfectly still, she could feel death like scudding grass touch her back. But when she had a seizure, it scratched like pins and drew blood, until she belonged to death a little more each time. She liked getting closer and closer. She stroked his penis again until he was hard, and then she lay on her back, her arms straight down at her sides, while he pushed himself into her, then she gave a little shudder and said, "It can be quick. I don't care. Every time you see me, think of this."

She was missing the next day at the tug-of-war. All week long he'd been encouraged to do things—things unthinkable for him: diving into a lake and climbing high ropes, walking on a beam ten feet above the ground and paddling a canoe by himself. In the afternoon they had study groups about epilepsy; he was learning about it—truth from myth—for the first time: all his responses were based on fear and misperception of his abilities in the "real world." The problem lay in the way people responded to epileptics—and an epileptic's dread of that response. But here he felt understood: his shame, his worry that he was being watched all the time or that everybody knew what he was; they all were like him here, and all of them had the same fear. "The best bunch of paranoid princes and princesses I've ever seen," his counselor told them, grabbing one end of the long rope. "You think that people have nothing better to do than wonder when some poor jerk is going to fall down and twitch awhile? Well, so what?" and he'd motioned all fifteen of them to the other side of the rope and tugged them right over. "Put some muscle into it, you weaklings!" And Julian had gotten furious, despite knowing he was being tricked, and he'd cursed and shouted, caught up in the battle with the counselor, who like the kids here, all the Camp Tu-Wa-Ka staff, everyone in the whole damn place, suffered from epilepsy. "A bunch of jerking, foaming, twitching, grunting, shitting fitters!" he yelled at them as they dragged him forty feet through the mud in pure rage.

Luchesca came up while they were celebrating their victory, whooping and gleeful over the counselor's mud-splattered clothes. "Hi," she said to Julian. "I was waiting for you." He didn't know what she meant. Waiting where?

"I have lunch for us."

She unzipped her pack and showed him two box lunches. "And here," she said, rummaging around in the pack until she found two cans of Coke. They weren't supposed to have sugar or caffeine up here, although nothing was expressly forbidden. "I smuggled these in from Melk's." Melk's was a small roadside store two miles from the camp, the closest sign of civilization. She must have walked there and back during the tug-of-war. "Are you ready?"

"Where are we going?"

"You know," she said. But he didn't. He wanted to stay here, with the other kids. His muscles ached with the pleasure of the drubbing they'd just given their counselor.

"I thought I'd hang out here."

Luchesca blinked at him. Her rusty, hacked hair was soaked with something he hoped was only water. A single red legging on her right leg—her left leg was bare—made her look as if she were wearing a Christmas cast. She'd put on lipstick and wore eye shadow the color of a purple bruise. In the bright noon sun, with everyone else in bathing suits and T-shirts, their hair sweaty, their faces pink with exertion, she looked ghastly, like a lost spook. He was embarrassed to be seen with her but had become involuntarily hard just standing next to her. He wondered if she had put a curse on him. He'd never known anybody who was a better candidate for being a witch. "Okay," he said, and followed her down to the lake.

Once there, she'd told him about her parents. They'd emigrated to this country thirteen years ago. She hadn't spoken a word of English until she came here at four years old. When she was seven, they'd driven through an intersection in Reading, Pennsylvania, where they lived. During the night, some kids had stolen the stop sign for traffic coming from the cross direction. A trucker, unfamiliar with the intersection, had driven straight through, thinking he had the right-of-way. Her mother and father died in the accident. Luchesca had been thrown thirty feet from the car. Two hundred stitches had been needed to sew up her leg, torn from thigh to calf on a metal post.

She touched the red legging that extended up her thigh. Julian realized he'd never seen her in shorts, until today. When they'd had sex last night, it had been dark. "I wore this because I wanted you to know," she said, and pulled down the red covering. Her leg was a mass of dimpled scars, smoothly disfigured, like the white trunk of a birch tree carved with hundreds of signatures.

He didn't know what she wanted him to do, whether he should touch it or say he was sorry for her or ask did it still hurt? He thought, too, she was waiting for him to kiss her, reach for her hand, something that would make a connection to last night. But in the daylight, just a few feet from the dock, secluded only by a line of tall pines, where they could hear the voices of the other kids shouting as they did cannonballs and can openers into the lake, he couldn't make his hands move. It felt as if he'd never touched her. A mingling of fear and repulsion made her leg look contagious, like some outward growth, their shared affliction slipped down from brain to leg and alive with wormy evil. He wanted to get away immediately.

"I think we should go back," he said, standing up. She pulled the legging back on, the nakedness—more than what he'd seen last night—covered now.

She sat still for a moment, then got up, too, but walked a little ahead of him. When they came to the dock, he stopped to talk with another girl he'd met at the camp, Karen, who lived in Baltimore and whose father was a pharmacist too. They'd paddled a canoe together in a race the first day. She had said in an afternoon group session that she had some special kind of epilepsy she was supposed to grow out of after adolescence. But she worried sometimes she wouldn't. She had seizures only in her sleep, and nobody at her school, none of her friends, not even her relatives, knew about it. She played tennis and was on the swim team and was a majorette in the band. "Why are you here, then?" Luchesca had asked her. "We must all seem like real freaks to you."

Karen had said no, apologizing. She didn't mean to make it seem as if she were trying to separate herself, as if she didn't belong. Inside she felt like everyone else here. It was just confusing, that's all. The messages—the group leader had started off the session by asking them what hidden messages they get from people about their epilepsy—she got from everybody was how normal, even exceptional, she was, but she had to take these pills three times a day and nobody, not even her parents, who always changed the subject to her accomplishments, talked directly to her about it.

"We're a different species," Luchesca had told her, and then had been wordless for the rest of the session. It was true, Julian thought, watching Luchesca walk on around the lake and not stop to talk. She liked to be by herself. She had severe seizures, sometimes two or three in a day, and once had been in status epilepticus, something he dreaded, all of them dreaded—a continuous two hours of convulsions, the direct road to death, not just a stop along the way as with a brief forty-second seizure. Nobody could top that. And she was an orphan. How much bad luck could one person have? "I'll see you later," he called out to her, but she didn't turn around. He walked toward the bunk-houses with Karen, and they talked about getting together sometime in Baltimore. Seeing a movie. Going to the wharf. He'd already forgotten about Luchesca by the time he got back to his bunk, and then it was time for their afternoon session.

They had a visitor, a retired doctor from Baltimore. He'd been diagnosed as epileptic when he was eleven years old—back in 1933, when there was such a stigma attached to the disorder that he'd been put in a special school. He'd had as many as a hundred petit mal seizures in class a day. His teachers had thought he was lazy, stubborn, unwilling to pay attention. He'd often been struck across the hands for losing his place during a reading lesson. He would remember nothing of the five or six seconds when he was out; he'd hear nothing—not the teacher's voice, not the crack of her pointer.

Finally, he'd had a major seizure during lunch. His father was a Baptist minister, and his mother had died in childbirth. He'd been raised by an aunt, who was too feeble to take close care of him. When his seizures became worse, despite heavy doses of phenobarbital, which only made him groggy and irritable, he was sent away to the state institution, where he stayed for fifteen years, until he was twenty-six years old, living among the retarded and the psychotic, patients who couldn't control their bowels, who couldn't dress themselves, who thought they were Jesus, who regularly tried to slash themselves with bedsprings. His father visited him twice a year, on Easter and Christmas, and prayed for him in the ward.

The doctor paused here and looked, Julian thought, straight at him, although he was such an impressive presence, with his leonine white hair swept back and his intense blue eyes, that everyone's gaze was locked on his. "I became a surgeon at Johns Hopkins. I came from a background that dictated failure and worse. By all rights I should be dead, or a drug addict, or still in that institution. You don't spend fifteen years, your entire adolescence and young manhood, imprisoned in a ward, strapped to a bed for a good portion of that time because of disorderly behavior, without having it kill your spirit. The reason I'm alive is because I had one person recognize my humanity and tell me I had something important to do. That's the only reason I'm here."

Naturally, during the question-and-answer period, everybody wanted to know who this person was that had changed the doctor's life. Karen was the first to shoot up her hand. During the talk, she had whispered to Julian, "I love stories with happy endings." Luchesca, who had walked out in the middle of the doctor's presentation, evidently didn't. Julian imagined her spitting on the ground once outside, muttering curses in Italian, cynical and contemptuous of the whole business. She'd told him last night, when they'd had sex, that she couldn't stand these rah-rah sessions. They were for soft-headed people who couldn't face reality. She would go out of her mind if it weren't for her books and sex. He had a moment of jealousy then, wondering how many times she'd done this with boys, maybe even up here—with somebody else. But except for him, the other kids avoided her, or made remarks about the gypsy clothes she dressed in, the single legging, the leather miniskirt and black mantilla she'd worn at the dance, the large rings with fat, colored stones on her little fingers, the walks she took by herself (to get Cokes at Melk's, Julian knew; she was hooked on Coke), the way she'd come up to a conversation for a while, listen, and then walk away. Even here, where they were supposed to all be a team, supportive of each other, she'd become an oddity at best—the glances exchanged when she entered or left a room, the giggling and whispering. "She looks like a fifteen-year-old pree-mie," one boy had said to Julian, while they watched her stand still on the trampoline when it was her turn.

Julian had wanted to get away from her, associate himself with the popular, cheerful, upbeat Karen, who never had fewer than five people around her, who was always in motion even when she was sitting, nodding encouragingly at speakers, putting a tender, supportive (and nonsexual, unlike Luchesca, whose fingers lay heavy with want) hand on a knee or arm, and who believed in happy endings, including her own, her disorder programmed to expire after adolescence.

"The person was myself," the doctor said, and Karen applauded at this surprise. Cute, Julian could imagine Luchesca saying about the punch line. The doctor went on to say that he'd discovered an inner strength, a part of himself that had been buried for years, a memory of an eleven-year-old boy who had been one of two children left in a spelling bee. Given "millinery," he'd seen the entire word flash before his eyes and was about to spell it when he'd had a brief petit mal convulsion that everyone thought was a blank stare of uncertainty. When he came out of it, his turn had passed, he'd been disqualified; his competition had spelled her word, "presbyter," correctly, and he'd begun his descent into the institutionalized hell of the state asylum.

It was back to this boy that he'd gone one day, when he'd been let out of isolation after forty-eight hours (for punching an attendant). Back to that boy who knew the right word, who knew he had been cheated of his victory, whose rightful prize had been snatched from him by a disorder he didn't understand and that caused so much fear in other people that he had to be hidden away. Polio, tuberculosis, scarlet fever, influenza, all the terror diseases of his time couldn't match the intensity of dread people felt when they saw a full-blown convulsion. And why was that?

Karen raised her hand. "You have no control over your body?"

"Yes," the doctor said, and added, "More to the point, you have no identity anymore. For several minutes, you cease to exist as a recognizable human being. What people see is something primitive and darkly atavistic. A creature."

Karen asked what "atavistic" meant and wrote down the definition "ancestral." The doctor continued: "Where does this come from? they ask. What happened to my child, my wife, my husband? What happened to the little boy who had spelled every word correctly, with swift intelligence? I had to ask myself that question and find that boy again. My whole life has been dedicated to bringing that little boy home."

Luchesca returned at the mention of "home." Meanwhile, Karen's hand had shot up again. She was eager to know how he'd become a doctor, a surgeon! Wasn't it dangerous to practice? Didn't he put his patients at risk?

Julian suddenly had a flash of Karen married, with six kids, making lemonade for everyone on a hot day, far away from her adolescent epilepsy, a good mother who would teach her children to be kind to the unfortunate—thankfully no longer one of them herself. Imperceptibly he moved away from her and looked at Luchesca, who had crossed her arms in defiance and stood against the wall.

"I've been free of seizures for many years. That doesn't mean they couldn't come back at any time. There's not a day I wake up that I don't wonder if I'm going to wind up back in the asylum, strapped to my bed, soiling my clothes, screaming with incoherent rage.

"But it wasn't medicine that saved me. It was only when I began to look back on my seizures as something more than an electrical malfunction that I started to value my actions again, begin my journey back into the world. For years I feared that what happened to me during those convulsions was the work of the devil. I didn't think that consciously, of course. I didn't believe in God. I was a confirmed atheist, convinced that I'd been badly wired and this was my lot, pure chance. I had no head injury, no trauma. My disorder was elusive, idiopathic, without cause, only symptoms. It could have happened to anyone. But underneath that belief was another one, which I suspect you all have shared: I'd been marked for failure. I remember my father telling me he would pray for my soul—drive away the evil. Apparently, however, prayer failed, because I was abandoned to the institution and the devil there. I tried twice to take my own life."

The doctor paused here and waited for this to sink in.

"One day, while I was working on the grounds, I felt a hand on my shoulder, and when I turned around, there was my father. He didn't look like himself. That is, I experienced a tremendous compassion and love in his presence that I'd never felt before. He said nothing, but I had the sense that he'd come because he wanted my forgiveness, my blessing on him. A phrase came into my head: 'sin chaser.' Like ambulance chaser. I thought this was enormously funny, and I said to him, 'You're a sin chaser, aren't you?' and he nodded and said to me, 'The place you go is free of pain and pleasure.' Later I learned that I'd been experiencing a convulsion during this time, a major seizure that induced me to sleep for sixteen straight hours afterward. I was semicomatose, actually. Repeatedly, doctors tried to wake me up. My father had died during my seizure, and I was quite sure his spirit had come to visit me upon his passing."

Luchesca burst out with a groan, interrupting. "How can you listen to such nonsense?" Julian, sitting closest to her, shut his eyes, hoping the moment would go away.

But her voice grew louder, her inflected English chopping words into thin, clean shapes like cucumber slices on a cutting board. "Do you ask this man if he has any proof? Do you ask even if he is a real doctor? Would you trust me also if I told you the Virgin Mary appeared to me outside and asked if she might have a word with me about my poor attitude regarding religious matters?" There was cautious laughter. Everyone had become painfully quiet, afraid of what she might say next. "How can you let this man talk and not challenge him? Every one of you must know there is nothing special about what has happened to you. We are carriers of accidents. We walk down a dark path, but we do not bump into things out there. Only *in here*—" Luchesca jabbed a finger at her temple, so hard that Julian winced. "What more do you want from this man? Yes, we are cursed, if cursed means knowing the truth."

She walked out.

There was silence in the room.

The doctor—and such was the bite of Luchesca's protest that Julian himself now doubted whether the man was in fact a doctor—seemed unaffected by the speech. His eyes were closed, and he appeared to be meditating, sitting cross-legged and breathing sonorously through his nose. Finally, he spoke: "I think it's time for a break."

Julian went outside, while most of the others stayed behind to ask more questions.

Luchesca was sitting in the shade of a tower they'd all built earlier (except for Luchesca), a twenty-foot structure of cardboard boxes that they were encouraged to crash into, letting it topple down on them, letting their world fall apart, losing control. Julian had first bumped it with his shoulder, then used his hands on the second try, and on his third attempt had thrown his whole body at the structure, boxes everywhere, collapsing on him harmlessly. He'd had a memory of diving under the waves at Ocean City, before he'd been warned to avoid swimming.

He sat next to Luchesca, his back against the boxes, gingerly. "You didn't give him a chance," he told her.

She was reading, a fat book about the history of Italy. She wanted to return there eventually, just as soon as she could get out from under her foster parents' rule. They lived in Baltimore and had three other foster children. "Professional loafers," she'd called them. They lived off the income from their charges. He dreaded hearing about one more bad thing in her life. By chance alone, it seemed there would have to be *something* positive. But he knew that when she opened her mouth, more tales of misery, betrayal, and horror would be revealed. And he felt unable to walk away, ignore her, make light of her troubles, not gaze fascinated into her bottomless pit of woe.

"You thought it was inspiring, I suppose."

"Well, interesting," said Julian.

"Interesting," Luchesca repeated, smirking. "Let's get out of here before you become 'interesting' too."

The next day he'd gone to breakfast late, trying to avoid her, but she was waiting for him outside the dining hall. After they ate, she walked with him back to the bunkhouse. It was Sunday, visitors day. His parents had not come last week; some last-minute illness—imagined or real—of his mother had prevented them. "But definitely next week," his father had promised. And he'd called today to confirm that yes, they would be up, Mother was feeling much better, looking forward to the trip! Julian knew this was a lie. His mother dreaded going anywhere, even in the neighborhood. He was used to being alone with his father. In restaurants the two of them ate by themselves, wifeless, motherless. Or they would shop together for school clothes, make visits to the greenhouse and nursery for plants (his mother's hobby). After he was five, he'd stopped asking—the repeated question to his father of where was Mom being followed inevitably by the answer "resting"—and concentrated instead on explaining her absence to others. "She works a lot," Julian would say, and created a profession for her as sales director for a large drug company, Elemeno Pharmaceuticals, since he knew from his father's drugstore how much time sales reps spent on the road. "Elemeno" came from his studies of the alphabet with her. In her accented English—she had a pretty voice and would sometimes sing to him in Hungarian—LMNO had sounded like linked notes.

Being alone with her all day had been a kind of asylum, he realized, just like the doctor's, lining his blocks up and spelling simple words with her, their mornings sewing (he'd learned how to sew, but he'd never told anyone, would never admit it), their afternoons pulling weeds in the garden. They lived in a neighborhood with no other children on the block, and he never went anywhere—his mother couldn't drive—until his father came home after seven, and it was near his bedtime then and too late to see other kids, and where would they be at that hour anyway except home?

When he started elementary school, he didn't know what his mother did by herself, except more of the same—waiting for him to return. "I thought something happened to you!" she said once, when Julian had dawdled with the kids on the way home, throwing rocks at a construction site. He shrugged and walked past her to his room, while she stayed outside and called to him through the door: she'd made him some fresh apple pie; she had filled three books of Top Value stamps. They could look through the catalog and pick something out for him: a clock radio, a hockey stick, a sled. He wouldn't come out or answer her. She became frantic, at first knocking lightly on the door, then pounding on it—he stuck fingers in his ears, buried his head under the pillow—pleading with him to unlock the door, not to do this to her, he must answer her, weeping finally. He stayed inside until his father came home and found her sitting mutely, in a ball, outside his door. Two hours she'd been like that, while Julian remained on the other side, himself not moving, for fear his will would weaken.

"My parents are coming," he said now, stopping with Luchesca in front of the bunkhouses, hoping to separate from her here. "I need to wait around for them."

Luchesca elevated her eyebrows. They stood out like dark licorice, or horseshoes over a doorway for good-luck. He wondered if she could cast a spell with her eyes under those shadowy arches. His mother had talked to him about the evil eye, all the peasants in Hungary who believed in it, the maid and the cook who worked for her parents in Budapest before the war, how the help would sit with her in the kitchen and tell her stories about hypnotizing squirrels and rabbits to make them dance in the woods together until they dropped dead from exhaustion. In a rare moment of talking about the war, she'd told him that in the camps once she'd had to stand in the snow because she'd hidden a piece of bread, stand without clothes for five hours; in her mind, to keep alive and warm, she'd danced with her brother, as they had before the war at their private school.

"I don't belong here," Luchesca said, and he suddenly had a desire for her to meet his mother. Finally, somebody would understand her. In grade school the kids had called her Mrs. Katz the Bats, and he would pretend not to hear. Later they just ignored her. She never answered the phone or the door, so they would see her only in the sewing room on the way upstairs to Julian's room. She'd look up at them and nod, and they'd say, "Hello, Mrs. Katz," and Julian could hear the silent "Bats" hang in the air. "I'm getting out of here today," Luchesca said. "For good."

They still had another week of camp. It was an eight-week session. Next year they would be eligible to be counselors themselves. Julian had already been told by the director that he was a good prospect. Would he be interested in coming back as a counselor? He'd be paid twelve hundred dollars for the eight-week session. At sixteen years old—he'd be seventeen next year—it was more money than he had ever imagined making. He didn't want to do anything to jeopardize the job. "I think you should finish the time out," he said.

"And I think you should come with me." They walked down to the woods behind the bunkhouses. He'd known they would wind up here. He could smell the septic system and wished they could go sit by the lake. Karen had invited him earlier to take out a canoe with her. They just had to let the head counselor know they would be going and wear life jackets. The idea was that unlike home, they could do anything here. Swim, climb, even—why not—become a surgeon like the doctor. "Restrictions" was the only dirty word. Did this include sex too? He thought not.

Luchesca unbuttoned her wine-colored leather vest. Underneath were small white breasts with dark nipples. She was skinny, and he could see her ribs and her bony shoulders—and the incision that began above her waist and ran down her leg. Her nipples hardened in the breeze through the pine trees. She leaned over and put her tongue deep in his mouth. She tugged impatiently at the button of his shorts, unzipped them, and rubbed her flat hand against his penis through his underwear. He heard himself being paged on the loudspeaker. Come to the main office. He pulled away. Luchesca, breathing hard, told him to hurry, there was time, but he got up, zipping his pants over his erection and hoping it would subside by the time he reached the office.

His mother and father were waiting for him outside the camp office. His mother! She'd made it up here after all. "Hi!" he said, running toward them. "It's great to see you." They seemed taken aback by his good spirits, as if they'd expected to find him depressed, homesick, resentful (he'd been reluctant to come here). Instead, he was jubilant, as though he'd built the camp himself. He took them on a tour.

His mother had overdressed—tan slacks and a wool sweater. She'd at least taken off her raincoat, slung it over her arm. Chronically cold, she kept the wadded newspapers in her shoes even in summer. Julian tried to ignore the sound while they all walked to the obstacle course. ("You climb that?" His father whistled about the series of ropes that crisscrossed between trees.) He was determined not to let his mother's fears contaminate him here, diminish the satisfaction he'd taken in his achievement. He'd swum in the lake, paddled a canoe alone. He'd climbed a twenty-foot rock face, using hand and toe holds. He'd flown through the air in a harness. He'd been passed atop the shoulders of his fellow campers, his eyes closed, trusting they wouldn't let him fall—and if they did, so what? He'd get up. He'd crashed through a tower of boxes—blocks for big kids!

Julian told them everything he'd done (except losing his virginity), and they marveled, his mother sighing and saying, "You must be careful. Do you have a supervisor for this?" but he could tell from her voice that it excited her too, made him heroic, and he took her hand

and pulled her along toward the lake, so grateful that she'd made the trip.

They ate lunch with all the other parents and kids, at the long pine table in the dining hall, with its high, exposed rafters. Karen's parents, Mr. and Mrs. Leward, sat with them. Julian's father and Mr. Leward talked about their respective drugstores. Even his mother talked! She asked Mrs. Leward several questions about their oldest daughter, who was attending the University of Wisconsin in Madison. Julian's aunt Tula, his father's sister and the only relative who visited them regularly, had been to Madison on her travels and spoken highly about the place. It was, for Julian, the most normal meal of his life—lunch with other people, his mother making conversation, and underneath it all, everybody knew. There was nothing to hide. Every person in here knew about his epilepsy, and he knew about theirs.

The head counselor stood on a chair and tapped a knife against a glass for quiet. The counselor needed to make several announcements. The schedule listing the small workshops for parents and children was posted on the bulletin board at Cramer Hall and also in the main office. For those parents staying after six P.M., there would be a cookout at the lake. Any parents wishing a private conference with their child's counselor should see Jim Mahoney at Cramer Hall to sign up. And yes, one more announcement: Aren't these kids the greatest bunch of winners you ever saw!

The hall broke into thunderous applause, the parents giving their children a standing ovation. Julian's father leaned over and shouted in his ear, "You should never forget this!"

After lunch, Karen's parents had to leave to make a flight to Wisconsin to see their other daughter. "You must come over to visit us sometime," said Mrs. Leward. "We're only a couple miles away and never knew about each other!" Karen stood between them. She had on blue tights and a Camp Tu-Wa-Ka T-shirt. Her hair, which had dried from swimming before lunch, fanned across her shoulders like a gold harp. While their parents said goodbye, she whispered to Julian,

"I really like your parents. They're so gentle," and she squeezed his hand. She was, he thought, beyond good, almost saintly. Her epilepsy, unlike his, seemed something Christlike to make her human and to know suffering. As she stood alongside his own mother, he tried to imagine how two people so utterly different—one who never went out next to one who experienced the world as a big, joyful playground, one who had lost her self in a human slaughterhouse beside one who could have been queen of the May float—could stand next to each other and not explode on contact?

They all walked back to the camp's entrance. At the turn where the path led off to the bunkhouses, Luchesca sat on a wooden bench, reading her fat book on Italian history. He hoped for a moment that they could pass by without her noticing. He even turned his back to her and walked sideways along the path. But Karen stopped to inquire politely, How are you, Luchesca? We didn't see you at lunch. Luchesca, this is my mother and father. It didn't matter that Luchesca loathed her; Karen could not control her bubbly enthusiasm and kindness any more than Luchesca could her contempt and despair. Luchesca said not a single word, not a peep of acknowledgment, and Mr. Leward soon withdrew his extended hand, left suspended in space. Mrs. Leward likewise retrieved her smile, as Luchesca stared at Julian, only at him, and it was plain for all to see that something was very wrong and it had to do with sex and even Karen—trusting, innocent, unquestionably virginal Karen, an unearthly beauty who might as well have had a sign hanging from her that said THIS PROPERTY PROTECTED BY GOD, DO NOT MOLEST—knew that they'd done it and Luchesca had some rights here. Everyone waited, while her eyes pried into him like the tines of two delicate shrimp forks and demanded some explanation. What did she want from him? What in the world did she expect?

He turned and walked away, and soon he could hear the others following after him, conversation returning, an aberrant moment passing. Strange girl, the Lewards were probably thinking, the darker side of this disorder, glad our Karen isn't afflicted like that; what did that look mean? his own mother and father might be wondering; nothing I do makes her like me, Karen would say if she could admit to such concerns; but he himself, he'd just plain snubbed her, abandoned her, strolled off with his and Karen's parents while her foster parents were God knows where, and he felt nothing but guilt burnished into relief.

After their parents had left, he spent the rest of the afternoon boating with Karen. When dinner was finished, there were relay races. Each runner had to grab a bowling pin, a kerchief, a Frisbee, a carton of eggs, a water balloon, and five other items, then turn in a circle three times, do a jumping jack, wiggle the hips, bow, run back, and pass the whole armload to a teammate in line. Julian was the last to go. The cheering—his team was ahead—became deafening as he squeezed a lightbulb under his arm and gripped a squishy bunch of grapes under his neck and did his jumping jack, hip wiggle, and bow, then raced back to his line and sat down with his team, their hands shooting up in victory. Karen, on his team, in the thrill of winning, kissed him on the mouth. He would indeed marry her and live in the suburbs of Baltimore, merging their fathers' drugstores and growing prosperous and old with her.

Sometime after this, before it became too dark to see and they would have to use their flashlights to walk back to their cottages, an announcement came over the PA system for all counselors to report to the main office. Word got around that Luchesca was missing, and Julian had a moment of hesitation about whether he should reveal her whereabouts. Finally, he went to the office and said that they'd find her at Melk's. She often went there for a Coke. But he was surprised to hear that they knew this and had known it and had already checked out the place and Luchesca wasn't there. Where else did he think she could be? they asked him.

He didn't know. He'd been so sure they would find her there that it hadn't even occurred to him that she might really be missing.

Everybody turned out to search the camp, moving in groups of three, Karen and a boy named Harlan from New York in Julian's group. "I feel as if this is my fault," said Karen. "I should have been more sensitive when we stopped to talk to her," she went on, as they pushed their way through some sticker bushes, scratching their arms and legs.

About an hour later, one of the counselors reported that she'd been found, down by the obstacle and ropes course. She was sitting in the dark on top of Big Mac—the nickname they'd given the telephone pole that one had to climb and stand on, all of eight inches in diameter, before leaping for a trapeze six feet away. Julian hadn't done it; nor had many of the other campers. Though you were attached to a safety rope, it was still the most frightening part of the course: crouching shakily on the top of a telephone pole, standing up, and then jumping into thin air to grab a trapeze. It was that gap, that empty, blank space between letting go and holding on, that stopped most of them.

Flashlights shone up into Luchesca's face. She sat there, immobile. Was she dead? So still, so implacable, so refusing. She would not climb down. If someone came up for her, she would jump. She would jump all the way down and kill herself. Stay where you are. She made this very clear, and no one moved.

An hour passed, with the head counselor trying to talk her down. She disliked him, she said. She wanted him to know that she disliked his camp too. It wasn't fair to treat people as if they were rats in a maze, put them through these silly obstacle courses, give them all these pep talks, all this phony inspiring nonsense about what precious people they were inside and then turn them loose in a world that laughed at them. Do you have any *idea?* she said.

About what? somebody called out.

She didn't answer. For a moment, in the beams of light, her dark face with its rusty tuft of hair looked sadly wise, as if she were pitying *them* but was unable to redeem them from way up there.

She stood up. Twenty, forty, fifty flashlights followed after her, their unsteady beams flooding her in light as she turned in a complete circle and then faced them again.

She lifted her leg. Her hands smoothed themselves along her calf and thigh, as if in a striptease. She was going to shed her clothes for them—but no, it wasn't to be that; it was much worse. Her hands stopped at the top of her legging and unrolled it, while she balanced on her other leg. The scars glimmered like tiny silver fish in the flashlights; there was a collective hiss of shock. She held the limp legging in her hand and, like a bridal bouquet, tossed it down to them. Everyone jumped back as if a snake had landed.

Think about what you're doing, Luchesca! pleaded the head counselor. Please!

But she'd already put her arms out, stretched them toward the trapeze, to the heavens, to the night sky, to her home country, to her dead parents, to Julian, now so far away.

Part Four

sonainnu

Chapter Ten

MORE THAN ONCE CELIA HAD THOUGHT, THIS IS ALL JULIAN'S FAULT. It was wrong to speak unwell of the dead, but she was furious at him. If he'd given her a chance, he wouldn't have been hit by that train.

The whole class had found out about the accident on the morning of the final exam. Right away, Celia knew something must be wrong: Professor Kels had come to class and stood shakily in front of them. She usually sat on the edge of the table and joked around for a few minutes to get them awake and ready to listen. And she'd always managed to appear neat in the mornings, wearing a dress or slacks and a sweater with a necklace. She'd wear makeup too, and her hair was always just washed.

But on the morning of the exam, Professor Kels's hair was mussed and tangled at the ends. She wore no lipstick, and her lips were white. Her eyes were puffy and red, from the cold or crying or not sleeping—Celia didn't know. When she opened her mouth to speak, she stopped and excused herself, taking a tissue from her bag and wiping her nose. "I'm sorry to tell you that Julian died last night when he was struck by a train." She looked down at the tests that she was holding. "Under the circumstances, we won't be having an in-class final, as planned. You may take the exam home and return it to the economics office by noon tomorrow." Then she hurried out, explaining that she was sorry, but she had to go immediately. She left the stack of exams for them on the table.

Celia sat in shock, as did the others. She didn't remember much else about the morning, except that she went home and stayed in bed for the rest of the day and tried to figure out how it had happened. The newspaper said that the engineer had seen Julian trying to cross the tracks just before the train approached the intersection. Julian might have slipped on a piece of ice, or misjudged the train's speed of twenty-five miles an hour. The engineer had tried but couldn't stop in time. Julian had died upon impact.

A day later, after Celia had somehow managed to turn in her exam, the rumors started. Maureen Kels had left town immediately after grading the exams. She wasn't coming back for the spring semester. Or coming back at all. She'd quit or been dismissed or was headed for California, pregnant. Finally, there was the most unbelievable rumor of all: *Julian* had gotten Maureen pregnant. Near the end of the semester, Maureen had started wearing baggy clothes. There had been whispering among the class that she looked pregnant and who might it be, which faculty member? But Julian . . . ridiculous! And unfair. The accusation angered Celia, because Julian wasn't around now to defend himself. Supposedly a boy in their class, someone who lived near Maureen's apartment, had seen the two of them walking out of her building early one morning.

Then other things started to add up. There was Julian's abrupt departure from her farm at Thanksgiving. After she came back, he avoided her; he put her off in class, promising he'd call her but never doing so. And once, Celia had asked Maureen a question after class, and Maureen had been brusque, a bit irritated with her—telling her to look up the information in the library; surely Celia was smart enough to do that. Celia had passed it off at the time to Maureen's just being in a bad mood, but now she wondered if it fit into an overall pattern.

All she knew for sure was that Julian shouldn't have been wandering around at that time of night, and she intended to find out why he was.

There was a memorial service in the small nonsectarian chapel at the university. Celia stood up and said how smart and kind Julian was, and how he cared about others and went out of his way to help them. She didn't mention the meat-out, but she thought of him sitting next to her and looking as confused as she was about what they were doing there. Other students took a turn at the service, saying they had liked Julian and wished they'd gotten to know him better. They were going to miss him. Gaylon had come into town, his first time back since the branding. He gave a fiery and inappropriate speech about Julian being a radical at heart, a crusader: once again the world had lost one of its best fighters. The branding hadn't, Celia decided, made Gaylon humble. If anything, he now had the credential of martyrdom and would probably become even more shrill and obnoxious in his protests. His life had been only threatened, ultimately spared. She had the terrible thought that it should have been him instead of Julian who'd died. She found herself glaring at him while he talked.

She turned away and forced herself to look up at the altar, tastefully arranged with a blue velvet cloth and white orchids. On it was a picture that she'd taken of Julian at her family's table on Thanksgiving. She'd put his green jacket up there, too, and a few of his textbooks, and a letter from his mother that Celia had found on his desk. She'd collected it all from his apartment, going there with Dr. Kaplan, who was seeing that Julian's belongings were packed up and shipped home. When she had called the police for more information, they'd referred her to Dr. Kaplan. Celia told him about the memorial service she wanted to organize and asked him to invite Julian's parents. Understandably, they'd been too upset and caught up with their own funeral arrangements to fly out. Julian's father had sent a check as a donation to the small chapel. Did the things on the table add up to Julian? She didn't know, but she'd tried to make it be somebody specific, a person she thought she knew and had wanted to know better, whom she had thought of much more, she realized, than he had ever thought of her.

Dr. Kaplan stood up to speak now. He introduced himself as a friend of Julian's and explained that he was here on behalf of Julian's parents as well as himself. He wanted everyone to know how much Julian's mother and father appreciated this service. They were touched by it, by the caring it showed for their son. He paused a second, then said that he had known Julian for a while and during that time had become very fond of him. He wished Julian could have seen his classmates here today. It would have pleased him to know that so many people would miss him. Julian's good heart and keen intelligence would not go unremembered. It was hard to mourn someone so young—there was so much pain, frustration, and searching for a reason—but he hoped a service like this could be the beginning of a healing process. On behalf of Julian's parents and himself, he wanted again to thank Celia for organizing the memorial and everyone for being here.

To close the service, Celia read a poem, "No Coward Soul Is Mine," by Emily Brontë. She'd never read a poem to a group before. Nervous, she started off too fast, but she slowed down when she came to the last two stanzas:

> "Though Earth and moon were gone
> And suns and universes ceased to be
> And thou wert left alone
> Every Existence would exist in thee."

She looked up. People were attentive. It wasn't silly. She went on.

> "There is not room for Death
> Nor atom that his might could render void
> Since thou art Being and Breath,
> And what thou art may never be destroyed."

She waited a moment at the end, then closed her literature text and thanked everyone for coming. With Dr. Kaplan, she stood at the door to shake people's hands as they departed.

After the service, she went out for coffee with him.

Snow flurries had started outside, and Celia watched the traffic moving slowly through Pierre's main street. It was December 16; usually she'd be home in Alamosa by now. But she wasn't even packed yet and wasn't sure if she'd go today or even tomorrow. Things felt incomplete, unfinished here, despite her classes being through, her exams finished, her roommate gone, the service over. She'd expected to have more of a feeling of completion, once the memorial was done. Organizing the service and notifying people before they left for the holidays, getting the class to pitch in for flowers, shopping for a dress, finding an appropriate poem to read, all this had distracted her for the past week. But now she felt emptier than ever.

They walked to the coffee shop, three blocks from the chapel. On the way, they crossed Central, and she looked down the block at the West Martin intersection, where the accident had happened. She saw Dr. Kaplan looking too, but neither of them said anything.

They found a quiet table in the corner, and both ordered tea. Dr. Kaplan told her she'd done a fine job of organizing the service. He'd been moved by her talk and reading, and he could see that Julian had meant a lot to her.

She knew he was a psychologist, and he admitted on the walk over that he'd been Julian's therapist, not just his "friend," but what she really wanted to know was about Julian and Maureen. Was it true?

"Did Julian ever mention anything about his economics professor?" Celia asked him now.

He looked out the window. He had his hand around his tea mug, but he had yet to drink any. She'd once run into Maureen in this coffee shop. Celia had said hi and then not bothered her. She didn't want to be a pest. In class, Maureen had never seemed to treat Julian any differently from the other students. Everybody thought she was interested in Gaylon, if anyone, the way they would joke back and forth during class.

"I guess this is putting you in an awkward position," said Celia when he was slow to respond.

"I wish I could answer, but it's confidential information."

"But Julian is dead. Why would it matter now about anything that was said? Does confidentiality apply after the person dies too?"

"Yes and no," said Dr. Kaplan.

Something about the way he drew out "no" made Celia think there was more to the story. She took a sip of her tea. "Do you *know* Professor Kels?"

He stared at her blankly, no change in his expression. She'd never been to a psychologist, but she imagined this was the way they acted when you asked them a direct question they didn't want to answer— as if it were your problem.

"I know that she was Julian's teacher for environmental economics," he said matter-of-factly, adding nothing more.

"Did you know if he was having an affair with her?"

"Celia," said Dr. Kaplan, and she could tell by the way he said her name—sort of concerned but more as if he were drawing a line in the sand—that he did know a lot more than he was saying. "Is there anything else I can say to you to help?"

He looked tired himself, bags under his eyes. His hand was unsteady when he finally lifted the teacup to his lips. A pang of concern for him hit her; he'd been Julian's therapist, after all. She couldn't imagine what it would be like to have your client die.

But he didn't seem angry about it, as she did. Or maybe he already knew the truth about everything, so it didn't dig away at him as much. If she could at least find out what exactly had happened, she could eat and sleep better again, begin to let it all go.

"I'm really upset about all this . . . ," she said, and started to cry. Stupid tears. Of course she was upset; who wasn't? She didn't want to cry now. She wanted to find out things. Crying wouldn't help, especially around a therapist; he'd certainly seen boatloads of people cry. She didn't want him to think, either, that she was manipulating him into telling her anything. Yet she had a right to know. "Would you tell me one thing?"

Dr. Kaplan rubbed his forehead. She saw that this was more than he had expected, that perhaps he regretted coming here. He'd overseen the autopsy and signed the papers to have the body shipped back. That must have been hard enough, without her grilling him too. "If I can," he said.

"Why was Julian walking around at three in the morning?"

"I can't say, Celia. I don't know."

"What did you tell the police?"

"I'm sorry, Celia." He looked out the window. "I think you know I can't go into that."

She put another packet of sugar in her tea; it was what she'd subsisted on during the past week, tea and sugar. She didn't want to make Dr. Kaplan angry. Rather, she wanted him to like her, because he had been Julian's therapist, someone who had gotten inside him, and this connection to Julian was all she had left right now.

She had one other question. "Did Julian get Professor Kels pregnant?"

"What?" He looked genuinely shocked by this information. His whole face seemed to tighten; his cheeks reddened.

He looked so disbelieving, in fact, that she herself doubted now that it could be true. "It's only a rumor," said Celia.

"Oh," he said, as if greatly relieved. His hands relaxed around his cup.

"I guess you don't know where Maureen Kels is now?" asked Celia. She'd called the M. Kels listed in the phone book, but service had been disconnected. Then she'd tried to get the economics department to give her Maureen's forwarding address, but they wouldn't. It was so hush-hush that she knew they were trying to hide something. If she liked Gaylon a little more, she would have gotten him to dig up the truth. He'd announced to her—at the memorial service, of all places—that he was going to be a lawyer, as if the world should be thrilled.

She was angry at everyone.

The truth was she was most angry at Julian. He should have let her help him, and it made her wonder what was so wrong with her that he didn't, or couldn't.

"I have no idea where she is," said Dr. Kaplan, indicating nothing else about how he felt.

Celia asked if she could walk with him a little bit. She didn't want to be alone, couldn't go back just yet to her empty apartment. Whether she would even return to school next semester she wasn't sure. She kept telling herself she shouldn't let it bother her as much as it did. She'd only brought Julian home for Thanksgiving and sat next to him in class and kissed him good night once—what was the big deal? She'd slept with boys whom she cared about less, much less. That was the part she couldn't explain to herself.

More than a head taller, Dr. Kaplan slowed himself down when walking beside her. Like her, he was dark-complected. He wore a burgundy tie under his gray sweater and kept his jacket unzipped, though it had turned cold. She wore only a blue blazer, which she pulled tight around her. For the service, she'd found an almost black dress, which she'd worn with matching hose. She hadn't been sure what she should wear, how short or how long, how tight or what color. Even with her big family, she'd been to just one funeral, her grandmother's, and that had been years ago, when she was a child. Nor had she wanted to look too morbid, so she'd put a peach-colored headband on and three silver-and-turquoise bracelets that had belonged to her grandmother.

Dr. Kaplan asked her now if she was cold. He offered his coat, but she refused it. She just wanted to walk; the cold took her mind off things, forced her to remember that her skin was alive.

"Can I ask you something else?" Celia said. The snow squeaked under their boots. Shoppers were out in full force, nine days until Christmas, maneuvering gifts into open car trunks. She should be shopping herself; her family always drew names, and she'd gotten her oldest brother's this time—but she liked to buy extra presents for her littlest nieces and nephews. Her family would only sort of understand her feelings, and she herself wouldn't know how to explain them any more clearly. After all, she hadn't been Julian's girlfriend, had she? they would ask. No, she hadn't. He'd only come to her house for Thanksgiving. There wasn't anything more serious between them, was there? No, there wasn't. She shouldn't be so upset about it, then. So why did it feel as if leaving town meant she was deserting him? "Was Julian Jewish?"

"Yes," said Dr. Kaplan.

"I thought so," and she told him about what she'd been thinking lately. She hadn't known many other Jews, but she always felt—it sounded silly, but it was true—that she might be one. She'd read an article once about Mexicans who lit candles on Friday night and made a blessing over bread, and other Mexicans who used separate dishes for dairy and meat in their house, and this one family where all the men wore hats when they read the Bible, and the crazy thing was that they had no idea why. None of these families knew each other, but they all had these peculiar—that is, peculiarly Jewish—customs in common, which they went on practicing without being Jewish. Some-body had the theory that it was because they had been Jews in hiding, a long time ago during the Inquisition, Sephardic Jews who had over the generations forgotten their heritage but continued to practice traces of their customs, as if by instinct. She'd read the magazine article five times and then gone to the library and looked up everything about Sephardic Jews.

"I've heard about that," Dr. Kaplan said, "but I'm just wondering why you might be thinking about it now."

She was going to tell him that she liked the way Jewish people could complain without making it sound awful, just funny. She wished she could make complaining seem funny. "Are you Jewish?" she asked him instead.

"Yes," he said.

They'd reached Skookum Park. There was a Christmas village set up, little houses with frosted windows and ivy wreaths on the doors. The miniature homes glowed inside. Elves worked on toys, and red-cheeked doll families sat peacefully around a hearth, opening presents. She stopped to look in at the reindeer barn. Prancer and Dancer and Rudolph stood decked out for a sleigh ride.

He stopped and turned toward her. "I'm sorry," he said. "I'm sorry that Julian didn't take your friendship more seriously. I think it would have made a difference in his life."

And then she started to cry, because all this stuff about being Jewish wasn't really about being Jewish. How could it be? Nobody in her house said a blessing over the beer, nobody wore a hat except to keep the sun off, and although her family used two sets of dishes, one was plastic and one was the good stuff, with pictures of the saints on it. What she wanted to say was that this whole thing about being Jewish wasn't about being Jewish, it was about loving Julian. She had thought they were alike inside. She would never get a chance to tell him that now.

She took Dr. Kaplan's hand. As soon as she did, she realized it was okay. He squeezed her hand back and held on, as if he needed something from her too. And she knew that they were the only ones around who were grieving about Julian and, for a moment before saying good-bye, living through him.

Chapter Eleven

CAP AND HIS FATHER HELD UP THE HUPPAH ON ONE SIDE WHILE TWO OF Joan's brothers supported the other end. Underneath stood Joan and Allan, reciting in Hebrew after the rabbi: *Baruh ata Adonai, Eloheynu meleh haolam, borey p'ri hagafen.* First Joan drank from the cup of wine, then Allan. The rabbi, who was from Joan's synagogue in Haverford, motioned for them to come closer. "I've performed many weddings in my years," the rabbi said, taking Allan's and Joan's clasped hands in his own. "But this is one of the most satisfying occasions for me. I've had the opportunity to know Allan for only a short while, though in the brief time we've spoken, he's impressed me with his gentleness, courage, and quiet wisdom.

"I have known Joan since she was a little girl, since she would come see me in my office and recite her aleph-beth, a precocious, wonderfully bright and spirited child. I remember once saying to my wife, we have a young girl in the congregation who will someday be a rabbi—so quick a learner, so beautiful a voice." The rabbi stopped and looked down. Muffled noise came from Joan's mother's kitchen, where the caterer was at work. "We are among friends and loving relatives, so I feel I can speak freely here. When I saw this same gifted child struck by an illness for which we have no exact explanations, an illness so depriving and disfiguring to the mind that it breaks the strongest parent's heart, I questioned my faith in God."

The rabbi paused, raised his head again, and squeezed Joan's hand. "I say this because I could not understand what kind of trick this was, what kind of God would amuse himself with such terrible afflictions to his creations, what kind of God would take the brightest, prettiest, most life-giving and loving members of a people and shut them away in a dark world of fear and mistrust, strangers now to even their own parents.

"I cannot say I had some revelation about why this happened. I cannot say I accepted that this was the will of God. I cannot say that these experiences made sense to me as part of our suffering that helps us know God. I cannot say I became wiser for watching a transformation that made me witness a broken mind and behold the fragility of a young child's spirit. What I can say is this: We lived through it. We are here now. We witnessed happiness reawaken. In the chamber of these two people's hearts another sound has been heard, and that is the sound of joy. We can carry our anger and bitterness with us. We can ask, Why them and not us? Or why them and not my enemy? Most of all, why to children who have done nothing but try to grow up? Why again and again? Or we can say we will honor the source of this miracle. We will mourn the past. We will not forget, but we will have our joy too. We will live under God's gaze and make a joyous noise unto him. Our children have been given back to us today."

The rabbi stopped. Cap's mother wiped her eyes with a tissue. His father bowed his head. Joan's mother leaned on her youngest son's arm, her chin trembling. Joan's oldest brother, standing in for their dead father, pushed his glasses up on his nose. Farther back in the living room were Joan's two cousins and her three-year-old niece, who whispered loudly, "Why is everybody crying?" Allan had invited Everett Oost and his son, Cho. L. They both worked with Allan at Cap's father's business. They'd brought their families, these black people who stood around the huppah, murmuring "Amen," after the rabbi finished, and "Amen" again; and dabbing at their own eyes.

Wallis cried too, holding Claude in her arms.

Cap felt his own throat go dry. It was his turn to speak. He was to read from a short speech that he'd written, congratulating his brother and Joan. Sweat poured into his shirt under his suit. He always sweated when he had to read anything—he shvitzed, as his father would say. The rabbi turned to him. "Allan's brother, Cap, has something he'd like to say to the wedding couple."

Everett Oost and his son leaned forward to hear. Allan and Joan and Cap's father and mother and all of his new in-laws and Wallis and Claude (the first time he'd witnessed his father speaking in public) all waited.

He took out the folded piece of paper from his jacket pocket. He saw the words that he'd scribbled on the plane. What an honor . . . the pleasure of being here . . . the long, steep path that has brought you each heart to heart . . . wishing you a fine marriage . . . much happiness . . . looking forward to knowing our new family . . .

Wallis reached over and put her hand on his. He hadn't realized how much his hands had been shaking.

"I have a few remarks which I *won't* read," said Cap, to the laughter of the small group. The truth was he hadn't liked what he'd written, though he'd struggled over it. He folded the paper and put it back in his pocket. "This wedding commemorates, like all great rituals, the division of the old from the new. I have to admit to being stuck in between, in all the newness of this, resting momentarily in the doorway, but I'm making my way slowly across this threshold, with enormous anticipation and excitement. For two people like Allan and Joan to find each other is, of course, a dream come true. But it is also a dream for the rest of us, a dream that wakes us up to possibilities in life we could only imagine before. We celebrate your courage and your healing. Mazel tov to you both."

Everyone murmured approval. It had been honest, for which he was grateful, his discarded remarks insipid and at best obligatory, but he worried now that he'd introduced a moment of doubt, with his talk of hesitation, into an otherwise triumphant occasion.

The rabbi thanked him and then asked Allan and Joan to bow their heads.

"The Lord bless you from Zion. May you live to see your children's children. May we hear again in the streets of Jerusalem joyous voices, voices of bride and bridegroom. *Y'vareh'ha Adonai mitzion, ure'ey b'tuv yerushalayim, kol y'mey hayeha.*" Allan raised his foot and smashed the glass, to loud applause.

Allan wouldn't go near the water. Not that it was any big deal. Some six-year-olds were afraid of water, of swimming. But Allan screamed, shrieked, every time they even tried to get his feet wet or have him sit at the edge of a lake. Water didn't just bother him, it terrified him, and after the first day he would stay up by the pine-shaded picnic area, not come down to the lake at all.

"This water business isn't working out," said his father, a kind of apology to Cap, who loved swimming and fishing and could spend hours jumping waves at the beach. "We'll see other sights." And sure enough, on their way up Route 1 to Maine, they'd started seeing signs for "The Thing." Don't miss it! the signs said. Only twenty more miles. And by the time they'd driven half that distance, they were seeing billboards every mile, advertising "Unforgettable! Amazing! Shocking! Don't pass by *The Thing.*" Cap had wanted to go. His father had said absolutely not; it was a tourist trap and not worth the money. (Money! His parents argued about every cent on the vacation—the new bathing suit for Cap they'd had to buy in Boston because his old one had been forgotten, the price of a hot dog at Howard Johnson's, his father saying it was a crime. You had to eat, but who could afford these turnpike prices? . . . Money was every second breath the family took.) But Cap insisted. They had to see "The Thing." Maybe because he could finally read passably at ten—way behind the other kids—

and believed everything he did read, he became convinced that this "Thing" was the most important experience of his life and that if he didn't see it he'd miss the whole point of the trip, something really amazing to tell his friends about. Finally, just one mile away, he opened the car door and threatened to jump out unless they stopped. He got his way.

The Thing was in a shack behind a roadside restaurant—a luncheonette that had a counter with swivel seats, pies in glass on metal pedestals, and swami boxes that would tell your fortune for a penny. His parents slid into a booth. Allan was caught up in moving the selection hooks of the jukebox at their table. Something like this could occupy him for an hour or two. He liked dumb tasks where you had to do the same thing over and over. And over. He was clumsy and not much fun to throw a ball to. He didn't even try to catch it but let it hit him in the face or chest, and then he just stared at it, as if it were a strange fruit that had dropped from a tree. Cap didn't care about him now, though. Outside, behind the luncheonette, in a small, windowless shack, was The Thing. You had to go in one at a time. That meant he couldn't take in his dad, who didn't want to see it anyway. It was fine if Cap wanted to go in, but hurry up, they had to find a clean motel before dark. Their mother hated to travel at night.

So Cap went inside the shack. It took a moment for his eyes to get used to the dark, but then he could see a brick wall with a curtain over it. He waited for a moment, not knowing what to do. Should he open up the curtain and peek? Or wait until something happened on its own? He wished his father were here to help him, but his father often made fun of him for his interest in scary stuff.

"Hurry up, Cappie!" his father called from outside. Cap looked at the curtain. Why not. If he didn't pull it back, he'd have nothing to tell Robbie Goldman and Lewis Klein. They collected horror magazines, too, and watched all the movies. Lewis's parents even let him have a subscription to *Gore*, a really raunchy magazine, with monsters' heads cut open and black pus and carbuncles festering on the wounds.

It was sickening—they'd pretend to puke—but they looked at the magazines together for hours.

He parted the curtain.

When he went home, he didn't mention The Thing to Lewis Klein or Robbie Goldman. He didn't tell them anything, except that he'd had an okay time. And when Lewis Klein brought over the latest issue of *Gore*, with pictures of a ten-foot lizard who drooled sticky, hot acid that burned through your flesh and oozed into your bones, Cap said he wasn't interested anymore. Monsters were boring; they were for little kids. He went outside and whomped a rubber ball against the wall. Upstairs, Allan watched him from the window, crouched down so just his eyes looked over the sill. He knelt like that, watching, until it made Cap feel too creepy. He wished his brother would do more stuff like other kids his age. Not stay in the house so much and peek over windowsills. Not that crazy stuff he'd done at the luncheonette after Cap had gone back inside from seeing The Thing, after his father had asked, "Well, was it worth two bits?" and Cap had shrugged and wouldn't talk about it. He sat down next to his mother in a red vinyl booth. They ordered some food. Then his brother Allan climbed on the table, and before anyone could pull him down, he had stretched out his arms and was looking up at the ceiling. "Save me! Save me!" he shouted. A waitress turned around, and the cook glanced out. A family buying souvenirs all looked over at them. Somebody laughed, maybe the waitress, maybe a customer. Cap couldn't remember. What he did remember was that Allan looked around, as if suddenly realizing where he was, and he became frightened. More than frightened. Both his mother and his father tried to tell him that everything was all right, there was nothing here that was going to harm him, no monsters, no bad people. But Allan just sat on the table, shivering like an animal with a leg in a trap, scared to let anyone touch him, and Cap thought of The Thing, how it had been nothing, just this little tiny mummy, a *child* mummy, and he'd known it wasn't even real. You could see only the eyes (like Allan's peeking over the sill), everything else covered in bandages. Not a child at all, just a doll. But he never could be sure.

Cap stood by the food, sipping champagne. He glanced over at Allan, who was tossing a giggling Claude over his shoulder. Whatever the drug did, it made his brother's spirits irrepressible, as if he were making up for years of entombment. Cap, out of habit, in fixing himself and Allan breakfast this morning (everyone else had been sleeping), had gotten down Allan's orange plastic plate with the molded dividers for his bacon, eggs, and toast (all food had to be separated, nothing could ever touch). "Is that still here?" said Allan. "Throw it in the trash."

"Well, I wouldn't throw it away just yet," said Cap.

"Why not?" asked Allan.

"In case you change your mind."

There was a long silence, and then his brother said, "You don't believe this is real, do you?"

"I just would go slow. Sometimes drugs can be disappointing. They lose their effect, their potency weakens, or, in the case of clozapine, they can endanger your immune system." And perhaps cause death, he thought to himself. Cap looked down at the plastic plate, twirled it in his fingers. He didn't know why he was trying to scare Allan into compliance. It went against every instinct he had to be encouraging.

His brother got up to pour himself a cup of coffee. Another change. He would never drink coffee before; it was too black, and if he mixed it with cream he saw faces in the murky liquid.

"Want ketchup for your omelet?" asked Cap.

"You don't think I know all this?" said Allan; his breathing had quickened. When he got angry, he couldn't control how fast he breathed, and he could faint from hyperventilation. "You don't think it's been explained to me a hundred times by my doctor and my therapist?"

"Take it easy, Allan. It's all right. I'll put it away."

"I don't want you to put it away. I want you to *throw* it away! You, Cap, not me. *You* throw it in the trash."

But at that moment their father had come downstairs, his face sagging, his bones noticeably heavier than when Cap had seen him in Colorado ten months before. He sat at his regular place, in front of the wall clock. Cap watched him and hoped that when he died he would go quickly, without pain. Why couldn't he stop thinking about death today? It was his brother's wedding day; he should be joyful; his father should be joyful. But everyone he looked at seemed tinted with the same sallow, grim light. Was his father worried about Allan? After all these years of taking care of him, was it like losing your only child? His father did seem more fearful lately, more like his mother; they'd started to fuse into a single unit.

Cap had felt a tightness in his throat and turned around to peel the omelet out of the pan. He realized he'd always thought he would be the one to take care of Allan after their parents died or when they were too old to care for his brother. And now Allan might take care of them in their old age, or even Cap himself one day. Anything was possible with this medical miracle. "A hard-boiled egg, Dad?" Cap had asked. His father nodded. When his brother left, he put the orange cafeteria plate with its molded dividers back in the cabinet, high on a shelf that Allan was still unable to reach because he'd always been so much shorter than Cap. Then he took it down again, held it for a moment, and finally dropped the plate in the trash.

The doorbell rang. Cap went to answer it.

"So can I come in?"

It was Cantor Zommick. Cap was speechless. His old nemesis, here at his brother's wedding, come to mourn and nosh. He was notorious for showing up at catered affairs; weddings, bar mitzvahs, funerals, it didn't matter: food was food. "Come in," Cap managed to get out.

He helped the old man over to the table, where the cantor sat down with his cane. He squinted up at Cap, trying to recall who he was—

the memory like a dusty pot deep in a drawer. "So you're doing well?"

"Yes," said Cap, half afraid the cantor would ask him to read.

The cantor poked the handle of his cane forward into Cap's stomach. "Where are you now?"

"I'm out in Colorado."

"Good, good," said the cantor. "You don't have to travel so far."

"Pardon?"

"Collingdale. It's not so far."

Cap smiled. Across the county line. "Yes, you're right."

"Still hearing voices?"

"Voices?"

The cantor crooked his finger for Cap to come closer; Cap leaned down reluctantly into the same sour, smoky breath of thirty years ago. "I hear them too," said the cantor. "It's why you sing like an angel. Don't lose them. Then the angels fly away."

He realized the cantor was confusing him with Allan, who had, in spite of his disorder, read his haftarah with such lyrical grace that he was asked to join the synagogue choir. The cantor had literally wept over the performance. Cap had felt a mixture of pride and abysmal jealousy.

Wallis came up. Cap introduced them. "*You're* Cantor Zommick?" said Wallis. The man had been a myth in their house, Cap regaling her with tales of the imposing personage, who now, in his frail and advanced age (he would have to be in his middle nineties), was a husk of his former self.

"Who else?" said the cantor. "Ah, help me up. Let's see what's to eat before I kiss the bride."

The two families drove into center city to take Allan and Joan to the Bellevue Hotel for their honeymoon. Cap thought it was like being driven to the prom by your parents, but neither Allan nor Joan seemed to mind (Allan had never driven, and Joan experienced night blindness from her medication). If anything, they enjoyed having their families accompany them to their hotel. Everyone sat down in the lobby, while Cap's father helped the couple get checked in—the honeymoon was his wedding gift. It was the first time Allan had ever been away from home overnight without his parents.

"Watch this!" Allan said, and he grabbed Joan around the waist and danced her across the lobby, a fox-trot, a *good* fox-trot, both of them in sync and not stumbling over each other's feet. Joan tossed her head back at the end. Allan came over and asked his mother to dance. She blushed but got up and waltzed across the room with him. "We've been taking lessons!" Allan called over his shoulder. Cap's mother put a hand on her flushed cheek, laughing as Allan twirled her around. He sat her down with a kiss on her cheek, suave, gracious—a son to make any mother proud. "Naomi?" said Allan, extending his hand to Joan's mother, who made an embarrassed wave like an audience member on TV being dragged up to participate. "Oh, please?" said Allan, and coaxed her from behind the coffee table, helping her to do a rusty cha-cha. Afterward she collapsed on the couch next to Cap's mother, both women obviously thrilled by the attention. Allan, shy, reclusive, terrified, was conducting himself like a seasoned social director at a Catskills resort. Cap watched with a mixture of awe and trepidation.

"May I?" It was Joan, asking him to dance. "We can't help but show off what we learned," she said, her face glowing. "And the brother of the groom has to dance with the bride at least once." Her voice, full of bell tones, overcame his reservations about dancing in a public lobby, and he waltzed with her, the staff looking on. She had changed at the house from her wedding gown to a simple beige dress, her new gold ring gleaming on her finger. She was eight years younger than Allan, thirty-one, with fine brown hair and deep-set gray eyes, a thin mouth that would spring open suddenly in a laugh to show bright, white teeth and then, just as abruptly, shut, as if to keep her pleasure in check with watchful solemnity. She was very pretty, Cap thought.

She took his hand. Though he'd tried to put her at ease, she'd been shy of him; mostly it had been Wallis who drew her out and talked easily with her. Joan thanked him, his new sister-in-law curtsying like a young maiden. Touched by her carefulness, her effort to befriend him, he felt his eyes moisten.

Allan came over to Joan and whispered something to her. She recovered her high spirits with a girlish giggle, and Cap had some idea of what they were like alone, how they whispered in private and talked like any couple in love and how his brother made her feel safe.

Reluctantly everyone said goodbye, as if the spell might end and everything switch back. Allan, who had changed into slacks and new loafers, wove his way among the lobby's sofas, shaking hands and thanking everyone for coming. He would lose his virginity tonight, Cap thought. Or maybe that had happened already? Allan, clean-shaven, his wavy brown hair still full, embraced him. They'd all stay in touch and maybe even come out to Colorado. Cap's heart jumped at the possibility, all the old wishes for family, for closeness with his brother, possible now after all these years—if he wanted it.

They drove home along City Line Avenue. Claude, up way past his bedtime, had finally fallen asleep in the backseat.

"Wasn't that beautiful?" asked his mother.

"It was," said Wallis, who looked tired. Claude had been clinging to her the whole time here. Cap himself could barely keep his head up now.

"Joan looked like a dream," said his father.

"She did," said Cap, perfunctorily. He and Wallis, out of habit, were taking turns acknowledging their comments.

"I'm so glad the rabbi could marry them," said his mother, a comment both of them let go by, directed still, after all these years, at Wallis's refusal to convert. Do you care? she had once asked Cap. He had said no. They'd raise Claude like themselves, confused and agnostic.

"I hope they enjoy themselves at the hotel. The place isn't what it used to be."

"Oh?" said Cap, yawning.

"Those poor Legionnaires."

He prepared himself. He knew what was coming. "You'll have to send us pictures of the wedding," said Cap, trying to change the subject to something pleasant.

"It was terrifying what happened to your father," said his mother. She was in the backseat with Wallis and Claude. His father rode up front with him.

His father gripped Cap's arm, like a blood pressure cuff. "The look on her face. You should have seen the hatred."

"Okay," said Cap. "It's late and everyone's tired. We've had a wonderful day. There's no reason we need to talk about this now." His father had been in the hotel during the time of the Legionnaires' convention. He'd been there on unrelated business and had eaten in the coffee shop downstairs. An employee, a redhead who had been busing tables, had given him a nasty look. He later found out she'd worked there only that one day, before being fired. His father's theory—if only it had been a joke!—was that the redhead had poisoned the coffee and caused the illness. He'd offered his views to the Centers for Disease Control officials from Atlanta when they'd interviewed him in the hospital. Never mind that not all the Legionnaires would have drunk the coffee. Never mind that a bacteria in the air-conditioning system had been proved to be the cause.

"Like a witch. I call her Lizzie Borden the Second," said his father, talking about his favorite redhead.

Wallis reached from the backseat and squeezed Cap's shoulder. "You doing okay?" she said. He needed to spend time alone with her; he couldn't stand it much longer, being with his parents constantly. The three days he'd been here felt longer than his whole childhood.

"Your father almost died."

"I know all about it already, Mom. We all do by now."

"I aged a hundred years going through that."

"Right," said Cap.

"I couldn't tell if he was saying hello or taking his last breath. That's how weak your father's voice was."

Cap started whistling. Wallis patted his shoulder more urgently from the backseat. He had thought it would be easier to take this route home, less traffic, but they were getting stopped by every light, and now an ambulance made them pull over. He drove into the parking lot of Denny's, ironically his parents' favorite place to eat.

He put the car in park and turned toward them. "All right, what's the problem? What are we really talking about here?" His voice was tense and low.

"You're upset," said his father. "That we can see. You looked nervous during your speech. Everybody gets nervous. No big deal. Nobody noticed."

"This isn't about my speech! It's about your schizophrenic son, who's been dependent on you all his life and couldn't tie his shoes in a bow because the loops would strangle him and who almost burned down the house by setting fire to the couch—"

"That was your fault. You should have stayed home—"

"Forget about fault! Think about us all being honest for once. You expect me to believe that this crap about some witch being responsible for Legionnaires' disease is what you're upset about now?"

"You should have seen her, Cappie, that look—"

"Please," he said, almost crying from exhaustion. "Please listen to yourselves. This is about Allan. Allan and Joan. It's about them living with the threat of losing this new life. Can't we admit that's what's going on here instead of believing it has to do with being lost in the wilderness on the way to airports or with evil redheads spiking coffee?"

"Airport?" his mother asked. "You're going home early?"

"What's he talking about?" said his father. "You're working too hard, son. You're seeing too many funny-paper people in your office."

"Don't you think he needs to take a rest, Wallis, darling?"

"Please get out," said Wallis.

"What?"

"I would like you both to get out of the car so Cap and I can have a minute alone to talk. You can go sit in Denny's and have coffee."

"It's too late. Even the decaffeinated keeps you awake at this hour."

"I will count to three, and then I am going to walk home with Claude down City Line Avenue on a Sunday night by ourselves. If you are not out of the car by then, you will be responsible for whatever happens to us."

He stared into the parking lot, his wrists dangling over the top of the steering wheel. They were somewhere near Overbrook Park, though he couldn't tell exactly how close. His old college girlfriend Susan had lived around here. He wondered what she was doing now, whether she'd ever married Sam the sammy and moved into a mansion on the Main Line. Whenever he imagined living out here, Cap always thought of her house, with its back and front staircases, a symbol of wealth to him, as his father's rows of broken vending machines represented toil. He'd never be from that class. He could almost imagine being married to her now, his office in a high-rise downtown in Society Hill. He would have become a psychiatrist, a "real" doctor, to please her, prescribed drugs, and saved his patients—not clients, but patients. The whole profession was becoming drugs anyway. Biochemical engineers with hotshot diagnostic labs and gobs of brain mapping. He would soon be obsolete. Hadn't clozapine saved Allan? Enabled him to get married? So what if his family, with their talk of Legionnaires' disease and demons in the bowels of the Bellevue Stratford making coffee-flavored witches' brew, acted schizophrenic themselves? It was all a genetic glitch, his whole family, a chemical aberrancy.

"I'm feeling so goddamn bitter," he said to Wallis. "I shouldn't have yelled at them like that. They're such children. I keep forgetting." She had moved up front next to him after his parents went inside. Claude lay in her lap, awake again now from all the raised voices—he wasn't used to this at home—but happy, looking up through the windshield at the parking lot lights, sucking his thumb and swinging his foot loosely between the two of them. Cap, restored to them, relaxed a little.

"Don't be so hard on yourself," said Wallis. "It's difficult enough to come home, let alone under these extraordinary circumstances."

"You seem to be able to make the best of it."

"They're not my parents and not my brother. And you're right, I'm scared to death for Allan out there, for both of them."

Cap shook his head. "You know, clozapine has its own problems —drowsiness, drooling, constipation, weight gain, increased heart rate, occasionally dizziness or seizures." He stopped short at seizures. He had been unable to think of Julian without freezing up, some fiercely lethal combination of sadness and guilt over having failed the boy. "And he could develop agranulocytosis—either of them could."

"What's that?" asked Wallis. He had been holding back telling her this, hoping they'd decide not to get married, put off the wedding until they were on the drug longer, adjusted, or didn't adjust.

"The bone marrow loses its ability to make white blood cells for the immune system. Infection and hemorrhaging become a risk. If the blood cell count drops too low, they have to get off the drug. Back to square one."

Wallis shook her head. "Your parents know all this?"

"Of course they do. They had to be told about it. Allan and Joan have to be monitored and take blood tests every week. At least I hope they do."

"Well, let's hope, too, they never have to face that situation."

He could see his parents inside Denny's, cupping their hands against the plate-glass window to see out to the car. As though they might be able to tell if he and Wallis were finished. Wallis had instructed them, in her best junior-high teacher's voice, to remain inside until they were called.

"My father took me to a movie here one time," said Cap. The theater was long gone. Thirty-five years ago, it had been on the site of Denny's. "I was nine years old. It was a matinee, and Allan was sick with the flu at home, and my father said, 'Why don't we go see a Western?' I was amazed. He hardly ever did anything with me alone. So we went down to the theater. It was *Rio Bravo*, with John Wayne. When I sat down, a nickel dropped out of my pocket. It rolled under the seats—all the way down. My father said, 'Get that nickel.' He made the usher shine his flashlight in the first row so I could find the nickel. It was dark. The previews had already started. The theater was packed. It was only a nickel. If anybody in town shouldn't miss a nickel, it would be him, with his vending machines full of change. But there I was, down on my hands and knees, with bubble gum and spilled soda sticking to my palms, with stale popcorn crunching under my knees, with kids kicking me in the face. All for that goddamn nickel."

"Did you find it?"

"Of course I found it. I had to. I suppose he did it to teach me the value of a nickel. But you know what? It just taught me to hate him."

"He couldn't help himself," said Wallis. "Just like tonight, with the witch cooking up a big cauldron of Legionnaires' disease. They're primitives. They have to ward off the evil eye. Losing a nickel can start a whole chain of unpleasant events, nickels coming loose everywhere."

"Lose a nickel, find a Cossack. I think that's the saying."

Wallis laughed. "Is it?"

"No," said Cap. "But it might as well be in my family." His stomach had loosened as he listened to her voice. "How come you're so smart about my family?"

"Because they're not my family," she said with a laugh. "I just thought of something. Does all this have to do with Allan getting better? Does it scare you that he's no longer sick? I know that sounds crazy, but if he's better, then where does that leave you?"

He leaned over and kissed her. She opened her mouth wide, and he remembered how sweet she always tasted, how she used to kiss him hungrily at the door when they'd first been married. She had put all her will into those kisses, every bit of belief in him and their marriage. He'd felt the force of her devotion and thought he must never disappoint her; no one had ever loved him like this before.

He'd told Julian once, You'll know you're in love when you're more of your self rather than less. It embarrassed him now to remember; such ludicrous, impotent advice. A lot of good it had done the boy. He thought of the young woman, Celia, who had organized the memorial service for Julian—how sad she had been, how little Cap could tell her. He pulled away.

"What's wrong?"

"We better get him," he said, and realized only after he said it that he meant *them*, his parents, not him—not Julian. Julian was dead. He was gone.

In the morning, he drove to the warehouse with his father. Cho. L moved along, dusting the new electronic machines. Their numerical panels required Nintendo wizardry. The pull-knob models from Cap's childhood had long since vanished, along with the caramel chewies with their soft white centers, his favorite candy. He'd been coming here since he was two years old, his father's warehouse still in the same block of West Philadelphia, though every store around it was now boarded up.

"*Vend machine ain't got no go*," rapped Cho. L, to no one in particular. He had barely given Cap a glance, while Cap's father went to the safe, the same one they'd had for years. It worked only intermittently, but his father believed it was good luck and the reason they hadn't ever been robbed. Cap could hear him cursing the dial in the windowless office.

Cho. L whirled in his high-top pumps. "*Ho, big boss, let my people go.*" He flattened his palms against the black glass of a machine that contained none other than an assortment of condoms destined for the boys' dorm of the University of Pennsylvania. Such a placement would have been unthinkable back in the early days of the business. Cap could remember only one condom machine, with a picture of some saucy starlet in a woolly bathing suit, pushing her breasts out while she waited to be rescued on a tiny two-person island with a single palm tree.

A whole new generation of machines lined the walls, even if the building was exactly the same. Smart units. Talking soda machines, a candy machine that fired a laser image of the chosen selection, even a popcorn dispenser that steamed out the smell of melted butter, or its chemical equivalent—Cap wasn't sure.

"*Downtown, you know I'm holding the crown . . .*" Cho. L moved on with his squirt bottle to the cigarette machines that Cap had tried many times, unsuccessfully, to talk his father into dropping. "*Dirty ware, I got fire to make my lair!*"

Cap wandered into the shop, where Everett Oost, Cho. L's aged father, serviced all the machines. Everett was there, asleep atop bags of change. Bags everywhere. Cap's father, for all his worries about not losing a nickel, had a puzzling disregard for storing the profits right out in the open. Money sacks lay spread around the room, their little goose necks cinched locked with steel wire. One sack, taut as a pigeon's breast, kept the shop door from blowing shut. How much money was in this room alone? And just Everett Oost snoring atop all these bags, waiting for the Brink's pickup.

His father called to him, and Cap went into the office. "I wanted to show you this," he said. "In case something happens and nobody knows. It's my will."

Cap nodded. What could he say? It meant talking about death, and this was the only way to do it in the family, in terms of money and possessions. "That's fine."

"But you haven't heard what's in it yet."

"Whatever," said Cap.

"Everything's split fifty-fifty, after your mother dies. All my savings, the house, the furniture, etc."

"Good," said Cap, turning to go.

"Except the business. Allan gets that."

Cap turned around. "Allan? You're going to let Allan take over the business?"

"Why not? You never wanted it."

"No, but . . . I'm just surprised."

"Why the surprise? He's well. You can see for yourself."

"I just wish you had consulted me before you made the decision."

"So I'll ask you again—do you want it?"

"No—"

"I didn't think so."

His father sounded bitter. Cap felt himself apologizing, or apologizing like a therapist would: "Does that bother you, Dad? That I don't want it?"

"Why should it bother me? I know you never had any interest. At least Allan always liked to come down here."

"I liked coming here too!"

"Even with all his mishegoss, he wasn't ashamed of what his father did for a living."

Oh, so that was it. "I was never ashamed of what you did," said Cap, but he could hear the hollowness of his own words. His denial rang with more sympathy than truth. His father kept one hand on the dial of the safe, reluctant to let go. The will, a copy with Cap's name on the envelope, was in the other hand. It was stifling hot in the office, the way his father preferred it. One of them would have to break the silence soon, or else, as his father liked to say, they'd plotz in here.

"I guess, then, that Allan will continue working here," said Cap.

His father shrugged. "It's his choice, but I'd be surprised if he didn't. Already he's talking to me about all the changes. He wants to move and automate everything. You know, bring in a computer specialist who will charge a small fortune to make your file cabinets disappear, poof. Give you a whole new life in business. Everett!" his father yelled, knowing without even being in the room that the senior Oost was sleeping. "So we're going to move."

"Well, I guess it's for the best," said Cap, wanting to sound more enthusiastic about Allan's new involvement, about Allan. "Can I ask you something, Dad?"

"Ask."

"Have you been feeling all right lately?"

"All right is all right."

"What's wrong?"

"Some things are wronger than others. What can you do?"

"Such as?" asked Cap, not liking the sound of this evasion.

"It's nothing to worry about. I'm going to have a little operation. They'll take a nickel's worth off my prostate."

"Dad—"

"I told you it's nothing to worry about. Your mother doesn't know yet. I just found out. And don't tell Allan, whatever you do. He's too excitable. Who knows how this could set him back."

"Answer me honestly. Do you have cancer?" asked Cap, struck by the analogy to the lost nickel.

"Please, let's not make a public announcement. There's just a little something on the end they want to cut out. It's just a nuisance at this point."

Cap sat down at his father's desk, stunned. He would call his father's doctor and find out the actual extent of the problem. He realized now that they'd come down to the store for this—that his father could speak of such things as cancer, if indeed it was cancer, only in the stronghold of his business.

"So you're doing well in your profession," said his father, changing the subject, Cap knew, for good. He would not want to discuss it anymore—directly, that is. They would talk about business instead. His father had a business, he a profession. Professions didn't have dips, nor did they make a killing, nor could they eat you alive. They were supposed to be too dignified for that. Nor could they make you ashamed. No wonder his father had taken him here; it was perhaps a last attempt to gain filial approval, standing here in the building that was the best history of his father's life, the place where he had given his finest hours, and waiting for Cap to tell him that it had all been meaningful.

"I'm doing well," said Cap. "Thanks for asking."

They stood in silence. His father took off his glasses and rubbed his eyes. "I saw Hershiser shut out your Rockies," he said.

Cap nodded. He'd seen the game too, knowing his father was watching on cable. Claude had sat on his lap, as Cap had sat many years ago on his own father's at Connie Mack Stadium in Philadelphia, the little, perhaps only, physical contact he'd ever had with his father as a child. "Nied was pitching a no-hitter into the fifth."

"He blew it," said Cap's father. "Self-destructed. His slider kept getting away from him. He should have used his fastball more—that's what Orel got your boys on. They're a young ball club, your Rockies. They'll get better." His father said this sympathetically, reassuringly, as if it mattered to Cap inside or could help somehow.

They looked at each other; they'd run out of things to say.

Cap took the copy of the will from his father. His father's hand remained in the air for a second longer, waiting for Cap to grasp it, but then dropped to his side—too late—before Cap could hold it without embarrassing them both.

Cantor Zommick waited in Cap's office. The old man sat on the sofa and tried to talk, but nothing came out. The cantor a mute! All those times the cantor had chastised him. Now it's your turn, thought Cap. But when he looked closer the cantor had become Allan, and his brother was trying to tell him that he'd been poisoned. Allan pointed to his throat. Help me. You must help me.

Cap cried out, and Wallis sleepily patted his back. They'd pushed the twin beds together in Cap's old bedroom so there would be space for them all—including Claude, whose kicks in his sleep to Cap's back really hurt.

Cap sat up against the headboard where he'd carved World Series scores as a child. His old Phillies baseball pennants were still up above his dresser. Somewhere in that dresser was a baseball signed by Richie Ashburn, and in his closet a stack of comic books that were probably worth a good sum of money now.

They slept under the dormer that Cap had been careful to slide out from under ever since he'd been thirteen, when he had already needed to shave twice a day (he was five feet ten at his bar mitzvah). Generally, everyone expected him to be the adult he looked like. "Do you know," Cantor Zommick had said to him the week before the miserable event of his bar mitzvah, "what the Hebrew word *sonainnu* means?" The cantor's brow trembled with frustration.

"I guess not," said Cap.

"The closest meaning is 'our persecutors.' A more literal translation perhaps would be 'our haters.' But that still doesn't tell you the real meaning. Do you know why?"

Cap shook his head, which had started to throb in pain.

"*Because there is no translation!* In English, such terrible things don't keep happening to one people over and over. Only a language like Hebrew, with its understanding of endless evil, can speak of these nightmares in a single word! *Now do you understand why you must learn to read your haftarah?*"

The house was completely dark now. Cap got out of bed and went downstairs. At the bottom of the steps was Allan's asthmatic dog, wheezing in its sleep. Who would take care of him now that Allan and Joan planned to set up housekeeping in their own apartment? Allan had called yesterday morning to tell them he and Joan were about to check out of the Bellevue and would soon be on their way to Longwood Gardens, by bus. They'd be home in another day or so, a short honeymoon but equivalent to light-years for a first outing. "So far so sane," Allan had joked on the phone.

My God, Allan with a sense of humor about his own delusions. Not talking about conspiracies or room service leaving a newspaper outside his door with a knife wrapped in it for him to kill himself. Instead, he had said, "We had breakfast in bed and Joan spilled orange juice on us. Fortunately we only had our skin to clean." Even sex wasn't off limits anymore.

After opening a soda from the refrigerator, Cap ate three Oreos—the food of his childhood, his bad habits instantly resurrected here. He couldn't stop thinking about Cantor Zommick. Would his old tormentor start popping up in his dreams all the time? And why had the cantor turned into Allan? Allan holding his throat, pleading with Cap to help. Help him talk? Help him sing? Help him breathe?

Cap got up from the kitchen table. The atlas was still in the same place, above the phone books in the utility cabinet. He thumbed through it until he got to Maryland. They were supposed to go sightseeing today, just the three of them, visit the art museum and even the Liberty Bell, which Wallis had never seen, before they flew back to Colorado tomorrow.

He went upstairs and gently shook Wallis awake.

"What's wrong?" she said, looking around—unsure, Cap could tell, where she was.

"I have to go to Baltimore."

"Umm . . ." She pulled at her face. "Baltimore?"

"I have to go, Wallis. I'll be back before dark."

"It *is* dark."

"I'll call you once I get there."

"Cap . . . drive carefully! Please!"

He drove along the beltway, looking for the exit to Woodlawn. He had the address of the drugstore, but it was Julian's mother he wanted to see. Back in December, when he'd called to notify the family of the death, he'd reached Julian's father at work. The number had been in Julian's file at Cap's office. He remembered that Julian's mother never talked on the phone, and it made sense that Julian had listed his father's business number for emergencies.

He assumed now that the residence would be in the vicinity of the drugstore and had marked all the Katzes in the surrounding area, stopping at a Baltimore coffee shop at seven A.M. and unfolding a map.

Exiting at Woodlawn, he found the main street, Crestview, easily enough. The first Katz home was off Lime Avenue, though Cap couldn't imagine Julian growing up on a street called Lime. Nor the boy's mother living there. He made a left turn after waiting through two lights at Crestview—gridlock: welcome to the East—and drove three blocks before finding 809 Lime.

The house was a small brick bungalow, with two Big Wheel trikes on the lawn. He got out just to make sure it wasn't the place. A woman with a snake around her neck answered the front door.

"What?" she said. The snake, half asleep, but husky and menacing with its silver and black scales, slid lazily down her chest.

Cap took a step back. "I'm looking for a Mrs. Katz—" He realized he didn't know Julian's mother's first name. "Do you have a son named Julian?" It was foolish to ask, but he was hoping she might be related (though he didn't expect that either). The woman shut the door in his face. He walked across the lawn, almost tripping on the hand-lettered sign that said, "Guard snake on duty."

Julian had been hit by a Burlington Northern freight train at approximately three-fifteen A.M. The engineer had seen him out the side window, but the boy appeared too far away to be in danger. Nevertheless, the engineer had repeatedly blown his horn going through the intersection. In his statement, he reported that the victim appeared to have jumped in front of the train at the last moment.

Cap had identified him. The sheet was lowered off Julian's face for a brief moment. Julian's brown eyes stared blankly. His lips were parted as if whistling or letting out a breath. Cap had nodded, then put his hands over his face for a second to compose himself.

The injuries sustained, according to the coroner, supported the engineer's testimony. A dissection of the aorta near the neck area of the spinal column—his most massive injury, most of his blood lost here—had been brought about by the body twisting one way and the internal organs another. It was all consistent with a blunt-force trauma of perpendicular impact, the coroner told Cap, after Cap requested a meeting with him. If the victim had been lying down on the tracks, passed out from alcohol, as happened occasionally with transients, his injuries would have been those of laceration and dismemberment rather than the upper-torso wounds they'd found. "There is no doubt," the coroner said, showing him the pictures of a section of Julian's chest, pictures that Cap forced himself to look at, "that he was clipped and thrown away from the train."

That left two possibilities. Either he slipped on the ice in making a run to beat the train or he intentionally jumped into the path of the train.

The coroner had put away the pictures in a sheath like a manila envelope, except it was rubber. Everything was rubber or steel down in the morgue, it seemed. He was letting Cap draw his own conclusions about the second possibility.

"So you're saying it could have been a suicide."

"It's not my best guess," said the coroner, "unless you can fill me in on some history that would persuade me of this." He knew Cap had been Julian's psychologist.

"What about a third possibility?" asked Cap. "What if he had a seizure?"

The coroner had lifted his head from the filing cabinet in his office (also in the basement), where he had taken Cap to talk. "It's curious you should say that," said the coroner. "Did you know we found edema in the lungs?"

"Edema?"

"Saliva. During a seizure, saliva can be inhaled into the upper bronchi. Such uncontrolled inhaling could be a symptom of a convulsion."

"So it could have been a seizure, then?" asked Cap. "It could have occurred just before he tried to cross. That would have slowed him down a second or so too long, right?"

"Perhaps. We would have to depend on peripheral evidence. Edema can be found normally, just from excitement, rapid breathing. What do we know about the victim's history? Was he taking medication?"

"Not the last time I spoke with him."

"It was the middle of the night, so fatigue could certainly have contributed to the cause of a seizure." The coroner—the assistant coroner, actually (the regular coroner was out of town for the holidays)—had sat down at his desk and seemed to be considering. "I think we could reasonably conclude that the cause of death here was accidental, with a strong possibility of epileptic convulsion. But why he tried to run across in the first place, his poor judgment of the train's speed . . . well, I can't account for that."

Cap would have thought he'd be more relieved. After all, he had the assistant coroner's best opinion that the cause of death was accidental. Still, he knew that when it came to suicide, some were more accidental than others. The continuum of accidental to intentional left a wide and tormenting range of uncertainty for survivors to anguish over. He had been unable to get the thought out of his head that Julian killed himself. When he made the call to Julian's father, having been asked by the police to do the notification, a woman had answered, "Katz Pharmacy." In less than ten seconds—Cap had counted the beats of his heart—Julian's father got on the phone. "Mr. Katz, this is Dr. Kaplan. I'm calling from Pierre, Colorado. I have some unfortunate news. I'm sorry to tell you that your son died this morning." Cap had written the words down to keep himself from saying any more than were necessary. It wasn't the first time he'd had to report a client's death; a man had died on the ward when Cap was an intern at Denver Psychiatric. And once a woman had died of a heart attack in his office. He'd had to notify their spouses. But in both cases, he'd been telling one adult about another. He'd never had to say this before to a father about his son. Mr. Katz had not been able to talk. He had asked for the number where Cap could be reached. He would call him back when he had recovered enough to speak. Cap had imagined the man, this father who'd taken care of others all his life, in his store and at home, sitting down at his cluttered desk in the pharmacy and making the terrible call to his wife. It was not something Cap had volunteered to do, nor should he have been expected to, but over the last six months he had come to understand that he would have to see her himself.

He left Lime Street and followed his map three miles to Potash and Irvington, an intersection manned by boys. Two of them pounced on Cap's car and did his windows, front and back. "Two be good," said the older of them, and Cap (what did he care, he was from Colorado, what did he care if they laughed at him afterward, no East Coast what-do-you-take-me-for-a-shnook? was he anymore) gave them two dollars and drove through. He turned down Leicester, a side street off the busy commercial thoroughfare of Irvington. The houses, after a brief run of modest bungalows, suddenly became imposingly large, like one of those tiny dinosaurs Claude had that grew to two hundred times their size in water. The expansive homes seemed to have appeared from nowhere.

The white-brick house had green wooden shutters and trim. The flagstone walk in front was immaculate, with winding rows of impatiens on either side. A low cedar fence ran along the length of the trimmed shrubbery. Everything was quiet, orderly, and looked as if no one lived inside, the downstairs shades drawn.

He rang the bell. He hadn't allowed for the possibility that Julian's mother would be gone or that she wouldn't answer the door. She must go shopping, or to have her hair done, or to her husband's store occasionally. But he had trouble picturing her anywhere but here. When no one answered, he tried knocking. After a few minutes, he stepped back and looked at the upstairs windows. The lace curtains were open, but nothing moved.

A noise came from the backyard, and he walked around, undoing the heavy bolt on the side gate. A black woman was dragging a garbage can over the patio, toward the back. "Excuse me—" said Cap, and the woman turned, startled. "What you want?" She gripped the garbage can as if she might be ready to throw it at him, should he come any closer. It had been so long since he'd been back East. He could have actually done this in Pierre—walked into someone's backyard without their suspecting the worst.

"Could you tell me where I might find Mrs. Katz?" The woman looked at him in silence, as if he'd better have more to say. "I've come to see her from Colorado."

"What you want, bothering her out here!"

It wasn't a question.

"I knew her son."

"Oh," said the woman, who had on rubber gloves and had, Cap saw, been washing out the trash can. "You wait right here."

He sat down on the back steps of the porch. Rows of yellow, white, and pink rosebushes on trellises bordered either side of a fountain, its bottom checked with small blue and white tiles. No red roses, though. A birdhouse, with detailed white shutters and a miniature French door, sat on a high steel pole. Toward the back of the garden stood an immense magnolia, its branches with their purplish-gray bark sweeping the ground. He looked around for some sign of Julian—an old bicycle, a basketball hoop, a rusting swing set—but found nothing.

"Can I help you, please?"

It was Julian's mother. The black woman—a companion? the maid?—stood behind her and watched Cap carefully. If he'd expected a tiny immigrant woman in a babushka, with gnarled hands and a sidelong glance to divert the evil eye, she wasn't this Mrs. Katz. She was taller than he'd imagined. Julian had been on the small side. Her hair was gray but cut stylishly short. She wore a necklace of dove-gray pearls over the front of a russet dress printed with the red roses absent from her garden. She looked indisputably as though she belonged in this house, on these grounds, and had found elegant refuge here.

Maybe he'd expected a broken-down woman, paralyzed with grief, wheeled out to face the sun every day. Maybe he'd even hoped for that, to justify all his fears.

He stood up to introduce himself. "I'm Casper Kaplan, Mrs. Katz. I was Julian's psychologist in Pierre."

"What can I do for you, Dr. Kaplan?" Her voice, too, was sturdier than he had expected. There was a tension between her strong accent and the exacting English, neither side willing to budge, it seemed.

"I first want to tell you how sorry I am about Julian's death." Mrs. Katz nodded and waited. "I thought we might talk about Julian," he said, having never really imagined what he might say.

"Is there something you wish to know?"

He was still standing. Over Mrs. Katz's shoulder, the maid watched him with her hawk eye. "Is there somewhere we could talk?" he asked.

"Certainly," she said, and led him inside.

The interior of the house matched its outside in neatness but was more chambered and uncharted. The stairway, which seemed to go on up to the attic, had a crisp floral runner. Dark cherry paneling lined the stairwell, each third panel recessed, as if one of them might lead to a secret vault or hidden passage. An antique sideboard, set with pink tapers in silver candleholders, stood below a family portrait. Cap glanced at the painting, done in oil. Julian, whose expression seemed as solemn as that of an elderly burgher, looked resigned to the sitting.

Mrs. Katz led him into a room lighter than the rest of the house, with white wicker furniture, and flowers (from the garden?) on a glass coffee table. He sat down across from her in one of the wicker chairs, its green seat cushion warmed from the afternoon sun. She placed herself in the middle of the sofa, the cushions profuse with languid hibiscus and leafy green stems. She had offered him coffee or tea, or some other beverage, using that word. He wondered whether Julian had sat much with her in this room, all these rooms.

"I was actually thinking you might have some questions for me," said Cap.

"I did not know you existed until this moment."

"But I called your husband. I spoke with him several times, once about the arrangements for shipping Julian's belongings, another time about a memorial service for Julian in Pierre. Surely he told you."

"My husband told me nothing."

She offered no more explanation. Had Julian never mentioned therapy either? But why would he? And Cap had always sent the bills to Julian's father, who would have screened this news from her, as he evidently did most everything.

"Anyway," said Cap, after it became clear she was waiting for him to go on, "I thought perhaps you might have some questions about what happened."

"I know what happened. My son was struck by a train."

The bluntness with which she stated the fact was unexpected and took him aback. "Yes, that's true."

"Is there anything more?"

"No," said Cap, "I suppose not," though he was surprised she wouldn't ask him about any of the details. He felt himself grasping for a connection, something to show her why he'd come here. Elsewhere in the house, a phone rang. Mrs. Katz ignored it, as if it weren't ringing. "Is there anything you would like to ask me about Julian's therapy?"

"As I said, I did not know he was in therapy until ten minutes ago. Was he having difficulty adjusting to school?"

"Mrs. Katz," said Cap, "were you aware of Julian's turmoil about his disorder?"

"If you're referring to his epilepsy, I am certainly aware he suffered from it. Is there something else I should be informed of?"

"I don't know," said Cap. "I suppose I should tell you that he talked about you a lot in therapy too. That is, he felt protective of you."

"Why was that?"

"Your background affected him." Why couldn't he use specifics today!

Mrs. Katz said nothing.

"Your experience during the war."

"Yes, I was in the camps," she said.

"I realize this is a difficult subject to talk about, but I'd think you'd want to know everything you can."

"Why is that, Dr. Kaplan?"

"Because it might help."

"How would it help?"

"It would help you to know who Julian was. And I believe he'd want you to know him. I would think, too, you'd care enough about that part of his life to find out."

She stood up abruptly. "Excuse me, Dr. Kaplan, but I feel it is time for you to leave."

"I'm sorry if I've upset you, Mrs. Katz. That wasn't my intention."

"Yes, I understand it wasn't your intention, and yes, I care very much, but is there any reason why I should tell you? I do not know you from Adam, as the expression goes. And I am not in the habit of telling my thoughts to strangers."

He had wanted to protest that he wasn't a stranger, but of course he was, therapy and good deeds for the dead aside. He was a stranger; he would need no more proof of that fact. To press her further, to search her for answers he himself wanted, would only cheapen her already incomprehensible sorrow. Her comportment in the face of such a loss offered her the only relief left, the comfort of dignity.

"I'm sorry," said Cap. "I understand," and he slowly pulled himself up. He wouldn't be absolved here, if that's why he'd come. He followed her out of the room. They walked in silence past the kitchen, where the maid was oiling the cabinets. She glanced at Cap warily again. It seemed to take them forever to reach the front door.

"Do you have any children, Dr. Kaplan?" Mrs. Katz asked when they had gotten there, a first note of curiosity about him in her voice.

"A son. He's eleven months old."

"Would you wait here one moment, please?"

When she came back, she had a child's blanket with her. It was old and worn, but with vivid colors still, a blue background with sleeping ewes stitched in gold. Hebrew lettering arched around each corner of the blanket. "This was Julian's when he was a boy. Before that it belonged to my brother. My mother made it. It was one of the few articles I found left in my home in Budapest."

"It's beautiful," said Cap, running his fingers across the gold Hebrew letters. "Do you know what this means?" He was unable to stop touching the letters.

" 'Be strong and let your heart take courage.' Would you have it for your son, Dr. Kaplan?"

"I couldn't, Mrs. Katz. It belongs to you. How could I take it from you?"

"Please. I would like you to bring it back to Colorado, where Julian lived."

Cap looked at the sleeping sheep, with their forehooves tucked under them. "All right," he said. "Thank you."

She folded the blanket into a square and brushed her fingers over it a last time before handing it to him.

"Mrs. Katz, Julian was important to me. I cared about your son very much."

"I can see that, Dr. Kaplan," she said, and stepped back to let him pass. He went out the door, the blanket tucked under his arm.

Part Five

survivors

Chapter Twelve

"Take out your carpet squares, everyone! Erin, come over here by me." Erin had a runny nose today, as did Kira and Burton. Wallis had spent a good part of the morning blowing little noses. The kids were cranky too, their colds making them tired and impatient. It was everyone's first day back since the Christmas break. "Okay, what did we bring?"

"Screwdriver," Burton said, holding up the tool with its red rubber grip. "That's a very strong one, Burton," said Wallis. Burton, the oldest member of the group, had a black front tooth. The first day Wallis opened her school, he'd fallen on his face and knocked the tooth loose. Wallis had rushed him to the emergency room at the hospital, then called Burton's parents and frantically explained what had happened (he'd tripped going up the back steps)—an awful, inauspicious beginning. But that had been almost a year ago, and now she had five kids, all over two years of age, like Claude. And Burton was still here; not only did his parents not sue, but they'd kept him in the school: accidents happen, they said. She'd been immensely grateful for their trust and understanding, Burton's fall her initiation into the hazards of running a preschool.

"Do you know what kind of screwdriver this is, Burton?"

"Phillips," he said. Burton knew all about tools. One day, he'd amazed her by asking for a miter square to draw his picture.

"Very good," said Wallis. "And what did you bring, Kira?"

"Scissors," she said, and held out the pair of metal scissors in cupped hands, as if to show them all a baby bird. Wallis had asked the parents to let the kids bring a real tool or utensil, not a toy, to help them learn responsibility and safety.

"You're very careful with your scissors," said Wallis. "We have to know how to hold tools, don't we?" Everybody nodded so vigorously she could hear their little necks popping. So different than teaching eighth grade! Her eighth graders would have stared impassively at her or sulked or laughed outright at her attempts to pique their interest. No one at fourteen years old would dare risk the embarrassment of being an enthusiastic learner. "And what did you bring, Nicholas?"

"Patch of love."

"Pardon?" Wallis asked. "Can you show us?"

Nicholas opened his bag. She'd told them to bring their "making" tool in a bag to surprise everyone.

"Oh," Wallis said, laughing, though she was the only one, of course. If there was a drawback for her about being around only kids, it was having no one with whom to share her amusement at the funny things they said and did. "Spatula, you mean," said Wallis.

"Patch of love," Nicholas insisted. So be it, Wallis thought. His parents had just separated. Should she tell them about this? She didn't want to read too much into his mispronunciation, but maybe that's the way he felt: that he needed to patch up their marriage—or, worse, could expect only a small patch of love now.

Wallis turned to Claude. "Can you show us what you have, Claude?"

Claude opened his brown paper bag. Last night, he'd prowled around the kitchen for a good hour before he'd come out with something in his bag. Except now she felt a sudden dread. A kitchen knife or an ice pick would be flourished—never mind that she didn't know how he'd get either item. She breathed with relief when he held up a nutcracker. Last week he'd scratched Kira across the eye, and just yesterday he bit Nicholas on the hand. Having to share his toys, his house, and especially his mommy with five other kids every morning had made for a hard adjustment. Sometimes he acted so aggressive toward the other kids that Wallis considered closing the school. But she couldn't, or wouldn't. With Cap so moody and unhappy lately, the school was the only thing she looked forward to anymore. She'd get excited about making peanut-butter bird feeders, or shopping for macaroni at the market to do noodle jewelry, or figuring out how to design Indian vests and headbands from paper and old clothes. She even enjoyed changing their diapers assembly-line fashion on the bed, singing "Old MacDonald" to them as she went down the row. "You're hooked," said Roberta, Burton's mother, with whom Wallis had become friends—yet another benefit of the school: she'd finally met some other moms. "I guess I am," she'd said, and flushed, as if she were confessing to liking a boy.

"You all brought in wonderful making tools," said Wallis. "I guess nobody wants muffins and apple juice for a snack," and all of them shouted Me! Me! Me! "I didn't think so," said Wallis, and they yelled louder, giggling now and scrambling after her.

A few minutes later, a new mother came by. Her name was Sheila, and she was thinking about enrolling her daughter in Wallis's school. They were from California and just wanted to look the place over. "Your daughter is a little young yet," said Wallis. "The other kids are all over two." The little girl, whose name was Julia, had light hair and gleaming auburn eyebrows, beautiful almond-shaped blue eyes, and a thin mouth that she kept shut tight over her thumb when her mother carried her through the house. She was about one and a half. Wallis showed them the playroom, the shelves of kids' toys, the bulletin board with Monday through Friday's activities, the snack area. But the woman seemed more interested in pictures of her and Cap on the mantel and picked up one (their wedding picture) to study it.

"Well, thanks," she said, after Wallis had taken her outside to see the backyard, with the two pet rabbits, the children all following. She left quickly, with Julia, who had never taken her thumb out of her mouth and, with her moody, quiet intensity, seemed to have her mother's temperament.

After their snack, they listened to a story, then had some free time to run around the yard. At noon, parents came to pick up the children, and soon the house was quiet again.

Wallis sat down on the couch to rest, while Claude walked around from room to room. "What's wrong, Claude? Do you miss the kids?" He didn't answer. "Are you hungry?" No answer still. He looked up at her, then went outside to wait on the steps, searching, she knew, for Cap, who, though he spent more time at home than ever, hardly played with Claude anymore. "Daddy will be home soon," she said, and wished she could say something else so he wouldn't miss his father so much, or the father Cap had once been.

Last night they'd argued about money—again. Cap had brought out his legal pad, with the latest budget for them, revised as of the day before—and the day before that. "I hope nobody gets sick," he said. "Including Sam and Sam." A skin disease on big Sam had cost fifty dollars to treat. They'd been dipping more into their savings than ever and had borrowed money from Cap's family.

Wallis told Claude now, "Let's wash dishes." He wore his cape, which he never took off. Cape days, as she thought of it. He'd slowed down in growth, wasn't as big as the other kids. His hair was the tawny smooth color of hers, but not so thin and straight, with a little wave from Cap's curls. She wiped at his eyebrows with her wet finger to get some food off, something her own mother had always done.

Wallis pulled up a chair to the sink for him. He'd spend an hour there washing plastic plates under a pencil stream of water. In the meantime she could look through some library books for new projects, now that the holidays were gone. They could always go back to Halloween, a favorite occasion with the kids. Witch hats had been easy enough to make.

When she went to the shelf where she'd left the books, they weren't there. She searched through Claude's room, inside the window seat, where Claude liked to hide everything from celery sticks to stuffed animals. Nowhere. It drove her crazy. She'd purposely put them in a spot where they wouldn't get lost. She tore through the house again, opening closets, feeling under the mattresses, turning over cushions, and sweeping her hand beneath the couch, though she could clearly see that nothing was there except Claude's discarded pacifiers.

She heard Cap pull into the driveway, finished for the day. At one time she would have been thrilled that he'd come home early and broken away from a ten-hour Monday, his busiest day, clients especially distressed after the weekend. Now she found herself wishing he'd go somewhere or just stay away. Then she felt guilty, because he was having such a tough time. He didn't eat much, hardly slept, and had no energy to do anything with them as a family, though he worked less than ever. His father had died two months ago. "He's suffering," Dick had told her, when Wallis made a call to him out of desperation. "The usual pressures of the profession getting to him in an unusual amount," was how Dick had phrased it. "Intensified by his father's death." And Wallis knew, too, that things were slow now, not as many referrals, which made Cap worry about money and doubt himself. Getting off the phone, she'd thought that if she went back to her job, Cap would snap out of it, but she knew that wasn't the answer. Things had gone beyond the practical solution. She'd never seen him like this in her life.

He came in the back door from the garage. He sat down heavily on the couch. Claude looked around from the sink, climbed down, and came running. At least that hadn't changed. His son was still crazy about him, though Cap acted more drained than energetic, wouldn't play Runaway Elevator or Tornado Terror or Monster Truck Pileup. (He had made steel barriers with crunched-up aluminum foil and once even used olives, grapes, and kumquats as exploding debris for the monster trucks to roll over and squish. They'd made a horrible mess! Pulp, seeds, and juice all over the kitchen floor. She'd scolded them both. But now she would have given anything to see Cap down on the floor, making a mess with Claude, who hung on him while Cap just said, "I'm tired, Claude.")

Wallis took a breath. "Let's bake something, Claudie," she said.

"Daddy time," he said.

"Daddy's tired," Wallis told him, though she didn't know why she was making excuses for Cap, who stared at the TV. That was another thing. As soon as he'd come home he'd switch it on and flip through the channels with the remote. He did it so mechanically that he reminded her of a museum guard counting people with a clicker as they passed through a turnstile.

"Do you want some lunch?" Wallis asked Cap. Lunchtime. Her stomach sank at how early it was, how many hours they had together until bedtime. She rubbed her head, wanting to banish such thoughts. They were dangerous, the kind she imagined her own mother had had about her father.

"No, thanks," said Cap, stopping his channel-hopping for a moment to watch four long-limbed, bikini-clad girls on ESPN spike a volleyball at a beach tournament in Venice, California. She walked over and switched off the set.

"Why'd you do that?" he said.

"Cap . . ."

"What?"

She felt dizzy, hot, light-headed. "Have you seen my library books?" she asked, not knowing what else to say.

"I returned them," he said, his eyes drifting back to the blank screen.

"You took my books back? Why?"

"They were overdue."

She stared at him. Claude brought out his red trash truck and put it on Cap's lap. "Go in your room, Claude, please." She didn't like to yell in front of Claude, and she was afraid she was going to lose her temper like never before. "I needed those books, Cap."

"They were overdue."

"A day! All of five cents. My God," said Wallis, and turned away to go into the kitchen, then came storming back. "When? When the hell am I supposed to get to the library?" She couldn't believe he'd put her on the defensive. "How dare you take back those books without asking me first!"

"Wallis," he said softly. Her name sounded sad in his mouth, like being surprised by the sudden press of someone's lips, a forgotten sensation; he so rarely called her by name anymore—or kissed her, or wanted to touch her. "You have to understand," he said, "we're not in the same position—"

"Shut up!" She couldn't stand to hear it one more time, the same lecture. He was relentless!

"I'm sorry," he said, "but we're just going to have to conserve more—"

She grabbed Claude and took him upstairs, out of range of Cap's voice. She wanted to hurl the screwdriver Burton had left behind. Kick his TV set onto the floor. Yes, she'd give herself a time-out, just like for the kids. She sat breathing heavily on the bed, Claude looking at her expectantly. She waited for Cap to come up the stairs and apologize. But after a few minutes, all she heard was the TV clicking on, the channels being changed.

Chapter Thirteen

"HE'S NOT THE SAME PERSON," SAID WALLIS.

"And how is that?" asked Dr. France.

"He seems uninterested in anything."

"You mentioned his father died recently."

"Yes, but Cap's been like this for a while now—too long, it seems."

Dr. France nodded. Wallis's second-grade teacher had been named France too. How common was that? Two Frances in one lifetime. But it was the reason she'd picked the name from the therapists listed in the yellow pages. That and because Dr. France—Wallis preferred calling her by her last name instead of Ella—was new in town, and Cap didn't know her. Wallis had been delighted to find out Dr. France was black. Somehow it was easier to tell all this to a black person.

And then she wondered what that meant; did it make her prejudiced?

The fact was she thought black women were more motherly, whether it was true or not.

"Why are you sniffing the air?" asked Dr. France.

"Was I?" said Wallis.

Dr. France nodded. Wallis couldn't stop staring at her jade earrings in the shape of flutes. She wanted to touch them. She'd seen Dr. France three times already and had found it comforting to look at her clothes and jewelry, vivid corals and shell whites and tropical blues. It was as if they were together on a dive, with Dr. France signaling her silently along underwater.

"I thought I smelled smoke."

"I don't smoke," Dr. France informed her.

"Maybe the person before me."

"I don't allow smoking in the office. Why do you think you smelled smoke?"

Dr. France wasn't going to drop the issue.

"I don't know."

"Are you remembering someone now who used to smoke?"

"Remembering?" Wallis said, feeling as if she were fourteen again and had been caught staring at herself naked in the bathroom mirror after her shower. "My mother used to smoke a lot."

"And what does that remind you of?"

"Pardon?" She wanted the hour to end. She looked at her watch.

"We have plenty of time," said Dr. France.

"Well, I really should leave early. Claude's not used to being away from me. I don't leave him often, even with Cap." She was babbling but couldn't stop. Dr. France didn't say anything.

"Were you left a lot when you were younger?"

"Not a lot. Well, a little. Some," said Wallis, and she felt herself on the verge of hysterical laughter or tears. "I really think we should get back to Cap and me. I'd like to take something specific home with me that we can both work on."

"I had asked why you were remembering your mother smoking."

"Can't we just drop that subject?"

"If you wish," Dr. France said without annoyance. "But I believe it's useful to talk about what happens here in the office. What comes to mind? Any specific occasion you remember?"

Was this therapy? Being a witness at a trial of your own foggy past? "It's not important."

"Why don't you tell me anyway," Dr. France said, and tilted her head, her brown eyes not leaving Wallis's.

"My mother was smoking when she told me something once."

"And what was that?" asked Dr. France, reaching for her blue ceramic coffee mug with the face of Sneezy—Wallis's least favorite dwarf. Should she tell Dr. France this? Was this significant too? That she abhorred germy Sneezy?

Dr. France had pictures of two grown children on her desk. But no husband. Was she a single mother? Divorced?

"I'm sorry. Can you repeat the question?" asked Wallis.

"What sorts of things do you remember about that conversation with your mother?"

"Oh, I remember my mother looking at me and being amused by my interest in her smoking."

"What happened?"

"She was in the bathroom, getting ready to go on another trip. She traveled a lot, as I told you. Her cigarette was in an ashtray on the sink, with pink lipstick on the filter. Anyway, she put the cigarette to my lips, and I puffed on it. I don't know why she did it. I was only seven. I can still taste the smoke going down my throat. It snaked into my lungs and made me cough. The smoke exploded out of my nose because I'd shut my mouth. Afterward my mother said, 'Don't tell Daddy I told you.' She put her cigarette out in the bathroom sink, and it sizzled. There was never any explanation for her giving me that cigarette, but I knew it was very important and was meant to seal our pact."

"Yes, and what exactly did she not want you to tell your father?" asked Dr. France.

Wallis looked away. Heat rose up from her chest. "My mother told me about somebody she liked. Somebody in Portland, Oregon. She'd met him at some sales meeting. He would call when my father wasn't home. If I answered the phone, he'd hang up. I figured it out and asked my mother."

"And she made you promise that day not to tell your father."

"Yes."

"It must have confused you."

"I guess," said Wallis.

"And did you promise her that you wouldn't ever be angry?"

"I don't know," Wallis said. "I was only seven."

"Yes, but seven-year-olds see and hear everything—more than adults, often."

"She was my mother."

"She is your mother still. Did you trade your mother's secret for something?"

Wallis put her hands under her legs, a little girl in the nurse's office. "I can't remember."

Dr. France waited.

"Maybe," said Wallis, "she promised that she'd never get divorced if I kept her secret. Or that's what I believed as a seven-year-old."

"Do you still believe it today?"

"How's that?"

"With Cap. If you promise not to tell, which means show how angry you really are, he won't leave you." Dr. France smiled comfortingly. "Some part of you stopped feeling back then, Wallis, so it wouldn't hurt."

Wallis Lark is tough as bark.

Wallis stood up, then sat down. "It's very upsetting to talk like this. Can we stop, please?"

"Yes. I'm sorry. You've had more than enough for one session."

Wallis left in a daze, neither relieved nor unhappy. She rode the elevator down to the basement, having forgotten to push the first-floor button. She walked back up the stairs. At a stoplight on the way home, she saw a little boy on a bike, about eight years old, and like the smoking, another memory jumped out at her: getting two bikes for her tenth birthday, one from her father and one from her mother. Neither parent knew about the other's gift. And Wallis kept it that way: rode her father's bike at her father's apartment, her mother's at the house, keeping out of sight in case one or the other parent should drive by. She had never said a word to them, protecting them even today from being hurt.

Each of her parents had seen Claude only once. Her mother had visited Pierre overnight and been with Claude for a total of eighteen hours, counting sleep. Her father hadn't even done that: he'd called from the Denver airport to have Wallis bring Claude down between connecting flights. And she'd gone, rushed there to take advantage of her opportunity. It made her furious to realize that she was still afraid of losing the pittance of attention they gave her on Claude's behalf.

She envied grown children who had successfully disengaged themselves emotionally from their parents. That such an operation was truly possible! And she had once thought that she too was satisfied with the yearly birthday and Christmas cards she'd gotten from her parents, the occasional visits when they were in Denver on business. She'd even believed the arrival of Claude would become the strongest reason yet to turn inward and feel untroubled by their indifference. (Though it wasn't indifference so much as their own discomfort at seeing her, she knew. Their only child, did she remind them too much of their awful marriage?) Who were they punishing by not coming here? Wallis asked, realizing she was still talking to Dr. France. Who do you think? Dr. France asked back, returning the birdie. Wallis thought no one. There must be some name for it. Afraid of your own kin. She suffered from it herself; what child didn't, to a degree? Maybe it was a double standard, but when parents did it, they were cruel— deserters, not rebels.

She couldn't stop talking to Dr. France in her head, the floodgate open now. Another memory: After the divorce, her parents couldn't agree on how to cut her hair. One wanted it long with bangs, the other a pixie cut (it had become *their* haircut, her own wishes getting lost in the battle). So one of them—she couldn't remember who did what—took her to get the front cut, and the other to get the back done. It was nuts! And she went along with it and thought it was normal. Didn't all kids have parents like that?

Cap had been the first person who hadn't made her feel split in two—or as if she had to hold her emotions in with some elastic belt like movers wore to keep their backs in place. The first winter they'd been married, right after they moved to Pierre, she would meet him at the front door after work. She'd bought him an English tweed overcoat because he'd been wearing some mangy pea coat from the sixties. She wanted him to stand out from all the other Colorado men in their parkas and ski jackets, wanted him to look sturdy and dashing, wanted his face with its silky dark beard to rise up out of his shoulders like some mad sea captain's (he tended to hunch over, as much to hear people as to make himself more their height), wanted him to use all his strength and heart on her and not hold back, though she knew, too, that she confused him by withdrawing, jumping up to grade papers at odd times, deflecting something complimentary he'd say with a verbal kick of her heel, pushing him away when he spontaneously put his arms around her while she was folding the last two pieces of laundry, because she couldn't stand to be interrupted from a task, any task, especially so close to the end, and it didn't matter whether it was laundry or the last line of the dissertation she was finishing that first year they were married—she couldn't make such distinctions, much to her dismay.

She liked meeting him at the door. It was old-fashioned, unliberated in 1975, something Donna Reed or June Cleaver (but not Wallis's own mother) would have done. She'd get home from teaching, and she could barely wait until she heard his footsteps on the porch, returning from work, where he'd just started getting clients. Her arms would slip into the loose sleeves of his new overcoat, and she'd stand like that for a few moments, some strangely comforting position, and after a while they'd kiss, and affection would turn to deeper urges, and they'd hurry upstairs and make love. She didn't even know how it had gotten started, but it happened every day for six months, as if this was what newlyweds did—waited for their husbands to come home in their English tweed overcoats. This man coming up the steps was her husband (not her "old man," as all their unmarried friends referred to their men). It was important that he be her husband. *Her* husband. Her *husband*. It didn't matter how she said it to herself, it was amazing, like a password to a back room. People looked at her differently. An immediate acceptance of her as belonging to someone. For months after they married, she'd used the word every time she could squeeze it into a sentence, eschewing pronouns. My husband isn't home yet. He'll be back shortly, and then I'll have my husband call you. . . . My husband will want to look at this chair too. . . . My husband was just talking to your husband. . . .

All the indirect and not so indirect ways people had had of letting her know they found her stiff or cold: from an aunt who would tell her, "Little girls need to smile more if they want to be considered pretty"; to a date, memorable only because he'd informed her, "You need to move your hips more when you dance"; to the occasional person who would still ask, "Was that a joke?" (her sense of humor having reached its peak in obscure sarcasm during college)—most every experience in her life, not the least of which had been her parents' divorce, had convinced her never to expect she'd be married, that anyone voluntarily spending a lifetime with her would be seriously misguided.

So she'd called off the engagement with Cap.

What was wrong with him that he wanted to marry her? She'd left him a note that she wasn't ready to marry him (or anyone) and driven up Flagstaff Mountain in Boulder, on her way to Turnerville, an abandoned mining town, a place where nobody would bother her and she could sit in the woods in the hot springs and figure out how she'd almost made the worst mistake of her life.

Marriage was a lie. How could he understand that? He'd come from a family with parents who had stayed together their whole lives; they were celebrating their thirtieth wedding anniversary, while her parents had been divorced for most of her life. And then she had looked in her rearview mirror, and there he was, following her up the mountain in his beat-up Volkswagen van, which had no compression left, straining its gears in smoky pursuit.

No one had ever followed her, stuck so gently close to her, been chugging behind her so stubbornly loyal and in love with her. She had to admit it: after years of looking for a father in men, she'd finally found herself a mother.

A few months later, they were living together in an apartment in Denver, after Cap transferred to a new graduate program there. They'd been sitting on the couch, reading. Cap was studying case notes for his graduate practicum, when Wallis had glanced over and seen him squinting. His neck was a knot of muscle. Beads of perspiration had come out on his forehead. His throat was working to swallow. He gripped the manila folder with both hands, as if he were holding up a shirt from a store rack or, more to the point, a robber by the lapels.

"Is something wrong?" she'd asked him.

"No," he said quickly, and shifted his position, relaxing his shoulders, placing the case notes in his lap. But in five minutes the folder was back up, and he was tensely examining it once more, his throat making those strained noises. "Do you need glasses, Cap?" Wallis herself wore glasses for reading.

"No. I'm fine." He got up to go into the kitchen for some juice.

When he came back, she said, "It must be a difficult case."

He shook his head. He looked at her a long time, then told her, "I have a reading disability."

She remembered that she'd been amazed he hadn't told her before. Or, worse, that he'd thought she might love him any less. If anything, she was even more impressed by what he'd accomplished. Unlike Corman, whose only handicap was snobbery, Cap with his struggles had touched some place in her that felt disarmingly human.

She pulled into the driveway now and saw Cap playing ball with Claude—in the snow. At least they were both outside, away from the television, and Claude looked thrilled, holding the oversize red rubber bat while Cap threw him the white plastic ball. Claude hit it, and Cap ran up to him, hurrying him around the bases, Claude giggling, Cap shouting for him to *run run run*, it was a homer for sure, quick, here comes the throw from center, and Cap fell down at home plate, with Claude crashing on top of him.

"Mommy!" shouted Claude. "I hit a home her!"

"That's wonderful!" said Wallis, going over to him and hugging him. She had told Cap she was meeting Phyllis for coffee, not able to bring herself to tell him yet about therapy (worried, too—greatest of ironies—that he'd complain about the cost). "Hi," she said to him now.

"Hi," he said back, and he touched her neck, so that she smelled smoke again. Except this wasn't from her mother, this was from her, her own smoky aloneness, a stale odor that she associated with full ashtrays and empty rooms, new housekeepers and echoey holidays, and such unstoppable needs as seeing Dr. France.

Chapter Fourteen

Dear Cap,

I was very pleased to hear from you again. I am sorry to
take so long in answering, but as I've told you I am a very
slow writer, my command of English being limited on paper
by a tedious use of both dictionary and thesaurus. My
greatest worry is that I will not make sense, but I must
admit to some secret and prideful wish of becoming a
writer. It was my most favorite daydream before the war. I
remember at thirteen years old writing in my journal that
today I have made gold from the dross of words, so proud of
myself at having written a poem for my father's birthday
(which he read with great flourish at the dinner table).
So this is my very roundabout way of asking for your forgiveness at my delay in responding these past two months.
You must believe me when I say it is not from a lack of excitement about your letter to me. You have told me so much
and given me so much to think about that I perhaps needed
the past months to prepare my response.

I am first deeply sorry to hear of your father's passing. You do not indicate in your letter at what age he
died, but I believe, judging from my estimation of your
age, he must have been in his seventies. My interest in
his age must seem curious if not rude to you, but it is a
preoccupation I have had ever since surviving my own parents and siblings. I can't help but ask, as if I might understand through age alone, why time has ended for some of
us while it continues for others.

Your letter also tells the good news of your brother and
sister-in-law's coming child. You confess that you feel
some trepidation about this for fear the child will inherit your brother and his wife's disorder. I can understand that fear, for it is what kept me from wanting
children for so many years after the war. Many unpleasant
things, acts of sadistic inquiry by the camp doctors,
were done to me during my time as an inmate. Afterward I
was convinced that I could not bear children. My own fear,
I now believe, kept me from having children any earlier,
and I cannot help but wonder if my late pregnancy caused
Julian's epilepsy. I have no reason to think this, there
are certainly epileptic children born to younger women,
but I did believe for many years that I was contaminated
by my experiences in the camps, by a succession of operations. You will understand that for me the shame of my experience was doubled by being a very young woman and used
like this—as brutal as any rape. Diseased tissues from
other species were implanted inside me, the viruses of
animals. It was beyond comprehension as a human act. I was
fifteen when this was done to me. These experiments would
go on for two more years until we were liberated at the end
of the war. What people of this time call science fiction,

I experienced as truth. So I could never think of myself
again, nor anyone from my womb, as fully human. When Julian was conceived I was frightened and repelled and
filled with shame that I must now admit to you: I have
never been able to see my son without thinking that I bore
a deformity—the cruelest curse of those days that I have
had to live under. I have never said this to another living soul. I know, however, that Julian was aware of these
feelings of mine and that he came to you to understand
them better. From my behavior that first day we met, you
would never guess how relieved I was that he did. I believe, too, that is part of the reason why he died, and
that I am fully responsible.

I am telling you all this because you have asked me a
difficult question in your letter, and I must speak honestly to you before I answer, otherwise you will not believe my answer, and it is very important that you do.

You have asked how I can go on. You apologize for asking, but you say that it is a desperate plea from you for
an answer which you admit now you came to my house for in
the first place. You want to know how can I accept this
world that first wipes out my whole family and then my
only son on his twenty-first birthday. And you say that
two years later his death and your part in it continues
to trouble you.

I have to answer you by referring back to your brother
who, once mentally ill, now finds himself about to become
a father. Can he truthfully make a fair decision about
bringing a child into the world who has a fifty percent
chance (as you say, quoting a study) of becoming schizophrenic himself? And what would your brother and his wife
think of themselves knowing they had borne a child only to

face this fate? How could they ever live with themselves? That is the question you are really asking. Why would anyone bring a child into this world, knowing what can happen? Why would I have let Julian be born, with all that I had experienced, with all that I feared could happen to him? And is it so much different from any child brought into this world, whose future has no front or back to it, whose parents' past is the only floor he will have to stand on?

I must answer you now. I cannot avoid your question much longer, I see, because it is getting dark here and my husband will soon be home. His sadness is such that I sometimes wish I had cut my throat rather than have him find me. He did find me, however, wandering with a friend from the camps alongside a riverbank. I remember whispering to my friend, who spoke only German, "Ist er Jude?" and my husband looking up at us and seeing me with his very sad blue eyes. I was only just seventeen and he not much older and I have thought many times how filled with sorrow his life has been because I took the chocolate bar from him and lowered my eyes shyly, but even in my shyness, even in my confusion about where I was––we had been walking for two days with only a little water and fruit given to us by a rare friendly Polish farmer––I could not help but flirt with him, show him the one side of my mouth that had full teeth, and then brush against his arm as he led us to the DP camp at which he was assigned.

I think it was then that I wished––and perhaps deep inside knew––that one day I would have a child like any other woman. I would love someone from a place that was not rotting like my womb, filled with vicious tampering, but from my heart, which would never let love rot, which could never let all that I had inside me for my own mother and

father and my brother and sisters go to waste. I believe
it was true: that I thought it better to smile with half my
mouth at my future husband than not at all for fear of ex-
posing my decay.

Such love, however, causes unbearable pain. I cannot
think of Julian today without a violent pain in my womb
where no anesthetic was used to lessen what was being done
to me. I hate this pain, I hate it with all my heart, I want
you to know this; but I do not hate the people who caused
it. That is perhaps difficult for you to understand,
given what has happened to me. My parents and youngest
sister, only seven at the time, were killed in the gas
chambers. My older sister died of typhus in the camp. My
brother, for whom I had the most affection and who resem-
bled my Julian, was shot in the back when he tried to run
into the woods during a roundup. Only I have remained, and
now remain again. I see in your letter anger that wants to
find who is responsible for this harm, and that you cannot
rationally accept it without a cause. You must understand
that the only way—and here is the answer to the question
behind your question—that I have gone on is to hate the
pain while not hating the hater. Otherwise, I would give
up this drug of hope that offers me reason not to be done
with myself, a possibility that I have faced every day
since the war. I cannot bear my loss, and yet I have only
one choice and I am not willing or brave enough to use it.

You have been very patient to listen to all this. It is,
I now must admit to you, this correspondence that has
helped me to continue after my son's death. I only know
you through your letters, and our one brief and ungra-
cious (on my part) meeting, but I know, too, that you must
continue in what you are doing.

Now I must tell you my exciting news. I have saved it for

last because I myself am not quite believing it. I will be
speaking to a public school class on Monday, as part of
the week's festivities here in Baltimore commemorating
Martin Luther King's birthday. Perhaps you can understand
what a momentous occasion this will be for me! I will
speak to them of the Holocaust (my husband's store manager, who knows of my background, has a little boy in the
sixth-grade class). I have heard so much lately about how
the Holocaust was exaggerated or did not happen at all
that I feel I cannot remain silent any longer. Though the
occasion remains a week away, I have been barely able to
control my fright at the prospect and am sure my mouth
will go dry, my voice become a mere squeak. Do you know
that, except to my husband, I have not spoken on the
phone for most of my life? I am terrified of speaking
to strangers, even children. I will try to imagine that
I am writing to you when I perform this event so I may
talk from my heart without terror. I wish to do this for
Julian. I feel he would be proud of me, as I believe you
will be too.

Will you write to me soon? And please tell me if I have
said things here for which I should be deeply sorry. You
mentioned your mother's great grandparents were from Budapest, a detail I have read over and over hoping, however
futilely, we have some small relation in common. Perhaps
it is only a foolish wish to believe that I am not without
family in the world. As a little girl I dreamed I had cousins on every continent and one day we would all be united.

You might know that Hungarians continually speak of
misfortune. I believe our pessimism is exaggerated, however. It is a strategy, mind you, a need to speak of all
our gloom on the chance that it may be averted. We rescue

ourselves moment by moment as such. For myself, I am so
restrained in person, so afraid of the world in many,
many ways, that it is only in writing to you that I can be
brave.

In friendship,
Anna Katz

Cap put down the letter and took out a piece of paper from his desk.
He stared at his own letterhead: Cap Kaplan, Psy.D.; Licensed Clinical
Psychologist. He dated the letter, and wrote at the top:

*Dear Anna . . . Thank you for your wonderful letter. It meant much to
me that you wrote so honestly and wisely of your experience . . .*

He crossed out *honestly* and put in *truthfully*. He crossed out *truthfully*
and started over again.

*I have something I must tell you about Julian. I've wanted to inform you
of this news for quite some time, but complications prevented me from . . .*

He crumpled up the letter—too portentous—and started over.

*I've been wanting to tell you for some time good news that I've been reluctant
to reveal . . .*

He took out another sheet of stationery.

You'll be very surprised to hear that you have a grandchild . . .

Cap closed his eyes and laid his pen on the desk. He couldn't write
to her about it. How could he explain why he'd withheld the information for so long? Because he still owed his clients, no matter how
undeserving, the privilege of his confidence? Because he feared Maureen would somehow use the situation to her advantage, extract promises, extort favors, somehow menace the woman with her only living
descendant, a grandchild Anna didn't know she had and would be, to
say the least, shocked to discover? Or more likely Maureen would just
refuse to cooperate, and then he would have tortured the poor woman
further by having let her know of the child, whom she would never

see. Wouldn't it be better for Anna not to know, if the outcome was so doubtful, if she'd have yet another person made alive, then forbidden to her?

He knew the child existed because he'd received a picture of her, sent to him at work but with no return address, just a California postmark. He wasn't sure why Maureen had sent it to him, but it confirmed the rumors he'd heard about a baby. Cap had studied the picture for quite some time, trying to decide what to do. The little girl was definitely Julian's, the same watchful eyes and somber long brow, set half in defiance, half in wonder. On the back, Maureen had written: "Thought you'd like to see my daughter . . . our future president." Signed her initial. Nothing else. He'd put the snapshot away in Maureen's file, but had gradually, over the past six months, with every letter to Anna, begun to feel urgent about telling her. He had hoped the picture was a calling card from Maureen—that he eventually might persuade her to contact Anna—but nothing more had followed. He'd tried to track her down through the university in the town on the postmark, but with no luck.

The fact was he hated Maureen. Contrary to Anna's generosity, he hated the hater. He hated her for the indecency of fleeing town even before the service—her callous retreat, if indeed it was a retreat and not just a whim to leave. He'd been the one to notify Maureen about Julian, calling her from the police station. She hadn't believed him at first. Then she'd realized there was no reason for Cap to be joking. She'd call back; she had to go to class to give a final. But she never called. He'd wanted to know if Julian had been at her apartment. Had he left because of a fight? Did Maureen send him away that cold night? She hadn't murdered him, but it was possible that she'd driven him to the act, sufficiently possible to make Cap hate her.

But even this act of hers didn't quite explain his feeling. Ah, the levels of *sonainnu*—the cantor's great riddle to Cap on the occasion of becoming a man. What was the exact translation here? How precise, how pure could he get about the hate? Anna had been right. He couldn't give up the irresistible conviction that someone must be hated. He or Maureen, by some turn, some small degree of deflection, could have steered Julian out of the path of the train that night. There were only three choices: hate her, hate himself, hate God, if He existed, for not stopping this.

And even if he could find Maureen, Cap couldn't imagine her welcoming Julian's mother into her life, or even bringing the child to Baltimore for a visit, making it easy on anyone but herself. So he should just remain silent, the consummate neutral therapist, careful not to get entrapped by his clients' predicaments. What a joke! He'd already stepped over the line long ago with Anna, some quirky form of ethical impropriety that now had him corresponding passionately with his dead client's mother.

He'd been writing to her for over a year. The correspondence had started when he'd sent her a thank-you note for the blanket she'd given him for Claude. He'd never expected a response, but to his surprise, amazement even, she'd written back a long, informative letter, apologizing for her brusqueness, explaining she was two people, one in person and another in writing. She wished he had written to her initially instead of visiting; he would have received a more generous welcome. She needed the distance of words on paper to give her a way to speak to people, without feeling as if she would be misused by their presence.

"I see no reflection of myself in a looking glass, only on paper," she'd written to him, the words impressed strongly in blue ink on crisp sheets of beige stationery. "On paper I can speak not as a hollow thing but as a person, not to be pitied but to be challenged and engaged and remembered for myself, not my history. I do not wish to be an object of pity or morbid curiosity. Sometimes, I must tell you, I write my husband letters and leave them on the bed—more than sometimes. This is how we have been a married couple all these years, not out of pity for me. Do not pity me," she had written, and since that first letter he'd sent her his own unbridled torrent—his father's death, confusion about his career, news of Joan's pregnancy—surprised that he could tell this woman such things through the mail, a complete stranger whom he knew from only inside his client's head, and to whom he was unable to stop baring his soul.

Now he pushed his own letter to her aside. It was a waste of time to write back. Anything less than telling her that she still had one living descendant left in the world would be a lie.

He took out another sheet of paper to practice his Hebrew. Lately, when he'd been unable to sleep, he'd been trying to relearn Hebrew, without the hovering judgment of Cantor Zommick. He'd gotten a Hebrew dictionary from the library and studied a different letter each night. His goal, difficult as it might be for anyone, let alone for him, was to make his way through the Midrash Rabbah in Hebrew, the Judaic legends and wisdom in their original tongue. Interestingly, he had an easier time reading Hebrew now than when he'd been bar mitzvahed. The letters appeared more distinct to him somehow, as though they were indeed carved in stone tablets and stolidly deter-mined to have meaning, even for his eyes.

What he'd discovered was that Anna Katz had omitted the full translation on Julian's—now Claude's—blanket. Claude had lain on the couch last night, sick with the flu, the whole school sick, in fact, and Cap had stayed up with him. Eventually Claude dozed off, and Cap didn't want to move, so he'd taken out his dictionary and begun translating the words on the blanket with its ewes that covered Claude. "Be strong and let your heart take courage" was there, but preceding it was "Hope in the Lord."

Had she left this off intentionally?

Certainly he could write her with a question about the words on the blanket, but what did it matter? Compared to knowing that she had a grandchild, what possible importance could a few extra words have?

Even these extra words.

He grew tired and put down his pen.

Not wanting to turn on the heat, he took the quilt from his office closet and went into the living room. He sat on the couch and flipped through the channels of late-night television. The Bob Babcock Strategy was on. Cap, if he heeded the call, could make upwards of two million dollars. After all, Bob, who would be onstage in a minute, after the testimonials about his greatness were through, had started out small, a shoe clerk (though last week, Cap could have sworn, Bob had been a high school guidance counselor) and presumably despondent until he "took the chance of a lifetime." It would be only a matter of calling the 800 number and getting the necessary tapes, books, and special investment tips that would revamp his financial life. The Strategy—Cap thought of Anna's "strategy" for avoiding Hungarian gloom—was so simple. He could start using it tonight, while waiting to sleep. Yes, anybody, even you depressed and disillusioned therapists out there, could become new people if you'd put your silly old dreams aside and get on with the Strategy.

He clicked off the set. He'd deposited a check from his brother today. His father had been sending money, but now that he'd died, Allan, fully in charge of the business, signed the checks—a measure of just how much progress Allan had made. Allan and Joan lived with Cap's mother, in a new house. They'd sold the old one, the one Cap grew up in, after Cap's father died. They all worked in the business now; even his mother, as a bookkeeper. Joan helped Allan out with sales, the people end, never Allan's strong point, even on medication. Every week, Cap's mother called to find out about Claude and to give Cap reports of the store, of Joan's pregnancy, of the new life. She seemed happier than ever, much of it because Allan had not only taken the place of their father but found a way for her to contribute. He'd become the true head of the family, a mensch. Cap watched from a distance with longing, admiration, resentment, and, more and more, resignation. Allan had been on the bottom, after all, for so long. Would he, Cap, now take his turn down there indefinitely?

He should work more on his Hebrew, fill out some insurance forms, check his messages, type up some scrawled case notes.

At the very least he should immediately write to Anna and wish her good luck on her talk. He went back to his desk.

Last night he'd dreamed of Julian for the first time. Julian was with Claude at a playground, crouched down to be on Claude's level, as any smart adult would do. He'd taken Claude over to the fire pole, which in real life Claude was so afraid of falling off. Julian made a hoop with his arms around Claude, so he'd feel secure. Cap called out to them. Julian had turned sideways, as if unable fully to face Cap. "You're a good father, Julian!" Cap had said, and his eyes had filled with tears in sleep, the only place he allowed himself any relief now.

He sat for too long, a half hour, he guessed, and just stared at Anna's letter and at his own crossed-out efforts to reply. He thought about his father's funeral. They'd gone into the rabbi's study for the Kreah. At the appointed moment, the funeral director had cut the black ribbons pinned to their clothes, the rending of the garments that symbolized a tear in the heart—though the tear didn't go all the way through. There were still memories. Allan and Cap had their ribbons on the left side, over the heart. Uncle Morty, Cap's father's only living brother, had his on the right side, as did Cap's mother. The rabbi explained that children wore the black ribbons close to the heart because parents could never be replaced. A parent gave you life, and there was nothing you could do to repay that debt. You might have another sibling or another husband or another child if yours died, God forbid, but you lost only one father and mother. The ribbons were to be worn for thirty days.

They'd filed into the synagogue, where they sat in the front row. Wallis was waiting there with Claude. So was Joan and her family. Then Cap had seen the coffin. It took him by surprise. A simple mahogany casket with a Star of David carved on the lid, the coffin lay on a wheeled platform in the center aisle—closed, of course—with the mourners seated on either side.

After the service, the family rode to the cemetery in a limousine. Claude, hushed and still, sat on Cap's lap. Allan and Joan comforted Cap's mother, who wept quietly. At the cemetery, the rabbi said Kaddish, and then the coffin was lowered slowly into the ground by a pulley. One by one, mourners came up to drop a shovelful of dirt on top of the coffin as a way to say goodbye. The soul floated off. The body, the soul's carriage during life, would be respectfully returned to its resting place. Cap walked up and dug the shovel into the mound of dirt that had come from the grave's hole. He sprinkled dirt on the coffin's top; the soil skittered across the lid. It looked offensive, dropping dirt on his father, on this gleaming coffin, but the greater good was that he was speeding the body to its final resting place. Or so the rabbi said.

Cap waited behind a moment with Allan, while their mother was helped back to the car by Wallis and Joan. Claude, who had clung to Cap's leg while the Kaddish was said, quieted by the solemnity, followed after his mother.

"Do you remember what those stones are for?" asked Allan, pointing to the little stones on the top of the gravestone next to them. Allan had looked tired and pale during much of the ceremony and had risen to get a drink of water in the middle of the rabbi's eulogy. In the past, before his medication, he wouldn't have been fully aware of the circumstances, lost in a delusion that screened out reality. Now he faced it head-on, like Cap.

Some of the headstones had only a few stones, some had many, stacked on top of each other or in a neat, crowned row across the top. Cap had never known the reason; he'd thought it was just an old custom. "I know you're supposed to put one on top every time you visit, but I've never understood why."

The rest of the mourners had left them alone.

"It's from nomadic days," said Allan, "when the Jews wandered through the wilderness. They'd gather large stones to make the burial markers. Sometimes the mounds would break up in a storm, or a wild animal would knock the rocks apart. The markers would have to be put back together. So every time you visit, you leave a stone to build it again."

"How do you know all this?" said Cap, impressed.

"Joan and I are taking a Hebrew history class," Allan said.

They'd stood silently together and looked down at their father's coffin. Allan began to cry, great heaving sobs that Cap would not allow himself. Instead, he thought of some history he did remember from Hebrew school: David losing his beloved son Absalom and throwing himself on the ground, tearing his clothes in anguish, the original source of the Kreah. Would his father have wept for him like David for Absalom? Cap put his arm around his brother and wished that his own grief for their father could be so straightforward and explosive, not complicated, not withheld, himself as stingy with it as his father had been with his love for him. He was not willing to give back in grief what he'd never gotten in love, stubborn as the old man, dead now, any chance lost.

He put the letter from Anna inside his desk drawer and went upstairs. He sat on the side of the bed. Wallis turned over in her sleep, opened her eyes, and saw him sitting there motionless.

"What's wrong?" she asked.

"I don't know. I can't sleep again." About Anna's letters, Cap had said only that they were to do with old bills, not able to speak of this even to Wallis. Indeed, the circumstances surrounding Julian's death he'd kept largely to himself, telling her only that the boy had been his client, leaving out Maureen, the baby, and just how heavily guilt dragged on his neck.

Nor would he talk about his father, unable to mourn one death without the other.

Wallis brushed a hand across her face, trying to erase her tiredness. "Cap, can we talk in the morning? The kids will be here at eight-thirty."

"Sure," he said. "I shouldn't have woken you. I just found myself up here."

She reached out a hand to his leg. "We do need to talk. I've been wanting to so much."

"Yes," he said, though he didn't know where to start. The end. "Wallis, I think I'm going to quit."

"I can't believe you're telling me this now."

"I want to start letting clients know."

"Well, I have something to tell you too. I'm seeing somebody. Oh, God no, that's not what I mean." She put her hands over her face. "I'm so tired, Cap, I don't know what I'm saying. I mean a therapist. I'm seeing a therapist."

He laughed. "Well, I'm relieved it's only a therapist, I suppose. Who?"

"Dr. France."

"Oh," he said, and felt jealous anyway.

"Is that okay?"

"Sure. It's just a surprise. Why?"

"I wanted to. For myself. And because I didn't know what else to do."

He didn't say anything. He had the sensation of falling, vertigo, from lack of sleep, from nothing in his stomach. *The closest meaning is "our persecutors" . . . there is no translation . . . I hate this pain, I hate it with all my heart . . . but I do not hate the people who caused it . . .* Cantor Zommick and Anna Katz, his conscience and his anticonscience sitting on opposite shoulders, only which was which?

"I guess we can talk about this more in the morning," said Cap.

"Would you go see Dr. France with me? Or somebody else?"

"Maybe," he said. He lay down on the bed. "You're not going to give up on me, are you, Wallis?"

She took the bottom of her nightshirt and dabbed at his eyes. He hadn't realized he'd been crying. "No, I'm not giving up on you," she said. "I still love you, Cap. I wish I could make that sink in more during all this."

Subhuman creatures flickered at the corners of his vision, genetically engineered griffins and phoenixes and hydra-headed organisms, mutating at an exponential rate. Animal viruses on the loose.

"You're shivering," said Wallis. "Come under the covers."

It was all right, he reminded himself. Claude was downstairs in his bed, safe, with Julian's blanket protecting him, protecting him all through the night.

Cap knocked lightly on Dick's open door.

"Come on in," said Dick.

Dick motioned for him to sit down on a white muslin couch—new. Dick had redecorated his office: track lighting, three landscape paintings he'd brought back from a trip to Santa Fe; indeed, the whole office had a Southwestern flavor to it, Dick's desk now a long washed-gray table with sturdy trunk legs. Between the two east windows, small Zuni pots lined themselves up on a Spanish oak chest with painted leather door panels. Cap, meanwhile, pictured his own office: its Ansel Adams black-and-white photograph of two aspens. The picture, along with the furniture, had been there forever. Only the stuffed animals were recent. He'd been meaning to upgrade too, but not now. He was down to fewer clients than ever before. He wondered naturally if there was some word about him out there. Dick's practice, after all—just look around—wasn't suffering. Last week Dick had sent four referrals his way. Two had specifically wanted Dick, but the others were open to trying him out, Cap informing them (oh, so subtle the persuasion had to be; you could never sound like a vacuum cleaner salesman in this business) that Dick and he had been associates for a number of years and often referred clients to one another.

But all that didn't matter now.

"How are the Johnsons?" asked Dick.

"They terminated."

"Oh?"

"She got pregnant again; they're happy."

"How about Irv Cafferty? You were doing some nice work with him about his father."

"He left too."

"I would have thought he'd want to continue."

"Well"—Cap shrugged—"he didn't."

Dick was silent.

"Listen, Cap, maybe this isn't the time to bring it up—I know things haven't been going well—but I'm wondering about your share of the building."

He hadn't paid his half of the mortgage for three months now.

"I owe you for that," said Cap. "I'll have to come up with it somehow."

"I can carry us a little longer, but after another couple of months . . ."

"Looks as if you could carry us longer than a couple of months." He regretted the words as soon as they'd left his mouth.

Dick regarded him silently. He had such a different style than Cap. Dick would never get down on the floor to help a client hit a pillow or put a hand on someone's chest to help him breathe or drift too far from analysis into interviews with parent introjects. He was too much the careful practitioner for that. For him, psychodynamic therapy required more decorum and distance. Too much risk of malpractice these days anyway. And maybe Dick was right—maybe the regressive, experiential work was just one more way Cap got too involved. Even Dick's clothes showed tempered goodwill. Today he wore a light-blue sweater and charcoal wool pants, warm, while Cap had shown up for work in sweatpants and sneakers. And Dick clearly ran his practice like a business—Cap's father would have approved—charging clients for phone calls, hiring an accounting service to do his billing, making first-time clients sign a long waiver form. All good business sense.

"Dick, I'm going to be leaving," said Cap. Finally, it was out. A great relief.

"What's wrong, Cap?"

"I've had it," said Cap. "I'm used up."

"There are other ways to take care of yourself besides quitting. Find activities that get you away from your clients' burdens. Exercise helps. You used to do that religiously. We haven't played racquetball in months, despite my goading. You don't need me to tell you all this, Cap."

"No, I don't." He thought about Dick's outside interests: he flew a plane, he skied, he went to professional training seminars, he played racquetball, he even belonged to a model railroad club—and he had a wife and three children.

Untouched, it seemed, by the seeping despair of his clients.

"Maybe I'm just not as good as you about keeping my own stuff separate," said Cap.

"You've had so many changes in the last two years, Cap. Think about it: You had a son. Your brother is functional. Your father died recently. Have you dealt with all these things?" And before Cap could answer, Dick added, "And you can't let one client determine your future. You don't seem to have ever gotten over what happened to Julian. You're an outstanding therapist. I know that, and so does everybody who's ever worked with you. I can't say it any more clearly, and I wish you'd take it from me, not as your partner or a therapist, but just as a friend who's known you a long time. I envy what you do, Cap. I can't do it myself, but I appreciate success when I see it."

"Success," said Cap, hearing the magic word. *So how much did you pull down last year, Cappie?* His father's voice more alive than ever in his head.

"It's a cycle, Cap. We've all been through it and survived. Next week you'll suddenly wonder why you were ever complaining about so few clients."

"I don't think so, Dick. I somehow slipped out of the loop. Something's off for good."

"Things have *happened*, Cap. Just agree to give it some more time before making the decision. See a colleague for a while. We both know lots of people you could go to. We'll work something out about the building."

Cap looked around the office again. He and Dick had found this house in ugly disrepair: dingy rooms, moldy carpeting with skid marks from the motorcycle gang who had lived here and driven their bikes right into the living room, broken windowpanes, water stains on the ceiling, exposed wiring, squirrels in the attic and mice in the walls. They'd bought it cheap and commenced working on it. They had pulled up the rugs, torn down walls, sanded the wood floors and stained them back to their original high gloss, rebricked the fireplace, gutted the old kitchen and bathrooms, and hung wallpaper. That had been eight years ago; they'd just started their partnership, after working together occasionally on family services cases, and decided that remodeling the house would be a good way to forge their association. They worked on weekends and late at night, hammering and sawing and talking to one another about joists and headers and select lumber and furred-out walls, never mentioning a single client. It had been a fulfillment of Cap's old fantasy—to build a cabin out here in Colorado; instead, he would make a sanctuary of his office. And Dick (whose father had been a carpenter in Ouray, Colorado) had taught him how to do everything from plumb an old sink to hang drywall. Once the entire south wall, propped up with two-by-fours, had nearly fallen on Cap, and Dick had pulled him away at the last moment. He would have been crushed, no question about it. Dick took it in stride, but Cap had been in shock, then overwhelmingly grateful. In some ways, Dick had been the brother he'd always wanted, but now Cap could feel himself pushing him away too. It was too hard to stand up straight under the threat. That wall, that wall that should have collapsed on him, finally had—only there were people behind it, the broken and the haunted; they'd all come crashing through. They could not forgive themselves their terror.

"Please don't ask me what else I'm going to do," said Cap. "I haven't got that far yet." He stood up and walked tiredly out of Dick's office.

Wilmella was waiting for him, faithful, dogged Wilmella. "Can you feel the winter in your bones, Mr. Cap?" asked Wilmella.

Cap nodded. He could indeed. "Wilmella, I have some news for you. I've decided to close my practice."

"But we've been through this before," said Wilmella. "You were going to give me another chance. I've even come prepared today!" She dug into her ample straw bag and took out a newspaper. "I've brought you something."

Blue eyeliner made her eyes look as if they were lost in orbit. A pert red tam was pinned to her thinning hair. Fluffy white bangs dipped over her forehead. Her mouth had dropped even further in the corners at his news, so she looked like an old, forgotten rodeo queen. "You've done nothing wrong, Wilmella. It's me who's decided to leave."

"But where? Can I take lessons from you somewhere else?"

"Sessions."

"Can I?"

"No, Wilmella. I'm terminating my practice."

She looked aghast. "But how?"

"I just do it."

"Don't you have to get special permission?"

Cap smiled. He'd miss her. She kept it all in perspective. One day, in the other world, he'd meet her and find out she was really his guardian angel in disguise, with perfect pitch as Wilmella Hoder of Wyoming. "I simply leave. I don't have to turn in my collar."

"Oh, my," said Wilmella. "I guess you won't want to see this, then." She handed him the news article. It was a story of a murder that had taken place over fifty years ago. A man had been brutally hacked to pieces and buried under the floorboards of a pump house. An excavation of the structure by the new owners of the ranch had turned up the bones, already ten years old by that time. The article, from the *Wyoming Eagle*, was dated November 2, 1953.

"I did that," said Wilmella.

"You did what?"

Wilmella straightened her back. "I killed that man. He was my uncle. See, there's his name in the second line. Corbett Myers, my father's brother."

"All right," said Cap, taking a breath. "Why tell me now?"

"Because I'm going to die," she said, and he heard a snap in her throat. She chewed gum politely when one of them wasn't talking. Cap associated their longer silences with the sound of her gum snapping.

"Could you tell me why?"

"I'm sick. I have an inoperable brain tumor."

"Oh," said Cap. "For how long now?"

"Ever since I began therapy. You see, I knew that once I told you the ending to my story, I'd die. You know about Scheherazade, don't you?" Cap rubbed his neck. He'd expected it would be hard to tell Wilmella he was leaving, but he hadn't quite anticipated this. "Don't you think that's what everyone wants to do? Put off their own demise?"

"I don't know," said Cap, not understanding endings, deaths, or why people lied to themselves, though he'd done it all his life too.

"You should know that I enjoyed myself."

"Here?"

"No, I enjoyed hacking my uncle to pieces. That's the true condition of my mind."

Something caught his eye on the news clipping. In very tiny print at the bottom could be found the information that the paper stock was 65 percent recycled. "Since when did newspapers use recycled paper in 1953?" he asked her.

Wilmella looked contrite.

It was one of those mock newspapers you could get printed up in a novelty store, with your name in the front-page headline: CAP KAPLAN RETIRES—TIME STOPS.

"There is no brain tumor, is there?"

She shook her head.

"Is there an uncle?"

"No."

"No uncle?"

"No uncle."

"No headaches?"

"No."

"No loud booming noises?"

"No."

"No voices?"

"No."

"No fears of smothering in a basement or shadowy figures on the edge of the bed?"

"No."

"How then, Wilmella, how did you mimic all the symptoms of sexual abuse?"

"I read an article in the *Reader's Digest*. It showed a check-list."

Cap winced. "That's very upsetting, Wilmella. Lots of people come here with real cases. Why did you pretend to be abused? Don't you realize it's not something to be taken lightly?"

"But Mr. Cap, you were so concerned that I have a problem that I made one up to please you! When you gave me an assignment about my uncle, I wrote this instead," said Wilmella, the first real tear in her eye he'd ever seen. "You've been so nice to me when no one else bothered to care. I've enjoyed every moment of our talks."

He made some final notes in Wilmella's case file. He'd hugged her goodbye and assured her that he wasn't angry with her for fabricating the story. Her final words to him had been, "You made me feel as if being alone wasn't a good enough reason to be in therapy. But isn't that what's wrong with most people you see?"

Rare wisdom for Wilmella. If only she'd been this sharp throughout, they might have actually gotten somewhere, provided there had been somewhere to go with her. Maybe not. In his search for the Big Problem, he had made her think she needed to come up with something better. Was that just another vestige of wanting to excel, that he needed clients with superior problems, or problems that would lend themselves to his dramatic intervention? Or ones he might someday dream of writing about so that he, too, could land on the best-seller list with the other self-help gurus? Was he back to this again, full circle at the end of his career? Or was he really being fair to himself? Wasn't Wilmella wasting both her time and his: he still believed that therapy, despite his decision to leave, amounted to more than heightened chatting and had to be used wisely and selectively, like any good medicine.

What did you do anyway after being a therapist for twenty years? *I used to be a psychologist.*

The statement had an ominous tone. I used to fight fires . . . *until the accident.* You couldn't leave a job like this without the departure hinting of controversy and scandal. You couldn't go back on your vows; it was a lifetime commitment, like nuns marrying God (Wilmella's comparison to a priest not that far off, after all). You couldn't practice long without realizing that it was your insight that had become the word, and you the therapy. Doctors had their stethoscopes, lawyers their casebooks, teachers their curriculums; every profession had its tools that distanced the doer from the act. But therapy, his kind of therapy, had no such boundaries. You were it. The answer to your own questions. The self without tickets to any other show. How could he ever have another job? With what other job did you always ask, after every word, every handshake, every hour, Am I enough?

He walked out to the waiting room to find his ten o'clock, a new client. He'd have to give her the disappointing news that within two months he'd be closing his practice.

Cap stuck his head around the corner, only to find Maureen sitting there.

"What are you doing here?"

"I wanted to see you." Maureen smiled and recrossed her legs.

Cap stepped closer and loomed above her with barely controllable rage. "I have a client coming in at ten o'clock."

"I made that appointment," she said.

"What are you talking about?"

"I didn't think you'd agree to see me—if I called as myself, that is."

How stupid could he be. She'd asked for an appointment, barely disguising her voice. And he'd told her, I'm looking forward to meeting you, Sheila. She could make a fool of him like no one he'd ever known. "I'm not your therapist anymore."

"I tried to see someone else, out in California." Gone was her black dragon outfit. She had white drawstring pants and a plum-colored blouse, sensible fleece-lined boots. She'd cut her hair, too, and looked her age, with very little makeup. He wondered if this was just another act.

"I'm not interested in your case anymore, Maureen."

"This other therapist I went to in California . . . he suggested that I should come back and finish my work with you. He said it was clear that I trusted you in a way I didn't trust him or anyone else. I'm not the same person, Cap. A child changes things. You should know that. Give me a chance."

"You've got fifty minutes. Start talking."

"You always gave me a full hour before."

"Shut up and talk," he said, wild to get her out of his office. Hunched over his chair, his breath sour from coffee and too many Tums, he'd caught a glance of himself in his office window. His hair stuck out asymmetrically from one side in black shrieking spikes; his face had a brutish shadow of bristles running down to his throat; one wing of his blue shirt collar was rolled under like a neck bandage. He looked the epitome of every joke about a crazy psychiatrist. "Start," he growled. "I'm listening."

He actually saw a flicker of fear cross her face. It wakened and stirred him—shaved a fine dust off his dead bones and made him lock his eyes onto her, wired for details.

"Where?" she said. "At least help me start."

"You're at the pond. You're four years old. You're alone." He leaned over and held her milky wrists with their pale veins.

"Stop—you're hurting me." She pulled away from him, rubbed her wrists, looking at him from the side like a frightened bird.

"Tell me your father's name."

"Azal."

"What are you doing at the pond, Azal?"

Maureen shook her head. "I don't want to."

"You have forty minutes."

"Stop reminding me about the time!"

"What are you doing at the pond, Azal?"

"Looking for my cows." She shrugged, as if to say, Why not?

"Why are you down there so late? Aren't all your cows in the barn by now? Where are they?" asked Cap impatiently.

"One's lost."

"Who's with you?"

"My daughter's with me."

Cap leaned back in his chair. He could hear the slight change in Maureen's voice; she'd found the slot, the father's index, discreet as an entry on a silicon chip. This wouldn't be as easy as the mother. This one was trouble. He'd hit trouble, all right.

"Is that the daughter you had second or first?" Her face went blank. "Answer me, Azal."

"She ain't mine."

"Oh, what makes you say that?"

"I know. I just know she ain't."

"You have anything besides your own suspicion as proof?"

"She's like her mother. Always misbehaving."

Cap put his hands behind his head. Big Azal. Big Azal was finally in the room with them. He had a few things to say to this fellow. "She's four years old, Azal. Four-year-olds are supposed to misbehave."

"She's bad. Like her mom. She ain't any of mine."

"You got it in your head that's true, Azal. I guess there's no convincing you otherwise."

"There ain't."

"Any particular reason you're so sure?"

"She don't look like me."

"Who's she look like? Azal?"

"I don't want to say."

"Why not? Are you afraid I'll laugh at you?"

"I don't even belong here. It's for sick people." Maureen sat straight up in her chair, her lips pressed together. She stared right at Cap, comfortable finally, as set in her role as in the molded seat of a tractor. She knew she was good. She knew Cap knew it. He could see the farm girl behind the professor, behind the rapacious siren, behind the will to match his own will. She was going to try to have her way with him, her father's way.

"Azal, can you tell me who you think your daughter looks like?"

"She looks like my wife's brother."

"Oh, your brother-in-law."

"He ain't no kin to me."

"So you're saying your wife and her brother had sex."

"That's filthy talk."

"But you're saying it."

"It's filthy. You said it."

"But you thought it. Is that what happened to you, Azal? Did someone in your family do something inappropriate to you?"

"Nothing inappropriate about my family."

"All right, then, did you do something filthy to someone? Azal, why won't you answer?"

"I'm finished with all this. I had just about enough."

She stood up; so did Cap. "Sit down, Azal."

"You can't keep me here."

"I said sit down. We're not finished."

"I'm free to go as I please. You just move aside—"

"Sit the fuck down, Azal!"

She sat down, shrinking from him into her chair. Some small part of Maureen hidden inside peeked out to watch, with relief. He was protecting her. He'd stood up to her father, knocked him down to size, promised her safety to go on.

"That's better, Azal," said Cap. "You're a bully, aren't you?"

"I don't have any idea what you're talking about."

"You like to bully people smaller than you. Children, for instance."

"Listen here—"

"All right, Azal, don't worry. I want to talk to you about something else today. Something that's important for my client, your daughter Maureen. Can you tell me what happened when Maureen was four?"

"I don't know what you're talking about."

"Oh, I think you do, Azal. I think you know exactly what I'm talking about."

"You keep talking, but you ain't saying anything. Spit it out, if you got something on your mind."

"What did you do to Maureen at that pond, Azal?"

"I didn't do nothing. I don't have to sit here and take this."

Cap put his hands on either side of Maureen's chair. "We're not finished yet, Azal. I'll tell you when we're finished. I'm concerned about what you did to my client Maureen. I'm watching out for her, Azal, and something isn't adding up here. So either you tell me or we'll get it out some other way."

"Don't you threaten me. You goddamn people think you're smarter than me—"

Cap leaned in closer, his breath on Maureen's face. He smiled. Her eyes didn't even blink. How many clients he'd done role-playing with; how few would go this far. He was going to push it today. Bad pushing, good pushing—it didn't matter. One last push. "You listen to me, Azal. I've got a client here who has a real problem. Something happened to her a long time ago. Something you won't let her forget. She's carried you around long enough, Azal. The free ride is over. Now you're going to tell me what happened back then."

"You got a helluva nerve talking to me that way. You people are all the same. Hell, you didn't come by any of it honestly, always Jewing honest folks out of their money—"

"Azal, let's get something straight. I don't give a damn what you think of me or my 'people.' " He saw one more screen drop. Money money money. Her father despised her because she had cost him money. "What happened down by the pond? Did you throw Maureen in the water?"

"You dumb son of a bitch."

"Okay, what happened, then?"

"She slipped. She was playing by the edge and I turned back and she was in the water."

"Azal, you're lying to me."

She spit in his face. "Go fuck yourself."

He tightened his hands on the arms of her chair, his knees touching hers now. Maureen drew back, her face ashen. "What's the matter, Azal? Something wrong? Is this what you used to do to Maureen?"

She lifted her hand to scratch at his face, but he caught her wrist. "That's not going to do you much good here, Azal. There isn't anyone to bully like you did your family. Like you did Maureen. Didn't you get her on the floor in a headlock once and tell her, 'I could break your neck in two right now'? Didn't you? Answer me!"

She stared wide-eyed at him.

"What else, Azal? Did you sit by her bed one night with a kitchen knife until she woke up and saw you?"

She started to gag. Her face drained of color. She gagged again. Cap didn't move. He kept his hands on the sides of her chair and made a cage with his elbows. She motioned that she couldn't speak. She was choking.

"Where are you?" asked Cap.

She shook her head. A foul, brackish smell rose up between them, putrid and green to its depth, although maybe he imagined its odor because he understood now she was drowning. She was swallowing the pond water. She swayed in the chair, holding her sides. "Breathe," said Cap. "Keep breathing. You're not going to die. I have you." She gagged again, dry-heaving gas in his face. "You're drowning. Who's there? Where's your father? You said he was there. Is he pulling you out?"

Before he could stop her, she scratched him twice across his cheek, clawing at his face, blood streaming down his jawbone. He grabbed her wrists, his face stinging with searing heat. "Please," she said so softly—speaking as herself—that he made the mistake of releasing her. She sprung at him and knocked him back over his desk, tearing at him, drawing blood again, this time from his neck, before he could grab her shoulders and wrestle her to the floor. Her knee jerked up into his groin, and he grunted, curling in a ball, a cloud sinking without sleep, his body sweating and soaking his clothes, and he thought for a moment, seeing her stand up and lift the desk lamp to bring it down on his head, that he would die now, and then he swept his leg out and knocked her down. He pressed his shoulder into her back, catching his breath and grunting to keep her struggling body pinned down. They lay panting on the floor, Maureen still. He kept his weight on her. Her tongue tried to lick the side of his head—getting too close— and then her teeth snapped viciously at his cheek.

When he spoke again, it was in a thin rasp, his own heart pounding, blood in the back of his throat. He put his teeth on the back of her ear, touching the cartilage with his lips. *Let him go, Maureen.*

He felt the air go out from her then, her rage collapse, a chambered cave between memory and breath sucked clear.

"He's watching me."

"What?" asked Cap.

"He's watching me drown."

"Where is he?"

"He's crouched down at the edge of the pond. I can't swim well enough to get out. Water is coming up above my chin, into the bottom of my mouth. I can taste pieces of leaves. I'm splashing and flapping my arms as hard as I can, but I can't reach the edge. I'm too tired, and too frightened. There's scum on my hair and my lips, and I keep going under, then forcing myself to the surface. My legs are turning underneath me, and it feels as if I'm going backward, over my head—too much dizziness to make my arms work anymore. I'm screaming and screaming and screaming and screaming and screaming and he gets off one knee and I think, Daddy's going to help me. But he steps back and just watches me. He just looks. And I know then I'm dead. I've already died. No matter what happens after this, I'm dead inside."

Cap relaxed his grip. "Who saves you?"

"He looks over his shoulder. My mother is calling me. He reaches for me because she's coming. I never forget how he looks at me. Every year afterward he tries to finish it."

"You're alive, Maureen. You're here. You exist. He's dead and you're not. He can't harm you anymore from where he is." Cap rolled off her.

"Don't. Please," she said. "Don't go," and he lay there with blood on him, holding her.

The session with Maureen had finally exhausted him, too, into a brief sleep. They woke up together on the floor of his office and looked at each other, Maureen drawing a hand across her face. "I feel as if it's the morning after," she said with a laugh, and went off to the bathroom down the hall, as if it really were, a shyness he felt also. When she returned she had washed up, and it was his turn. He splashed water on his face, cleaned up as best he could, then went back. Maureen was waiting for him on the couch, her hands folded.

The room smelled of mingled odors, sweat and too much heat and gastric juices. He opened a window. He had lost track of the time. His muscles ached, and he wanted a shower—signs of life inside him. They sat in silence for a few minutes.

"Well, where do we go from here?" Maureen finally asked.

"That's up to you. But at least you won't have Azal on your back."

"And I suppose you think I'll be fine now?"

"It does make a difference when you don't believe every man is secretly trying to kill you."

"You haven't forgiven me, have you?"

"About what?"

"Julian."

Cap remained silent. He couldn't be calm or reasonable about the subject.

"You know that I had nothing to do with it," explained Maureen.

"I know nothing of the sort."

Maureen took out a cigarette. He thought it was a measure of just how much he'd already left the job that he didn't try to stop her.

"I know one way I could forgive you," said Cap, realizing he couldn't wait any longer to ask.

"Oh?" said Maureen, leaning forward. He'd piqued her interest. She hadn't been expecting this. "What would that be?"

"You could let Julian's mother see her granddaughter."

There was a stony silence. She had frozen, her cigarette held out in front of her.

He stood up and went to Maureen's file and took out the photograph of the child, leaned it against the back of his desk lamp so she could see. "Have you forgotten you sent this to me?" he asked.

"No," she said. "I won't."

"Why not?"

"This is my child. She belongs to no one else."

"She was Julian's too, Maureen. He still has a claim through his mother."

"A claim? A claim?" Maureen stood up and paced toward the door. Her voice was so tense and thin it came out in a strained whisper. "How dare you talk to me about *claims*."

"You're frightened she'll be taken away from you, aren't you?" He could see by the vicious glance she gave him that this was true.

"Not for discussion."

He'd try another tack. "I know Julian's mother. Let her have the happiness of holding her granddaughter. It would mean everything to her. She's lost so much already. Not just Julian, but others."

"All the more reason," said Maureen, "not to let her near us. She's jinxed."

Cap dropped his head. He felt as if she'd just rammed him with a forklift at ninety miles an hour. She had found Anna's weak spot without even knowing her, or maybe Cap's spot on behalf of her. It took him a few minutes to catch his breath. "Maureen, what do you want from me?" It was a plea. "Please."

She considered him a moment, watching his eyes. "I want you to make love to me."

Cap sighed. His desperation was so nakedly apparent now that there was no use in hiding it. "You're just telling me this because you know it's the one thing that I won't do."

"That's right," said Maureen, standing up. She smiled at him. He couldn't believe they had reverted so swiftly to their old positions on the game board. Had the past hour meant nothing?

"Maureen, don't you think you owe me this one favor—"

She started to leave.

"All right," said Cap. "Give me the number where you're staying."

She wrote it down on the back of Wilmella's file, turned facedown on Cap's desk. "I'm house-sitting for an old colleague until next Friday," she said. "Then I'm gone from here for good."

"If you get what you want, will you agree to let Julian's mother come see the baby?"

"I'll wait for your call," Maureen said, making no promises.

Chapter Fifteen

DR. FRANCE STEERED WALLIS BACK TOWARD HER PAST AGAIN. "WHAT did you do when your parents argued?"

Wallis didn't want to talk about her childhood anymore. She answered with a bored sigh, the way her eighth graders did when they didn't like to give themselves away. "I suppose I tried to stop them at first."

"How?"

"I'd ask for a glass of water, make a nuisance of myself until they screamed at me. Anything to break into their locked horns."

"And did that work?"

"At first. But then after a while they just completely ignored me and went on screaming at one another." She remembered how she would get cramps in her stomach and lie across a rolled-up beach towel on her bed.

"Do you feel that you can't break through to Cap in the same way?"

"Yes." God, it was a relief to say it, to tell someone what it was like trying to get through. "I keep staring up his nostrils to see where the aliens have done the implant. He's acting completely unnatural. Now he's decided to quit being a therapist altogether."

Dr. France shifted in her chair. She wore gray slacks and a crimson sweatshirt from Harvard. Her son, a student there, had sent it to her. Dr. France admitted she had debated whether to wear the item to work, whether it would make clients think she was trying to impress them with her children's achievements. But she'd gone ahead and done it anyway, she said with a laugh, because she liked the color. She'd told Wallis all this in the first five minutes of the session, when Wallis asked about the sweatshirt. It had significance, Dr. France said, so it was worth pausing over, and indeed, Wallis had listened with fascination to every detail.

"I told him we need to talk with someone, but he hasn't agreed yet to see you, or anyone for that matter."

"Why not, do you think?"

"Embarrassment, or pride, maybe. He doesn't want to show any weakness in front of a colleague. And anyway, aren't therapists the last to get help for themselves? Aren't they always filling themselves up with their clients' problems partly as a way to avoid their own messy lives?"

Dr. France grunted, a deep, hungry grunt of either sympathy or disagreement—Wallis couldn't tell for sure, only that it had touched a professional nerve.

"And of course," Wallis continued, "there's the money. Most of all, maybe."

"You mentioned your parents fought about money."

It was true. That was the worst part of hearing it from Cap; it reminded her of all those arguments about her mother's extravagance. Wallis felt as if she were being accused in the same way.

"Wallis," said Dr. France, and Wallis closed her eyes for a moment at the sound of her name. "Are you afraid I'll abandon you too?"

After a while, when Wallis still couldn't answer the question— every time she tried, her throat would dry up into a wordless crisp— Dr. France said, "You've never shown me a picture of Claude. Might I see him?" and it made Wallis start to cry. It was ridiculous how easily she cried in here. Her parents' disregard of Claude was, in some ways, as bad as having them divorce again. The same dreadful, infuriating, gut-wrenching (yes, that was it, like pressing down over the rolled-up towel, praying they would stop fighting before her belly exploded) rejection.

She was crying so hard she had started to gulp down air. She was so emotional these days, a grotto of weeping walls. Dr. France came over and patted her back. "All those tears from long ago still there," said Dr. France. She placed a box of tissues on Wallis's lap. Wallis counted the rings on Dr. France's fingers—four—and tried to get control of herself. She took the pictures of Claude from her wallet and laid them out on the couch, in order of years, narrating for Dr. France—a first taste of banana, a toss in the air by Cap during Runaway Elevator (a lump came back in her throat as she looked at that one), Claude's first-birthday party, a pony ride at two—who made warm, throaty sounds. "Do you think he looks like me?" asked Wallis.

"You bet he does, girl!" said Dr. France, completely out of her role for a wonderful moment.

Chapter Sixteen

EARLY FRIDAY MORNING, CAP CALLED MAUREEN FROM A PUBLIC PHONE two blocks from his house.

"I was just packing," she said, without much blame or disappointment in her voice. A cool fact.

"Can we talk?" he said.

"Talk?"

Sighing, he pulled the collar of his coat tighter. The temperature had dropped to ten below last night and was supposed to get even colder tomorrow for Martin Luther King's birthday. Cap could see that the parking meters along University Avenue had already been bagged for the parade.

"You're one of those guys who like to keep a gal guessing," said Maureen, though it didn't sound as if she had her heart in the repartee. If anything, he heard anxiousness in her voice—he had actually called her, broken professional protocol. It was a first, all right.

"I'm calling you from a phone booth, Maureen. It's very cold, and I'd like to keep this brief." He held the chilled receiver away from his ear. "Will you see me or not?"

"I have some errands to do."

Hard-to-get. "Okay, when?"

"At three. Two hours should give us enough time, wouldn't you say? Or do you need a lot less or a lot more?"

"Sounds like you're afraid I'll really come over," said Cap.

"Sounds like you have nothing better to do." Had she already figured out that he was leaving therapy? For the next two months, he would be going through the termination process with his remaining clients, but today had wound up open.

"I can make time," he said, not wanting his words to have any hidden meanings, a hopeless effort, because he had after all called her on the basis of a proposition.

She gave him the address and told him three would be just swell.

He must have panicked when he hung up; at least that was how he explained his impulse to call Armond immediately afterward. It would have made more sense to call Dick, but perhaps he'd wanted advice from an old father figure, and perhaps he'd just wanted to tell the figure that the real father had died, bring it to a close with his surrogate. He hadn't expected Armond to be there, much less answer his phone.

"It's Cap Kaplan, Armond."

"Hello!"

"I thought we might talk sometime."

"Today at twelve."

"Today? I didn't mean so soon—"

"Otherwise it will have to wait for two weeks. I'm going to Vail."

"Armond, I hadn't even planned—"

"Must go. Noon, then?" and he hung up.

The traffic moved slowly on the interstate to Denver. Drivers were cautious because of the icy roads, and Cap followed a line of cars in a slow procession. At this rate, he'd have to turn right around after his meeting with Armond and rush the sixty miles back to Pierre to make sure he got to Maureen's house by three. If he'd expected that quitting would gain him more separation from the job, he was starting off poorly, heading straight to his old therapist and then to his worst client.

He found Armond's office on Second Avenue in Hilltop, one of Denver's most affluent neighborhoods. Cap had never visited him here before. Armond had worked out of his office at Denver Psychiatric Hospital before going into private practice.

Cap walked up the steps to the large double doors with their heavy brass knocker. The building appeared to be a small renovated mansion. The right door opened without a squeak. The hallway, its walls lined with hand-carved walnut molding, stretched deep into the back. On top of a black marble side table stood a slender pearl-white luminous vase, with three tall tan cattails. From the cove ceiling, accented with hidden fluorescent lighting, hung a chandelier worthy of Versailles. Its pendants twinkled and spun slightly in the wind Cap had allowed in before he shut the door silently and took a seat on a lacquered bench in the hall.

All the office doors—all psychiatrists—were closed, but in a few minutes he heard Armond's voice. Cap watched him escort a man out the front door with a tidy pat on the back.

He stood up as Armond turned around. Armond hadn't noticed him waiting. "How are you, Armond?"

"Yes, hello."

"It's me—Cap."

"I know who you are," said Armond. He wore plaid suspenders, a silk tie, and a powder-blue shirt with gold cuff links. He'd grown a mustache. His hair, which had turned gray twenty years earlier, was now dyed back to black. Gone was the "Valtano's Electric" windbreaker and the derelict look. Evidently he'd decided to stop dressing down.

"You're looking good," said Cap, thinking rich.

"Thank you," said Armond, but didn't return the compliment.

Armond motioned for Cap to follow him. The office had its own monumental scale: High windows reached toward the fourteen-foot ceilings. Oriental rugs stretched out, like prostrated servants, under the antiques. A fireplace, its opening wide and tall enough for a Mountie to ride through, the whole structure built of massive quarry stone sparkling with mica and quartz, fortified one long wall. Cap whistled. "This is quite a step up from your cubicle at Denver Psychiatric."

Armond made a small nod of acknowledgment. His eyes had the hooded look of a well-fed man who knows breakfast is being prepared even as he sleeps.

Cap noticed a metal cube with numerous tubes, gauges, and dials on a low counter in the corner. "What's that?" he asked.

"An espresso machine. Quite a nice model, don't you think? It's commercial size. Care for caffè latte or cappuccino?"

Was this supposed to be a joke? "I just stopped by to see how you were," said Cap, disappointed now he'd actually called him.

"Excellent, as you can see," said Armond, raising his eyebrows into grand arches that seemed to enfold the room's treasures. "I was just about to leave for Vail. I never time-share. I have my own condo there."

Cap suppressed a yawn. "Nice you can get away."

"Anytime I wish."

"Is that right," said Cap. He had to get out of here. He couldn't believe he'd ever gone to this quack. But obviously other people did too, as he could see.

"Did I ever show you a picture of my baby?" asked Armond.

"Baby?" Armond's children were grown and dispersed around the world. "You have a new baby?" Was he remarried at his age? Perhaps they'd have something in common, after all.

Armond reached into his desk drawer and withdrew a leather case monogrammed with his initials. He slid it across the wide desk.

Cap opened the snap. Inside, he found pictures of a sports car, a Jaguar, photographed from different angles. Front, back, side. Looking at the grille. Straight down on the sunroof. Sideways at the extra-dark tinted glass. Even one from underneath the chassis, showing the silver-piped exhaust system. He turned the plastic pages. More glossy pictures of the white Jag's interior: seats that smelled, even from the photograph, of money—dark-green leather, smooth as sea grass. There was something obscene about the sequence. He felt as if he were examining dirty pictures on his lunch hour.

"You like it?" asked Armond.

"Why are you showing me these?" asked Cap.

"No reason," said Armond, retrieving the leather photo case, carefully closing the snap. "I thought you'd be interested."

"Do you feel competitive with me, Armond?"

"Why should I? Do you have a Jag?"

Was Armond putting him on? It was impossible to tell with the man.

"I have some property up your way too," said Armond, racking up more assets. "A man up there breeds horses for me. Arabians, Appaloosas, and Belgians. Very high quality."

Cap squirmed in his seat. This was unbearable. He must be mirroring Cap's own lust for success. It was some therapeutic technique, a lunch-hour presentation, a quickie treatment—Armond showing Cap that he still had the stuff. It couldn't just be raw boasting. "You already mentioned your horses in a note after I sent you the baby announcement."

"Oh, yes. He's very cute," said Armond. He looked around his desk for something, then picked up a demitasse of rich chocolate-smelling coffee and, after sipping, set it back on its delicate gilt-edged saucer.

"I've decided to close my practice," said Cap. Was he trying to get concern from this man—this braying egotist? "My father died recently too," he added, helpless to stop himself, out of an old habit of spilling everything. "Lots of changes, obviously." He could feel himself growing shrill in a plea for sympathy.

Armond made a low, rumbling noise of condolence. Suddenly he perked up. "By the way, I still have your umbrella."

"What?" said Cap. "What!" This umbrella business again! "Are you out of your mind!" He stood up, furious, ready to punch the man! My God, he would hit his old therapist!

"Just a minute," said Armond calmly, impervious to any threat. "I'll give it back to you, but first I want you to meet someone."

Cap, still simmering, reluctantly followed his crooked finger.

They walked down to the cellar. Armond pulled the chain for a lightbulb in the ceiling. Down here, the space was cold, damp, and unfinished. He led Cap through a warren of windowless rooms with concrete floors, cobwebs tickling his face. Finally, the maze ended at a paint-strafed door with a hand-lettered sign: DR. MOHAN VAISH, PSYCHOTHERAPIST. "Please," said Armond. His self-satisfied tone had become conciliatory. "Would you go on in and pretend to be a patient."

"What are you talking about?" said Cap.

"My father wishes to have patients. In India, as a medical doctor, he had many people come to him for help, but here no one pays any attention. I have set him up in"—Armond made quotation marks in the air—" 'practice.' You see what I mean?"

"No, I don't see."

"He needs to feel useful before he dies."

"This is absurd. And cruel! Putting him down here like this!"

"He wants to be here. It is his choice. Please, enter."

Cap opened the door. Sitting at a student desk, one that would fit a small elementary schoolchild, wearing a blue blazer that drooped from his shoulders, his face brown and wrinkled as a baked apple, his hair white as midday sand, his dry hands clawed arthritically on the hinged desktop, his teeth crusty brown with bloodstained gum lines, his eyelids thick in sleep as walnuts, was the tiniest, most barely alive man Cap had ever seen.

It was The Thing. Unmasked. The Thing, here in Armond's basement.

"Armond, is he . . . okay?"

"Say something to him," whispered Armond.

"What?"

"Tell him you are unhappy. You suffer from inordinate feelings of futility. You are receiving no pleasure from your job and your marriage."

"Don't be ridiculous."

"Tell him you can't get close to people and are afraid of intimacy. You suffer indigestion, constipation, loss of appetite, insomnia, bilious rage, and fear of VDT terminals."

"That's it, Armond. I'm leaving."

"Wait! Then just tell him that you're here for your appointment. Please go inside, I beg you."

Armond left Cap in the dim room, quickly shutting the door.

Cap took a seat across from the tiny, shrunken man. What was he doing here with these lunatics! His day off, and he was involved in this absurd charade. Cap closed his eyes and spoke, as if reciting for Cantor Zommick. "I'm here for my appointment, Dr. Vaish." Armond's father opened his eyes—a startling amber, lucid, and searing as marbles in a stove's fire. The sudden light caused the pupils to shrink into tiny metallic luminous dots, concentrated pins that stuck on Cap's face. Both eyeballs rolled back in his head, white, shorn of sight. They reappeared, bulging and glistening with moisture, then the lids closed tight as spaceship doors. Nothing more. The show done. The Thing gone. "Are you all right?" asked Cap.

The father opened his eyes again; they looked normal and restful now. "What problems are you experiencing?"

His voice, unlike Armond's, sounded tinny and electrical. "Oh, just the usual," said Cap, playing along.

"Would you be more specific, please?"

Why not? He had a captive audience, so to speak. "Trouble sleeping, not much appetite, fatigue, aimless thoughts, a little dread here and there."

"Anything else?"

Why not go on? The father appeared actually to be listening, more concerned than his son. "My father died two months ago. A young client of mine died a couple of years before that. He was going to be a father. His mother, that is, my dead client's mother—she's a Holocaust survivor—doesn't know about her grandchild. . . ." Cap stopped; it was preposterous explaining all this to the man.

"You know many dead people," enunciated Armond's father. Cap couldn't tell if it was a question or a statement.

"I told you, two." Though he thought of all the dead he knew through his clients, the brothers and babies and lost relatives, the walking dead, the grieving dead, the unremembered dead, the once dead, the haunted dead, the shamed dead, the pieces of the dead that he had held every day, the dead who came and left their bones with him, the dead far inside him. He'd looked under the earth and seen the mazed tombs; he'd seen the dead waving him away, now beckoning him toward them: stay back . . . come to us. The dead as confused as everyone.

He felt his chest break open, tears erupting. When he looked up, he saw Armond's father's eyes, vacant of judgment, though dimmed now, weary of tears, or was that himself who was weary of the dead and their tears—Dr. Vaish the perfect conduit, an instrument of exquisite projective accuracy?

"What is it you wish from me?" Armond's father said, perhaps sensing that Cap was drifting into some corner of intellectualization, stuck there like a wind-up toy. It was a question Cap had asked so many times of his own clients as he tried to keep them from losing contact with some emotional pulse, though he had always said "want," giving the statement a slight tone of being put upon: What do you want from me? Tender as he might ask.

"Why would I wish anything? I feel sorry for you, if you want to know. Your son leaving you down here . . . it's cruel." Cap turned away. He knew he was lying to the old man. He didn't feel sorry for anyone but himself at the moment, a shameful admission.

"Are you angry with me?" asked Dr. Vaish, looking above Cap's head, as if at a bubble that showed his knotted thoughts.

"I don't even know you. Why would I be angry with you?" He saw the old man shiver. "You're cold. You shouldn't be down here."

"It's you who are shivering."

"I am not," said Cap, feeling petulant about the accusation. The man made him feel like a defensive child.

"You're shivering inside."

"This is silly," said Cap. "I'm perfectly fine."

"It's with rage."

"Oh, please," said Cap, chilled, if anything, by the echo of his own words to clients.

"Would you like to take my hand?" asked Dr. Vaish.

"What?"

"I asked if you'd like to hold on to my hand."

"I don't know why."

"You don't know why," said Armond's father with unsettling flatness, so the answer appeared less a response than a motto or an instant slogan of collective dismay and bewilderment. "Is that your thought?"

Cap looked at the shriveled brown hand, its skin thin as cellophane. Death, he had thought of dying. It was his father's hand, resting at his side in the coffin, no commands left in it, no anger, no force—that hand with its baggy pored skin and bristled gray hairs, the hand he could not bring himself to truly touch in life or in death, gone to the earth now.

"Are you ready to take my hand now?" Dr. Vaish stretched his hand across the small elementary school desk, two feet away from Cap. The old man held it there, suspended in the air. Cap looked in his eyes. "Are you ready to take my hand?" he repeated.

Cap's wooden chair squeaked against the hard cellar floor as he pulled himself closer. Pains shot through his chest, and he thought he might have a heart attack. Breathe, he told himself, breathe. Keep breathing. He winced, some terrible blockage in his sternum, he needed something to break this up, all this hot ice in his chest. Space trapped within space. Dead air.

He let out a mammoth burp, a horrible foul-smelling expulsion of gas. It humiliated him, though the old man didn't even seem to notice. Dr. Vaish's voice whirred in the air like a tiny surgical drill. "Are you ready to take my hand?"

Cap grabbed it. The old man's hand somehow enveloped his own larger one. Each of Cap's fingers was petted, his palm stroked, every pore and hair follicle nudged, the bones awakened. It was a massage so peculiar—some mix of the deeply healing and the fetishistic—that all thoughts and desires had rushed into his hand, his self shrunk to receive this caress. When it finally stopped, it took Cap a while to realize that Dr. Vaish's hand now lay small as a baby's in his own— the dry flesh, the old bones, the grip weightless as dust in light.

"He's sleeping," said Armond, when he came to fetch Cap afterward. And truly, Dr. Vaish had dozed off immediately after Cap touched him. "He's happy. Thank you, thank you so much for speaking to him. Thank you, Cap." Armond grasped Cap's hand, the same hand, kissing it—as supplicating as he'd been imperious before. "You don't know how much it means to me. You can't imagine what it's like."

"For God's sake, what do you think you're doing, keeping him down here in this dungeon?" He'd recovered his indignation at the fact of the old man's confinement.

"Oh, no, no, you don't understand!"

"Understand what? That you're trying to kill him? Is that what you're up to here? Is this your idea of euthanasia for the elderly?"

Armond smiled. His eyes brightened. "I've made him a child again. He thinks he's a prodigy. A ten-year-old therapist! A son to make his own father proud. He's forgiven me everything. Fantastic! Such peace with your parent, you just can't imagine," said Armond, and he motioned Cap out of the room, quietly shutting the door on his still father.

So he'd brought the umbrella back with him, this idiotic umbrella, which was falling apart and had lost, not two, but all *but* two of its spokes. With its wood handle and rickety spreader, its exposed rod-and-groove mechanism, its lusterless steel tip and frayed black canopy, the item was ancient, a relic. Somehow he'd wound up with it at college.

My God, the umbrella had been his father's! He remembered now. He'd taken it with him to Boulder his freshman year. It was really an antique, a little piece of history. Cap looked under the knob and saw his father's initials on the base, put there before World War II.

What was all this supposed to mean? He didn't believe in signs—never had—yet this item, this forgotten old beat-up heirloom, ironically the only belonging he had of his father's, having taken not a single possession of his father's from the house, not even a watch, was back in his life. And Armond had given it to him. Armond the quack. Armond the avaricious. Armond the ostentatious. Armond the keeper of his willfully or not-so-willfully ascetic and questionably sane or mystical father. Armond the dutiful or wicked son? Either corrupt or honorable. One or the other. How could a therapist be only a little corrupt? Like a little pregnant, or a little dead.

He felt tears come up again. His grief wasn't the grief he'd thought he'd known—what he'd observed of his clients who lost lovers and parents and pieces of themselves. Grief for him was not agonizing and keening and pitching forward into the grave to drag out the departed, was not cavernous with ache; it was soft and creeping, and it had finally come to him. It had baby fingers that lifted him lightly by the elbows and swept him inside himself, to a peep show of sorrows.

He pulled off at a gas station outside Longmont to buy some Tums; it felt as if a small steel rake were scraping the inside of his chest. The

Tums helped enough for him to make it forty more miles to the address Maureen had given him back in Pierre.

At the house where she was staying, he pulled up behind a Subaru with California plates. He could take down the numbers and find out her address. But so what? What good would that do, unless she consented to let Julian's mother see the baby. And he didn't just want her to see the baby; he wanted her to know the child, for which he needed Maureen's cooperation. He wrote the license plate number down anyway.

She answered the door in a coat and scarf. He couldn't tell whether she was getting ready to leave or had just come back from her errands. But when he saw her bags behind her, he understood she was set to walk out the door. It was one minute before three, and she hadn't intended to give him an extension.

"I'm glad you're still here," he said, and waited for her to invite him in. He realized she was hesitating because of her daughter. She didn't trust even him, so protective of the child was she.

Finally, she let him inside.

The house had plants everywhere, thriving in winter, large ferns and even a small pine tree in a giant pot. Pottery lined the fireplace mantel—mugs, pots, pitchers, and odd, impractical-shaped containers fired to a high glaze. A warm, cozy home with an unobstructed view of the mountains. Maureen looked comfortable enough, having sat down on the long couch in front of the fireplace and taken off her coat. She wore white tights and black hiking shoes, a forest-green turtleneck. He glanced around for her daughter, who was nowhere to be seen. For a moment, he had the fleeting fear there was no child, no grandchild, no reason to be here, that he'd been trapped into coming (which, any way he thought about it, he had), but then he heard a child cry out, and Maureen went to her.

Maureen had not said a word since he'd gotten here.

Then again, he hadn't been listening. He seemed to be following Dr. Vaish's hand through the house, leading him as if with a bridle, dissolving into dust and recomposing itself. The meeting, whether wretched or fruitful—he couldn't decide which—had left him with little emotional guile. He simply wanted her to help him.

When Maureen didn't return in a few minutes (or call out her whereabouts to him), he wandered into the kitchen, large and open, with tall cherry cabinets and a view out back to the mountains. Maureen came up behind him, holding her daughter.

The child looked exactly like Julian, with Maureen's fair skin. Cap saw, too, in the child what he'd never seen before in Julian: the resemblance to himself. She could almost pass for their own child.

"Whose house is this, Maureen?"

"An old colleague," she said, and he guessed this must be a former lover. "He's in Oregon. Don't worry; no one will know you're here."

"What's your daughter's name?"

"Julia."

Cap shook his head. "Why? How can you name your daughter after Julian and not let her grandmother see her?"

"My sister picked out the name after I told her Julian's."

"Of course. You had nothing to do with it yourself."

"That's right," said Maureen, and flashed him a tense smile.

She put down the little girl, who ran over to Cap and used his leg to stop herself. Cap picked her up and held her, while she pulled curiously at the beard he'd begun growing. Julia. Julian's daughter. She snuggled against his chest, rested her head on his shoulder, then wriggled to get down. He carefully put her back on the floor, afraid she'd fall. She went scrambling away, making an *unnnnnhhhhh* noise. She looked back to see if he was noticing her, and pushed open the kitchen door with a bang as if it were a saloon gate, heading off to her toys, in an open suitcase in the living room. Cap put his hands in his pockets; they still felt her body, alive and squirmy. He hadn't wanted to let go of her.

"Maureen, can we reach some kind of agreement? If you cared anything about Julian—"

"I cared plenty for him. You have *no* idea how much."

"Is that why you left town so quickly? Because you cared so much? Come on, Maureen."

"I couldn't deal with it. I didn't want to be in the middle of Pierre's version of a scandal: Pregnant teacher forces lover to his death. That's the way it would read, right? About me it would."

Cap said nothing.

"Well, it wasn't that way. I don't know why he left that night. Maybe I did push him too far. . . ." She looked away. "Anyway, it's on my conscience, not yours, so why don't you just drop it."

"What about it, Maureen?" He felt more determined than ever.

"What about what?"

"You know what."

"I haven't let my own mother meet Julia. Why should I let some stranger?"

"She's not a stranger. She's your daughter's grandmother."

"So is my mother."

"This is different," said Cap.

"You have quite an interest in this person," said Maureen. "Any other reason you're acting as her agent?"

He could feel her sensors moving for the hidden truth—what exactly it meant to him. What did it? "It's the decent thing to do."

Maureen snorted. "Decent. You're going to lecture me on what's decent? I would have thought you'd seen enough in life to believe that it's the *indecent* we have to worry about. Why should I do this? I know all too well what becomes of decent intentions."

"Maureen, you're depriving your daughter too. Can't you see that?"

"Depriving her of what?"

"Of affection and love."

"Too bad. Love loses," she said, and angrily picked up Julia's plastic juice cup from the kitchen counter. "I can't take the chance. Another person could, obviously. But not me. If anyone should understand that, you should."

"You have nothing to lose. How can I assure you of that?"

"You can't. What if she decided to make trouble? What if she got it into her head I wasn't a fit mother or something, because of what happened to Julian?"

"That won't happen."

"You're right," she said. "It's not going to happen."

Cap sighed. He sat down on a stool at the breakfast bar. Maureen sat at the other end, her eyes not leaving him. He was fatigued from hunger. He felt dizzy and slightly nauseous; he hadn't had anything to eat since early this morning, when he'd woken up picturing this conversation.

"What do you want from me?" he said finally, the familiar refrain. He heard the echo of Armond's father: *What is it you wish from me?*

She stood up and walked around to the other side of the counter, so she was directly in front of him. He felt the pain in his chest again as he had on the interstate coming back from Denver, as if glue had settled inside his breastbone. He didn't believe she wanted sex. That had never been the issue. It was something else.

"I want to know what you think of me."

Cap stared at her. Her face had lost its tight screen.

"Maureen, I care about you—"

"Don't," she said. She put up her hand for him to stop. "That's not what I want to know. You know that's not what I want to know." Her hand dropped to the counter between them, resting there for him.

He realized now what she meant. "Are you asking if I love you?"

She looked back at him without answering. Her hand lay halfway toward him. The grand conjugation: love, loved . . . lovable. He thought of Armond's father, alone in the dank basement, waiting for clients, offering his aged hand.

It was what he'd always wanted to know too. The riddle of The Thing: Am I loved?

"I'd make you happy, Cap. I could do that for someone I love. We could all be very happy." She looked toward Julia in the living room.

He saw no trickery in her face; she was making her offer: marriage, home, family, sex—even a child, a mirror of his own life. And love, from her remotest parts, sprung and beating. Alive, amazingly.

"Maureen, things are no different than before."

"Aren't they?" she said, and he wondered if she was referring to Wallis and him. Her wire to him stretched that far, detecting the slightest seismic movement in his marriage.

"I can't," he said. "I can't give you what you ask, Maureen. I'm sorry if anything I did ever encouraged or promised otherwise."

But he had a flash of himself living with them. Anna Katz visiting. A life so skewed it momentarily appeared attractive in its rupture.

"I have to leave," she said abruptly. "Help me with my bags."

They went outside together. Snow had started to fall, big floppy flakes that looked like miniature three-cornered hats. Cap put the bags in the trunk and got Julia buckled into her car seat. Maureen slid in the driver's side and closed the door. He stood there, his heart thudding more than he wanted her to know, waiting for her answer. Finally, she rolled down the window. "I'll send you my address and a letter that you can forward to Julian's mother. But I make the rules. All the rules. Do you understand?"

"Yes," said Cap.

"I'm finished with therapy," she said. Her face was streaked with tears.

He watched her go. She was like an ex to whom he'd never been married. Their involvement had been long, exhausting, savage, and bitter, and now, finally, they'd had a drop of peace, enough to say goodbye forever. She'd keep her word, and he wouldn't ever see her again; he knew that much about her: she hadn't stayed alive, made it this far, without her own wily pride. She'd stolen courage from the tyrants of childhood; such daring was what had brought her into therapy in the first place and now would get her out. It was the end of something for him as well.

Chapter Seventeen

Cap bundled up Claude and hurried with him to the march for Martin Luther King Day, coaxing him along with a cheese stick and a juice box in a dinosaur holder, so he wouldn't squeeze the juice in front of him like the water cannon he'd seen on the Turtles. A group of people heading for the march hurried past them on the sidewalk, carrying signs that said FREE ALL THE PEOPLE and BAN BIGOTRY—VOTE YES ON FIVE, a city ordinance that would prohibit discrimination against gays. Every day, letters about the issue battled back and forth in the *Pierre Guardian*. Cap had contributed his own letter of support for the ordinance, quoting the old adage that all it takes for the triumph of evil is for enough good men to do nothing.

He put Claude on his shoulders now, Claude having made it only a very slow block and a half of the eight they had to go. At this rate, they would miss the parade. The temperature had risen, and snow mixed with rain was forecast. Just in case, Cap had brought his father's umbrella, having become attached to it. Gutters thawed and dripped, and he stopped occasionally to let Claude break off icicles. Each time he broke one, Claude—whose red cape over his puffy down jacket made him look like a junior hunchback—shouted "Cowabunga!" the only four-syllable word in his vocabulary. And this was supposed to be a march in honor of nonviolence.

When they turned on University Avenue, he could see the marchers coming toward them, led by the mayor of Pierre, a woman with a doctorate in psychology and a former practice she'd given up for politics, with its larger if more fickle clientele. Cap had gone out to lunch with her once. She'd explained her reason for leaving the profession: it was too solipsistic, she said. At one time, she'd thought the individual consciousness was the bottom rung, and after that, everything else would fall into place. But nope, empowerment was a social problem. It was the community that counted most. All the other issues, the classic concerns of psychotherapy—childhood traumas, parental conflicts, the oppressive past, the shame, the abuse, the lack of attachment, the thwarted drives, the whole confusing mess of the self: wounded, grandiose, deflated, nonesteemed, marginalized, unintegrated, isolated, repressed, false or true—it all came down to belonging. So why not get on with the business of living as a person within a family, within a town, within a nation, within a world, within . . . who knows? It was endless, if people just let themselves get outside their own heads.

Cap had listened patiently. He'd heard it before: thinking too much about your unhappy thoughts just encouraged them to stay around. "A little doom and gloom goes a long way," the mayor had said, when Cap told her it sounded as if people in pain made her uncomfortable (it was to be their only lunch). But she had gone on: Wasn't it presumptuous to think you understood people better than they did themselves? Wasn't it a little naive to think you could find the meaning of anyone's life when philosophers had given up on the general question a long time ago? Weren't those studies notable that showed forty percent of clients in therapy got better, forty percent showed no change, and twenty percent became worse—figures that corresponded *exactly* to the control group without therapy?

What studies? interrupted Cap.

"And as for being nurtured," the mayor continued, ignoring him, "sure, one can find belonging in therapy, but it lasts only until the money or insurance runs out. Admittedly, therapy can be powerful, but isn't it, in the end, store-bought caring? Somehow that never tastes quite as good as the homemade kind."

Whew, she had been tough, and maybe that's what she needed to be to make the jump from therapy to politics. He wondered what the mayor would have thought of Anna Katz and Julian, not exactly community people, either of them, or Maureen, or his brother, for that matter. Last night Cap had come back from Maureen's, pleased, happy as he'd been in years, and the phone had rung, a call from his brother. Joan had had a miscarriage. She'd been in her third month. Allan had wept on the phone; all the strain of the last year had finally caught up with him. Getting married, taking over the business, Dad dying—all of it hanging by a thread on a new drug. He was going so fast, but he couldn't stop; he was afraid to stop. What if something happened tomorrow? He wondered—did Cap think it possible?—if stress, his stress and Joan's together, all these incredible, wonderful, but maybe too big changes, had caused the miscarriage?

No, Cap said, he didn't. It happened, and it happens to other people. Allan shouldn't read anything into it. There was no punishment here. It was a misfortune, not a rebuke. Allan had thanked him profusely, but for what, Cap wondered. He'd gotten off the phone and looked at Claude's blanket. Be strong and let your heart take courage. Hope in the Lord. Hear O Israel the Lord our God, the Lord is One. He'd remembered praying at Claude's birth, really praying for the first and only time in his life, not faking it as he'd done all those years for Cantor Zommick. He'd finally known the right words that night, read them in the air where they'd always been. He'd made a noise unto the Lord, all right. And he'd been heard, or had he? The Lord giveth and the Lord taketh away. A son for him, a miscarriage for his brother. It couldn't possibly be that simple.

This morning, the mail had brought a postcard from Anna Katz. "I spoke," she wrote to him. "For one hour I talked without pause.

When I finished, I was amazed to see children still in front of me, some with their eyes wet. They asked me to please come back and speak to them again. What is someone like me to do with such kindness?"

And now he could see the city council members in front, their arms joined together in solidarity, and right behind them, in the second row, was Wallis, her elbow linked with Dr. France's. He knew it must be Dr. France, because Dr. France had called early this morning and asked if Wallis would go to the march with her. Out of line? Unorthodox? A therapist calling a client for a "date"? But he'd given her the benefit of the doubt. Dr. France evidently had her own ways of establishing a positive transference, there being no rules about how it should be done, barring exploitation. And Wallis had been flattered, thrilled, off to march with her therapist, her therapist with her African hat shimmering with colors braided purple and gold under a pink winter sky, who was mothering Wallis all over the place. It made him feel nostalgic already for the profession, and he wasn't so sure now that people like the mayor wouldn't goad him back into it.

They marched under a banner displaying clasped black and white hands. Wallis saw him and waved. She had never looked happier.

He waved both arms back at her. "There's Mommy," he pointed out to Claude, who stretched up to see. She looked lovely, with her scarf pulled around her ears, her pink cheeks and red lips framed inside an oval of white linen. He kept his hand in the air a moment, waving to her, and she smiled back warmly at him before turning the corner.

And then the marchers suddenly stopped. Coming from Lupe Street, from the direction of the post office, was a group of men. In parkas and ski vests and snow boots and gloves, they looked like everyone else, except for the swastikas on their sleeves. They turned the corner at Sullivan, cut across the gas station parking lot, and ran right into the marchers.

"Daddy," said Claude, kicking him to get closer. "Go there." And Cap did, walked in to get a better look.

Cap recognized Bill Sable. Bill Sable with a swastika on his coat. A beefier, more florid, and less conciliatory Sable, perhaps, but definitely him, the salesman pitching hate instead of appliances. Indeed, Sable turned out to be one of the leaders—a spokesman for the group. He climbed up on the back of a bench and began addressing the marchers through a bullhorn: "We're not here to make trouble," he said, always reasonable. "And we're not against the minorities in this country!" he explained, in case anyone should get the wrong impression about the armwear. "We're just for white people gaining back their fair rights."

"Pigs!" someone in the crowd shouted back.

"What about the working people of this country?" asked Sable. Two young boys (his sons? was this what had become of the custody battle?), with swastikas on their jackets too, held his feet in place on the bench's back, as if to fix him there like a statue, unmovable. "What about you working people out there whose children can't get into college because some person from a favored group gets a free ride right through an open door?" He tapped his forehead, as if the point were irrefutable. "Isn't that like being able to butt in line anytime you want? Now, is that fair?"

Someone picked up a trash can but was restrained from heaving it. "No violence! No violence! No violence!" the marchers began chanting. The police moved in to protect Sable and his men.

Sable smiled magnanimously at the crowd, having stirred them to where he wanted: "That's why we're marching out here today, folks! We're against this holiday. We're losing all we've worked for, just because we're not the right skin color or religion. I ask you again, is that fair?" The cordon of officers had moved directly in front of him now. "It's Martin Luther King Freebie Day, as far as we're concerned!"

Cap crossed through the gas station parking lot, then squeezed between a dumpster and a tow truck and slipped behind the line of police. Claude hung on tighter to his neck, sensing that something was not safe here.

He had to do something. He hadn't been carrying his father's umbrella all morning for nothing, he realized.

He came out right at the spot he'd aimed for, directly in back of Sable but unseen by the police, who had their backs to him and were concentrating on controlling the crowd. Cap could see Wallis. She was watching him with a mixture of curiosity and disbelief. And worry. What was he doing over there? With all those evil men? Was this one of his disaster games? Some live version of, say, Klan Attack?

"I mean," Wallis said afterward at the police station, although Cap suspected she was secretly proud of him, "were you trying to be a hero?"

Maybe. Maybe he had just wanted to open his umbrella—which had been closed up for more than twenty years: this worn, clunky, rickety umbrella, which connected him to his father's dead bones and to Claude and to Claude's children to come. Maybe good or bad acts didn't matter as much as he'd thought. Maybe the real mitzvah was forgetting, and if you did that, if someone could look inside you and could say yes, you had forgotten how to hate, then you'd done your true job.

So there was no reason not to reach up and give Bill Sable a little love poke in the fatty tissue.

Sable fell off the bench with a yelp, dropped his megaphone, and turned around to see what had attacked him. "Afternoon, Bill," said Cap politely. And for a moment everything stopped, until the police rushed to grab Cap and take him away—but gently, because Claude wouldn't let harm come upon his father.

DUTTON

 PLUME

COMPELLING NOVELS

☐ **SINGING SONGS by Meg Tilly.** Written by the acclaimed actress, this novel explores how one family lives, centerless, caught in a flux of emotion and violence that touches and transforms each of its members. It is the masterful realization of a young girl's journey to adulthood in a chaotic, abusive, and fragmented world—an affirmation of a child's ability to use her judgment and imagination alone to light her way. "A triumph . . . absolutely believable, completely irresistible."
—Chicago Sun-Times (271657—$9.95)

☐ **THE BOOK OF REUBEN by Tabitha King.** Reuben Styles has spent his entire life in Nodd's Ridge, Maine trying to do the right thing according to the standard American success story. While nothing turns out as he expects, his incredible spirit and strength keep him struggling to become the man he envisioned. Capturing the searing, gritty reality of small-town America of the '50s, '60s, and '70s, this stunning, deeply involving novel touches a common nerve and casts a light on our own lives. (937668—$22.95)

☐ **RIVER OF SKY by Karen Harper.** This magnificent epic of the American frontier brings to vivid life one woman's stirring quest for fortune and happiness. This is Kate Craig's story—one of rousing adventure and heartbreaking struggle, of wildfire passion and a wondrous love, as strong and deep as the river itself. It will sweep you into an America long gone by. (938222—$21.95)

☐ **MIAMI: A SAGA by Evelyn Wilde Mayerson.** Spanning a hundred years of challenge and change, this breathtaking panorama of Miami, Florida traces the tragedies and triumphs of five families—from the hardy homesteaders of the post-Civil War era to their descendants who bravely battle the devastation left by hurricane Andrew in 1992. (936467—$22.95)

Prices slightly higher in Canada.

DUTTON

LITERARY FICTION

☐ **UNDER THE FEET OF JESUS by Helena María Viramontes.** This exquisitely sensitive novel has at its center Estrella, a girl about to cross over the perilous border to womanhood. What she knows of life comes from her mother, who has survived abandonment by her husband in a land where she is both an illegal alien and a farmworker. It captures the conflict of cultures, the bitterness of want, the sweetness of love, the power of pride, and the landscape of human heart. (939490—$18.95)

☐ **WHEN THE RAINBOW GODDESS WEPT by Cecilia Manguerra Brainard.** Set against the backdrop of the Japanese invasion of the Philippines in 1941, this brilliant novel weaves myth and legend together with the suffering and tragedies of the Filipino people. It shows us the Philippines through an insider's eyes and brings to American audiences an unusual reading experience about a world that is utterly foreign and a child who is touchingly universal. (938214—$19.95)

☐ **THE UNFASTENED HEART by Lane von Herzen.** This is surely the most lyrical, extravagantly sensual novel ever to address the splendors and sorrows of love. Anna de la Senda possesses an extraordinary empathy, that draws to her a marvelous collection of lovelorn souls. A novel about the succor of true friendship and the marvel of true love. (938907—$19.95)

☐ **ENTERTAINING ANGELS by Marita van der Vyver.** Griet Swart's life is not exactly a fairy tale. Her once marvelous marriage has ended in divorce. She has lost her husband, her home, and her baby in yet another miscarriage. But late one night an angel appears or her doorstep and breaks her spell of sadness with a joyful sexual adventure. A modern-day fairy tale that is outrageously witty, unblushingly candid, and magically moving. (939180—$20.95)

Prices slightly higher in Canada.